FOR TWENTY DOLLARS IN GOLD

A Story of the Civil War

A. C. "CARL" WARD

The novel **For Twenty Dollars in Gold - A Story of the Civil War** is a work of fiction. Apart from the well-known actual people, events, and locales that are presented in the narrative, all names, characters, places, and incidents either are the product of the author's collaborative research, imagination, or are used fictitiously. Any resemblance to any actual persons, living or dead, events, or locales is entirely coincidental to this story.

This book was printed in the United States of America.

DEDICATION

This novel is dedicated to my family, friends, and soldiers of the United States Army for their relentless protection of our personal and national rights and freedoms. Whether you like them or not, we would not be a nation without them.

I also extend my deepest appreciation to all of the military services, having personally collaborated with all of them at some point in my 30 years of military experience and over 22 years of consulting for the Department of Defense and Department of Homeland Security.

For over 52 years, I have used the wisdom and talents of three teachers from my high school, in Greensboro, North Carolina to move through life.

Ms. Peggy Joyner was my English Literature and Composition teacher.

Ms. Peggy Woodlief was my Journalism, English Composition teacher, and my Advisor for the award-winning school newspaper.

Ms. Mary Gamble was my History teacher and she taught me the importance of both World and US History.

Those women, put a "poor country boy from North Carolina doing the best he could" onto a road, to a success I never imagined for myself. I'm glad they pushed me.

I also dedicate this novel to Mister Terry Fox, a dedicated Gettysburg Battlefield Guide Emeritus at the Gettysburg National Military Park. He provided both personal tours for me and my family as we explored our historic past. His help for this author, in this endeavor, was monumental in the research and development for the key events and battlefield intelligence of the book. Thank you, Terry, couldn't have done it without you!

A special thanks to the wonderful artist Melanie Eger for first taking the time to read the entire manuscript. And second, she found the relevant objects and placed them into her painting. She captured the essence of the story and a tear comes to my eyes each time I look at it. Thanks Melanie.

Finally, I want to dedicate this book to my son, Brian Wesley Ward. Brian represents the next chapter in the history of our family. While he was born in North Carolina and knows this story, he is no "poor country boy doing the best he can." In his seemingly brief four decades, he has achieved great things in Los Angeles, California. He has made us proud many times over.

He constantly reminded me that one day I needed to finish telling this story. Now, I leave the story for him to write the next chapter.

Here it is Brian, for all to read.

TABLE OF CONTENTS

Chapter 1 – Gettysburg, June 29, 1863 1

Chapter 2 – "How do you feel about that?" May 1861 13

Chapter 3 – Camp Crab Tree, August 27, 1861 35

Chapter 4 – Coastal Christmas, Winter 1861 53

Chapter 5 – "How do we survive?" New Bern, 1862 69

Chapter 6 – Campaign North Summer 1862 87

Chapter 7 – Going home, Fall of 1862 105

Chapter 8 – "We pray and hope", April 1863 135

Chapter 9 – "Take it to 'em boys!" May 1863 155

Chapter 10 – "They're fools!" May 1863 171

Chapter 11 – "Shoes for my feet" June 30, 1863 183

Chapter 12 – "Steady boys, steady" July 1, 1863 193

Chapter 13 – Day of rest, July 2, 1863 211

Chapter 14 – A Loud Serenade! July 3, 1863 229

Chapter 15 – "Lord, help us!" July 1863 249

Chapter 16 – "How long do we run?" July 1863 261

Chapter 17 – "Papa let's go home!" July 9, 1863 269

Chapter 18 – Long Journey Home, June 24, 1864 289

Epilogue 315

Author's Final Thoughts 327

About the Author 335

CHAPTER 1

GETTYSBURG, JUNE 29, 1863

Private James Ward of the 26th Regiment of North Carolina Troops lunged forward, using the triangular shaped bayonet on the end of his musket. As the blade plunged into the flesh, he gave the weapon a sharp twist to the right as he had been instructed in his training.

The results of his effort were successful. The "twist of the wrist" broke the bayonet free from the fallen tree. James then rolled it to a shaded area on the side of the road where the regiment's march had come to rest.

The soldier slowly looked up to the sky and saw a bright and hot late June Sun. Sweat rolled off his face and down his back. His uniform was darkened by collected perspiration around his belt, armpits, neck, and crotch.

As he examined himself, he couldn't find very much of his butternut-colored Confederate uniform was not damp or just plain soaking wet. He guessed that it was at least ninety degrees, based on his experience working on the farm in Southeastern North Carolina.

Down home, there would be considerably more humidity involved, not like the Pennsylvania countryside. It was only a few weeks ago when the unit had received new uniforms made by the local textile industry in the State. As he looked down at it, he noted it was not as clean as that day on parade.

Given their previous excursions on the North Carolina coast, and the trips up North, the uniforms were not in the best state of repair either, at this point. James pulled the bayonet socket off the musket and placed the sharp weapon into its scabbard on his hip. He laid the musket against the fallen tree and slowly unslung the additional rifle he carried for only special purposes.

His cartridge belt came off next and was carefully laid on the fallen tree. Then he removed the oil-treated haversack that carried so much of his life as a soldier. The oil treatment helped keep most personal items dry on those wet days. Next, he pulled his wooden canteen from his neck and laid it on the ground where he intended to sit down and rest from the march.

His expectation was a short break for water and a quick meal. They had been marching North, North-East into Pennsylvania during the previous day and most of this morning.

Rather suddenly, around noon, they were told to rest in place. They were also told to be prepared to smartly move out on command. He gave his canteen a quick shake, realizing he had very little left. James knew he would need to refill it very soon. As a country-boy from North Carolina, he knew the importance of keeping water on hand. This fact was especially true when out on the march. At that moment, a yell came from deep in the woods behind him. James immediately reached for his musket leaning against the fallen tree.

"Creek down here!!" someone shouted.

James drank the remaining water in the canteen as he headed for the woods, with musket in hand. The creek turned out to be a little larger than a "creek" and the water was fast-moving and clean.

He did not hesitate filling his canteen and took a long drink to quench his immediate thirst. He then re-filled the canteen. Given the clamor of men rushing down to the creek, he worked his way to his gear left by the fallen tree.

As was his prediction, in no time, the narrow path to the water looked as wide as the road from foot traffic.

Everyone knew, on the march, water was a special commodity. James made his way to the shade of the fallen tree and finally sat down to rest. He closed his eyes and faced the high Sun above him.

"Thank you, Lord, for the water and another day. Amen." He whispered.

He reached for the haversack and pulled out an apple he found on the ground near a tree that morning. He went a little deeper into the sack and found a piece of hardtack biscuit leftover from last night's meal. A small piece of cheese was also saved and put in a cloth wrapper.

He smeared a portion of the warm cheese onto the hard biscuit and knowing how hard the small ration could get, he took a quick swallow of water and began to slowly chew around the biscuit. Between bites of the biscuit, he pulled his knife from his belt scabbard and sliced a piece of apple. The fruit gave the rather bland taste of the biscuit and cheese a much-appreciated flavor to his humble meal.

In short order, he was halfway through his noon meal when he saw a motion to his left. A rabbit appeared on the edge of the woods leading to the creek. The prey sat only fifteen feet away from James' position. The animal seemed to acknowledge him but offered no indication of fear or greeting toward the man. James chuckled to himself.

"I would run as far away as I could old rabbit. These boys are going to be looking for supper tonight." He said.

The rabbit took time to raise his right paw, give it a quick lick, and then wipe his eyes. James would have sworn, the rabbit was saluting him. He chuckled again and cut another slice from the apple, tossing it at the rabbit. Once again, the rabbit wiped the other eye, reached down to the apple slice, and nibbled it. The animal saluted once again, and silently hopped back into the woods.

James turned back to the remaining portion of his meal and took his last few bites between more deep swigs of water from the canteen. A deep burp rumbled up from his chest.

He paused for a moment to think about what to do next. Should he lean back and try to catch a quick nap? Perhaps he should clean his equipment one more time.

No, there was a letter from home. It was kept inside a special place within the haversack to keep things like paper, ink, and pencil safe from the weather. He had been saving letters from home for a couple of days now and was always amazed that mail was still being delivered to him on a reasonably regular basis despite the distance.

Because of the quick march, and lack of sleep, he had not yet found the opportunity to read the small moments of peace. Let alone having the time to prepare a proper response for it.

James heard an approaching horse on the road and saw First Lieutenant John Emerson coming his way. He was a young officer of Company E, "Independent Guards," of the 26th Regiment of North Carolina Troops, mostly from Chatham and other surrounding counties of North Carolina.

Lieutenant Emerson was a Corporal when James first met him at Camp Crab Tree back in the late Summer of 1861. He rode up right about the moment James was anxiously pushing the letter back into the haversack.

Private Ward moved as quickly as his tired body could, to stand at the position of attention and give the proper salute.

Lieutenant Emerson brought the horse to a halt, smiled, and said, "Private Ward, why don't you just set down and rest for a while?"

James responded, "Well, Sir, it seemed to be the proper thing we do in this here army. You know, you being an officer, and me being a private in this here same army."

"Yes, I know," the Lieutenant said.

"But nobody's close by, so we can dispense with the formalities between us. Hell, James, we been together for over two years now. Besides, I just came to tell you that we're going to be here for at least tonight." He added.

"Let the others know as soon as they come back from the creek. Captain Brewer will be by later this afternoon with orders. Also, inform Sergeant Jones, we need him to stop by the company headquarters about an hour before sunset back that way about a quarter mile on the right. A big ass Oak Tree is where the tent will be." He continued.

The young Lieutenant turned in the saddle and pointed in the direction of his arrival. "Sounds like something big is about to happen, please tell me it's not Malvern Hill all over." James said.

Lieutenant Emerson leaned onto the saddle pommel and whispered, "Can't say for sure right now but we got some people up at Regiment pretty excited. King is just about to worry himself to death."

James gave that shy grin of his and reached up to the saddle while he patted the horse's neck, "That boy is excitable." He laughed.

Then the Private got serious, "Do you think this is the one that's going to get us home?"

"I heard Captain Brewer say more than once that if we could press them up North, maybe they would back off and leave us alone. Hard to believe though, you know how they fought near Richmond last year and Malvern Hill. Didn't act like they were the kind of folks that would just back off, if you know what I mean." The Lieutenant straightened onto the saddle.

James shook his head, remembering that night, lying on the ground at Malvern Hill, firmly imprinted into his memory. "Yeah, I think you're right about that. But he's the Captain and he knows a lot more than I do."

"Well, he's a good officer and I trust him, but not completely sure he believes it either. I think we're getting close to this thing, one way or the other," he said.

The Lieutenant pulled the reins of his horse to the left, gave the horse a nudge with his boot, and moved down the road.

James watched him disappear around the bend of the road and trees and then turned back to his temporary resting place by the fallen tree. As he sat down, he closed his eyes and let the hot Sun hit him again.

Immediately his thoughts led home to Columbus County North Carolina. The heat combined with the warmed breeze that washed across his face and the many days he sweated under a similar hot Sun, a more humid sky, and fields filled with crops of corn, cotton, tobacco, sugar cane, and the earthy smell of a huge garden filled with vegetables.

Private James Ward was twenty-eight years old when he enlisted into the Confederate States of America's Army on May 28, 1861, in Cartersville, North Carolina. That was a fateful day on so many levels for James and his family.

At five feet and ten inches, his brown hair, hazel eyes, tanned body from too many hours exposed to the Sun, presented a lean but muscular body built through a young lifetime of farming. To some, he seemed a little thin for his 162 pounds, as most people would describe him.

On that day, he was in Cartersville on a chore for his father. His father had recently made a purchase of a new and much larger wagon needed for the increase in crop harvest. It would be a two-day trip from the family farm to the small crossroad community and back.

Since that fateful day, he had seen another couple of birthdays and was thirty years old. He was one of the "old men" in the Regiment. Many of the much younger men looked to James and those like him to help them learn their trade in this new adventure.

The next thought was of his young wife, Miss Anna Wallace Ward. That warm thought sent him reaching for his haversack and the latest letter from home. He recalled from a recent letter that important things were happening on the family farm.

Just as he touched the letter with his hand, another voice from across the dusty road called out, "James!! James!! Help me out!!" Private Stephen Ward, James' first cousin, ran to where James sat on the ground.

"What's going on Stephen?" He replied as he carefully pushed the letter back into the haversack another time.

The boy was grinning from ear to ear, teeth showing like a bear. "I got to run a bunch of messages for Captain Brewer, and I need you to watch my haversack and my gear. Going to take a while."

Stephen had his brogan-style half boots strung around his neck. James pointed his finger at the boots, "You going to take those with you?"

"Yeah, Captain says I got to wear my boots when I report to each officer, 'cause I am supposed to represent him with those other officers."

James chuckled, "Well, I find it hard to believe you could ever 'represent' him very well. Him being an officer and gentleman, and you, well NOT an officer and gentleman with no boots on." He said.

Stephen laughed as well, "Yeah, but those boots slow me down when I'm running. I got to go, you'll watch my gear and take it with you if they start moving again?"

"Yeah, I got it Stephen, lay it over there, on the other side of the log so it's not seen," James nodded his head to his left.

The young boy, quickly moved his extra gear as directed and immediately turned toward the road, "I'll see you later tonight unless he makes me stay at the company headquarters to deliver more messages."

"Won't you need the gear to sleep tonight?" James asked.

"Nah, I got a cubby hole at the back of the tent where they store the supplies and headquarters equipment. Nobody even knows I'm there." Stephen adjusted his musket, cartridge box, and canteen as James watched.

"You be careful, and I'll have everything wherever I am tonight. Lieutenant Emerson was by here a while ago and he said we might be here overnight. If you don't hear about us moving, look for me over by that big Oak Tree," James pointed his thumb to the left at the designated tree.

"I'll do that, if the Captain don't have any messages to run by the end of the evening." With that said, Stephen turned and began running, his brogans bouncing around his neck as he ran.

Private Stephen Ward was age 23 at his enlistment June 1, 1861, at Cartersville, North Carolina. He enlisted because his cousin James had enlisted three days before him.

The young farm boy was a little smaller than James but was strong at five feet and eight inches tall and weighed in on the cattle scales at 142 pounds. He was known in the family for his quick smile, infectious humor, and always seeing the brighter side of life. He was hard working, fully committed to whatever was asked of him, always trying to please the family, but all the leaders of the senior Ward families sometimes felt he was a little too impetuous with his decision-making.

However, what they did like was even when making the wrong decision, he seemed to make it work out better than most people imagined. Even with his smallish size, he was strong and could endure a long day on the farm with that smile on his face. What amazed everyone the most was his running.

No one in the county had been able to race and beat him at the county fair in five years and there were many who tried. There was one story that was popular at family gatherings where his running saved another cousin's life when they were clearing woods for the lumber and new fields for crops.

A large yellow pine tree split while being cut with cross-cut saws. One of the limbs caught the cousin and pinned him to the ground. It was obvious there were broken bones and internal bleeding. There were no horses or mules with them that day since they were just cutting the trees down and would be milled on another day.

The closest doctor was nearly five miles away to town. One of the other cousins ran to the Ward home for help over two miles away. Knowing a doctor was needed, Stephen chose to run for the doctor. He ran to the doctor's house in under twenty-five minutes.

After making the doctor aware of the situation, the doctor quickly gathered his medical bag and supplies he thought he might need. They got into the doctor's wagon and rode back to the farm. All of this took less than one hour. The doctor found the cousin in bad condition, but they had successfully stopped the bleeding of the external wounds and kept the boy awake.

He was moved, using the doctor's wagon to the Ward homestead where after some surgical procedures, the doctor was able to save an arm, leg, and hand from being amputated. Meanwhile, the boy's family arrived almost at the same time. However, everyone recognized the cousin would not have survived if the doctor had not arrived so quickly.

As James' first cousin on his daddy's side of the family, Stephen was very familiar with the Ward Farm life. As one of the older cousins across the entire senior Ward Brother's farms, he was expected to help each one of the four farms when extra hands were needed.

This system worked well within the family. The Ward Family farms had lots of boys and quite a few young women as well. Each played a critical part in not only the survival of the farms but the moderate success they had achieved over time under their father Brice Ward's leadership.

With Stephen gone, James decided to gather the equipment and gear and relocate to the big Oak Tree he had indicated to Stephen.

Once James had everything positioned within close reach, he settled himself between two extending surface roots of the tree. The roots were just high enough for his arms to rest on them like a rocking chair.

He looked around the area and saw other men beginning to claim similar positions for comfort whether short-lived or a longer stay. He gathered the haversack into his lap and once again found the letter he had been trying to read for over two days.

* * * * *

May 1, 1863

To Private James Ward, Company E, 26ᵗʰ Regiment, Pettigrew's Brigade, Heth's Division, General Hill's Corps

My Dearest Husband,

I wish to inform you that we are well on the farm. Your father complains often about your absence and the loss to the farm. Not to mention the foolishness of your participation in this war. Your mother seems a little more settled with the situation.

Recognizing that, as she puts it, "James is in God's hand now. We must pray for his safety."

This year has been a great labor for us since so many of the younger men have been levied into service and sent away. I am now convinced, if you had not joined when and why you did, you would have been eventually drawn into the war regardless. Our families are getting by on food. Miz Lizzie and I have grown a wonderful garden and we have plenty to eat for our entire family. We occasionally share with neighboring farms when they drop by seeking our help. We give what we can.

We struggle milking the cows with so many fewer girls available in the barns since they are busy working the fields to support the older men folk and the few boys we have left to farm. I am well and the baby seems to be settling in my large belly for the last few weeks before coming out. It is another reason why I am having trouble sitting on the stool trying to milk those cows.

You may be interested that I feel like I am just about as big as the cows are. Knowing you, I am sure you would like to squeeze my breasts too (please don't let others see this letter!).

Oh, the hinges and latches that were purchased last year have been put into place. Your father, with help, finished the barn and stable we began last Fall when you were here on furlough to recover.

We nearly have the house ready for us to finally move into our own home. Miz Lizzie has sewn some beautiful cotton drapes for the windows. Your sisters dyed the drapes a beautiful light blue. When we held them up to the windows in Miz Lizzie's house to make sure of the length of them, we were surprised that as the Sun shines through drapes, it looks like the sky comes into the house. It will take your breath away.

The money you provided was greatly appreciated and your short stay last Fall made a big difference, not to just the house but to our entire family. You gave us hope. Please be safe and know that I love you very much. I am sorry to bother you with our problems.

Your loving and devoted wife,
Anna Wallace Ward

CHAPTER 2

"HOW DO YOU FEEL ABOUT THAT?"
MAY 1861

James woke up that morning before the Sun came onto the horizon. As he crawled out of the bed to get dressed, his very newlywed wife reached up and gave him a hug. They had been married for nearly two months. She was a smart, young, strong, attractive, twenty-year-old woman raised on her own family farm just a few miles away. And Anna Wallace thought she was the luckiest woman in the State for getting James Ward as a husband. They had known each other for years and both families were close and trusted neighbors.

Anna Wallace, as everyone called her, was aesthetically a very attractive girl, with light brown hair, blue eyes, and a few freckles across her nose from the Sun. She stood five feet and eight inches and weighed 135 pounds.

Being a farm girl, she was physically strong and the pounds on her body were nearly all muscle. While many a boy would have loved to tussle with her, they would have found out that pretty package had a real mean streak when riled. Growing up, she had proved herself on more than one such occasion.

Anna Wallace had one older brother, two older sisters, one younger brother, and closely followed by one younger sister. With just a few brothers to work on their family farm, she was necessarily required to learn the family business, girl or not.

She was not just a girl on the farm, working in the house or kitchen; her working knowledge and years of experience, made her an indispensable member of her family's daily farming life.

Most people thought the two would get married years before the recent wedding. However, both James and Anna Wallace were of a very similar mind. They would be ready to marry only when they had their own farm.

It was not lost on either of them that on this morning, they were living with James' family until they completed their recently started homestead down by the "Green Swamp." It was one reason that James was anxious to take on this chore for his father this morning. The wagon and horses were to be part of the bargain between him and his father for their new homestead.

The hug was too much for James and he immediately fell into the arms of his wife. It was dark and they could barely make out each other in the bed but it did not take long to find what they were both looking for.

He kissed her softly on the lips, stroked her hair, and gently caressed her firm breasts. She reciprocated by guiding him carefully over her.

They took a few extra minutes to passionately say goodbye, and they enthusiastically consummated their love once again.

They both knew he needed to get dressed and leave. Anna Wallace Ward crawled out of the bed before her husband and moved to the wash pan located in the corner of the room. She quickly cleaned herself, threw on her shift, a light dress, and apron, and moved out of the room.

James was also moving quickly, realizing they had taken a few more minutes than planned. After dressing, he quickly reached for the cloth bag he had filled the night before with a few personal items he needed for the overnight trip.

He stepped into the kitchen area to find his mother and wife working feverishly at the stove and pantry. James remembered that the family farm was just that and the lady standing at the stove was the one that kept it moving.

"James, I don't care if you two carry on like that, but you got to be quieter about it. You'll drive every boy in this house crazy." Louise Ellen Martin Ward said.

She was better known as "Lizzie," was fifty-seven years of age that particular morning and she never looked at him or his wife as she spoke.

"Sit-down over there and get yourself some breakfast before you go. Coffee is on the stove; plenty of milk as well. I got some ham biscuits, wrapped in a cloth for your ride," she said. nodding her head toward the sideboard against the wall of the house.

Once again, she never looked up from the stove. Her pots and pans were constantly moving around to various places on the woodstove ensuring nothing cooking was too cool, overcooked, or burned.

James swiftly moved to the long table, sat down long enough to wolf down the sliced ham, four eggs, grits, bread smothered in freshly churned butter and Miz Lizzie's last season grape jam.

He looked around to ensure his mother was not watching and grabbed a couple of extra slabs of ham, cheese, and bread and started to stuff it into his jacket.

Miz Lizzie was more observant though and knew her son well enough, "James put that in that burlap bag over there before you mess your clothes up. Boy, you're going on business for the farm. Act like you know how it's done proper." She lambasted him.

"Yes ma'am, I promise not to bring shame to the family farm." He knew her reaction before he even said it out loud.

For the first time, she turned, with a large wooden spoon shaking in her hand, and looked directly at James, "Boy, are you sassing me?" She asked.

James was already up and moving for the door grinning from ear to ear, "No Miz Lizzie, I am just a poor country boy doing the best I can." He chuckled.

Miz Lizzie placed her hands on her hips, smiled as he reached for the door, and said, "Before you go, I got a short list for you to take with you. Don't buy it unless you got any extra from the sale."

James walked back to his mother, hugged her, and said, "I will try, Momma."

She slipped a carefully folded script of paper that contained her equally careful writings into his shirt pocket.

His mother leaned into him and hugged him as well. She patted his head softly. "You be careful, there are crazy people out there and some of them want to cheat you."

James eased her away from himself and looked at the glistening eyes of his mother. "I will momma. And I can't speak for Anna Wallace, but I promise to be quieter next time."

He turned and ran quickly out the door, as the wooden spoon was thrown against the door.

The young man trotted to the barn where he saw his father holding a lantern for light, already waiting with the mule harnessed to the wagon.

As usual, his father had bargained for the new wagon. The Ward family farm was not so large and profitable that such large amounts of extra cash were readily available for such significant purchases as a larger wagon.

James was going to take one of their smaller wagons with one mule, two bales of cotton, a large cask of tobacco, two gallons of cane syrup, a keg of grain alcohol, a dozen chickens, and two halves of smoked hog.

The plan was for James to exchange those goods for the new wagon, a set of new traces for the wagon, and two younger work horses, or mules if the price was too great for the horses. The night before, James had loaded the wagon and prepared for the next day trip.

His father, Thaddaeus Brice Ward, preferring to be called "Brice," was the patriarch of the Ward Family. He stood as tall as his son at five feet and ten inches and a bit heavier in weight.

While some of the weight was a bit of fat accumulated over the years, he was still a muscular man and one that no son would challenge without some fear of the results.

The old man had once told his sons that anytime they thought they could take him, to walk right up and tell him so. At sixteen years of age, young James did just that. "Father, I think I can take you."

In the blink of an eye, James had a fist on the left side of his head. He woke up moments later lying on the ground, with Miz Lizzie holding his head in her lap, waving a wet cloth on his face, "My God, Brice, you've killed our boy!!"

Brice Ward was standing with his feet between James' legs, clenched fist flexing. "You all right boy?" He asked.

James mumbled something that no one could understand. Brice nodded and walked away. Later, when James was fully conscious, Brice sat down by his son, who drew up with a bit of fear. "What did you learn today?"

After puzzling the question, James said, "I'm not ready to take you?"

"No, that is not what you learned. What you learned is that if you are going to challenge someone, you need to get the first hit. If he is bigger than you, it might be the only swing you get in the fight." Brice slapped him on the thigh, got up and again, walked away.

Brice's hair had once been an auburn color and prolific in mass when he was born in 1794 to "poor dirt farmers" with little to account for themselves. The only thing they had was the land they tilled and the fruits of their individual labors during each harvest season.

Yet, he was a restless young man on the farm. At eighteen years of age, he left home in 1812 to volunteer with the militia to defend against the British attacks in Maryland, Virginia, and the District of Columbia.

Having seen some military action there, he was transported to Louisiana to complete military operations against the British. He remained away from home for over two years. With the experience of war behind him, some of that previous restlessness was requited.

Many that knew Brice in his early years suggested that when he returned home, he was different. He had changed. When asked about his war experiences, he would immediately look down, maybe shuffle his feet, and say, "Not much to tell." Then he would start talking about something else.

Upon Brice's return from war, he married a young farm girl in 1816 only to lose both his newborn child and wife during a childbirth that went terribly wrong. This tragic event made him even more sullen, independent-minded, and focused on the large Ward family.

With his loss and disappointment, Brice committed himself to life as a farmer. By 1826, he had become so proficient in his farming abilities, that as the oldest and fittest son, he assumed responsibility for the Ward Brothers' farms. Each of the Ward brother farms included his younger brothers Joshua, called "Josh," at age sixty-five. Jeremiah, called "Jer," at age sixty-three, Issac at age sixty-two, and Nehemiah, called "Nem", at age fifty-seven.

Five years later, in 1831, he married a lively young lady named Louise Ellen Martin. They would have six children including James as the oldest. He was followed by Rebecca, Henry, Joshua, Ruth, and Sarah.

On this pre-dawn morning, Brice stood holding the reins of the lone mule required to pull the wagon for James.

Even in the darkness, James could see his father was dressed in his usual farm attire consisting of black or dark gray pants and a similar colored suit coat. It stood out because of the pressed white shirt he had beneath the coat. His brown felt hat sat on his head at a slight angle to the right.

This was Brice's work clothes of choice. Very little deviation was acceptable to him. He considered himself a gentleman farmer and would dress as the refined gentlemen he saw in Washington, in the South, and in New Orleans during his war years.

On the hottest days of Summer in Southeastern North Carolina, it was the same. Occasionally, he would remove the coat to get down into the earth, if necessary. However, he would never allow himself to be seen in public or in the presence of a lady without the coat.

For more formal occasions, such as a trip to town, there would be a vest and tie to accompany the suit. Miz Lizzie was always responsible for the cleaning, pressing, mending, and folding the same three sets of clothing he had hanging in a large cedar wardrobe in their bedroom each day.

"James, put that bag your momma gave you under the seat. You can eat while you're riding. Don't hesitate to stop by the river and creeks along the way and let the mule drink either." Brice hesitated as if thinking of other instructions.

"There is one of the double-barrel shotguns under the seat. Use it if you have to. You got some valuable goods for this load. Lot of people would covet it and take it from you if you're not prepared." He handed the reins to James.

The eldest Ward son understood what his father was saying. What he carried was a very valuable bargaining cargo for something this farm would need for many years. "I understand Father, I'll take care of it and use it only if I have to." He said.

James climbed onto the wagon seat and straightened the leather lines. Brice offered, "You'll do fine. You always do. I know your mother gave you a list. Try to get what you can, and she'll be satisfied. Don't waste any of the cash though if you can help it. But bring something home just for her." Brice patted his son's shoulder.

"Alright, get out of here, it'll be light soon. Probably takes most of the day to get to Cartersville from here. Tell Henry I said hello and tell him I said not to take advantage of my son." Brice slapped the rump of the mule and the wagon started lurching forward.

James looked back, "Should be home by late tomorrow. I'll take care of Momma's list and Miss Anna Wallace's list too!"

Brice thought he would get in the last word, "That girl's gonna drive you to the poor house boy!!"

"I know, Father but I do so love her!!" he shouted, riding away.

James settled in for the long trip to Cartersville down the two-track dirt road and had only gone about two miles when a lone figure stepped out of the wood line.

His first reaction was to reach for the shotgun under his seat. He just about had it up to his lap when he recognized the dark shape in the early morning light. "Stephen, is that you?"

"Yeah, it's me! Don't shoot me!!" He was laughing as he walked toward the wagon.

"What are you doing out here this time of morning?" James brought the mule to a stop.

Stephen patted the mule's rump, "Dad told me Uncle Brice was sending you over to Cartersville for the new wagon. Thought you might like some company?"

"Surely your dad's got work for you to do. Won't he miss you?"

"Probably, but we had a slow day planned anyway. Nothing he and the brothers and sisters can't handle by themselves. So, what do you say, can you handle an extra passenger?"

James looked a little unsure but knew Stephen would not do anything to make his dad mad. "Sure, I see you got your poke sack there, so pretty sure you got what you need to stay overnight. But if your dad gets mad, I'm saying it's all your fault." James said as both of the young Ward men laughed.

The two Ward sons stopped three times to water the mule. They took the early afternoon stop to pull out the burlap sack that Miz Lizzie had packed for him.

"Good Lord, she's got a whole fried chicken in here. Looks like four or five biscuits, even got a baked potato." James said, pulling smaller cheesecloth-wrapped packages out of the rough woven fabric bag.

He then reached into the bag for the slices of ham, bread, and cheese he had tried to sneak out of the kitchen that morning.

Stephen watched James continue to pull each small package out, "Miz Lizzie out-did herself, again! I thought you said you were only going to be gone two days!" Stephen said.

"Well, maybe she knew I was picking up a freeloader along the way," James laughed.

"I got my own stuff in my bag but not that much for sure. Let me pull some things out and see if we can make a couple or three meals out of it." Stephen started pulling similar small packages of wrapped food out of his bag.

"Let's see, I got a couple of pork chops, I got two cooked sweet potatoes, a jar of sweet pickles, some fresh-baked bread, and a chunk of butter." James watched as Stephen continued to pull the food out.

"Lord, Stephen. We must be rich! Can't get any better than this?" James leaned back against the willow tree and enjoyed what they had selected for their midday meal.

The two young men haggled over what they would eat for the Noon meal and then started bargaining for the evening meal. That complete, they looked at the leftovers and then felt they had enough for breakfast as well.

Stephen leaned back on the grass as well, and chewing on his chicken leg, he said, "Rich men indeed!"

While running into people moving along the same route in both directions, other than an occasional wave or tip of the hat, they didn't meet any difficulties.

They made it to Cartersville at about five-thirty in the afternoon and well before dark. James headed straight to Henry Jones' foundry to get the bargaining out of the way before dinner.

Cartersville, North Carolina was not a large city, town, or even village by most accounts. There were few shops, stores, or real business establishments congregated on what would be called the main road of the community.

As they rode into town, James could see, a general store, certainly, one of the more busy and larger stores. He saw a building with a sign hanging outside that looked like the building held the town doctor, hospital, dentist, and apothecary in a single-story building perhaps sixteen feet wide and perhaps thirty feet deep.

The town's most prominent building was a well-built, feather-edged boarded, white-wash painted community church capable of seating over one hundred souls for communing with God. It had a tall front steeple having several bells, no doubt provided by the Jones foundry.

There was another two-story building that posted a sign saying Jones Boarding House. It evidently had meals being served as part of boarding there. As they progressed past the boarding house, James noted there was a gathering of several men and at least two men in uniforms.

Stephen saw it as well, "I wonder what that's all about?" he said.

"Don't know, but I need to get to Mister Jones' pretty quick before dark." James answered, giving the mule another nudge with the reins.

They continued their tour of the town as they moved closer to the foundry office. But before that they saw a butcher shop where beef, pork, sheep, chicken, rabbit, squirrel, and quail could be bought. Right beside the butcher shop was a bakery that also carried eggs, fresh fruit and vegetables, and some pies were placed in the window. Then they saw a rather small building not more than ten feet wide and twelve feet deep; it was the post office.

One did not have to be a businessman to recognize the primary industry of this town was the making of farm implements and wagons. The twenty-five or thirty houses surrounding the town were all focused on the Henry Jones Foundry and its supporting businesses.

James did some quick multiplying in his head and calculated that the entire town was probably less than two hundred people. He chuckled to himself as he looked back at the church, "I'm guessing that church was built to hold about two hundred people. What do you think?"

Stephen did the same and glanced at the church, "I'm guessing that's about right." He added.

The foundry contained three large buildings. One was a barn and office for the foundry. One building held the actual forge for the metal works and the blacksmiths were hammering away. The third building had a lot of lumber and housed the wagon-making activities.

They arrived at the foundry office and pulled to a stop in front of the barn. Stephen jumped down and gathered the reins of the mule. James stepped down from the wagon and walked to the front door of the office.

Before he got to the doorknob, a tall slim man came out, "James, is that you boy? I haven't seen you since you turned twenty! You're full grown now!" He said.

"Hello Mister Jones, yes, it's me. Father said to tell you hello and don't take advantage of his son." James was smiling when he said it.

"Yep, that's your old man. We been doing business for a lot of years and he still thinks I charge too much for things at times. How is he doing these days?" The foundry owner said, reaching out with his right hand to shake James' hand.

Mister Jones continued while finishing his firm handshake of friendship, "I got his letter about a month ago. He was pretty specific about what he was looking for. Is this what you brought me to bargain with?" Henry asked.

"Yes Sir, it is. I'll be happy to let you look over everything and decide what its worth for bargaining." James reached over and pulled the canvas-covering away.

The wagon-builder looked over the edge of the wagon wall and then flipped the cover back over the goods. "If what he suggested is in here, I am good with the number. I'll have the boys pull everything out of this wagon and store it tonight in the barn. You want to see that new wagon?"

"Yes, Sir if you don't take offense. I am sure it is exactly what you and Father agreed upon, but he bragged about your fine work, and I would love to see it." James exercised his charm.

"It would be my pleasure to take you through our business. Hoping you will be impressed enough to recommend us to your entire family. Every farm needs wagons and we would love to sell them one." Jones was very proud of his reputation and knew James and Stephen were farmers of a new generation.

"Mister Jones, this is my cousin Stephen Ward. His dad is my Uncle Jeremiah Ward." James introduced his younger cousin.

Stephen shifted the reins from his right hand to his left and stepped forward, offering his hand to the foundry owner.

"I'm pleased to meet you Mister Jones. my dad has bought off at least two of Uncle Brice's smaller wagons that you built. They're still working just fine." Stephen shook the owner's hand and stepped back to the mule's side.

Mister Jones shook his hand and said, "Well, Stephen, I'm glad to meet you as well. Maybe your dad will like Brice's new wagon and want to buy one too. C'mon boys, let's go around the back. We got your wagon ready to pull."

They moved through the foundry building and it was impressive. The barn had several wagons of various sizes and purposes sitting on the ground floor level. Above, in the many stalls, were lumber of various size and lengths. They continued through the extraordinarily large barn to the back.

To say James was impressed with the new wagon would be an understatement as they stepped out of the back barn doors.

"My Lord! It's huge!!" He slowly walked up to the wagon and touched it with both hands. He just wanted to make sure it was real.

Stephen was following behind, just as stunned. There was a large stump close by, he sat down on it and said, "How big is it?" The cousin was almost whispering.

Mister Jones proudly responded, "Well, she is four feet longer than the wagon you brought. She is six feet wide from wall to wall. Got four feet high side walls as you can plainly see. Side boards can be lowered to half depending on what you're hauling. The back gate can be unlatched and drops into two pieces to use as a loading ramp. There's a toolbox located underneath the driver's seat." He said grinning with pride.

"James, I took the liberty of putting some tools in there for your father in case you have to do repairs. Wheels are five feet high and about two inches wider. She can take two, four, or six horses at a time, depending on the traces you're using and the size of the load." The owner added.

Henry Jones moved around the wagon, showing the features built to Brice Ward's precise requirements.

"Mister Jones, how do we get this monster home?" James said. He was overwhelmed with the size and his immediate thought was that "Red" the mule would never survive pulling this wagon back home.

"Well, I think your father had that in mind as well. C'mon and let's go over to the other barn." Henry Jones started walking away.

Both James and Stephen sat or stood where they were for a moment before realizing that Mister Jones was walking away.

They both followed the older man to the barn. There he stood beside two eighteen hands high solid black Morgan draft horses. Their bodies shined in the dimming afternoon light. They were well-mannered and stood perfectly straight. "Boys, meet Demon and Satan!"

James spoke first, "They're beautiful. Are they named that for a reason?"

"Well, I'm pretty sure they can pull anything from here to Hell and back with no problems." Henry Jones laughed.

"I can't imagine that Father can afford those two animals. He suggested that I look for a couple of mules if we couldn't find a horse we could afford." James was shaking his head.

Henry responded, "I don't think you understand James, your father already bought these as part of the deal. Given what you got in that wagon you brought, I'm sure I can make a pretty sizeable profit to offset the price."

"Mister Jones, I am stone cold numb right now. I don't know what to do?" James Ward said.

"James, I suggest you take your good fortune and go home tomorrow. Where you boys staying tonight?"

"Well, I was thinking we would stay under the old wagon tonight and then hook up in the morning, if you don't mind us staying here." James paused.

"Not going to happen! You boys can stay at the boarding house tonight if you don't mind bedding together. Got chicken and dumplings, cornbread, lots of green beans, and turnip greens for dinner tonight," Jones handed the horse reins to one of his handlers and pushed the boys back to the front office.

As they walked, Henry Jones asked, "Correct me if I am wrong James, but I believe I saw a keg in your wagon that might contain some strong moonshine? Am I wrong?"

James was quick to respond, "Yes Sir! I believe Father made that run himself very carefully and just for you."

Henry Jones slapped James on the back, and they laughed as they gathered their personal items from the old wagon. Their mule had already been taken away and the wagon stripped bare of its cargo.

The boys checked into the Jones Boarding House and enjoyed a great meal. Henry and his wife were with them and about eight other guests. Three of the guests were in military uniforms.

There was conversation about local events, current business ventures, and news from the state capitol in Raleigh.

Eventually someone asked the men in uniform, what was going on with the possibility of war after the attack on Fort Sumter, in nearby South Carolina.

The gentleman named Captain W. S. Webster was calm and deliberate in his explanation of the current conditions. "I'm afraid our neighbors to the South have created a problem that is going to draw us into something North Carolina has very little interest in."

Henry responded, "Captain, I have to use the port down near Fort Fisher occasionally to get my supplies. Do you think someone will do like they did at Fort Sumter at Fort Fisher as well?"

"There are some hotheads that may attempt it, but the Governor has made it clear that he won't tolerate such notions in North Carolina." Captain Webster offered.

"Do you believe this rumor of secession from the Union will impact us?" Another guest asked.

"Only the legislature and the Governor can make that decision. I know there is a lot of debate and discussion, but I believe the Governor is talking to President Lincoln's administration about how to minimize the danger." Captain Webster continued to push his dumplings around on his plate.

"Captain, may I ask why you are here in Southeastern North Carolina?" James asked.

Webster looked up and said, "I am in this area to recruit individuals, like yourself and your cousin there, to join the militia of North Carolina Troops if such a decision is made to defend the State."

The Captain pushed his unfinished meal toward the center of the table. "One of the steps the Governor thought prudent was to prepare for just such a levy of regimental soldiers in the event the North Carolina legislature makes that decision."

Webster continued, "He even offered to pay recruitment bonuses to those willing to sign in the near future." He said.

The officer reached into his jacket pocket and pulled four five-dollar gold coins and placed them on the table.

Everyone at the table leaned forward to see the very bright coins. "For twelve months of service, the Governor has authorized a monthly payment of six dollars and an enlistment bonus of twenty dollars in gold coins freshly minted from Charlotte."

Both James and Stephen looked at the coins and each other. They gently leaned back in their chairs. Stephen responded first, "Where would you have to go for that service?"

With a tight-lipped smile, the Captain said, "Well, at this time, we expect our militia regiments to be readily available to quell any mischief toward the Governor and North Carolina. However, I must tell you truthfully, if the State secedes from the Union, there is little doubt, we will eventually be deployed North."

James was next, "When would we have to leave?"

"It is our intent to get everyone enlisted, then we move near to Raleigh sometime in late Summer. Let's everyone get the summer harvest in before going to training. After that, you would be deployed to where the Governor considered necessary. Most regiments would probably be stationed near their regimental center point. For this area, which will probably be to the center and Southeast of Raleigh, not too far from here and close to the coast." Captain Webster replied.

"So, we would need to be trained first somewhere around August or September? And when do we get the money?" Stephen responded.

Webster looked at both of the Ward boys and certainly realized he had two potential recruits right in front of him at the dinner table. "Sounds about right but no promises. As for the money, you get paid at the end of each month on duty and during roll call. As for the bonus, you sign the contract, I'll give you the coins on your oath to return on May 28th for the unit movement."

Stephen looked like he was about to ask for the contract at that very moment, but James eased his hand onto Stephen's arm and said, "Sounds interesting but we got to get a wagon back home. If we knew somebody interested in this contract, how long before they need to sign?"

"I'll be in this area until the end of the month. If those interested parties show up, I'll make sure we have somebody here to sign the papers and give them their bonus. How do you feel about that?"

James paused, "Not sure about that quite yet, Sir."

"But you need to tell your friends, take the bonus, and not show up will go very badly for them. We have prisons for such people." Webster added.

The Captain pushed himself away from the table and gave his compliments and thanks for the meal and company. The other two men in military uniforms had remained very quiet during the discussion and they got up as soon as the officer stood.

Both James and Stephen waited an extra moment for the soldiers to leave the room and gave their thanks to Mrs. Jones for the meal.

"Mister Jones, if you don't mind, we'll go to our room for the night. We've got some errands to run for our families in the morning and we'll visit the general store first thing it's open. I expect we'll try to be out of here and on our way home within the hour after that, with your permission of course, Sir." James added.

Henry Jones stood for the boys and said, "You do that James. We'll have the wagon and horses ready about dawn. You can get 'em any time after that."

"If I'm busy and you don't see me, say hello to your father and tell him, I tried to take care of you boys!!" He gave a hearty laugh and sat back at the table.

The next day went pretty much as planned. The general store visit was successful especially since Mister Jones had offered his "family price" to the boys.

Miz Lizzie would be pleased with the ten yards of cloth for dresses for the Ward girls and the extra cloth would make some nice handkerchiefs for the men and boys. She was always thinking about Christmas no matter the time of year.

James found an unusual pan that he thought she would like to make cornbread into individual shapes. It would be his gift to Miz Lizzie's upcoming birthday.

Brice had asked him to look for some books for his wife and something special if James could afford it. He found a book of Shakespeare plays that was a little worn but serviceable. He also found a beautiful brooch with ruby colored glass. At the price, he was sure it was not real rubies, but he knew she would love it since her birthday was in July.

For Brice, James found a very nice two bladed pocketknife with pearl inlaid. It would be nearly useless on a farm, but it was too nice to be used like that. No, Brice would use it to open a letter, clean his occasional pipe, or trim his nails. It would be used as something that drew attention to its owner.

Stephen also made minor purchases in the form of writing paper and pencils for his mother and sisters. For the boys, he had nearly a pound of hard rock candy.

They started their journey home and talked nearly the entire trip about the dinner with Captain Webster. "James, with that gold I would be the richest man in our family! Why wouldn't I take the gold?"

"Boy you just might get yourself killed too. Then how you gonna spend that gold?" James gave his two new horses a quick flick with the reins.

"Well, how would you use the gold?" Stephen offered.

James mulled it over for a few moments, "I would be buying some new hinges, locks, and farm equipment for the well. And Anna Wallace is wanting glass windows. I guessing that would take up most of it."

Both of the Ward cousins were fairly quiet the rest of the trips, caught in their own thoughts and twenty dollars in gold.

* * * * *

August 5, 1861

To Mrs. Anna Wallace Ward, General Delivery, Whiteville, North Carolina

My Dearest wife and family,

Stephen and I successfully travelled most of the State to get to a place they call Camp Crab Tree. We're not too far from the Capitol of Raleigh but I am sure I will not be visiting it while I am here.

Our travel included train, wagons, and marching. I guess we better get used to all three. Probably more marching than anything else.

We're just getting settled in and best I can tell, there are hundreds of people just like Stephen and me. We are assigned to the 26th Regiment of North Carolina Troops. It has mostly men from our neck of the woods and Chatham County, just like Captain Webster said.

Most folks seem excited and trying hard to be good infantry soldiers. I'm sure we'll do you and the State proud.

Training is not too hard for a farmer, but it is different. Lots of drills for marching. Who knew moving around could be so complicated. But Officers and the Sergeants push us hard.

Lots of rumors about where we are going and ever since the Governor and the legislature pushed us into secession, we seem hell-bent on going to war with everybody it seems. The popular rumor is that we will be assigned near the coast once we finish training. That would be good for us since it would not be far to travel to visit us.

Tell Miz Lizzie that they don't cook the food here like she does. Takes a little getting used to it and surely doesn't taste as good as hers.

Tell Father, I am sorry he is so mad at me for doing this. I'll have to admit I don't really understand what everyone is so upset with but that twenty dollars in gold was just too much to pass up.

We were able to get the nails, hinges, latches, and other hardware to finish the house. Most importantly, we were able to order and pay for the glass we *needed for the windows. Hopefully, my monthly pay will help as well. I have enclosed two dollars for you to use as you think proper.*

Please wish your family the best for me and that I miss their daughter so much already. I wish we had one more night together.

Your loving husband,

Private James Ward, Company E, 26th Regiment of North Carolina Troops, Camp Crab Tree, North Carolina.

CHAPTER 3

CAMP CRAB TREE, AUGUST 27, 1861

The new recruits' movement to Camp Crab Tree, Northwest of the State Capitol was fairly uneventful. For many, this trip was the furthest they had ever travelled from their own towns, homes, and farms.

Such newly recruited soldiers watched from the window of the train with awe as they passed large farms, cross-roads, small towns, and then the larger city of Raleigh.

After arriving and then disembarking from the train, they were formed into some semblance of a military formation and began marching several miles to the new camp. At this point, if they could walk forward, the officers were satisfied.

James and Stephen stayed close to each other the entire trip. They had promised both of their parents they would look out for each other. And that they did.

Stephen said, "James, I've never seen this many people in one place before! How many you guess?"

James did the quick multiplication in his head, looked to the sky as if calculating the answer on an imaginary blackboard, "I'm guessing about a thousand or more and me neither. Never seen this many people in one place. This makes the county fair look really small."

He continued, "I heard one of the Sergeants on the train say there were about ten or twelve companies in each regiment."

It was six o'clock the next morning and Captain Webster suddenly appeared from the wave of white canvas tents to stand in front of the gathered men of Company E.

He stood on a small wooden box and shouted above all their voices, "First Sergeant Brooks, form your company!"

The Captain then stepped off the small platform. The man identified as the First Sergeant, stepped forward and onto the platform. He was dressed in a new, freshly pressed, and clean butternut colored military uniform.

At first, his head looked from left to right and then right to left. He then stared over the mass of over one hundred men before him, as if collecting his thoughts.

Four other men, dressed in similar military uniforms, moved, and stood right below and to the front of the First Sergeant. Two of the uniforms had Sergeant stripes and two had Corporal stripes on their uniform sleeves. They were standing at what the soldiers were about to learn was the position of attention. The crowd of recruits watched and mumbled to each other as the scene played out before them.

James recalled a brief description of camp training Captain Webster had supplied them the morning after their supper at the Jones Boarding House in Cartersville. "Stephen, correct me if I am wrong, but I believe this is where Captain Webster said all Hell would break loose?"

Stephen never had the opportunity to respond. The First Sergeant's face started to take on a look of severe pain. When it looked as if his face would burst from blood rushing to his head, he yelled, "Sergeants, form your ranks!!"

At that very moment, the two Second Sergeants and two Corporals ran to the group of new recruits and positioned themselves facing to the right and one arm's length beside each other. Once positioned, they extended their right arm out from their sides. The first of the Second Sergeants yelled to the group of new soldiers, "Tallest man in the company stand behind me, then the next man by height, tallest first!"

The latest soldiers of the Confederate Army were getting their indoctrination in the forms and functions of the order of drill. Their first lesson was forming the company. To say there was confusion is mildly describing the chaos.

After watching the confusion for several minutes, Captain Webster and his group of Lieutenants gathered by one of the canvas tents, "Watch the Sergeants and help when necessary but let them straighten the men out. The sergeants need to learn to command these men as well as you or me."

"Sir, I suggest we give the Sergeants the time to get them organized and at once begin marching in section, platoon, and company formation. I would also recommend we begin with a movement to the open parade field for drill practice, and then finish this morning's session with a march around the entire camp," offered the First Lieutenant.

First Lieutenant William Headen was a large man with the strong ability to lead and inspire men. His attitude and leadership were quickly recognized by all that met the junior officer. He would soon be called by the nickname, "Bull Headen."

Second Lieutenant Bryant C. Dunlap and his fellow Second Lieutenant Stephen W. Brewer smiled, saluted smartly to Captain Webster, as he turned to leave.

Both young men were from affluent families but still well-respected young leaders in their own communities. People tended to follow their direction as leaders.

After thirty minutes of Sergeants yelling, screaming, and pushing soldiers into their ranks. Lieutenant Headen, yelled in a deep voice,

"Attention!!" The Sergeants and Corporals quickly assumed the position of attention, arms at the side, standing straight, and eyes directed forward. The new soldiers quickly followed their example.

Headen continued, "First Sergeant, you will now take charge of these enlisted men and explain to them the proper actions to take in close order drill. You will begin with the proper way to form the company. Do you understand?"

"Sir, Yes Sir, I do understand and will comply Sir!" The First Sergeant crisply saluted the Lieutenant.

Headen continued, "Upon completion of that instruction, the Lieutenants will lead the troops, by platoon or section, to the parade field where they will be introduced to all section, platoon, and company drills and commands, and how they integrate with the entire regiment." No one appeared willing to argue the directions.

The First Sergeant again responded, "Sir, Yes Sir!"

"Very well, I offer this advice to you men. You are newly recruited members of the Independent Guards, Company E of the 26th Regiment of North Carolina Troops. You have sworn your allegiance and committed your lives to this Company, this Regiment, this State, and to each other. Your honor and survival in battle is built around that trust in each other. Do not forget that when you doubt your own resolve." He paused to let that thought linger in each man's mind.

"Your First Sergeant and Cadre are not your friends. They are your leaders in battle. You must listen, you must learn, you must practice, and you must execute orders as they demand of you. You are soldiers now, whether you know it now or later, their direction will save your lives. Do not fail them!" Once again, he paused for the effect.

"Every day, until we leave this Camp, you will conduct parade ground drills from Eight to Ten o'clock each morning and then from Three to Five o'clock each afternoon following the order of the Camp

Commandant, Major Burgwyn. You will not embarrass Captain Webster. Do you understand?" Lieutenant Headen waited for an answer.

The Cadre at once responded, "Sir, Yes Sir!!" The troops shuffled their feet and looked at each other.

First Sergeant Brooks immediately jumped in front of the group of soldiers and shouted, "Your superior officer asked you a question. Answer him!!"

Soldiers started to mumble in response and created only an almost muted sound. The First Sergeant stood in front of the group with an evil eye, and whispered, "When your superior officer asks you a question, you say, Sir, Yes Sir!! Do you understand?"

The group responded in chorus exactly as the Sergeant said and as he knew they would, "Sir, Yes Sir!!

The First Sergeant immediately shouted again, "I am your First Sergeant, do not call me Sir!! I am not an officer; your Second Sergeants are not officers; your Corporals are not officers. You address us by our rank, Sergeant, or Corporal. Do you understand?" He waited with his hands on his hips.

"Sergeant, Yes Sergeant" was the response from the troops.

The troops were beginning to get the idea.

The First Sergeant looked at the men and inquired, "Now troops, do you have an answer for the Lieutenant's question?" He then turned to face the officer.

As one, the group responded to Lieutenant Headen, "Sir, Yes Sir!!"

"Very well! First Sergeant, take charge of the drills and Lieutenants Dunlap and Brewer will assist where required. Conduct a proper roll call, then send these men to breakfast. Be on the parade field no later than Eight o'clock. No weapons required at this time. Carry on." Headen waited for the proper dismissal salute from the First Sergeant.

The First Sergeant responded, "Sir, Very Good, Sir!!" and awaited the Lieutenant's return salute.

Headen saluted and stepped from the platform and walked over to the other lieutenants where he provided directions for the younger officers as well. None of the new troops noticed whether they were just as new to their roles as officers and gentlemen as these troops were to being soldiers.

As was tradition with militia units, the officers and enlisted cadre of the 26th Regiment were recently elected to their positions. Many men were chosen for their professional or military experience, many by family affluence, some by education, others by appearance because they were large men and not to be disobeyed. A few soldiers would suggest those men were elected because they were bullies.

Captain Webster reappeared from his company headquarters tent to face his officers with a well-used book in his hand with small slips of paper hanging out of pages in the book. He motioned for his Lieutenants to step over to the tent.

"Gentlemen, Major Burgwyn, the Camp Commandant has directed a very aggressive training schedule for the men. I believe he has some knowledge of the expressed intent of our newly appointed Regimental Commander, Colonel Zebulon B. Vance, formally Commander of Company F of the 14th Regiment." Webster paused.

"If Major Burgwyn's information is correct, our Regiment will probably be assigned to the East coast of North Carolina as soon as the Regiment is prepared and ready."

Lieutenant Headen offered a personal thought, "I'm guessing that will be better news for the men since we would be staying in North Carolina and closer to home." The other Lieutenants nodded their agreement.

"I would agree Bill, but we have to make sure the men are ready for anything we're assigned. Most of these men have seen little more than a local fist fight for battle. They have to be organized, trained, and ready for war, regardless, if it's at Fort Fisher, the state of Virginia, or somewhere else North of here."

Captain Webster extended the book out to Lieutenant Headen, "Gentlemen, this is a used copy of the Gilham's Manual for Volunteers and Militia. If you have any doubt of your own understanding of forming and fighting with troops, you need to get educated in a hurry."

The officers looked at the book as Headen turned the pages to the preface and contents pages. He read the instructional preface out loud for the others. As Headen finished the preface, Webster took the book.

Webster continued, "I am not, personally, ready to command these troops into battle, but before we deploy, I guarantee, I will be much better than I am today. And you will be too."

"You will each read this entire book and be able to lead this company in its drill each day. You will read the next day's parade field drills and memorize them like you have known them all of your life. The men do not need to know, you're just as new to the art of war as they are. As officers, your job is to train, lead, and inspire your men." Each junior officer nodded their understanding.

Webster advised, "We start at the basic level and work ourselves through section, platoon, and the company level. We'll deal with the regimental portion as we collaborate with our Commander."

"Help each other, learn together, work together, correct each other. Your lives and the lives of these men depend on your ability to execute the formations and commands as effectively as practical. Perform your duty well; all our lives depend on it."

The Captain looked at each officer, "We will conduct drills each day. Each day, we will get better. We will become proficient enough to do our duty. We do this without weapons at first. Then we move to drills with weapons. We begin to move in formations with weapons for battle and commands later, when we can do it without hurting someone."

Captain Webster paused, "Finally, we go the firing range and practice firing in mass. Between those critical drills, we must teach these men about military courtesy, guard duty, camp hygiene, digging latrines, washing, and cleaning uniforms and proper maintenance of our equipment, and medical attention."

He dismissed the junior officers.

Breakfast was good, even for the Ward boys that lived on a farm. Eggs, grits, biscuits, ham, bacon, potatoes were in abundance. Coffee, milk, and water were ready to wash it all down.

James offered, "Well it's not Momma's cooking but it ain't too bad."

Between bites, Stephen added, "You could get used to it, it's really good! I might have to think about the army for a job."

"Are you crazy? As soon as this mess is over, I'm for home and the farm. The food's not that good!" James replied.

Later that day, the men of Company E, made their way to the parade field located at the center of the camp. It was a hot August day, and the Sun was high.

To be expected, at first, the men were disorganized, failed to quickly learn the proper commands, and the expected reaction to the commands. Dysfunctional was the proper word when describing the troops on their first day on the parade field.

Off to one side of the parade field, observing each unit on the field, was a very well-groomed young man in an officer's uniform that was pressed to perfection.

At one of the water breaks, James noticed the man had been there for at least an hour watching all of the units conducting their drills. In his hand, he had a small notebook or journal where he apparently made numerous notations with a pencil of those observations.

"I wonder what he's writing down in that book?" James asked more to himself than anyone in particular.

One of the Sergeants overheard James' rhetorical question and answered, "That officer over there is the Commandant of Camp Crab Tree, and he decides when you and this Company are ready for battle."

"Looks awful young to be a Major, don't you think. Don't look much older than me. How'd he get to be a Major?" asked Stephen.

The Sergeant chuckled, "Yep, he's young all right. He will soon be twenty years of age. But he knows his stuff. Just graduated a couple of months ago from the Virginia Military Institute near the top of his class. Comes from a pretty rich family here abouts. Pretty sure with his military training and family politics, probably helped get that promotion." The Sergeant walked away.

Major Henry King Burgwyn, Jr. was a most unusual young man. His family had connections to the North and the South. He was not raised to be a farmer by his family but his affection for the South made the family's North Carolina plantation near the Virginia and North Carolina state line, in the Northeastern part of the State, is where he really called home.

His early education, other than his own home instruction, was provided in preparatory schooling in the North. Then followed that up with school at an Episcopal College.

Being too young to enter West Point, he was sent to West Point for private tutoring.

Instead of staying at West Point, he returned to the place he called home and Chapel Hill where he attended the University of North Carolina. He graduated with honors in two years. Next, he attended and graduated from the Virginia Military Institute where he was instructed by his Professor Thomas J. Jackson.

Burgwyn's rank of Major and position as the Camp Commandant was by appointment of none other than the Governor of North Carolina on July 5, 1861.

The drills and training for all of the North Carolina Troop units continued throughout the months of July and August of 1861. As proficiency in battle drills and training progressed more attention was paid to weaponry and battle engagements.

James was especially interested in this portion of their training. He was an excellent shot but the process for the fast loading of the musket he received was a little concerning for him.

While the massing of over one hundred muskets firing at the enemy was new to his thought process, he understood it. However, his first thought was why not focus on one target and a careful shot to hit that target.

One hundred guns, essentially firing as one, seemed a terrible waste of time and ammunition to James.

The officers and cadre had begun to recognize that James was a little different than the young privates in their company. He was older and his maturity showed. He was confident in what he could do. He was seen as one of the smarter men in the unit.

They also saw how proficient he was with a weapon in his hand. Within one hundred yards, he was deadly with his musket.

After a particular day of training, there were other soldiers that showed similar capabilities. To James' dismay, challenges were being made to a contest of shooting skills and accuracy.

One of the cadre shouted out, "All right, we're going to settle this argument once and for all. James, you want to accept the challenge?"

James slowly looked up from the stump where he sat while he cleaned his musket, "Yeah, I'll take the challenge, but I get to pick my weapon. If that's all right with the others."

The Sergeant looked to the other four men, "Gentlemen, do you accept those conditions?"

All four of them laughed and one of them said, "It don't matter which one he uses, I'll beat him!" The others continued to laugh as well.

"Very well, you five, grab targets and move to fifty yards." The specified men grabbed the prepared targets, moved to the fifty-yard line, and placed the targets.

The Sergeant continued, "Any man that fails to hit the black of the target is eliminated after each shot. Is that understood?" All five contestants said yes, including James.

"Each shooter will fire at the target from the standing position, just like you would, if in battle. If they hit the black, then they advance onto the next target at seventy-five yards. This continues until a single shooter has hit the furthest target. Once eliminated, you will move back to the group to observe. James, since you were the one challenged, you will be the last to shoot. Do you agree?"

Without looking up from where he sat on the stump, James nodded and said, "I do."

As the group of five shooters moved to the firing point, James eased his haversack and kit onto his shoulder, along with something wrapped in a blanket to the firing line. No one noticed what he was carrying.

The first shooters stepped to the firing line and fired their 1840 .69 caliber smoothbore musket weighing in at over ten pounds. Each fired their weapon in turn. The third shooter missed the black of the target by an inch at the fifty-yard line.

After each shooter fired, a soldier located not too far away from the target verified each shot fired with a thumbs up or down. Three other shooters hit the black circle on the target. Each shot was greeted with hoots and cheers from the Company E men.

About that time, Stephen got really loud, jumped in front of the Company, and shouted, "I'll bet one silver dollar to anyone that will bet against James hitting all the targets!"

Someone from the Company group shouted, "Boy, you ain't got that many silver dollars for this whole company!"

Stephen still did not relent, "I'm not expecting everyone to bet against James. I'm thinking somebody will help me offset the bet."

He was laughing, "But, if he loses, I'll give my pay every month until I pay everyone who bets against me."

More hoots and profanity followed, but suddenly some people started shouting, "I'll take that bet!"

Minutes passed as the Sergeant collected silver dollars or slips of paper with "I Owe You one Silver Dollar" with the soldier's initials or their mark on the slip of paper. When it was all calculated, eighty-one bet against James and twenty-four men placed their bets for James.

James whispered to Stephen, "Cousin, are you crazy? What if I miss?"

"Ain't going to happen Cousin. I've already seen these boys shoot. Anyway, I know what you got on your mind." He smiled and gave him a quick wink.

"All right, we're ready to continue. Private Ward, it's your shot on the fifty-yard line." The Sergeant pointed to the firing line.

James, stood up, reached into a pocket, and flipped a coin to the Sergeant, "Sergeant, if it's all right, I'll bet a dollar as well."

The Sergeant caught the silver dollar in the air and said with a smile, "I'm guessing you're betting on yourself?"

"I am." He then reached down and grabbed the rolled blanket. He took his haversack with him to the line. He slowly unwrapped the blanket to reveal the beautifully polished wood of the 1841 Mississippi Rifle. The bore was rifled in its original .54 caliber round. He began to load the weapon.

"Hey, that's not your musket!" More hoots and hollers were heard throughout the group about cheating.

The Sergeant shouted everyone down, "If you will recall, Private Ward specifically requested if he could use his weapon of choice. Each of you can use whatever weapon you choose as well."

More grumbling ensued with the Sergeant's decision. "Continue Private Ward."

James completed the loading process, looked around at the trees, and then gathered a little fine dirt from the ground. He stood, tossed the sand up above his head, and watched it move back to the ground with the wind. He then licked his trigger finger and held it into the air.

He stood at the line, brought the weapon to his chest, then slowly brought the stock to his shoulder. He gathered a breath and let it out slowly. He repeated the process once again. His right thumb slowly cocked the hammer back, his finger slowly moving to the trigger. His left eye closed, one more breath, held it a little longer, and the finger caressed the trigger to the rear.

The explosion was nearly immediate. James allowed the rifle barrel to lift straight up and then slowly brought it down to the firing position again.

The soldier ran to the target and gave the thumbs up sign. People groaned and complained. A few men gave a light applause.

"We'll move to the seventy-five yards position." Everyone meandered to the next position.

One of the competitors shouted out, "I'm going to double my bet!"

James looked at him and said, "You really don't want to do that. I don't want any more of your money."

"Well, that's good because I'm not planning on giving it to you."

James shrugged as he gathered his gear and moved to the next line.

The three other men shot their next rounds in the competition. Two others missed the target at seventy-five yards. The one competitor made his shot hit the black. James made his shot again.

As they moved to the one-hundred-yard line, the man offered once again, to double his bet. This time, James refused the bet. Both made their shot at the one-hundred-yard line. James' competition shooter barely broke the line on the black of the target at the seven o'clock position. James was solid in the black.

They moved onto the one-hundred-twenty-five-yard line and saw the man miss about eight inches below the black. Many of the soldiers in the crowd groaned for the miss. Their silver dollars were nearly in Stephen's pocket.

"It ain't over!!" shouted the competitor. "He's still got to make the shot!!" The crowd felt as if they had a new life.

James looked at Stephen and started to load the gun one more time. "I'm taking any additional bets on this one shot! Any takers?" One person took the offer, the lone competitor remaining.

With the bets all collected, James carefully followed his process, raised the weapon to his shoulder, aimed and fired the weapon.

Everyone waited for the target minder to give the signal of thumbs up or down. After a quick look, instead of the thumbs up sign, he used his index finger to put the finger into the hole, indicating it hit dead center.

The groans were loud but not nearly as loud as the cheers of twenty-four winners that supported James.

James walked over to the competitor and extended his hand. The man hesitated and then reached to shake James' hand in congratulation.

Before taking his hand, James asked, "What's your name?"

"My name is Henry Rogers. I know your name," the competitor stated with some disdain.

James took Henry Rogers' hand but did not let go, "You're a good shot Henry Rogers and I would bet on you most of the time."

He smiled, finished shaking his hand, and withdrew from Henry Rogers.

As James walked away, the man looked down into the palm of his hand where he saw three silver dollars resting in his right hand.

The Sergeant walked over to Stephen and handed him the coins and IOU slips, I'll leave it to you to disperse this to those that also won on James. By the way, where did he learned to shoot like that."

Stephen smiled, "He's the best hunter in the county and won the annual turkey shoot every year at the county fair, that I can remember and that's for the last eleven years. His daddy bought him that rifle six years ago. Keeps all our farms in deer and turkey meat every year."

Not too far away, just inside the tree line, Company E's Company Commander, Captain Webster, and the Camp Crab Tree Commandant, Major Burgwyn were watching the proceedings.

Captain Webster turned to the Commandant and said, "Sir, I'll ensure that the Private Ward's weapon is removed and secured since it is not a service weapon."

Major Burgwyn looked at the Captain, "Why in God's name would you do that Captain Webster? If he can carry two, let him. There will be plenty of sharpshooters trying to kill you; it would be nice to have someone that could return the favor on our side."

* * * * *

August 21, 1861

To Private James Ward, Company E, 26ᵗʰ Regiment of North Carolina Troops, Camp Crab Tree, North Carolina

Dear James,

We sincerely hope that you and Stephen are well. I hope they feed you good.

The courthouse has now placed a board on the outside to show the latest news on the war. Where able, they provide rosters with the names of the wounded and dead. We see people from North Carolina on the list but none from our community as best we can tell.

Harvest time this year has been a little more difficult with both of you boys gone from home. We had a pretty good harvest, but we lost quite a bit of the fresh vegetables rotting before we could get it all canned or preserved. The hogs, goats, sheep, and cattle got quite a bit more feed from it though.

Cotton was a little more difficult and we needed more hands. Your father went to a couple of the larger farms and borrowed some of the slaves for help. You know how he feels about slaves, and he insisted that not only would he pay the owner, but he intended to pay each slave ten cents for each day of work. It wasn't much but he felt it was necessary and proper.

You know we both feel strongly that it is against God's will to hold a man in slavery. Exodus provides us with plenty of evidence of that. The slaves seemed confused by his offer to them. Some pushed it back at him, but your father insisted. One man said he was afraid his owner would find out and punish him for taking it. What human being would do that?

Anna Wallace is doing fine. She used the gold coins and the extra paper money from your recent letter to purchase the hardware for your cabin. Several of the boys have been over here, when they were able, to continue to improve the house. Hopefully, after your enlistment is over next Summer, you can move into your own home.

We did see an article posted on the courthouse bulletins that there might be more enlistment bonuses next year. Your father is hoping you will not take advantage of the bonus this time.

Knowing you are getting ready for Winter, I have sewed some additional undershirts, socks, and handkerchiefs for you for when it gets cold. Anna Wallace was able to get some wool cloth as well and we're making you and Stephen some gloves for Winter.

Anna Wallace said to tell you she loves you and remember her always. I can't imagine how that girl can think that well of you. You're a terrible husband to leave your bride like this.

I hope you know I am poking fun at you Son.

I know you took your Bible with you and hope that you are reading it regular. We're praying for you both and look forward to your faces in our fields again soon.

Mrs. Louise Ellen Martin Ward

CHAPTER 4

COASTAL CHRISTMAS, WINTER 1861

T he end of Summer was fast approaching and while the 26th Regiment of North Carolina Troops had made significant improvement on their camp and military skills they were still not fully ready for the battles that would surely come.

The First Battle of Manassas had already occurred in late July. With some effort and bravery, the Confederate Army had won that first major battle.

President Lincoln and the Union now understood, this was a serious threat to the very existence of the United States of America.

Hopes floated through the camp that perhaps President Lincoln would see the futility of the Union Army incursion into the South and let the secessionist states leave the Union in peace.

It didn't happen that way. President Lincoln ordered each State to provide a portion of the 75,000 troops required to set down any rebellion in the South. Several states soon followed the path of South Carolina and seceded from the Union. Some of those states seceded under great duress.

On August 27, 1861, after much training and drills, at Camp Crab Tree, the 26th Regiment of North Carolina Troops was officially formed and recognized as a Regiment. Within those regimental ranks stood men that called North Carolina home and every county where those men lived and toiled, had voted against secession.

The first newly elected officers of the regiment included the Commander, Colonel Zebulon Vance. Vance was from the mountains of North Carolina near Asheville. He attended the University of North Carolina and studied law. Within a year of completion of his studies, he was the Buncombe County Solicitor and then created his own private law office.

He was affable and outgoing. Easy to approach and yet, he always downplayed his own worth. He was a born politician. In a relatively short period, he was deep into state politics and elected to the US Congress representing North Carolina.

In Congress, he was an outspoken opponent to secession for North Carolina. It took Lincoln's failure to withdraw from Fort Sumter that turned the tide for him. He came home to Buncombe County and raised his own company of volunteer militia.

His attention to the needs of his personal militia company was notable to others. As he progressed to Camp Crab Tree, he was the beloved leader of his "Rough and Ready Guards." Many others at the camp saw his potential as well.

His regimental staff included recently promoted Lieutenant Colonel Burgwyn from Camp Commandant to his new role as the Assistant Commander, and Major Abner Carmichael was his Regimental Major.

The staff was rounded out with First Lieutenant James Jordan as Adjutant, Sergeant Joseph Young as Quartermaster, Lieutenant Robert Goldston as the Commissary, Doctor Thomas Boykin as Surgeon, Private Daniel Shaw as Assistant Surgeon, and the Reverend Robert Marsh as Regimental Chaplain.

The non-commissioned staff included Sergeant-Major Leonidas Polk, Hospital Steward Benjamin Hind, Ordnance Sergeant E. H. Hornaday,

Sergeant Jesse Ferguson as Commissary Sergeant, and Sergeant Abram Lane as Quartermaster Sergeant.

The orders to deploy were prompt and clear, move to the coast and prepare for the defense of the State, at Fort Macon, near the Bogue Banks. In a very few days, the 26th Regiment was packed and ready to move to the coast and take on its first mission.

While packing and loading the Regiment's equipment onto train rail flatbed cars, James wiped the sweat from his forehead. He looked to his right where Stephen had that silly grin on his face while whistling a tune. "What are you so happy about?"

"James, I'm tired of all this drilling. I want to get out of here and get closer to home." Stephen never stopped loading the boxes onto the train.

"Well, don't get too excited about that. We might be closer to home but not close enough to run to the farm for a visit. Don't forget, they shoot deserters," James responded while he gathered another box into his arms.

Stephen stood for a moment to puzzle James' last comment, "You really think they would shoot us for going home? I was planning on coming back."

James grunted and continued to put boxes on the train car, "I'm not willing to take the chance. But maybe we're close enough for the family to come to us, once in a while."

"Yeah, maybe that would work better. Probably avoid a lot of trouble that way. Mention that in your next letter." Stephen stepped over to his gear and grabbed his canteen of water.

He continued, "You think we're going to see any action on the coast?"

James joined him for some water, "Don't know that either. Can't believe they would put us out there for no reason. Besides, Fort Macon is there. Got to mean something."

The trip began by train and left Raleigh on September 2, 1861. It was not an especially eventful trip except the Ward boys saw the train pass farmland where they were reminded of the season of the year on the calendar.

Late Summer and early Fall are harvest times, and it was fast ending.

James thought of the farms at home, surely the Ward families were very busy. He suddenly yearned for his home, and he was reminded of a new wife trying to build their new home without him. "Nice field of corn over there."

James mused. "Should be a good year for the farm." Most of the farms were not unlike their family farms but they did seem a little smaller. Also, there appeared to be an obvious field hand shortage.

Stephen said, "Gonna take a lot of time to gather it up with that few a hands in the fields."

James nodded in agreement, "Yep, looks a little strange. Maybe they don't have several families working together like our farms."

The train worked its way down the track that day and eventually stopped in between Goldsborough and Kinston North Carolina. Officers came by and instructed the troops to offload and take a brief rest while the train took on water for the engine.

Local folks came to the train and brought food, water, and an occasional bottle of spirited beverages as well. Most of those bottles were confiscated by the officers in short order.

As the Sun eased higher into the sky, roll call was conducted. A small number of soldiers failed to answer at roll call. A couple of those were found "visiting" with local families, mostly young farm girls. Once they were discovered, they were promptly reprimanded and placed in custody for failing to appear at roll call.

The other missing troops were placed on furlough on the roll call until found and their reason for not being present was adjudicated.

Rumor quickly spread among the men that a firing squad or hanging was going to take place. Neither of those events actually occurred.

Once the troops were on board again, the train continued the trip East toward the coast of North Carolina. The train eventually came to a stop at the town of Morehead City late into the night.

The troops retained their personal gear and created a temporary bivouac area for the night. The next day found the former Camp Commandant, Lieutenant Colonel Henry Burgwyn establishing a new camp in the absence of Regimental Commander, Colonel Vance, who was still delayed in Raleigh.

The still raw soldiers were in a new environment. The coast was an entirely new adventure, both good and bad, for so many.

The surrounding countryside on the coast included the community of New Bern. It was once a productive seaport along the mouth of the Neuse River that ran deep into the Carolina interior from the Pamlico Sound.

Control the town and port and you control the river. A prize being sought by Federal forces.

Not only did a river run to New Bern, but the town also had a significant railroad connection to the West and with North and South connections. However, to get to New Bern from the coast, it required going through the Pamlico Sound.

Once into the sound and past Morehead City and Beaufort, both located at the southern end of the North Carolina Outer Banks, you could easily approach the prosperous community of New Bern.

Burgwyn and his staff determined the best place to position the troops of the 26th Regiment was on the eastern end of an island called the Bogue Banks.

One reason for the decision was the camp location was near the impressive fort known as Fort Macon. It stood watch over the sound and entry from the Atlantic Ocean. The busy port of Beaufort sat on the horizon Northeast and across the sound from the fortification.

This area of the South, and more specifically the North Carolina coast, was the most recent place of incursions by Federal troops. It was here that Union forces captured Southern troops at Fort Hatteras on the Outer Banks.

Most of the Outer Banks' forts would remain in Federal hands until the end of the war. Suddenly, the Outer Banks and the Carolina ports became important to the Southern cause for survival.

Burgwyn understood that point better than most. While hoping for deployment of the Regiment to Virginia, he found his role in defending the coast disappointing given its importance to the Confederate leadership.

While early in the occupation of the area, the Regiment relocated several times and in smaller dispersed versions for the companies.

However, anticipating a sustained presence, Lieutenant Colonel Burgwyn began construction of more permanent and effective winter quarters for their first Winter together, recognizing that Winter was fast approaching.

The construction of well-built but rough-hewn buildings required lumber. That required timber and someone with the skills to mill the lumber. When the call went out for such occupational skills, James and Stephen quickly volunteered.

In addition to building his own new home for his bride, James and the Ward family cut and milled timber for all of the family farms.

As forest land was cleared for new fields, Brice Ward made good use of every linear foot of cleared timber on the family farms. What timber that was not used by the family farms was sold or used for bartering with other farms in need of building materials.

James led the farms' clearing efforts and Stephen was one of his most reliable hands cutting, hauling, milling, and building with the materials.

When Captain Webster inquired of the company for such skills, James and five other men stepped forward. "James, march these men to the Regimental headquarters and report directly to Lieutenant Colonel Burgwyn. He will give you orders for this task. Carry your gear, you may not be able to come back to our bivouac area for a while. Let us know if you need anything."

James saluted smartly, "Yes Sir, I understand. Sir, can I take Stephen as my chief helper?"

Captain Webster chuckled, "James, I assume you are suggesting that Stephen would be your assistant for this task?"

"Sir, Yes Sir. He would be my assistant, Sir. I guess that is the right word, Sir, assistant." James responded with a quizzical look on his face.

"Very well, Private Stephen Ward is designated as your assistant on this task, whatever that task is, as directed by Lieutenant Colonel Burgwyn. Be on your way." Captain Webster returned the salute and then turned to the map located on his field desk.

James and Stephen led the other four men to the Regimental headquarters. The Adjutant, First Lieutenant Jordan, met them at the front of the headquarters tent. "Can I help you Private? What's your business?"

James quickly saluted, as did the other men with him. "Sir, I was instructed by Captain Webster, our Company E Commander, Sir to report directly to Lieutenant Colonel Burgwyn for a task regarding lumber, Sir."

"Ah, yes, Private, Lieutenant Colonel Burgwyn is expecting you. Stand-by while I speak to the Colonel." Lieutenant Jordan turned and stepped through the tent flap and disappeared from view.

He returned shortly, "The Colonel will see you Private, what is your name?"

James stood at attention, "Private James Ward, Sir."

"Have your men stand over by that tree while you meet with the Colonel." The Lieutenant pointed to a tree with good shade from the Sun about thirty yards away.

Jordan stepped inside and waved James into the tent. "Sir, I have Private James Ward from Company E regarding that task you had, Sir."

James quickly stood at the position of attention directly before the field desk where the Assistant Commander of the 26th Regiment sat reading over papers on the desk. James saluted, "Sir, Private James Ward reporting as ordered Sir."

James had seen the former Camp Crab Tree Commandant many times from a distance but never very close. As he stood before the senior officer, James noted he was neatly dressed in his well-tailored uniform and as he lifted his head from several drawings and maps, James saw just how young the man was.

The face was smooth to a fault. His mustache was thin, and the goatee was modest and nearly as thin as the moustache. At that moment he was about to reach his twentieth birthday.

Burgwyn pushed away the drawings and maps and looked at James, "Be at ease Private and take a seat on that field stool over there."

James nervously looked about and then at the Adjutant who nodded his head in the affirmative, and then James moved toward the stool, "Yes Sir."

"Private Ward, Captain Webster tells me you were most proficient in cutting and milling lumber back home in Columbus County, is that correct?"

"Well Sir, not sure about the proficient part but I've been clearing land, cutting trees, and milling them for lumber for as long as I can remember." He paused to see if that was sufficient for an answer.

"This Regiment needs Winter quarters, and they need them soon. We're only a couple of months from serious cold and wet weather and we need our men under good cover. If I can contract for timber to be cut, could you get that lumber cut and quarters built by late October or early November?"

James paused for a moment of thought, then responded, "Sir, it really depends on the type of timber or what you're trying to build. Hard woods like Oak, Hickory, Maple, Sycamore, and Cypress are hard and take longer to cut and mill. Pine is softer and easier to cut and mill. If you need it fast, Pine is the way to go."

Burgwyn continued, "We have over one thousand troops with us and more to come. As for what to build, I have some rough drawings of what I am looking to build. Private, take a look at these drawings." The Colonel handed several parchment sheets of drawings to James.

After a few moments of examining the drawings, James offered his opinion, "Sir, looks to me like you could have about six or seven of these for each company. Probably house about twenty or twenty-five men per cabin. Ten companies, times seven houses a company comes to about seventy houses. Guessing you're probably going to need some housing for your headquarters and people."

"James, I think you're correct with your numbers. And, yes, we'll need similar housing for our officers, supplies, and hospital. What do you need to make it happen and how soon can you begin." The young Assistant Commander stood up and moved around the desk to face the Private. He held his hand up when James started to stand.

"Sir, can you give me a few minutes to put a list together? I'm just thinking about what we used back home. Mostly, cross-cut saws, axes, wedges, mauls, skinners for the bark, several pretty-large wagons, mules. If you could find a steam engine for the milling saws, that would be a big help." He paused again.

"I guess you're going to need a lot of nails, hammers, hinges, could use leather for the hinges, and such for the doors. Got to have heat for the boys, so we need some fireplaces. Probably use stone or river rock for those."

"We could use all of the limbs and such for the firewood. I guess we need hands more than anything. Between me and Stephen, we can teach most of them what to do for the cutting and milling and then the actual building. If you got any carpenters in this outfit, we need to grab them soonest."

James stopped, took a deep breath, and looked at the young Commander, "Sir, if you can give me a few more minutes and some paper, I think I can give you a pretty good list. That list I just rattled off was just running around inside my head."

"Private, I'm thinking that brain rattled off a pretty good list. Yes, please step outside and start that more detailed list. Lieutenant Jordan will get you some paper and pen." Burgwyn stood up and extended his hand to James.

James stood again and met the Colonel's handshake. "Sir, I'm guessing with about ten men per company, we can get the men in quarters before it gets too bad."

"Thank you, James. I will also have Lieutenant Jordan prepare an order for you to carry with you throughout the camp. If you need something, order it and if anyone takes exception, show them my order. An order in this regard is an order from me. Use that power judiciously. Plan on seeing me as often as necessary and provide me with a report on your progress." The Assistant Commander returned to his desk.

James left the tent and met his group by the designated tree. He was followed by Lieutenant Jordan who passed along several sheets of paper and a new pencil as promised.

"Sir could you tell me where you want us to put up our tent? I don't want to lose any time getting the information to the Colonel." James took the paper and pencil.

Lieutenant Jordan looked around the immediate area and pointed to an area near a wood line, "That area over there meet your needs?"

"Yes Sir, that will be just fine. I'll have a list for you shortly." James saluted.

"Private Ward, the Colonel wanted me to pass along something else. We anticipated some of your needs but certainly not all of them." He pointed to a wagon near the place where the Lieutenant suggested they pitch their tents.

"Over there, you'll find a wagon with a few saws and axes. Not nearly what you need but a beginning. Here are the drawings the Colonel showed you. If you need these replicated, let me know, I'll have the headquarters folks copy as many as you need." He turned on his heels and returned to the command tent.

"Boys, we got a hell of a job to do and not a lot of time to get it done." James took a deep breath and started to describe their task at hand. The longer he explained, the bigger their eyes opened.

Progress was slow at first, but as James' team instructed and was provided the resources to complete the task, greater progress came with more experience in building each hut.

What really created a problem was an outbreak of measles. Suddenly, some of the new houses were used by the Doctor and Surgeon's staff to segregate those infected. Measles wasn't to be treated lightly and within a short time, it spread to those that had not been previously infected. A few cases of Chicken Pox were also noted. With the colder weather, several cases of Pneumonia led to multiple deaths.

For James and his team, they were fortunate not to have an issue with Measles since nearly their entire team had the infection when they were young. They lost only a couple of weeks of effort.

As the Christmas season came and the Measles epidemic subsided, the Winter quarters were turning into their own little town. Beaufort and Morehead City were a short boat ride away and the local saloons, bars, and roadhouses became favorite gathering places for many of the off-duty troops.

Not to be lost on many of the troops that had not previously been this close to the ocean and seafood, was suddenly finding the menu for meals included lots of fish, oysters, clams, and crabs. They also found out that seagulls, herons, and sandpipers did not replace turkey, quail, or doves for the dinner table.

The local harvests of crops had allowed the commissary and quartermaster to obtain vegetables and fruits in abundance. Also, meat was readily available with beef, pork, chicken, and venison nearby.

Christmas found the camp in good order. When not building and improving the camp and its defenses, the troops were required to continue their training in drills and fighting techniques.

Some of the troops were frequently heard complaining about the lack of battle action and the low likelihood of the Federal troops coming to this part of the State.

Regardless of the local sentiment, the Assistant Commander was constantly on the watch for guard posts not properly maintained, any lack of military courtesy, and improper use of command authority were not tolerated. The 26th Regiment was getting a reputation for no nonsense in military training and preparations.

True to form, James wrote his letter to the family back home and informed them the Regiment would not be relieved from duty for the holiday. He encouraged them to come to Camp Carolina and share some of the holiday with them when off duty.

James knew it would have been at least two days' travel each way and no guarantee of a place to stay when they arrived. James and Stephen were not concerned about the Ward family surviving in these conditions, but they recognized it certainly was a risk to be in temporary quarters during bad weather for others less prepared.

The 26th Regiment Commander, Colonel Zebulon Vance had given almost complete responsibility for training and drills to Lieutenant Colonel Burgwyn, creating a bit of controversy for the young officer.

Vance was the affable commander, Burgwyn was the disciplinarian and task master. The troops began to resent their suffering under the hand of a twenty-year-old boy Colonel.

Knowing that Burgwyn's middle name was King, troops began muttering under their breath, "He thinks he's a King!" With less than a half year, after Christmas Day and by New Year's Day, 1862, the threats and insubordination were becoming commonplace regarding the young officer.

During one of his final personal building reports to the Assistant Commander, James offered, "Sir, with your permission, you might want to let up just a little with the men. There is too much complaining by the men and they're not seeing the need for all the additional training."

"James, I appreciate your candor and honesty. I hear the complaints and muttering about the drills and training. However, I believe we are getting close to being deployed to address some of General Hill's concerns in the North Carolina Sector as well as the tidewater area of Virginia." Burgwyn offered a pitcher of lemonade to James.

James held the jar he was using for a glass and received the lemonade, "What are you hearing, if I may ask Sir? I can make sure that the right message gets out to the troops. It certainly couldn't hurt."

Burgwyn looked at James with those young but steely eyes for a moment. "Maybe you're right, but I am not able to give you a lot of details. However, I've heard that there is some movement by Union ships to get inside of the Albemarle and Pamlico Sounds. If that is true, it is only a matter of time before we have to turn them away."

James swallowed the bitter lemonade. "Sir, do you believe the boys will let you down?"

"No James, they are performing well in everything I have asked them to do, complaining or not. We'll do our duty and I'm sure the 26th Regiment will do itself proud. But we've never faced a trained force before. Men get scared and that can lead to disaster."

The older Private nodded his head in understanding. James had questioned his own ability to face heavy fire from the enemy himself and on many occasions during training. "Sir, when the heat of battle is on us, we'll do you proud. We'll follow you."

"Thank you, James. Feel free to share what you think is appropriate with the men but remembering, no details. If we are moved to another location, I clearly recognize we are in the middle of the coast and that means we can be ordered in several directions. When the Union does attack, it will be at Fort Fisher, near Wilmington in the South or New Bern to our North. Either way, we'll have to move and move fast. These men must respond to orders and perform to their best. Otherwise, our people will needlessly die."

James did as Burgwyn suggested and started a couple of conversations with some of the troublemakers. He explained he "heard a rumor" of why Lieutenant Colonel Burgwyn was training so hard in anticipation of an attack that may not be that far away.

The "rumor" got passed around Camp Carolina. Some of the mutterings started to subside.

Not lost on the troops were recent reports of Union troop movements on the coast. To assist in the validity of the rumor was a Federal ship stranded in the tidal waters off the coastline.

The stranded ship was eventually abandoned by the crew. Colonel Vance ordered the ship's supplies and equipment to be captured and returned to the camp. Other Union warships fired on the 26th Regiment troops during the salvage effort but no one was lost.

The 26th Regiment now had its first engagement with Federal forces. It was a minor conflict, but it buoyed the morale of the men, knowing they had faced the danger.

"King" was beginning to regain some of his properly due respect. However, there were still naysayers in the ranks.

* * * * *

January 1, 1862

To Private James Ward, Company E, 26ᵗʰ Regiment, located at Camp Carolina

My Dearest Husband,

I am so sorry we were unable to attend Christmas Services with you, Stephen, the troops of your Company, and Chaplain Carmichael. I am sure it was as wonderful a sermon as you described in your recent letter.

It was a quiet Christmas here. There were prayers and candles. The children opened their gifts on Christmas Morning after our morning prayers of thanks.

Given your description of your meal served by the officers of the Regiment, ours was nearly as fine a meal. It was most wonderful with the smells in your mother's kitchen. The table was full of ham, roast beef, and your father even shot a turkey on a recent hunt. The sweet potatoes, turnip greens, butter beans, fried okra, and cornbread were cooked to perfection by Miz Lizzie, herself.

I made a Persimmon Pie. Your mother made two Sweet Potato Pies, two Apple Pies, and even found some Strawberry Preserves for a Strawberry Pie.

After the Noon meal with the Ward family, we travelled over to my family for the dinner meal. It was more of the same except my mother prepared your favorite of two Pecan Pies in your honor. My Father provided a very solemn prayer of thanks for the meal and you and Stephen's safety.

I cannot tell you how much it has meant to me being with the Ward family while you have been gone these last several months. Your mother treats me just like your siblings and I prefer it that way. I don't think I should be treated differently.

Your Father was not pleased with some of the accounts we are seeing posted on the courthouse notice boards and newspapers. He saw the reactions of some people that were seeing the reports of injuries and deaths in the battles in Virginia. He is a proud man, and such public displays of grief reflects his attitude that such grief should be appropriately expressed in privacy.

We are all wishing you a safe and uneventful year ahead. As for me, I am anxious for your year of service to be completed in May. At that time, we can enter our house as a husband and wife. I will not move into it until you are home, and you can carry me over the threshold.

I am your most loving wife,
Anna Wallace Ward

CHAPTER 5

"HOW DO WE SURVIVE?"
NEW BERN, 1862

The new year's Winter of 1862 saw the North Carolina coast become an area of great interest to President Lincoln and the Federal Army.

Blockade Runners were smaller and fast-moving ships that brought supplies and support from foreign nations such as France, Britain, Spain, the Caribbean Islands, and South America. In return, the South was using the sale of tobacco and cotton as a major form of exchange.

With this new threat of foreign intervention, President Lincoln thought to take advantage of the moderate attitudes of the "Olde North State."

On May 20th, 1861, the North Carolina State Legislature voted to secede from the Union. What is often lost in history is that the Legislature had previously voted twice, and secession had been voted down by significant margins.

It was Lincoln's decision to levy North Carolina to provide part of the 75,000 troops to repulse any rebellion in the South that forced a change to the vote to secede.

Most North Carolinians found themselves in a war they never wanted and felt no need to actively support.

The Governor of North Carolina, John W. Ellis would be placed into a position he did not want to be. However, political pressure took its toll, and he was convinced he could not withstand the fever pitch for secession in Raleigh.

What was unknown to most of the residents of North Carolina was the message the Governor received from the new President of the Confederate States of America, Jefferson Davis, "Might I suggest you look about. You are surrounded by your neighboring states. How can you not join the Confederacy and survive?"

Even though promised by Lincoln that he would not send troops into the South, President Lincoln made Ellis' decision to accept the Legislature's bill on his desk easier to sign but no less painful. He signed that day.

Recognizing that North Carolina had seceded from the Union, President Lincoln recognized his affinity for the people of North Carolina's reluctance to leave and willingness to work with the Union. While not an ally, he thought them different than the rest of the zealots of the South.

With that thought in mind, he ordered his Generals and Admirals to find a way to leverage entry into the State via the coastline. The outposts along the Outer Banks had been relatively easy to overcome and those successes occurred by late 1861 and early 1862.

What followed were plans to enter the State in the major ports near Wilmington, New Bern, and Morehead City. Fort Macon became an early target on all Union battle maps.

Brigadier General L. O'Brian Branch had recently been appointed command of the District of the Pamlico for the Northeastern area of North Carolina and the responsibility for all coastal defenses. Newly appointed Brigadier General R.C. Gatlin commanded the center and the Southern North Carolina coasts.

Roanoke Island had fallen by early February 1862, with every expectation that an attack by General Ambrose Burnside's forces were imminent nearly anywhere along the Atlantic coastline.

With no Confederate navy to speak of in the North Carolina waters, entry into the entire Albemarle and Pamlico Sounds was under Union control and discretion. Given the most obvious targets on the map, it appeared an attack on the smaller port of New Bern was imminent.

The 26th Regiment, along with five other infantry regiments composed of nearly five thousand men, moved quickly in late February to the town of New Bern, North Carolina.

Other than being a quaint little coastal town, New Bern was at the heart of the State's coastal area. Not only was it on the primary coastal waters of the Pamlico Sound on the mainland side of the Outer Banks, but it was the entry way into the Neuse River that traversed deep into the interior of North Carolina.

Like the Cape Fear River in the Southeastern part of the North Carolina coast, near Wilmington, the Neuse River represented a major water roadway to the center of the State. Control those two waterways and you had straight arrow shots into the heart of the State and its many resources.

In addition to the Neuse River at New Bern, major North and South railroads ran near the town. Those connections were met by the East to West railroads that went straight to the State Capitol in Raleigh as well.

All these connections represented major military targets to reduce or eliminate North Carolina's favorable influence for the Confederate States and potential new resources for Union military forces. It was a supply chain that could not be ignored by either military force. For President Lincoln, controlling those railroads was critical.

Private James Ward was moving equipment and supplies into several wagons that were destined to shortly reach the railway station. The same flatbed rail cars that brought him to the Bogue Banks area in the late Summer of 1861 were now headed Northwest toward New Bern, North Carolina.

His cousin, Stephen handed him more boxes to load onto the wagon and as he did, he said, "I guess all that training is going to be used now. You think we learned anything?"

James looked over his shoulder at the younger cousin, "Well, we did our part and learned what they showed us. I'm guessing we're as ready as a bunch of farm boys could be. Does make you worry though."

"I have to admit, I'm a little scared but somehow, I'm excited to see what it's really like. You figure?" Stephen asked.

"Yeah, I know what you mean. You just don't want to let down the Colonel and all the other men. I don't like the thought of losing a battle though." He said.

James then patted the last bag of supplies and headed to his personal equipment laying on the ground.

Stephen grabbed his gear as well and heard Sergeant Jones as he yelled down the railway, "Private Ward, report to the Captain's tent and break it down. I want it on this rail car in the next few minutes. We're due to pull out at the top of the hour. Stay with it 'til we get to the dismount point. I don't want some yahoo getting it before we get set up."

Stephen looked at James, "I'll catch you when we get to the town. This being a message runner for the Captain is not as much fun as I thought it would be."

He grabbed his gear and moved at double-quick time with the Sergeant. Stephen's running skills had become something of a wonder to the company and his value was not lost on Captain Webster.

When Stephen showed up on the training field and delivered a message from the Captain, no one in Company E ever questioned the affable Private, usually delivering the message with no shoes on his feet.

The young man just hated wearing boots. One dressing down in front of the whole company on a day when someone did question Stephen's message with his boots around his neck, removed that dilemma forever.

Even Colonel Vance and Lieutenant Colonel Burgwyn had to smile when he showed up. The two Commanders had agreed that protocol required they should address the young man's appearance, "Soldier, are you out of uniform?" they asked, as they returned his salute.

When Stephen initially tried to explain his situation to the Regimental Commander and his assistant, they both listened and nodded their understanding.

Smiling, Colonel Vance replied, "I understand your problem Private Ward but as your Commander, I must always question your inappropriate appearance. I expect you to always reply in the future, 'I will take care of that immediately, Sir.' Do you understand me?"

Stephen paused in thought for a moment, then that big silly grin spread across his face and said, "Sir, Private Ward, Yes Sir, I'll take care of that immediately, Sir!"

It was now a personal joke with the entire Regiment, and the officers and men enjoyed it. No one ever said anything about those boots hanging around his neck after those instructions.

By March 12th, the 26th Regiment was ordered to occupy and improve the far-left flank of the Confederate lines near New Bern. Cutting trees, digging rifle pits, preparing trenches, and positioning troops was well under way.

Colonel Vance had been placed in command of the forces on the left flank, near the fort overlooking the Neuse River. On the day before the anticipated attack, the troops of the 26th Regiment were ordered to form their companies into regimental formation in front of their positions.

After many commands and even more movement, the companies were all formed and stood at the position of attention. The Acting Commander of the 26th Regiment, Lieutenant Colonel Henry King Burgwyn, Jr. stepped onto the higher ground for all to see.

He spoke to the group of soldiers, including many of them that didn't particularly like him. "Soldiers, the enemy are before you, and you will soon be in combat. You have the reputation of being one of the best drilled regiments in the service. Now I wish you to prove yourselves as one of the best fighting regiments. Men, stand by me and I will by you. You may rely upon a hard fight; but God's providence is over us all."

Several men, including James and Stephen shouted, "We will Sir!"

Already, both Colonel Vance and Lieutenant Colonel Burgwyn had, on numerous occasions, demonstrated they were true North Carolinians.

They were men that considered it an honor to lead and deeply cared for their troops. They did it by showing they were human in their concerns for their men but still very demanding in their training and execution of orders.

They had both promised those same troops standing before Burgwyn that day, they were with them, even in war.

Their men loved them for it. War be damned, the troops were accepted for the common men they were, and the men accepted their officers as people they could trust with their very lives.

"Company Commanders, take charge of your company and prepare for battle." Burgwyn saluted his troops.

James looked to his front. There was a small creek he was told was called Butler's Creek. To his right and for as far as he could see, another creek flowed through the marshland and swamps prominent along the Eastern coast of North Carolina.

Further to his left, James could see the banked railroad bed where they had disembarked and began preparations. Much further to his left, he had seen Fort Thompson well positioned on the West Bank of the Neuse River.

James felt a little better knowing that Fort Thompson had eighteen cannons available to defend that flank of the command. He also felt good that four of the command's regiments were located adjacent to the fort and spread to the West toward the railroad bed.

The 26th Regiment anchored the Western flank. To the East of the 26th Regiment was the thirty-third Regiment that also covered both sides of the railroad bed.

On the Western end of the four regiments facing the main forces of the Union Army, was a local militia unit. It was the Western anchor at the railroad for the main Confederate force.

From James' position in the line, he couldn't help but feel a little pride in his company's position. Captain Webster had trained and commanded them well. James went to sleep early that night with a full stomach and knowing he had guard duty at 2:00 AM in the morning.

General Burnside planned and began his preparations and movement for March 12th, 1862, having landed his infantry well South on the West Bank of the Neuse River and below New Bern proper. As a feint, he had his gunboats fire multiple rounds into the countryside in the hopes that the Confederate forces might take the bait and move toward the Union forces' current location, well down river.

James heard the cannon fire from his position and could tell it was some distance away. What he didn't know was just how far it was. Henry Rogers was in the same trench with James.

"Do you think they gonna hit us today, James?" Henry asked.

James looked over at Henry and could tell the young man was a little nervous. "Nah, don't think so. Looks like it might rain anytime. Not good for loading muskets. From the sounds of those guns, might be a little too far to hit us today."

"They don't want to try to find us in the dark tonight. It would be a mess with the rain and a lot of their boys killed just running into us. Half of them would probably drown in the creek or get swallowed by the swamp." James settled back into the trench.

His reassurance was followed by a quick and nervous look to the South toward the tree line on the other side of the creek. The rain began falling almost immediately.

Less than an hour later, Captain Webster ordered the 26th Regiment out of their positions and ordered them to form into company formation and follow the Thirty-Third Regiment to the South. "Be prepared for battle, boys. They think this is going to be a quick one. We're moving forward and engage them before night."

"Be prepared to return to your positions here." Company E fell into formation behind their battle positions and began to move down the railroad bed and headed to the South with a quick-step march cadence.

James looked up into the sky and could see it was getting darker with the clouds. Nothing made sense about the movement from his perspective.

In a short order, while moving, the unit could hear heavy fire forward of the formation. While firing was heavy, it quickly decreased as the rain and darkness fell on the area.

Captain Webster gave the order to reverse march and Company E returned to their breastworks for the night.

James looked at Henry as they settled back into their trench, "Sorry Henry, guess I was wrong. Them, boys seemed awful anxious to get past us."

"I never doubted you, James. Yep, they do seem pretty excited out there. Guess the boys up in Company A ran into them first. Hope nobody got hurt."

Henry shaped his blanket and pulled it over his shoulder. "Think I'm going to get some rest while I can. Something tells me, not going to be a lotta time for it tomorrow."

Private James Ward smiled and chuckled to himself. He grabbed his blanket and pulled it up around his neck on the cold and wet March air. "Henry, I think you got the right idea. Besides, I got guard duty later. Say your prayers, Henry. We might need 'em tomorrow."

Henry only grunted and pulled his rain slicker over his blanket.

When James went on guard duty at 2 AM that morning, it was still lightly raining, and a foggy mist was floating over the field in front of his position to the creek. He could not miss the noise coming from the woods on the other side of the creek.

There was a partial moon in the sky but mostly covered by fast-moving clouds. The noise was easy to follow but the movements were less so.

James reached for his haversack and grabbed a quick biscuit and a piece of ham he captured at dinner the previous day. He took a couple of swigs of water from his wooden canteen.

Then, he reached into the haversack and pulled out his extra ammunition for his rifled musket. He had a feeling he was going to need that in the morning when the Sun rose high enough to offer light.

Henry woke up about 4 AM as well. "You want to grab some more sleep, James? I can take a spell." He offered.

"Nah, don't think I need it right now. Besides, got me some biscuits and ham. Might grab my winter apple and finish it for breakfast. Don't think I have enough time for sleeping though, those boys seem like they been moving all night." James said.

He then shifted his musket on his lap and ensured his rifle was close by and unharmed by the morning mist.

General Burnside began to move his troops inland on March 13th and well below Fort Thompson. His plan was to head directly toward the town of New Bern.

Bypassing the fort with its heavy guns would relieve any pressure from the fort's strength, the cannons. He intended to create another feint by having his gunboats fire at the fort from a distance and in parallel with the Union forces.

With the fort's occupants' attention focused on the Union gunboats, Burnside intended to reduce or eliminate the fort's advantage on the river and the adjacent land facing the road leading to the fort.

Burnside never lost his focus on his primary goal and that was the railways and the river landings to his front.

He began his more direct attack on March 13th, 1862, with thirteen infantry regiments consisting of over eleven thousand troops and more importantly fourteen gunboats that could provide indirect and direct cannon fire in support of troop movements as the battle went to ground.

By 7 AM, the attack on all fronts began. Union gunboats took on the Fort Thompson cannons, four heavy Union Regiments marched North perpendicular to the Fort Thompson Road and three heavy Union Regiments marched in a similar Northern direction West of the Atlantic and North Carolina Railway.

General Burnside initiated the attack knowing he had five additional regiments in reserve he could place anywhere he wanted or needed them. He anticipated being in New Bern before the Sun set in the West.

Between the rain, daylight, and Confederate preparations and resistance, the General would not make it to the town of New Bern that day.

James estimated that the attack had ended the day a little over a mile from his position. Only the heavy wooded area and creek stood between the Union forces and the 26th Regiment's positions.

When he shook his rain slicker and wet blanket, he stood, stretched, and looked across the dimly lit ground to see a heavy fog. The noise in the wooded area never seemed to cease.

From his position he could look to his left front and see a lot of movement in the open area directly in front of the Fort Thompson Road.

Hundreds of troops seemed to pore out of the woods and the fog. "Henry, get up!! They're coming!!"

James quickly wiped down his weapons, ensured the powder was dry enough, and his caps were ready to be put into action. He looked down the line on both sides to confirm the rest of the unit was awake and preparing for battle.

Captain Webster and the Lieutenants were busy walking along the unit positions and getting people ready for battle.

Webster stopped at James' position and looked down at him in the defensive trench and mound of dirt, "James, grab your gear."

James immediately started gathering his gear as ordered and climbed out of the trench line. Webster said, "I want you to move a little closer to the left and assume a good position a little higher and closer to the railway."

James nodded as he wiped the mud away, "Yes, Sir. What you got on your mind Sir if I may ask Sir?"

"You may ask Private. There is a depression over by the railroad where they have made and stored bricks. I'm worried the regiment doesn't have enough weapons covering that area."

The Captain wiped at his brow and turned toward the area he wanted covered. "Let's go."

James quickly followed constantly looking around as he moved closer to the location where Captain Webster had pointed. "James, you see that depression there?"

He pointed to a very narrow gap where the railway passed through. "Yes Sir."

Webster continued pointing with his thumb, "Back there is the Thirty-Third Regiment, they're facing in that direction. I'm not convinced they got that area down in the gap covered. I want you to find a good cubby hole and use that rifle of yours to take out anything entering that gap. Do you understand?"

James looked around in every direction before looking at his Company Commander, "Yes, I see what you got in mind. Let me talk to those Thirty-Third boys a little and see if I can grab that little hill back there. I just don't want them shooting me in the back. Might be a tree back there I can get a little higher look as well. It should take care of that area."

"Do what you need to do but don't let anything enter that gap unless we get pushed back." Webster hurried back toward the rest of the 26th Regiment.

Within a few minutes of receiving his orders, James selected the best spot he could find in the tree, conversed with 33rd Regiment Commander, and explained what he was ordered to do.

The Colonel smiled and said, "I like that a lot. You any good with that fancy musket Private?"

"You tell me after this is over," and James returned the smile and quickly moved to his chosen spot.

As the mist and fog moved away, the fields in front of the Fort Thompson Road looked like a massive parade. The biggest difference was those Union muskets were creating a lot of smoke.

James looked to his right to see the 26th Regiment preparing for the charge that was forming in front and across the creek.

He noted the looped position of the 33rd Regiment and its lack of connection with the 26th Regiment. He was beginning to see what Webster was so worried about. There was a clear area where, if breached, a mass of Union troops could nearly walk between the lines.

"Oh my God!" James whispered as he suddenly thought about Stephen and the rest of the 26th Regiment. They were exposed to great danger of being flanked, a cardinal sin for any military unit.

James saw a couple of large Confederate cannons being moved closer to the 33rd's location but just as they were deploying the weapons, the Union artillery began to focus on the large guns and the men quickly deserted the guns in place.

Not far from the guns, a small militia unit began to disintegrate from the heavy fire. James knew the unit and they had only been organized in the last few weeks.

The worrisome gap was becoming more than "just a worry." A large Union force had left the woods directly in front of the 26th Regiment. The attacks were being repulsed and the firing from the 26th Regiment became almost rhythmic. Units continued to fire, reload, fire again. James could see Union units holding their ground while being resupplied on the battlefield.

The Union troops continued to fall from wounds and death. It was not pretty but James couldn't take his eyes away from the carnage.

Both sides of the defensive line seemed to be holding Burnside's army back. But James saw a new push of Union troops from his front.

He could tell the next push would eventually overwhelm the Confederate positions. It was also at that moment he recognized the loss of the guns and the militia at that very spot was now the focal point for the Union attack. He was sure a breech was certain.

It got even worse. A general retreat had been called by the Confederate Commander from Fort Thompson.

Initially they fought well as they retreated but they had completely lost track of the 26th Regiment stuck out on the extreme right side.

James eased his thumb on the lock of the rifled musket and began to pull it back. He saw a Union Captain leading a group of men toward gap. "Dear Lord, please forgive me!" He whispered.

He gently pulled the trigger, and the Captain went down clutching his chest. The shot was taken from just over 150 yards.

At that moment, the 26th Regiment, completely unaware of a general retreat, was still pouring fire with great success into the Union troops.

James reloaded and realized the Regiment would be flanked and stuck against a swamp and creek they could not escape across if any of the Union troops made it through the gap.

He was firing and reloading well inside of a minute and hitting his targets as they got closer to the gap. The bodies were starting to build and becoming temporary obstacles for the troops trying to get through.

His shooting position in the tree was fairly-well concealed and the enemy just didn't see James as he fired round after round. After the last shot, he glanced to his right and saw the 26th Regiment was finally aware of their dilemma and were moving smartly toward the other retreating soldiers.

Unlike so many of the other units, the 26th Regiment had Lieutenant Colonel Henry King Burgwyn Jr. in command, and he would not allow such a rout by the 26th Regiment. They fell back in good order with each company taking its turn at preparing firing lines and dispensing death into the face of the oncoming enemy.

While "King" was leading his troops in orderly retreat, the 26th Regiment Commander, Colonel Vance was already at the River Crossing only to find the railroad bridge had been destroyed by other retreating troops.

Many units, including some of the 26th Regiment attempted to cross the river by swimming only to drown. Colonel Vance had not been idle and had found several small boats to help get as many troops across the river as time and their pursuers would allow.

The vast majority of the men of the 26th Regiment got across the river, one way or another. Unfortunately, over 400 troops of the Confederacy were captured on the wrong side of the river by the end of the battle.

General Burnside finally marched into New Bern the next day after the town was secured. The Federal forces would remain there for the duration of the war.

Though greatly outnumbered, the North Carolina forces fared well in their first major battle. The North Carolina Troops consisted of just over 4,000 troops, some with only weeks of training. As General Gatlin evaluated in his final reports, the Confederate forces lost 64 killed, 101 were wounded, and 413 were captured.

General Burnside's Union forces attacked with overwhelming ground and naval forces with heavy artillery. They also had experienced leaders and troops. And yet, Burnside realized he had lost 90 soldiers killed and 380 wounded.

Burnside won the battle and the ground that would remain in Union control for the rest of the war, but it was at a heavy cost.

Within the next 45 days, Burnside would take nearly every port along the coast of North Carolina except the port of Wilmington and Fort Fisher located at the mouth of the Cape Fear River guarding the port.

North Carolina was now decisively engaged in the Civil War, whether they wanted it or not.

* * * * *

March 31, 1862

To Mrs. Anna Wallace Ward, General Delivery, Whiteville, North Carolina

My Dearest Wife,
We have most recently found and fought the Union forces at New Bern and while they won the battle, we fought well. We lost many to both wounds and death, but we inflicted the same to the Yankees many times over.

I must admit that watching my enemy die as I fired gave me no great happiness. I asked God's forgiveness many times that day. I hope he heard my prayers. Please don't tell Momma. I am afraid I have lost my soul.

There was one troubling moment in the battle that turned out well. When we got to the river, the bridge had been destroyed to prevent the Yankees' access to New Bern. Unfortunately, many of the 26th Regiment were on the wrong side of the river.

Colonel Vance and King had found some small boats and we ferried as many across as we could. Stephen was helping getting people lined up for the boats and tried to keep some from trying to swim across the river. He did good, and we got most of our boys across.

At the end, as the enemy was beginning to approach, me and several of the boys had taken positions to keep a steady fire on the men in blue. The last boat was loaded, and they pushed off.

I yelled at Stephen to get into the boat, but he said there was no room, so he waded into the river, grabbed the back of the boat, and held on until they got to the other side. That boy is crazy!

With as many as could get across the river, me and the boys left behind found a lumber pile of rough-cut wood near the pier, we all grabbed a plank and put our gear on it. We jumped into the water and let the current carry us down and across the river. The boys and officers on the other side of the river cheered us all the way across.

As we got to the other side, we had to look back and could see the enemy approaching in small groups. We could see some of our boys on the other bank coming out of the woods with their rifles pointed down and hands in the air. They surrendered. We don't know what happened to them after that.

We are back in Kinston now and Colonel Vance is trying to get us reorganized and ready for the next attack from the coast.

Please tell everyone that Stephen and I are well and safe for the moment.

Please tell Father that I believe he would be proud of how we fought. I know he is not pleased we are here, but I fear for you and the entire family if we allow these men to push us around, we will lose everything. Best I can tell, they are merciless.

Given how well the boys in blue performed, I am afraid we are in for a long fight. I hope I am wrong. If it is a long fight, I wonder, how do we survive?

P.S. Please send more writing paper when you write again. I'm starting to run low.

I am your most devoted husband,

Private James Ward, Company E, 26ᵗʰ Regiment of North Carolina Troops

CHAPTER 6

CAMPAIGN NORTH SUMMER 1862

"James, I'm hearing we might be moving to Virginia soon." Stephen leaned his musket against the tree and hung his haversack from a low branch.

James let the younger Ward cousin fully recover from running to the fire. "Well, I'm sure we all knew it was only a matter of time. Any idea how soon?"

"I was catching a quick nap after dinner in the company tent, I heard Captain Brewer telling Lieutenant Emerson we would be leaving before the end of the week. Can't be more than two or three days at the most. He didn't say where though. Just said Virginia."

Finally catching his breath, Stephen sat down and grabbed a biscuit from the pan sitting on the rocks by the fire.

"James, how come you didn't take that election to be an officer back in April? You know the men wanted you to." Stephen slapped a thick slice of ham inside the biscuit and began to slowly chew it.

"Don't want to be responsible for another man's life. Not the kind of responsibility I need or want. I volunteered to do my duty and soldier. Give me a gun, cap, powder, and ball and I can do that. I didn't volunteer to be an officer. Don't know how." James finished his biscuit and took a long swig of water from the canteen.

Stephen pondered his response and offered, "Yeah, kind of know what you mean. I have to run those messages to the Regiment and back for Captain Brewer and I always feel like that when they write those orders on paper. All I had to do was just hand it to another officer. I was glad I didn't have to make those decisions."

He paused, "I hate it when they tell me to remember what they say and pass it on to the other officers. Makes me nervous I might get it wrong. Then it would be on me. Don't like that either."

James changed the subject, "Got a letter from home today. Anna Wallace said families and farms are passable. Got some Measles going around some of the young'uns, but everybody seems well enough."

He paused. "Men folk have started turning the sod over for the fields. Seeds in the ground not far away for sure."

James frowned like he was unsure what to offer next. "She said they got the bonus money we sent home. Said the money wasn't worth a whole lot when they use it at the general store though. She said your Momma said to tell you to be safe. That's about it."

He reached for his haversack and pulled out the letter to make sure he covered all subjects. James angled the letter toward the fire for light. Nodded to himself, "Yep, that about it."

As Stephen promised, Captain Brewer stood before Company E and proclaimed, "Men, the 26th Regiment and several others will be moving North by train within the next twenty-four hours. Get your gear in order and any excess baggage ready for the supply wagons. And no, we don't know where and for how long. First Sergeant, dismiss the Company."

The next morning began with the usual six o'clock formation. The roll call was concluded, and the troops were put at ease with no talking. Each company First Sergeant took their respective company rolls and passed them to the Regimental Adjutant, First Lieutenant James Bell Jordan, at the center and front of the Regimental Command Group.

There were short exchanges and brief discussions with each Company First Sergeant. The First Sergeants were then ordered to return to their companies. The only First Sergeant left at the front was from Company F.

There was obviously something wrong. Murmuring began to filter through Company F.

The Regimental Adjutant did an about face and moved to the command group, specifically Colonel Vance. Vance did not look particularly happy with what was being discussed. With a wave of his arm, the Commander had obviously decided a course of action.

Upon return of Lieutenant Jordan to the center front of the regimental formation, he ordered, "Private L.M. Blalock, Private Samuel Blalock, report to the front."

Every eye turned to Company F and their formation. Two individuals stepped out smartly and moved to the front of the formation. They stopped directly in front of the Adjutant. No one could hear what was being discussed.

Stephen turned his head slightly to his right toward James, "Ain't that the two soldiers we were watching on the parade field the other day?"

James studied the two soldiers as they stood before the Adjutant, "Not sure but could be, why?"

"I just got a feeling about this. But we'll see shortly, I'm sure." Stephen returned his eyes to the front, with that silly grin on his face.

As best James could tell from about fifty yards away, the two privates were from the group that had joined the Regiment just after the Battle of New Bern. They had only been on the roll for a couple of months at best.

The taller Private Keith Blalock, as he was known, was nearly six feet tall, maybe weighing around 185 pounds, with narrow hips, and of a slight muscular build.

James guessed the shorter Private Samuel Blalock was about five and half feet tall, probably weighing about 130 pounds, and of a stocky build. Other than being a little wide at the hips, James couldn't see anything extraordinary about the two soldiers.

What happened next was a pleasant shock to everyone.

Lieutenant Jordan pointed at the smaller Private Blalock's uniform. Sam Blalock reached for the buttons on the uniform tunic and began to unbutton the jacket. Still facing the Lieutenant, he then opened the jacket as directed. The Adjutant immediately averted his eyes and then looked at Colonel Vance.

The Colonel waved his affirmation with a brush of his hand and turned around and left the 26th Regiment's formation, along with the command group in tow.

Lieutenant Jordan ordered the soldier to button the jacket, but instead Private Samuel Blalock turned about, her jacket wide open and showed the entire Regiment an abundant and well-rounded set of breasts for all to see.

The entire formation went into wild cheers and shouting. The Company Commanders and First Sergeants lost all control over the Regiment. At least they maintained their formation although troops were falling over in laughter.

The Adjutant finally convinced her to close her jacket and stand at attention. She turned and complied. Both Privates Blalock were led to the Regimental Headquarters tent where they were summarily discharged from duty.

Private Samuel Blalock was none other than Malinda Blalock and the very proud wife of Private Keith Blalock. She said he could only enlist if she could go with him. Only three people knew she was a woman, the recruiter, the husband, and the wife.

Stephan looked at James and said, "I told you there was something strange about those two."

James' first reaction was sadness, when he saw the woman, not the soldier. His second thought was the young wife he had left behind and how much he missed her at that moment.

His thought was, "would my wife do the same thing to be with him?" James didn't think so.

Later, after everyone had calmed down, the company began their preparations for their imminent move. There was lots of scurrying about, packing equipment, gathering baggage to be packed onto the wagons, and breaking down and folding tentage for the movement.

The recent reorganization included assignment of the 26th Regiment to General Robert Ransom's Brigade. His brigade had orders to move to an area near Richmond, Virginia and prepare for major engagements under the newly assigned Commander of the Army of Northern Virginia, General Robert E. Lee.

Lee inherited his army with the serious injuries to Lieutenant General Joseph E. Johnston incurred by Union fire around Petersburg and Richmond. Those Union troops were under the command of Major General George McClellan.

General McClellan was under strong orders and encouragement from President Lincoln to put pressure on the Confederate Army and its Capitol in Richmond.

General Lee spent the late Winter and early Spring of 1862 fortifying the Capitol city and organizing his new army.

Colonel Vance led his Regiment into the North with great fanfare but offered advice to his troops that any battles they faced in Virginia would be even more deadly than the Battle of New Bern.

The 26th Regiment troops paid attention to their Commander as they arrived in Virginia in June as part of General Ransom's Brigade and placed under the command of Major General Benjamin Huger.

While assigned to Huger's Division, the 26th Regiment served in supporting roles but saw engagements in several smaller skirmishes. Each skirmish only reinforced the Regiment's troops with more experience in battle and convinced them they could go to the fight and win.

One such occasion was on the early evening of June 25 as the unit was being moved for placement into the battle lines. Colonel Vance led from the front. By nightfall, the Regiment moved to the side of a road to await instructions.

What was unknown to Vance and his command was a Union force lying on the opposite side of the same road. The ambush was massive and at close range.

The center of the Regiment took immediate casualties, but the unit found itself in a fight and immediately reacted with courage and strength using a continuous rate of fire.

The enemy was repulsed but Colonel Vance and his troops learned a deadly but valuable lesson. The enemy was to be found nearly anywhere.

Another lesson learned for the troops occurred on June 27. This lesson was about timing being everything on the battlefield.

James Ward stood in the newly improved trench for the Company E pickets posted to the front of the main unit. No one really wanted to be on picket duty because you were literally left alone with very little support to your left and right from other pickets.

He was no different, but James was here for two reasons. First, he was here to complete improvements to the trenches with log obstacles and abatis to restrict any enemy attack. The second reason was James' proficiency with his rifled musket.

On one occasion, the prying eyes of Union forces made the mistake of getting a little too close to the picket positions. They were looking through binoculars, from the wood line, searching for gaps or weaknesses in the Confederate lines.

Having seen the movement out of the corner of his eye, James slowly kneeled into the trench to put his shovel down. "Henry, keep working. I think we have a Yank officer over there to the left."

Henry looked down at James and knew what was about to happen. "You want me to keep throwing dirt with this shovel to keep him interested?"

James looked up at Henry and smiled, "Yep, but soon as I fire you get down. They may have a sharpshooter over there too."

"Don't worry, I'm down as soon as I hear that hammer drop." Henry stood back up and threw a shovel of dirt in front of the position.

He laid the shovel down on the dirt pile and stretched his arms as if taking a break from the chore of shoveling dirt.

James gathered his musket and moved down the line about ten yards. He slipped between a small gap in the dirt bunker. The musket slowly crested the dirt and gradually pointed in the direction where he saw the movement.

His first glance did not see anything, but the Sun offered just the right light into the shadows as he saw the binocular lenses momentarily flash. He eased back down and made sure the musket was ready as he cocked it.

The glaring lenses became his focal point, and those glasses were still very focused on Henry's movement. He eased his finger onto the trigger, placed his aim just a little higher on the target because of the distance, took a deep breath, held it, and eased the trigger back.

Just before the musket exploded, James did as he always did, "Dear Lord, please forgive me."

The musket ball went slowly toward its target, the glare from the lenses flinched, and the soldier's body fell backwards further into the bushes where he had been hiding.

The other pickets immediately looked toward James' position and then to the front. Each gathered their weapons and gear ready to move to the rear.

James yelled down the line, "Boys get ready, there's more of 'em."

Moments later, the woods erupted with Union troops moving down the hill from the wood line with the silver-colored bayonet attached to their muskets.

All of the 26th Regiment pickets did as James directed, and immediately placed effective fire on the oncoming blue uniforms. Several Union soldiers fell.

Seeing they were greatly outnumbered, the pickets reloaded and fired one more round each. Then one picket soldier, from each position, left for the rear, while the other picket soldier stayed to provide continuous covering fire.

When Henry refused to leave James in their picket position by himself, James did not quit firing and said, "Henry, get the hell out of here or I'll shoot you myself!"

Henry finally left the trench. Private James Ward was the last picket off the line.

After his fourth shot, he grabbed his other musket, gear, and ran for his life, with Union Minie' balls falling all around him.

Troops from Company E were yelling at him the whole way. Cheering and urging him to run faster. He ran through the small gap in the defensive positions and dove into a bank of dirt.

Company E troops opened with full and massive fire as soon as he was out of the line of fire. They continued to reload and fire for several minutes until the Union incursion was dismissed.

Stephen ran over to his cousin and shouted, "I don't believe I could run that fast across a hundred yards on my best day!"

James caught his breath, "I'll let you do it next time."

"Nah, I can't shoot as good as you!" Stephen smiled.

Captain Brewer came over to James, "Private Ward, excellent job out there. We were about to be relieved by another unit. Most of the troops were ready to move out."

He continued, "You gave us enough time to prepare for them before that happened. However, I would appreciate it if you would not stay on the picket line so long the next time." He patted James on the shoulder and smiled.

"I'll try to do better next time Sir." James suddenly realized what his timing had meant for the safety of the entire unit.

If the 26th Regiment had begun the withdrawal movement at that moment, the new unit would not be effectively in place to repulse the enemy attack. The result would probably have meant their position would be overrun during the transition between units.

By the evening of July 1, General Magruder's Division was engaged, in mass, at a place called Malvern Hill. Union forces were making heavy attacks at various points of the defense and having success.

After five other regiments had been engaged and pressed hard and with too many casualties, Magruder called for two more regiments to move forward and into the lines. Those regiments came from Major General Huger's Division and specifically, Ransom's Brigade.

The 26th Regiment was brought forward to reinforce a counterattack of the Union successes on Magruder's lines.

As they moved forward into the fray, Colonel Vance saw a rabbit running after being scared from the brush, as his troops pressed forward, "Go it cotton tail. If I had no more reputation to lose than you have, I would run too." The entire command roared a cheer for the Virginia hare!

Lieutenant Colonel Burgwyn was moving about the Regiment observing and providing detailed instructions where necessary. His message was clear, "There are many men dead and wounded to the front. You must keep your Company moving forward. Don't stop to help anyone, you must push forward and push the enemy off the high ground to our front."

The 26th Regiment moved at the quick step march and were placed into attack formations. It was formed into two large attack commands controlled by one of the Regimental lieutenants and reinforced with the remaining two Regimental companies in reserve and support. Each of the two large units were comprised of three companies. Each of the company attack formations were organized with two large ranks formed by each company.

When James looked down at his rank, the lines seem to go on forever. He remembered at that moment the formation looked just as Lieutenant Colonel Burgwyn had made them practice while on the coast of North Carolina for so many drilling sessions.

He muttered to himself, "Thank God for 'King' and all that drilling."

James looked forward and saw Captain Brewer positioning himself to the front of Company E. "Men, stand fast. Trust your drills. When we go, pay no attention to anything except the enemy to your front. Kill him before he kills you. I will see you at the top of the hill."

From his position, James could see that Stephen was standing just behind the Captain. He had that silly grin on his face again as he winked at James.

Stephen had recently been made one of three messengers and runners for the Captain. He also noted that Stephen had his boots on his feet.

"Lord, have mercy." James bowed his head in prayer. Everyone knew the messengers were favorite targets for Union sharpshooters due to the messages or information they carried.

Malvern Hill was a tough piece of land. Hardly worthy of serious farming. James wondered if maybe it was used as pasture. Either way James could not see the value of it except for the view on top of that damned hill in front of him.

Captain Brewer had asked James to pick a good spot to take advantage of his rifled musket. "Get me some Yankee officers, if you can James."

"Sir, I'll do what I can, but you know they have sharpshooters too. You keep your head on your shoulders Sir." James grimaced as he nodded.

Colonel Vance and his assistant, Lieutenant Colonel Burgwyn moved quickly through the Regiment quickly talking to company commanders and positioning themselves for the movement forward.

As the battle engaged up the hill, the Regiment was making good progress. The units moved in great form and shape.

Ranks moving forward, stopping for the forward rank to fire, quickly kneeling to reload, and allowing for the second rank to fire and then reload, always moving forward.

If a man on the forward rank fell from the enemy fires, the man in the rank directly behind the felled solider moved into his place in the rank. The process continued all the way back to the companies reinforcing from directly behind the forward companies.

The troops of the 26th Regiment stepped over many wounded and dead men as they moved forward. The noise from cannons and muskets was so loud, you could not hear the commands of your own officers. The white smoke drifted across the field and made the eyes water.

They stood, fired, reloaded, fired, reloaded, and moved forward steadily, for what James, thought were hours. It seemed the Sun moved slowly that day.

Third Lieutenant Orren Alston Hanner, a nineteen-year-old officer, was close at hand as James moved up the hill. The fever of battle was taking control of the young man. He kept yelling for the men of Company E to advance.

"Lieutenant, slow down, the men can't keep up with you and load too!" James reached for the lieutenant's arm.

"Come on James, we're almost to the wall!!" At that moment, the musket ball took the young officer in the right shoulder and knocked him.

James reached for him and pulled him down to the ground. Heavy musket fire raced over their heads. It was nearly dark and the Minie' balls that passed over them still glowed in the growing darkness like fireflies.

The Lieutenant rolled to the ground and moaned. James pushed him closer to the ground as the officer laid face up.

"Sir, I need you to be strong. I want you to push hard on that wound. We got to stop the bleeding!" James was quickly pulling a cloth handkerchief from this haversack.

"It's alright James, I'm sure I am about to die. Please tell my mother I died for my State and family." The lieutenant sighed, and James was afraid he might be right.

At that moment, a wave of cannon fire fell onto the Regiment. Commanders from all the companies began to shout, "go to ground!!"

The men followed their directions and hugged the ground as if their lives depended on it. And it did.

Most of the Regiment was only fifty yards from the Union forces. Time and darkness were working against them.

Nightfall was fast approaching and there was a strong military need to gain the high ground as soon as practical.

The Union forces were massing musket and cannon fire to defend and deny that same high ground.

Darkness came over the field very rapidly at that point but the fire from both the Union muskets and cannons continued to rake the field.

Captain Brewer loudly commanded, "Get down and stay down. Remain there for as long as necessary. They can't hit us if they can't see us."

Similar commands were moving through the entire Regiment. Every man was hugging what ground they could find. It was July and usually hot at night. For some reason, many of those men, on the hill that night, thought it was the coldest night of their lives. Some could not stop shaking.

No one raised a hand, much less their head, or shouted a command for fear the Yankee soldiers would continue to fire through most of the night toward any movement or sound.

Wounded men could not help but cry out in pain. Each moan or cry was met with indiscriminate musket fire from Union forces. Other troops held a hand over the mouth of those wounded to keep from drawing fire.

Around midnight, James heard a whisper, "James?"

James' first thought the sound came from Lieutenant Hanner. However, he realized the lieutenant was softly snoring in the night when he looked over at the dark shape in the night.

James was happy the lieutenant was still alive and able to sleep. Still not knowing who was calling, he whispered, "Yeah, who is it?"

A shuffle came just below him on the hill and Stephen stopped right at James' boots.

"It's me, cousin. Captain told me to find you." Stephen whispered in very hushed tones.

"What the hell does he want with me? And how the hell did you find me in the middle of the night?" James whispered in rather harsh terms.

"He says he wants you to find Lieutenant Hanner and prepare the men to attack those positions directly ahead on command in the morning. And he knew where you were before dark and figured you were smart enough to stay low. He just pointed me in your direction and said to find you. Here I am." Stephen finished.

James knew he had that silly grin on his face again without being able to see him in the night.

He whispered, "Well, the Lieutenant is right here beside me. He's been wounded in the shoulder. Not sure it's too serious but he needs medical help for sure. Can't be moved tonight though. Noise would get us all killed."

Stephen mumbled under his breath, "I guess you get to do it then?"

"What? Me lead the attack?" James couldn't believe he was being asked to lead others up the hill to positions about thirty-five yards from where they laid.

"Don't see any other way, cousin. I'll tell him about the Lieutenant being shot and all." Stephen started pushing away.

James whispered, "How bad was it?"

Stephen hesitated, "We got shot up pretty good, but we still got most of the Company around us right now. Pretty sure that Captain Brewer believes we can make that thirty-five yards before they can reload is his thought."

"Gonna be a mess, though. Tell him, I'll do the best I can. About all I can promise." James shrugged in the darkness.

"He knows. He said you would say that anyway." Stephen moved away and melted into the dark.

A few moments passed and James began to think about what he should do at that moment.

Lieutenant Hanner whispered, "You can do this James. I'll help as much as I can."

James turned toward the muffled voice, "Thanks Lieutenant, but I don't want to do this. I'm not an officer, you are. I don't know how to lead, you do."

"I think I said the same thing just a few months ago when I was elected by the Company. You're older. You're smarter, and you know how to survive. Let your instincts tell you what to do. Wake me before morning if I am still alive." The young Lieutenant then rolled over and went back to sleep.

James spent several more moments thinking about how they would rally and charge the hilltop. He wondered how he would know when Captain Brewer expected him to initiate the attack.

He finally realized he had no idea other than to stand and charge the hill. He hoped the troops would follow him.

It was almost dawn when someone yelled, "They're gone!!"

James was startled and quickly turned his head in the direction of the shout.

He could barely see the soldier that appeared to be kneeling and looking toward the hilltop. James slowly looked up but could not see any muskets or cannon in sight.

"Looks like you might avoid leading the Company up that hill after all James." Lieutenant Hanner slowly rolled with a grimace.

James looked down and reached for the bloody rag that covered Hanner's wound. "Glad of that, but I won't believe that until I get to the top of that hill."

He kneeled and took another look at the high ground and then stood, fully expecting a musket to fire, and put him out of his misery.

Nothing happened.

James reached down and gathered his gear. "Company E, stand if you are able. Come with me to the top." He promptly started walking the last thirty-five yards.

Lieutenant Hanner tried to stand as best he could. It was difficult. A soldier was starting to pass him, "Sir, can I help you up?"

Hanner smiled to the soldier and said, "I would appreciate it a great deal. I want to be with that man when he gets to the top."

The soldier looked forward and at a fast-walking Private James Ward moving away. "I'll help you Sir, but I'm not sure we can catch him."

Malvern Hill would remain in the memory of every living man of the 26th Regiment after that battle. All other battles would be measured against the results of Malvern Hill.

Ransom's brigade lost sixty-nine dead and three hundred and fifty-four wounded. The 26th Regiment lost six killed and forty wounded.

By mid-July, the 26th Regiment found itself back in North Carolina. And quickly found itself in another battle.

* * * * *

July 15, 1862

To Private James Ward, Company E, 26th Regiment, Ransom's Brigade, Huger's Division, near Richmond, Virginia

My dearest Husband,

We were most fearful of the news of the battles in Northern Virginia. Our worst fear was to see the death rosters the newspaper publish on the wall of the courthouse, and we feared to see your name or Stephen's name on it. Obviously, we were pleased to see that neither of you were on the roster.

Your father was most displeased by the public display of emotions shown by several families seeing members of their family on the roster. He said, it was just plain undignified.

All the children have survived our Measles sickness and the warm weather seems to be working in our favor health wise.

We are well into planting our second crop of wheat. The Spring crop was not particularly good. Corn has been fairly good, but we need some more rain.

Whiskey production will not be as good as usual. The Sugar Cane was good, and it will help with our cash sales with both syrup and rum made from the molasses.

We had to cut back on the tobacco and cotton planting because we just don't have the help to tend and harvest the crop with so many men gone to war.

Our garden continues to grow well and between Miz Lizzie and me, we have plenty to fill the root cellar and canning vegetables. We do have plenty of milk and we sold a couple of milk cows and their calves for some extra money. Unfortunately, people had to pay in Confederate paper. Your father had to barter as well.

We're planning on butchering several more cattle and hogs this Fall. Your father seems to think we'll be better off not having to feed the animals than having meat to eat. It also gives him more to barter for other supplies.

I had your brothers over to our homestead to do some work. They did a good job on Saturday of getting a good roof on the barn in place. They stayed over that night and finished some additional things like the fireplace in the main room and the kitchen.

They surprised me by finding some nice stones from the riverbed and used the wagon to bring them to the house. We're ready for winter when you get back home.

Right now, Miz Lizzie has a pretty good group of students. There are ten of the Ward family children plus one from my family for her classes in your main room or under the big Oak Tree by the barn on hot days.

She is spending three days each week teaching the young ones their reading, writing, and arithmetic lessons. Miz Lizzie has set aside Saturday and Sunday afternoons and Wednesday evenings for extra classes once chores are finished. Your mother is still using the same Bible and slate boards she used to teach you and Stephen so many years ago.

I have enclosed more writing paper for you, and I have included a new pencil I traded for at the mercantile store in town for a chicken. I also got eleven more pencils for the children's classes, as well.

Please write me when you can and know that I love you most dearly.

I am your most loving wife,

Anna Wallace Ward

CHAPTER 7

GOING HOME, FALL OF 1862

Success breeds its own rewards. The newspaper articles found on the courthouse walls and purchased on the streets of town, recollected many eyewitness testimonies and official accounts of the failure of the battles around the Peninsula Campaign for General George McClellan and the Union Army of the Potomac.

To such success, goes the spoils. Colonel Zebulon Vance's reputation and accounts of his Regiment's performance at Malvern Hill made him a formidable candidate for political office.

As it would turn out, the office he sought was the position as Governor of the State of North Carolina. In accepting the election results, Vance was required to relinquish his role as Commander of the 26th Regiment of North Carolina Troops.

He offered the not yet, twenty-one years old Lieutenant Colonel Henry K. Burgwyn Jr. as his recommended successor.

While the State and the Regiment were well satisfied with that recommendation, General Ransom made it abundantly clear that Burgwyn would not serve as a Regimental Commander in his command. He considered the "boy" too young to be a regimental commander.

Newly elected Governor Vance took Ransom's statement under advisement and passed the sword of Command to Burgwyn in a special ceremony before his departure.

However, politics being politics, Vance also made sure the 26th Regiment was transferred to the Command of General James Johnston Pettigrew's Brigade and away from Ransom's Command.

For everyone except General Ransom, the problem was solved.

This all occurred after Burgwyn was elected by the Regiment with less than two hands of fingers voting against him.

Those seven individuals were given the opportunity to leave the camp at their earliest convenience and for their own safety. Some would suggest those men were the same naysayers since the Regiment was originally formed.

To suggest that Burgwyn's new Brigade Commander was a pleasant happenstance was a great understatement. While there were many years of age separating them, both men were so much alike.

It was suggested that Pettigrew saw more of himself in Burgwyn than some felt was true. They were both graduates of the University of North Carolina and both had great academic records of renown.

Pettigrew was a world traveler with extensive travel, education, and experience in European affairs. He was very pleased with Spain and made the people, culture, and place a prominent part of his recently published book. He was a lawyer, politician, and very learned in military strategy, tactics, and weapons.

As to his resemblance to Burgwyn, they shared a love of literature, the planter's lifestyle, and the love of their home, the State of North Carolina.

More recently, both Pettigrew and Burgwyn had been in the Peninsula Campaign where Pettigrew was wounded. Pettigrew also knew of the 26th Regiment and its performance at Malvern Hill. He personally knew what was required to take that hill and push the Army of the Potomac back toward the James River.

More importantly, he was also aware of Burgwyn's performance at Malvern Hill and was duly impressed with the young man. He was also familiar with the Burgwyn family.

Captain Brewer found James in camp, preparing his gear for travel. The 26th Regiment was being sent home to secure the coast once again after saving the Confederacy from McClellan's campaign.

James saw Captain Brewer coming from around the tentage and quickly stood up to come to the position of attention. "Good morning, Sir."

Brewer returned the salute while shifting a large, wrapped package, "A good morning to you as well Private Ward. I think I got a gift from the Yankees with your name on it." He was smiling at James.

He handed the long package to James, "We found this while we were salvaging equipment from the battlefield at Malvern Hill. One of the units found it up near where the cannons had been located on the hilltop." Brewer began untying the leather straps holding the oiled-canvas wrap.

James' interest was heightened. He took the package into his hands. It was very heavy. He continued untying and unfolding the canvas. What he found was a very large musket with a strange device attached. "What is it, Sir?"

"Well, I'm not really sure of the right official nomenclature, but they tell me it's called a Leonard Target Rifle. Can't tell you who had it, how it was used, but a couple of folks at brigade seems to think it came from New Hampshire. Heavy thing, isn't it?" Brewer smiled.

James cradled the rifle in his arms, "Yeah, not sure how you could hold it steady enough to shoot it. It's got an octagon barrel, maybe about thirty or thirty-two inches. Looks like it might be a little smaller bullet, maybe .48 caliber?"

Brewer reached over his shoulder and pulled a large haversack that looked quite full. "You might want to take a look at the impedimenta in the bag. I think you got what you might need for a while in there."

"What's the big rod on top for? Can't see how you could see over it to properly sight the target?" James held it up to his shoulder and strained a little getting it to comfortably fit his shoulder.

He laid his cheek to the stock to illustrate his point, "Whoa! What is that?" He looked over the barrel again trying to see where the gun was pointed.

Captain Brewer was laughing, "That's a telescopic sight. It magnifies the target to your eye, so you can see it better."

James put the rifle to his shoulder again and selected a target about a hundred yards away. He looked into the telescope, "Good Lord! It does look like I can just reach out and touch the target. Might take some getting used to it, though."

"Take your time. When we get back to North Carolina, I want you to get as proficient with that rifle as you are with your own rifle. I think you are going to like the range on that one. I hear it is well over a thousand yards." Captain Brewer was smiling again.

James didn't even look up. He just kept looking through the sight. "Yes Sir. I'll do it."

Captain Brewer started to walk away after watching James getting familiar with the new rifle.

Private Stephen Ward came running up to the Captain, "Sir, got this message from Colonel Burgwyn. Says you need to be at the regimental headquarters at five o'clock for an Officers Call." He handed the folded paper to his Company Commander.

"Thank you, Private Ward. I'll leave you with the other Private Ward and his new toy." Brewer unfolded the message, read it, and gave a little grunt.

He folded the message and placed it into his jacket pocket. He walked away in a bit of a hurry.

"Damn, that's a big rifle James!"

"Don't cuss so much Stephen. We're too close to Heaven for that kind of language." James never took his eyes off the rifle as he continued to caress the fine, polished wood while bringing the rifle to his shoulder.

Stephen responded, "Well, I'm not planning on going to Heaven anytime soon."

James responded just as quickly, "The Yankees might have something to say about that and sooner than you think."

"Well, you might be right about that. But you can't be around these boys and not learn to cuss just a little bit more. Don't you think?"

"Yeah, but what would your mother say if she heard that come out of your mouth. I'm thinking a large bar of lye soap might be used on that shitty mouth!" James laughed as he put the rifle into the canvas bag and tied the leather retaining straps.

In late September, the 26th Regiment was still in the southeastern part of the State of Virginia, but orders were received to move South once again. Preparations were underway and equipment and baggage were being packed onto railcars once again.

That evening, around the campfires, the troops were eating their evening meal. Mister Mickey's 26th Regimental Band was centered in the camp and softly playing a tune from the Old North State.

The troops were tired. While buoyed by their successes against the Army of the Potomac, they were suddenly homesick. They belonged in North Carolina and the recent news of orders to return home were most welcome.

They were just too tired to celebrate the news.

James had gotten a nice meal of stew in his wooden bowl. He poked at the stew and saw several vegetables and chunks of meat. He thought the meat was beef. The bread was hard and difficult to chew. James dipped the bread into the stew to soften the bread.

It was filling but James thought it had an unusual flavor.

Stephen came over to where James was sitting on the ground and found a log to set his own bowl. "How is it?"

"Got a funny taste to it. Must be some special spice or something they added. Not bad, just don't taste quite right." James added after taking another spoonful of the stew.

His cousin poked at the stew in his bowl. "Don't think they used some bad meat or such, do you?"

"I don't think so. It is fresh meat. Maybe just killed today or yesterday. May not have had time to let the meat hang to drain the blood. That might be it." James continued to spoon the meal into his mouth.

Stephen got up and started back to the fire where the meal was being cooked. "I'm gonna go and see what they got in it. Maybe just eat some bread and cheese."

James watched him walk away and considered what his cousin was doing. "Good stew." He finished the bowl and polished it off with an apple.

The next day found many of the men with significant stomach issues. The "Camp Trots" had men running to latrines or woods to deposit what they ate the night before. James was one of those in pain.

Colonel Burgwyn made immediate inquiries as to why certain companies were having similar problems, while others were unaffected. Nearly half of the regimental companies had used water from a nearby pond, while the majority of companies used a running creek for their water supply.

Suddenly, the regiment was suffering from an epidemic of dysentery. The severity of each case was directly related to the amount of water or food poorly prepared in the water.

In James' case, he had eaten a bowl and then part of another. He had been to the woods no less than four times by early morning. He was sure he had emptied his bowels of everything in it. Unfortunately, he had not been able to purge the bacteria from the water in his body.

The unit continued to prepare to return to North Carolina, many of them sick with dysentery.

James struggled with the severe pain in his stomach. He wretched and fought nausea throughout the coming days. Since finding out the problem was water, he was reluctant to drink water. That only made the problem worse.

He had nearly stopped eating anything and when he did, it seemed to move straight through his body. More pain for the abdomen.

By the time they reached their destination by train, the unit had to move to their designated camp, James could barely move. Stephen carried most of his gear while they tried to march. He fell out of the formation on multiple occasions with dry heaves.

Doctor Thomas Boykin and Private Daniel Shaw the Assistant Surgeon were continuously moving throughout the tented hospital. Mister Mickey and the regimental band were also called in to support the medical staff as they had done on the battlefield many times already.

Captain Brewer and many of the other Company Commanders visited their troops in the regimental hospital. James was gathered with many of his fellow regimental soldiers in numerous hospital tents.

Brewer asked with concern, "Doctor Boykin, how are my Company E troops doing?"

"Sir, I believe most will be fine eventually, probably three to five days. We'll know more after that." Doctor Boykin wiped his brow with a white cloth smeared with blood and excrement.

He continued, "I'll tell you I've never heard or smelled so much farting, puke, and shit in one place before, but it is to be expected. Most of the worst fevers have come down but we need to keep an eye on that. They need lots of fresh water and rest."

Brewer walked slowly around the tent with the Doctor, "Any guess as to when they will be able to return to duty?"

"Oh, we got a ways to go with that. We need to get the sickness out of their stomachs, fill them with some solid food, and plenty of walking about in the fresh air." Boykin slowed his move from bed to bed.

"James, how are you today?" The doctor pointed to the shape wrapped in blankets on the makeshift bed of wooden boxes.

Captain Brewer frowned at the doctor, "James, it's Captain Brewer. You able to see visitors?"

The lump on the bed began to stir and looked like he was trying to untangle himself from the twisted blanket. "Sorry Sir didn't realize it was you. Give me a minute."

"No, that's not necessary James, don't try to get up." Brewer couldn't help himself and placed his hand on James to keep him from moving.

James' head finally appeared from the blankets and nodded in relief. "I'm so sorry Sir for being so disrespectful. I just can't move very fast."

Doctor Boykin intervened and stepped to James' bedside, "James, I'm going to remove some this blanket and I want you to sit up on the bed if you can. Let me examine you."

"I'll try Sir. But my head and my stomach may not act just right." James allowed the Doctor to pull the blanket away and he tried to lift himself upright on the bed.

Captain Stephen Brewer looked at a man near death, he was sure. The strong, muscled, and healthy man he knew just weeks ago at Malvern Hill, Virginia was nearly bare skin and bones.

James was clothed in small clothes drawers and cotton over shirt. He attempted to stand but only succeeded with the help of Doctor Boykin. He tried to stand upright, offered a weak salute with his right hand that could barely raise above his shoulder, "Sir, Private Ward, reporting for duty, Sir."

He almost collapsed with the effort and both Brewer and Boykin quickly caught him before he fell backwards.

"At ease Private Ward. We need you to get well. Falling over and hurting yourself is not going to make that easy."

Captain Brewer stepped back. "James, I want you to do exactly what Doctor Boykin says, no argument. Do you understand?"

James' head was already lowered as he spoke, "Yes Sir." Then he fell back into bed.

Doctor Boykin replaced the blanket over James' body and waved Captain Brewer to the side of the tent. James pulled the blanket back over his head.

"Captain Brewer, James and at least four others need long-term care. I can't provide that care for James and support this Regiment. There are too many that need attention for wounds and sickness that can recover sooner than these men." Boykin paused to let the statement settle in for the Commander of Company E.

"What do you recommend Doctor?" Brewer was sure he knew the answer but wanted the Doctor to say it out loud.

Boykin looked hesitant, "Your men all come from a proximity close to where we are located here in the Eastern part of the State. I suggest you send them home to recover. I think one, maybe as many as three months should be sufficient to recover from the illness. Then they can get their strength back."

He paused and then continued, "I would think they would be back in the Regiment ready for duty by Christmas at the latest. That means they would be ready for any Spring engagements that may arise on the coast."

"Very well Doctor. I will inform Colonel Burgwyn and prepare for James to be furloughed for three months for recovery. Please have the other four men ready as well. They are no more than two or three days from home as we speak." Captain Brewer extended his hand and thanked the Doctor.

"Very good Sir. I will have a small wagon and their gear ready for the ride tomorrow or at your earliest convenience." Boykin shook the Captain's hand.

Early morning two days later, the five men had corn-shuck mattresses laid on the bed of the wagon. Blankets were provided and the men were carefully placed into the wagon. Their personal gear and camping gear for stops each night were placed under the seat of the wagon.

Captain Brewer was there and provided furlough papers for each man. The furlough documents ensured that no one confused the men for deserters.

He offered instructions for each man, "Gentlemen, you are going home. You will recover there with the attention of your loved ones. Take advantage of that opportunity to become stronger and ready for return to your Regiment. Failure to return as specified within your furlough papers will result in your being declared deserters and subject to severe punishment. Do you understand?"

Each man in the wagon, other than the driver, was barely able to comprehend the question, much less than reply. James was able to say at a whisper, "Sir, we understand. I will personally make sure they return as ordered, Sir." He then closed his eyes and leaned back into the wagon bed.

Brewer then went to the wagon driver, "Private Ward, I expect you to take these men to their homes. Correct me if I am wrong, that's near your home, I believe. Once there, you will ensure they have ample time to settle in before leaving them. Upon determining they are being well-cared for; you will return to the Regiment at your earliest convenience. I'm thinking about three weeks from today should be about right. Do you agree?"

He winked as he handed his written orders to Private Stephen Ward.

"Sir, yes Sir! I believe that is exactly the right amount of time, Sir." Stephen gave that funny grin with all his teeth showing and put the packet with his orders in his uniform jacket.

Captain Brewer leaned in a bit, "Stephen, as you start to come back, check with each man's family, and give me a progress report when you get back. I want to make sure they are improving, and you can remind the men of what their furlough papers say. I don't want anybody shot or hung for desertion."

Stephen nodded his understanding, "I surely will Sir, but don't you be worried. These boys will be back in the Regiment soonest. Especially that ornery Private Ward back there. Never seen him like that in my life. He won't let this stop him though. He'll be back."

It took two full days for Stephen to get near the Ward family farms. They stopped for two nights and each time, Stephen set up a brief camp. He helped the men out of the wagon and to a comfortable spot he found for each man.

After that, he found a stream of fresh water and started a fire. With the one kettle pot from the equipment provided by Doctor Boykin, he placed a good portion of water and waited for it to come to boil.

After coming to a boil, he slipped a slab of cured ham, two cut potatoes, and a chopped onion into the pot. Since the cured ham had both salt and pepper on it from curing, he didn't need any seasoning.

Stephen let the supper boil for about an hour and used that time to finish setting up the camp for the night. The wagon mattresses were placed with care beneath the wagon in case it rained since it had been cloudy most of the day.

He went to the stream once again and filled the canteens with water. He returned one canteen for each man. As Doctor Boykin had instructed, he provided each man with a small, folded paper packet with some medication inside. Stephen helped each man take the medication with the fresh water.

Stephen reached into the wooden box where the cookware was stored and pulled out six wooden bowls and spoons. He also reached for a paper-wrapped package containing about twelve biscuits.

He poured a half bowl of the ham soup and gave each man a biscuit. All but James could set up and try to feed themselves with some effort. Stephen only had to help a couple of times.

James was different. Stephen recognized that whatever was wrong with James, it had almost taken the life out of him. Stephen helped lean James against the wheel of the wagon so that he could sit with support.

Stephen used the spoon to ladle it into James' mouth. James was barely able to open his mouth and swallow. He never spoke. His eyes were closed.

By the time he had finished trying to eat his bowl of soup, James just sat leaning against the wheel, still with his eyes closed.

Stephen got up and moved back to the kettle and filled the other men's bowls for a second round. When asked by one of the men for another biscuit, Stephen informed them he didn't have any spare biscuits. The rest would be for tomorrow's meal.

After everyone had their fill of the meal. Stephen sat down to have a bowl for himself. He ate quickly knowing he had other chores to perform before the evening and darkness set in.

The mules hobbled near the stream and a small meadow of late Summer grass. Stephen pulled a small bag of corn for feed as well and a half bale of hay from the wagon supplies. He split those out for the animals.

Darkness finally covered their campsite and Stephen began to move each man to their corn-shuck mattresses beneath the wagon. Since James was already leaning on the wagon wheel, he was last for placement on his mattress.

All Stephen had to do was gently move James to the right about a foot and let him lay back under the wagon. James opened his eyes for the first time in over an hour and said, "Thanks cousin." He closed his eyes again.

The next day of the trip was similar as the first, except the clouds were getting larger, darker, and the winds were picking up. Stephen recalled this was the season for big storms out over the ocean, hurricanes.

Supper that night was a repeat of the first night. One of the men was strong enough to complain, "You mean I got to eat the same thing two days in a row?"

Stephen just grinned, "No, you don't have to eat at all. You choose."

The weak man smiled and said, "I'll take mine just like last night."

For the rest of the night, things were like the previous night, except James was able to stay awake long enough to eat his soup from the spoon provided by Stephen's hand.

James was still too weak to feed himself. Once again, he only ate one bowl of the soup. However, he quickly went to sleep while still saying nothing. Stephen thought he couldn't even see any life in James' eyes.

The clouds stayed dark but never provided the expected rain. Stephen wanted to get an early start and get everyone home by tomorrow to avoid any weather issues.

Late the next day, at the Brice Ward Farmhouse, Stephen pulled the mules to a halt and yelled for help. He got off the wagon seat and moved to the back of the wagon. He pulled the rear gate out and dropped it onto the ground under the wagon.

Miz Lizzie Ward was the first out to see what the ruckus was all about. She saw Stephen, "My God, thank the Lord, Stephen, you're home!!"

Stephen waved and smiled. "Yes Ma'am, it's me and I got someone you know with me.?" By then Brice and other members of the family started filing out of the main house. A couple of younger brothers came running from the barn.

Anna Wallace Ward was the last out of the house. She was tentative in her steps as if a snake was somewhere to be stepped on. She briefly smiled at seeing Stephen and then stopped in her steps, afraid to know what was happening.

The family moved to the wagon to see what or who was in the wagon bed. Miz Lizzie was the first to see James, "Sweet Jesus, what has happened to my boy?"

James had his eyes open by then and he tried to smile. He thought it would hurt to do that. "It's not as bad as it looks, Momma." He passed out.

They moved James and his gear into the house. Anna Wallace was staying as far away as she could as she prepared their bedroom for his arrival. She didn't want to see James in this condition.

Stephen handed the furlough pouch to Brice Ward, while explaining what Captain Brewer's instructions meant. He spent another hour with the family before finally telling them he wanted to go home and see his family.

"Go ahead Son, you've done a wonderful thing for your cousin and this family. We're proud of you for bringing James home. We'll see you again before you go back." Brice shook young Stephen's hand as a man, with a firm grip.

Miz Lizzie was in full medical care mode. She was giving instructions left and right to every brother, sister, cousin, or husband in the room. Directions to find the local doctor were provided, beds were made, home remedy medicines were prepared, a bath was made ready, and Brice was told to stay out of the way.

Brice went to the main room and stoked the fire. It was early October and there was just a slight chill in the air. At that moment, that hurricane was passing just off the coast and pushing a lot of wind and rain into the farmstead. Stephen had just made it home before the storm.

Anna Wallace had still not gotten a clear look at her husband. She moved to the main room where Brice had stoked the fire. Now he stood in front of the large window facing to the front of the house, facing East, where he caught the morning Sun each day.

Brice Ward turned at the approach of Anna Wallace into the room. "Anna Wallace, are you alright?"

"Yes Sir, I am. I am just afraid for James."

"How would you know child? You haven't even gotten close enough to see him." Brice reached for his pipe on the fireplace mantle.

Anna Wallace winced at his observation, "Yes Sir, you're right. I am afraid. I sent my husband to war as I remembered him. I am afraid he is not that man, now."

"You're a wise young woman, Anna Wallace. He is not the man you sent to war. He is very different. From his letters, you only got a small sense of what he was seeing." Brice filled the pipe, took a small piece of lighter wood, put it to the fire, and used the flame to light the tobacco in the pipe bowl.

"I'm afraid Mister Brice. What is a wife to do for her husband in his present condition?" Anna Wallace sat down on one of the slatted rocking chairs in the room.

Brice looked at her for a moment and then took a draw on the pipe. He let a breath of smoke leave his mouth. "Well, I would suggest you love him as you did when he left. War has changed him, his love for you is just as true as the day he left. Of that, I can be sure. His letters say that each time."

Anna Wallace looked up at the patriarch of the Ward family and waited for more. "He needs you to nurture him, feed him, nurse him, and when able, love him as you did that last night together."

She blushed at that last advice, "Given his condition, I'm afraid that may be many weeks away." She turned her head with a flushed face of embarrassment.

Brice continued, "Lizzie is going to take care of his health; I will take care of getting his strength back; and you'll take care to ensure him you love him with your entire heart. I know he feels that way about you."

Anna Wallace stood up, nodded her head in agreement, smoothed the front of her dress down, "What should I do now?"

"Go into that bedroom and sit with him. Let him know you are there. It will be the best medicine for him right now. Give him a reason to live." Brice left the room and went to the front porch.

He sat down in the rocker and began a melodic rock. His thoughts wandered to a battle in Maryland in 1812. His eyes were closed, and his hands shook as he rocked faster in perfect time with each heartbeat.

Anna Wallace quietly moved toward the bedroom where James lay in their bed. He was conscious but was barely holding himself together with the stomach pains.

Miz Lizzie was hard at work providing directions. "Jonah, go get the metal watering trough out by the barn. Scrub it down and bring it here in the room for James to take a hot bath."

She paused, "Sarah, go get several of the large pots filled with water and heated on the stove. I think three or four gallons should do."

"Josh, go get about four gallons of cold water for the tub once it is clean. Help your brother bring the tub and put it in that corner over there."

The younger brother was about to run out the door when he stopped, looked at James, and said to Miz Lizzie, "Momma, is James going to die?"

"Boy, you say your prayers while you're doing what I said. Let me and God work on that answer." The brother ran out the door.

"Anna Wallace, come over here and help me get this boy out of his clothes. He smells like shit and I'm right sure he needs that bath bad." Lizzie Ward had already gotten a pair of shears and started cutting James' uniform pants away.

"What do you want me to do Miz Lizzie?" Anna Wallace said as she moved to the edge of the bed.

"Set him up and take that jacket off of him. We'll clean it later. After that, untie them boots and take those off as well." By then Miz Lizzie had finished cutting the pants from ankle to waist.

Anna Wallace did as Miz Lizzie instructed but she still avoided looking directly at James' face.

"Tell me I'm in Heaven, Anna Wallace. You must be an Angel." James' had a small smile on his face. He closed his eyes and fell asleep.

The young bride fell onto the bed beside her husband and stroked his long and curly hair. She leaned over and lightly kissed him on the mouth. "I'm here James Ward and you better not leave me alone."

"Stay with him Anna Wallace and help him through this. We got to get him back to wanting to live before he is going to want to get well." Miz Lizzie walked over and patted Anna Wallace on the crown of her head.

"I will, Momma, I won't leave his bedside." Tears fell off her cheeks.

"You people get out of here before the boys get back. We can take it from here."

The siblings moved with great efficiency and did as Miz Lizzie ordered. The metal trough was turned into a bath. A bedside bucket was placed close to the bed in anticipation of James needing to relieve himself of whatever was left in his stomach.

Between Miz Lizzie and Anna Wallace, they filled the metal trough with both cold and hot water. Sarah brought in some soft soap and cloth towels to clean James in the bath.

As Anna Wallace finished taking the last of James' clothes off, she gasped and swallowed hard. Her hands came to cover her eyes. "My Lord!"

Miz Lizzie saw the same thing and offered, "Stay strong for him girl. He needs you right now. Looks like he has lost about thirty or forty pounds."

Anna Wallace quickly returned to wiping some of the dirt and grime on his face, neck, arms, chest, and legs.

With that accomplished, the two women and Brice carefully raised and lifted James into the trough of hot water.

They had barely immersed most of his body into the water when James seemed to sigh and opened his eyes from the shock. "I didn't know Angels did this in Heaven." James nearly lost consciousness as he smiled again.

Brice left the room to wait for the Doctor until he arrived. Miz Lizzie stayed a few more minutes before gathering all the dirty and torn clothing and leaving the couple alone in the quiet room.

Anna Wallace looked upon her husband's form in the trough and kneeled to the side. She grabbed a washcloth and wet it. She then put soap on the wet cloth. She began with his head and worked her way down his body.

She stopped where there were scabs and abrasions on his body, trying to be as tender as practical. He remained unconscious until she had reached his abdomen. His eyes opened and he saw her working down his body. She looked at him and gently kissed him on his forehead. He responded, "I'm afraid I am not completely ready for you, yet my Angel. But I do love you."

Anna Wallace softly pursed her lips together and smiled at him. She quickly laid the wet cloth over his crotch area and the rising mound just under the warm water. "I may have to disagree with you about not being ready, but I do agree, you're not quite able for what I have in mind for you."

She was nearly done bathing him when they heard the front door slam. Moments later, the Doctor came into the room. James was covered with a towel, and she pulled the blanket over the metal trough.

"James, didn't want to see you under these conditions but seems like you are on the way to recovery." The Doctor put his black leather bag on the side table and began pulling out the tools of his trade.

"Sorry Doc, but not able to have full conversations quite yet." James grunted as he laid his head onto the pillow placed on the edge of the trough.

"Not a problem James. I'll do most of the talking and you just grunt with a nod or shake of the head. Understand"? The Doctor arched his eyebrow.

"Folks, let's get James out of his bath and onto the bed." The two men lifted James and the women offered help by drying off his wet body.

Once that task was completed, Brice, Miz Lizzie, and Anna Wallace moved to the side and let the Doctor perform his examination.

About an hour later, after all the questions and acceptable answers, the Doctor repacked his instruments into the bag.

James was propped up onto the pillows and against the headboard of the bed. Anna Wallace stayed with him after the Doctor and James' parents left the room.

The Doctor provided additional guidance and direction to Brice and Lizzie. It was relatively simple, resting, eating, getting up, and moving. He promised to send some medicines for them to give James on a recurring basis.

He continued, "I'm figuring James has lost at least thirty pounds, probably more. Got to get him to eat and drink. Brice, I'm thinking the quicker you get him into the barn and on the farm, the better."

Miz Lizzie quickly responded, "We'll do that Doctor. I know Anna Wallace will be hard to pry away from James."

The Doctor chuckled, "Nothing better for him, though. He fell in love with that girl for a reason. If it wasn't for this damn war, they probably would have two children already."

The Ward patriarch and matriarch both nodded their agreement as they walked the Doctor to the front porch.

Brice spoke in a hushed tone, "Doctor, we'll have a nice hog over to your house by tomorrow to pay for your services."

"You don't have to do that Brice. You gave me a dozen chickens the last time and I have so many eggs now, I'm starting to grow feathers. But I do appreciate it though."

"You know we don't take charity here. We pay our way in cash or barter." Brice Ward was proud of the Ward Family mantra.

"Well, do me a favor and just keep it until I need it. Then we can renegotiate the price. How's that Brice?" The Doctor smiled as he stepped onto his carriage.

Brice and Lizzie watched as the Doctor drove away. He kept watching as the carriage disappeared down the dirt road and said, "Lizzie, get that boy healthy. Soon as you think he can work the farm, let's get him strong again. I haven't seen a man broken like that in over forty-five years."

"Don't you worry about me old man. I'll have the boy on his feet within the week. You just don't kill him trying to do more than he can."

Both grunted at the other and walked back into the house.

Lizzie was true to her word. Within two days, she had gone from a heavy beef or chicken broth for James to something heavier. Anna Wallace also did her part by sitting and reading newspapers, books about famous people and places, and the Bible to James. She did this, even when he was not even awake since he was unawake most of the time.

After those first few days of supplementing the Doctor's medicines, James' mother provided a familiar thick chicken soup and some soft mashed potatoes. Some stewed turnip greens with a little salted fat back pork were also added.

Anna Wallace began the task of sewing and mending his uniform jacket and pants while she sat by his bedside. She did this especially when he was resting. She also began making him more small cloths and socks to add to his wardrobe.

In those first few days, James was making both physical and emotional progress. His Angel was beside him nearly all the time. He wondered how she was surviving his travails.

By the end of the first week, James was getting more alert and stayed awake for longer periods of time. His mother could tell he was moving in the right direction when he asked, "So, how about some pastry with that chicken for dinner?"

Miz Lizzie was quick to reply, "You think this is some fine restaurant in the State Capitol?"

James knew he may have stepped over his boundary. "No ma'am, just hoping."

"Well, if that's what you want, I'll see if I can get Joshua to get me a couple of chickens for tonight." Miz Lizzie paused and then said, "Maybe you could go to the chicken coop and pick them out with Josh."

"Not sure I can make it." He looked over to Anna Wallace and she smiled.

"Why don't you go as far as you can. You may surprise yourself. The Doctor said you must get up to get stronger." James hated it when Anna Wallace smiled at him like that. He knew he could not refuse her.

"Yes Ma'am, I'm going to give it a try." Anna Wallace was already starting to lay his pants and cotton work shirt across the end of the bed.

James and Anna Wallace were together and outside of the house for the first time since he arrived home. His younger brother Joshua was walking just ahead of him and joking about how slow he was.

"Shush boy! He's doing the best he can and you better recall, he has a good memory for those who take advantage of him." Anna Wallace wagged a finger at the younger Ward boy.

"Yeah, but I'm almost as fast as Stephen and it's going to be awhile before he catches me!" Joshua ran ahead to the chicken coop and opened the gate to the pen.

James pointed to several chickens for Joshua to gather and prepare for his mother's kitchen. Anna Wallace started walking him back to the house when they saw the wagon coming down the dirt road.

Stephen pulled the wagon up to the front of the Ward Farmhouse and stepped down. "Well Cousin, I got to head back or Captain Brewer's going to send someone to drag me back to the 26th Regiment."

"Can't thank you enough for getting me home. I think I would be dead by now from something. I am afraid that whoever cooked that stew that night almost killed me." James extended his hand to Stephen.

"Yeah, about the puniest man I ever seen when I drug your butt into that wagon. Thought I was going to have to dump you out in some ditch along the way to reduce the load." The cousins were both laughing.

Anna Wallace leaned James against the wagon and stepped over to Stephen. She paused in front of him, then leaned into Stephen and gave him a long hug. She whispered into his ear, "Thank you for saving his life."

Stephen felt very uncomfortable having James's wife hugging him, especially in front of James. "I didn't do much Anna Wallace. No need for thanks. I'm sure he would do the same for me or any other man in the 26th."

James chuckled, "I'm not so sure about you."

Stephen laughed but climbed back into the wagon. "Well, got a way to go and need to be back before Wednesday evening. If I play it right, I'll get there just in time for dinner."

"Did you check on the others?" James asked.

"Yeah, most of them will probably be back within the next couple of weeks. Not sure how strong they are but every one of them said they had to get back. I can't begin to tell you why, though." Stephen smiled at James.

James responded, "I believe you do know why Stephen. You can't leave them boys to themselves. Hell, they'll get themselves killed. Got to help 'em like they did at New Bern and Malvern Hill."

Stephen only nodded and took the reins of the two horses. He was about to give the two animals a good swish of the reins to get them started.

"Wait! I was out of my head most of the time we were coming, but I seemed to recall having two mules when we started?" James asked.

"Yeah, Dad insisted on trading them out for horses. My Dad's way of saying thanks to Captain Brewer for letting me come home, even for a short while." Finally, Stephen gave the horses the nudge they needed to start walking to the East.

The next week saw James taking walks with Anna Wallace to all the Ward houses, out buildings, and animal holding areas for various reasons provided by Brice Ward for his son. By the first week in November, he was able to bathe himself, dress himself, and feed himself.

While Anna Wallace had been by his side nearly all the time. She had not shared his bed. The chair from which she read and sewed, was as close as the two newlyweds truly got.

She was afraid of hurting him and he was afraid of disappointing her. Both of their fears were justified at that moment, but neither was willing to take that first step to a return to a more intimate relationship.

Anna Wallace was the first to suggest something a bit more intimate, "James, do you mind if I sleep on the bed tonight? I am just too tired to sit up and sleep tonight."

James paused a moment. "I am happy to share my bed with you. I promise I will not do anything untoward to you while you're here."

"No, I suggest nothing of that sort until you are fully recovered. I love you and I can wait." Anna Wallace moved to the other side of the room and began to change her clothes for bed.

She stood by a small chest of drawers where a small candle sat on the top. It burned with a small yellow flame providing only minimal light. It provided just enough light for James to see the shape and texture of her body silhouetted through the soft, thin, cotton gown she was wearing.

James could not avert his eyes as his wife climbed out of her clothes and slipped the night shift over her head. With her back turned toward James, he could see the shape of her body with strong shoulders, firm buttocks, and that thin waist.

She began to turn, and he held his breath. From the new angle, her firm breasts were not large but perfectly shaped. The distance to her across the small room was less than nine feet and he could easily see the firmness of her nipples. The light cotton night shift was so thin, he could see the outline of her pelvic area.

The sheer beauty of her body was nearly too difficult to bear. He almost said she could not come to bed. At that moment, he couldn't even speak. He still had not taken that breath.

But he didn't say that.

Anna Wallace was not much better. She couldn't help but notice James' attempts to hide him watching his wife changing for bed. She tried to move as quickly as practical. However, every motion only exacerbated her problem. Her body was there to be seen by her very sick husband.

The spouses were lightly dressed and attempted to sleep within twelve inches of each other in the small bed. They had a heavy hand-made quilt to push away the cold of the early Fall.

Neither of them had ever wanted the other any more than they wanted each other at that moment.

James had rolled to his side of the bed with this back to Anna Wallace. He pulled the covers close to his neck and closed his eyes. He hoped she would say nothing else.

She turned to the candle and blew the small flame away. Darkness fell over the room for a moment but given the lack of the small light from the candle, she could still see the shape of the bed.

Anna Wallace Ward also saw her husband's shape curled in the bed. Standing there, she closed her eyes and thought of the day she and Miz Lizzie had bathed James' naked body. She felt the center of her body quiver. She exhaled and drew another breath.

She pulled the covers back and slipped into the bed. Unlike James, she faced toward the center of the bed and near his back.

After she was settled in the bed, James could only whisper, with his back to Anna Wallace, "Good night." He paused a moment and then said, "I do love you so."

Unseen to her, a tear slowly worked down his wrinkled face.

She said nothing for a few moments, and for James, the pause seemed to be an eternity. "I love you very much and I will always do so."

Another tear fell from his eyes. He said nothing.

Without warning, a soft hand touched his back. It started at the back of his neck and gently moved down his backbone, then began to seemingly count each rib on his left side. The caresses moved slowly to his hips and gently moved to his muscled buttocks.

She stopped at that moment and gently whispered, "I would cuddle with you, if you would let me. We don't have to make love unless you are able."

James was afraid to roll over and face her. He was very unsure of his ability to make love to his wife but the thoughts of touching her was too much to let pass. "I would love that, if you are willing." He was still facing the outside of the bed.

Anna Wallace did not immediately answer his concern but very soon, moved closer to her husband. Her hand gently returned to caressing his body and each touch felt like heat moving through his body.

Her hands moved to places that he thought were lost to him. His thighs grew taunted with each touch and caress. His heart seemed to skip beats with each moment. Breathing almost became too difficult. His eyes were closed long ago gathering pleasure to his core.

She stopped and whispered, "I don't want to hurt you."

"If this is what you call cuddling, please finish it, if you will. I am sure I am ready to die." James moaned.

"No James, I will not finish until you have cuddled with me. I love you and miss you too much to let this happen without sharing each other." Anna Wallace eased out of the bed to grab a towel hanging from the empty tub still located in the room.

James felt like he was being abandoned at his moment of need, but he suddenly realized that he was being offered the very thing he wanted the most that night, the chance to be intimate with his wife.

Anna Wallace returned to their bed, pulled the shift over her head, and draped the shift and cloth across the headboard. She then moved to the center of the bed, turned with her back to her husband, and awaited his hands on her body.

James was a little unsure how to begin but mother nature took control at that moment. Anna Wallace was shorter than James and as such, he was able to reach nearly any part of her body he wished, and she desired.

He leaned in and kissed her on the neck, whispered into her ear, ran his fingers through her hair, and moved them down her neck.

His hands moved, like butterflies, gently down her back, just as she had performed earlier on him. Those hands moved quickly to her buttocks, where he caressed her for several moments. Her hips pushed against each caress.

James moved closer and rolled her to her back. He began to softly fondle and kiss her breasts. As he had properly noted earlier, her nipples were firm, and they took the new attention he provided with enthusiasm. His hands moved lower to the pelvic area and began to caress her in a place, wet with excitement. He knew she enjoyed this when they celebrated the beginning of their newly married life in the early Spring of 1861.

Anna Wallace was overwhelmed with emotions and passion. She too, had missed this loving experience for over eighteen months and she intended to enjoy it for what it was, a prelude to a fully marital sexual relationship with her husband.

And she enjoyed it! Her moans were heard throughout the household.

True to her word, after achieving her own sexual orgasm, she caught her breath and then pushed her husband onto his back.

While he pleaded to fully take her, she pressed him not to exert himself so much for this first time of intimacy. She replayed the cuddling of their first encounter that night and ensured he was able to complete his cuddled orgasm as well.

Both slept well that night holding each other with arms intertwined.

* * * * *

November 11, 1862

For Private James Ward, General Delivery Whiteville, North Carolina

Dear James,

 I am not the letter writer you and Anna Wallace are, but I am inclined to write you to let you know our current circumstance.

 It has been a quiet Fall, all things considered. But you know higher command is not going to let us alone.

 We made a foraging trip up to the Northeast near Rawls's Mills around Martin County. We ran into a pretty good-sized Yankee force up near Washington and Williamston. We think they might have come from the New Bern area as well.

 I heard Captain Brewer talking to Colonel Burgwyn and the Colonel offered he heard a rumor the Yankees were actually trying to find the 26th Regiment. Didn't know we had become so famous.

 Colonel Burgwyn earned his pay this month because we were just about caught, and he found a way to get us away from the Union boys. The Colonel waited until the Yankees made their play and then we escaped down another road completely. They chased us quite a ways, but we got to friendly lines in time. They turned and left us.

 God bless that "Boy Colonel!"

 Him and General Pettigrew seem to be getting along fine and work together like they really know what they're doing. Well, they are North Carolina boys after all.

 Thought you might want to know that you and one other is still on furlough. I think the other one is Evert Page. He was close to being the same as you, but we expect him back later this month.

 Based on your recent letter, sounds like you are getting better. I passed it along to Captain Brewer and he said that was good, but he didn't expect you until about Christmas.

Not sure, but you might want to write a letter to Captain Brewer, he might be willing to let you stay through Christmas.

It was good being home, even if only for a few days. The trip back was faster with the new horses and me by myself. Ran into a couple of boys trying to waylay me. I had two muskets beside me on the seat and two of them Navy Colt pistols in my belt. I think they eventually thunk it through and decided I wasn't going to be taken that easy.

They left me alone after a little conversation and me telling them I was on official business with the 26th Regiment. You'de thought I said we were assigned to the herald angels of God Almighty when I mentioned the 26th.

Give my best to the family and tell them I love them. I got to go. I hear Captain Brewer yelling for me to run a message to Regiment.

Private Stephen Ward

Company E, 26th Regiment of North Carolina Troops, Pettigrew's Brigade, Major-General D. H. Hill, Commander of the NC Coastal Department Command

CHAPTER 8

"WE PRAY AND HOPE", APRIL 1863

As time moved into mid-November, James began to slowly recover. Due to his mother's familiar home cooking, he began to get his weight to a healthier level.

Miz Lizzie's success at the table led to Brice Ward starting to press James into everyday chores around the home place. Each morning began with a gathering of eggs from the chicken coop. That was followed by a visit to the smokehouse to gather bacon or ham for breakfast and the Noon meal, and beef for the evening meal.

The root cellar was also included to gather potatoes, sweet potatoes, onions, carrots, and apples for the large family meal preparations.

Later, each morning, he was in the barn, milking the cows. It didn't take long before he was also churning the milk for butter, while sitting and resting.

Every one of these farm chores were carefully observed, from a distance, by Brice Ward to ensure James was getting strong enough for a return to farm life. Brice tried hard not to think of himself getting James ready to return to the war.

Brice hated the war and for what it had done to his son. Splitting firewood was a mid-day chore within a week of walking around the farm. Seasoned wood was piled near the house and beneath a large Oak Tree.

From that pile, James began splitting the cut logs of about eighteen inches and creating the firewood for the fireplace. He also split the smaller logs into wood for Miz Lizzie's cook stove. Her pieces of wood had to be more precise so that she could control the heat of the fire for cooking.

Seeing James' progress in strength and returning muscle, Brice suggested it was time to slaughter some hogs and cattle for the Winter stores. The temperature was about right, a cold thirty to thirty-two degrees at night during early November.

"You up to some hog slaughtering James?" He waited for his son's response.

James did pause while he looked down at the ground.

"Yes Sir. I believe I can manage it. How many you want to cut out?"

Brice mulled it over for a moment and replied, "I'm thinking five for right now. You go ahead and mark 'em. I'll send over to the other farms and get some help. We'll plan on getting started about late tomorrow afternoon."

"Sounds good Father. I'll get the blades sharpened, the cauldrons out and scrubbed, and the meat hooks ready. I'll have Anna Wallace get with Momma for the spice and rubs ready."

All the senior Ward families showed up with wagons, axes, butchering knives of various sizes and shapes, and more cauldrons. Each family seemed to be the resident expert in each phase of the butchering process.

James had marked six of the more mature hogs and placed them into a separate pen. The killing was quickly done, and the Jerimiah Ward family jumped in and began field dressing the animals for hanging to drain the blood. The innards were all removed and placed into slop buckets to be fed to the other hogs.

As the blood drained from the hogs, it was close to dark, and the fires had been burning hot. The large black cauldrons were moved onto large rocks that held the pots over the fires.

Joshua Ward's family immediately began cutting the outer fat from the hogs into slabs of fat back. Some of those slabs were cut into much smaller pieces and thrown into the large cauldrons to the hissing sound of the fat hitting the hot pots.

The small chucks of fat began to melt into liquid. The skins of the hogs curled up from the heat and floated near the top. The Ward ladies were busy scooping and collecting those skins to be used as treats for the children and some adults would grab a piece, after cooling, to chew on while they were working.

As the liquid fat melted, the ladies were also using large ladles and placing the liquid into large clay and metal jars. Once filled, the jars were covered with cheese cloth and candle wax was used to seal the jar. As the liquid cooled, it became a snow-white block of lard to be used in cooking everything on the farm.

After the fat was removed and rendered into lard, gallons of the grease were divided up for all the families to use for the rest of the year.

Meanwhile, the younger Wards were gathering the meat that was cooking in the cauldrons and all that remained of the fat. These morsels were cracklins and they were gathered up into more cheese cloth sacks, or at least as many that were not consumed at that moment by the bevy of Ward and Thompson children.

Lizzie Ward was the first to react to the minor thievery, "You young'ens quit eating all those cracklins. You're gonna make yourselves sick. You're worse than being in a Strawberry Patch. Save some!!"

It was finished with a grand meal while watching the fires go down. The butchered meat was covered in both salt and pepper rubs, carefully wrapped in more cheese cloth, and placed into the fired-up smoke house for curing.

This entire process would take most of the night. It was a practice used throughout the farms of North Carolina every year during the late Fall or early Winter.

The collected Ward families celebrated their good fortune of being self-sufficient by sharing a very well-earned meal late into the night with the small children lying on the ground, close to the fire, wrapped in a blanket to keep the chill of the night away.

The adults indulged in a little clear liquid sugar cane rum poured into a tin coffee cup that had been carefully distilled through a copper kettle at a hard-to-find location in the Green Swamp portion of the Ward farm.

James and Anna Wallace sat to one side of the fire and a little back from the collected families. Anna Wallace was curled into his left arm and looked up to his face, "James, are you well?"

They had a blanket pulled up around them and he had his eyes closed, "Yes, but not as well as I was. But I'm getting there. Why?" James looked down at his wife's eyes only to see her loosening the top button of her dress.

He spoke a little louder than necessary, "Anna Wallace, the fire is almost down, maybe we should go to the house."

She quickly unwrapped the blanket, "I think you're right James, I am a little chilled as well."

They both got up and walked toward the main farmhouse.

Brice just grunted, Lizzie smiled, and several other adults mildly acknowledged their departure from the fire.

"Now do those two think we're ignorant?" Brice said.

Miz Lizzie looked at him and had a cat's grin on her face, "No, but they are trying to be polite. Maybe we'll have a new member of the family by this time next year. Anyway, go to sleep old man."

The old man, eased his wife up and said, "Let's go to the house old woman."

Within a week, James was moving about the farm as he had for most of his life. All the minor chores had turned into something larger. Like repairing cattle fences, repairing farm equipment, and he even had time to plane some wood for their cabin.

It felt comfortable to him. He was where he was supposed to be.

Brice approached him near the end of the month and asked, "James, Jerimiah said he saw a real nice twelve-point buck down by the Green Swamp yesterday. You interested in a little hunting?"

James knew that portion of the Green Swamp was a couple of miles away, but he didn't think it would be a problem. "Sure, sounds good. Let me grab my gear from the barn."

Miz Lizzie came out the door about Noon time and asked when they would be back. "Should I plan a late supper for you?"

"Depends, if we find that buck sooner or later. We'll be fine and might stay out tonight and see if we can get him in the morning, otherwise." Brice yelled back at his wife.

She waved as they rode the horses in the direction of the swamp.

Once they arrived at the area that Brice thought was about where the deer had been previously seen, he dismounted from the horse. They spent the next few minutes setting up a small camp for the night. It amounted to a couple of bedrolls and campfire wood.

They set out toward a large corn field that had been harvested and chopped up for fodder for the farm animals. The field was relatively bare except for the plowed furrows where the previous remains of the corn crop had been plowed under for fertilizer.

Brice had noticed that James had brought two canvas wrapped cloths that he obviously thought contained two muskets.

It was about three o'clock in the afternoon when they positioned themselves on the edge of the plowed cornfield. They settled into their positions about a hundred yards apart.

There was not much to see around the field until about five o'clock when James saw something move out of the wood line near the swamp. His best guess was it was at least six hundred yards away.

From that distance, Brice knew James' personal Mississippi Rifle would not be able to come close to hitting the deer. He remained calm and watched the animal. It had to be the same deer that Jer had mentioned to him.

After a few moments of watching the deer, James looked toward his father leaning against a tree. He made a small noise, knowing the deer could not hear him from this distance, to get his father's attention.

Brice looked his way; James slowly pointed to the deer at the far side of the field.

Sunset was close at hand and Brice stood from his position and moved toward James. James noticed the deer's ears perked up as he looked in their direction. The animal watched Brice move toward James, and sensing no danger, dropped his head to eat more fallen grain from the field.

"Looks like our deer over there." Brice said as he looked that way.

James nodded as he stood and watched the deer saunter into the wood line toward the swamp. "He looks like a good-sized hundred and fifty pounds when he gets field dressed, don't you think?"

"Yes, probably so, but don't know how we get close enough to get him over there. I'm thinking we would have to get over by that corner early in the morning to get close enough to have a good shot at him." Brice looked at his son for confirmation, since James was the best shot in the family.

"Maybe. Maybe not. Let's go get a fire going and get warm. I'm sure Momma has some biscuits hidden somewhere in that burlap bag on your horse." James suggested.

Sure enough, Miz Lizzie had put together a small meal of biscuits, ham, cheese, and a couple of boiled eggs. The fire was big enough to keep them warm and close enough to feed slowly during the night to stay warm.

Brice asked, "So, what you got in mind for that deer in the morning?

James just smiled and reached to his left and grabbed the canvas bag closest to him. As he leaned back against the tree, he laid it across his lap, and began to untie the leather straps.

James pulled the Leonard Target Rifle that Captain Brewer had given him after Malvern Hill. "I don't think we're gonna need to make it skittish by moving around over there. I think I should be able to get it from where we were this afternoon."

Brice chuckled, "Son, I don't care how good you are with a musket, you can't hit that deer from that spot! That's easy six hundred yards. And what the hell is that thing?"

"Well, Father, this is a .48 caliber Leonard Target Rifle. It can shoot a really long way. I'm thinking that deer don't stand a chance."

"Son, that thing is so big, and looks heavy. How are you going to hold it steady enough to get a good sight at the deer? By and by, I don't see any sights on the gun anyway?"

James softly wiped the telescopic sights on the rifle and said, "Father, this sight lets you see the target up close. Makes it easier to sight the target from a distance. As for holding it steady, I'll use this."

He reached to the wood pile they had collected and pulled out a limb that was about four and half feet in length. At one end, there was a forked portion of the branch wide enough to hold the rifle.

"I just lay the barrel right into the fork, sight the deer into the telescope and pull the trigger." James smiled.

What James did not say to his father was how this particular weapon was used in the 26th Regiment. He thought that was unnecessary information for Brice. The thought of killing a man from that distance would seem almost uncivilized for Brice Ward.

As promised, the next morning they moved into a position, to the location where James had been sitting the previous day. They arrived just before dawn broke on the Eastern horizon.

James stood by the tree he had leaned on the day before and watched the corner of the field where they had seen the deer. James handed his father a pair of binoculars.

Over the next few minutes, the light of dawn creeped ever clearer, and James saw a brief movement across the field. He pointed in that direction and his father eased the field glasses to his eyes. Brice shook his head to confirm it was the deer.

James eased the rifle into the fork of the shooting stand. He sighted the deer and closed his eyes as he made mental calculations of the distance and the very light wind at the ground level.

He opened his eyes and once again sighted the deer. James waited for it to offer a profile of itself to him. He eased the hammer back until it clicked into place. He aimed just about twelve inches just above the shoulder of the deer as it leaned forward to eat loose corn off the ground. He waited for the deer to lift its head.

The rifle did its job. The deer quickly fell to the ground, shot through the lungs and heart. No pain, no suffering, just death.

They were back at the farmhouse by Noon time, and they took the field dressed deer to the smokehouse to hang with the hogs, cattle, and goats already being smoked.

Brice had said very little while in the field dressing the deer and preparing to bring it home. James had thought he would have congratulated him on his shot and clean kill.

But Brice did not congratulate him.

After finishing their family meal, Brice retired to the main room and gathered the tobacco into the bowl of his pipe. He lit the pipe and leaned against the fireplace mantle in deep contemplation.

James did not smoke a pipe but did enjoy the smell of his father's lingering smoke. Brice looked at James for a moment. He took another puff of the pipe and said, "Am I to understand that big rifle of yours is for killing a man at great distance?"

Without hesitation James responded, "It is."

"You know, of course, there are men on the other side with the same kind of rifle?" Brice watched as his son responded.

"I know it very well. I pray to God for forgiveness every time I pull the trigger." James waited for the lecture.

It never came. Brice Ward turned and walked out the door and to the barn.

James was unsure as to what he should feel at that moment.

By the end of the month of November, James knew his time at home must come to an end. Everyone in the family knew he was due to report back to Captain Brewer by the week before Christmas.

Miz Lizzie and Anna Wallace seemed especially busy during the last couple of weeks of November and early December. James saw very little of either woman after breakfast or before dinner.

His strength continued to improve, and Brice and the other Ward brothers kept him busy. Each day, Brice made sure the tasks for James got a little more strenuous. He was only a few pounds lighter than the day he had left the farm in May of 1861.

James tried to plan his return with the least inconvenience to the family. At dinner that night, James said, "Father, I'm thinking I'll have to hike it to the train station and then hike it to the regimental camp past Kinston the rest of the way. I will have to leave by mid-December to make it on time."

"No, I don't think so Son. I plan on taking a wagon and you there myself. Should only be about three or four days to get you there by wagon. Gives you more time here before you have to go." Brice, pushed away from the dinner table as if no further discussion was necessary.

Anna Wallace followed James to the main room of the house and sat with him by the fire. "James, I know you have to go back. But I don't have to like it. I want as much time as I can get before you have to leave."

James looked at her and understood, "I love you very much and if I thought they wouldn't come and get me just to hang me, I would stay. But I took an oath Anna Wallace, and I am beholding to God Almighty to meet that oath."

"What about the oath to me? What about what you promised me at the alter? I don't recall anything about dying in a war we don't even want." Anna Wallace turned her head away to hide the tears moving down her cheek.

There was little he could say that would assure her of his return. He gently pulled her to him and hugged her with all the affection he could muster.

She whispered into his chest, "Please don't plan anything for tomorrow afternoon. I have something to show you."

James grunted to acknowledge the request.

The next morning James completed his regular chores and when he asked his father for their tasks for the day, Brice responded, "Don't have any more work for you here, Son. I've promised Anna Wallace she could have you the rest of the day." His father only smiled.

"What's she got planned for me?" James looked amused.

Brice only continued working on the repair of a harness for a team of horses, "Can't speak to that. You'll just have to follow her lead. That's what we Ward men do for our Ward women. Don't you think?"

James followed Brice into the barn, and he saw the carriage standing ready for the horse to be taken from the stalls and hitched to the carriage.

"Where are you going?" James asked.

"You and Mrs. Anna Wallace Ward are going to town on an errand for the Ward farm. After that, you'll have to ask her. Here, take this harness and hitch the horse." Brice left James to the task.

Anna Wallace appeared shortly after Brice left. "Let's go to town Mister Ward!" She proudly proclaimed.

"What's in town that's so important for the Ward farm we have to go to town?" James asked with a frown on his face.

"We'll just have to see what Mister Brice has on his list." She was grinning from ear to ear at her husband.

The trip to town and the general store was only two hours by a slow carriage ride. The couple laughed and whispered naughty things to each other the entire trip.

James remarked, "My, Mrs. Ward, you're awfully pretty today in that yellow dress."

"Well Mister Ward, if you must know, I'm trying hard to find a good man and I want to present the best of me to catch his eye."

He hesitated a moment, "Well, I'm to understand you have a loving husband already Mrs. Ward. Are you not happy with him?"

"Oh, surely Mister Ward. He'll do, but you know we women must always look our best." She giggled.

The conversation was light and even with an overcoat covering the dress, to hold off the chill of the early December air, James could see just how beautiful she was.

For James, all other men were to be damned for even thinking about getting close to his wife.

Once they arrived, they went straight way to the general store. The owner immediately came to the front and greeted James and Anna Wallace.

"Anna Wallace, I got that shipment in for you. I think you're going to like it a lot. I carefully inspected it to make sure nothing was wrong."

Anna Wallace was quick to respond, "Well thank you very much Mister Thompson, James is unaware of its contents, but he can load that box onto the back of the carriage. James, please be careful. It is frail."

Mister Thompson winked at Anna Wallace, "Here James, come with me and I'll give you a hand tying it up nice and tight."

James had that look of "what is this all about," but figured he was better off not to inquire any further.

Anna Wallace took Brice's list from her hand purse and gathered a couple of other small items before James and Mister Thompson returned. She completed the purchase of the smaller items and James and Anna Wallace returned to the carriage.

They were just about to turn the carriage around when a woman screamed. James and Anna Wallace turned toward the scream and saw a group of people helping a woman off the ground where she had fallen.

"I wonder what that's all about?" James held the reins to the horse as he looked toward the side wall of the courthouse.

His wife lowered her head, "It's the death roster."

James turned to her, "The what?"

"They post the latest newspaper reports of the battles fought and that includes the roster of those wounded or dead." Anna Wallace was almost whispering as if she were afraid God would hear her thoughts.

She continued, "Most people only see it when they come to town, and they go look at the Courthouse Wall. Your father hates it. He says people should control themselves in public. Such emotions should not be shared in the public."

James tied the reins to the carriage and walked to the Courthouse Wall. His curiosity was getting the best of him. Anna Wallace stayed in the carriage, holding her hands in her lap, head down.

He stood in front of the two-story Courthouse Wall and walked slowly down the side to various newspapers pages tacked to the wall. He stopped at one article that reported on a battle at Rawls Mill in Martin County North Carolina.

James ran his finger down the article to the roster of dead and wounded. The 26th Regiment was listed. He paused, almost afraid to look at the roster.

His finger slowly went down the column and noticed several names in the wounded section of the list from both Company F and Company G. None were noted for Company E.

He slowly exhaled and turned away from the wall. An older gentleman stood in his way, "Why ain't you in the Army boy?"

"Sir, I'm here on furlough recovering from sickness." James moved around the man and headed for the carriage.

"You don't look sick to me, boy. You look like a deserter to me! My boy died at Malvern Hill. Where were you?" The old man continued to yell at James as he got into the carriage.

The carriage ride back to the Ward farm was quiet. The Sun was still bright enough to ward off the cold, but it did not turn back the tension in the air.

At one point near home, Anna Wallace spoke, "Now you see why no one wants to go look at that wall."

James completely understood what his father had told Anna Wallace about the public display of emotion. What he did not know was how to deal with being called a deserter. That truly hurt, especially about Malvern Hill.

As they got closer to the Ward farm, Anna Wallace's spirits brightened and her tone more excited. "Take the side road toward the swamp. I have something to show you."

He paused, "Don't we need to unload that box, first?"

"No. It will wait until later." She smiled.

Within about thirty minutes, they were deep into the Ward farm and near a flat area close to the Green Swamp. It was right where James knew they had started their new home.

As they turned around a bend in the well-worn dirt road and through a thicket of trees, he saw a large gathering of the Ward family farms standing before a nearly completed new cabin. At the back of the house was a small new barn as well.

Sawhorses with pine wood planks across them, were covered with white sheets, and held a feast of food on the temporary tables.

The families all cheered as the couple pulled the team of horses to a stop. Brice stood before the gathering and stepped forward to greet James and Anna Wallace.

"Well Son, welcome to your new farm. What do you think?"

James paused for a moment after stepping from the carriage. He thought it looked beautiful but then noticed a peculiar hole in the wall of the house.

"Well, it looks wonderful, but looks like you forgot a window in the front, and I'm noticing it's cut the wrong way." He laughed.

Brice laughed as well, "Thought you might notice that, but you see, we wanted you to put that one in yourself."

James continued to grin, "So where is it?"

"Son, you just brought it from town."

Jerimiah Ward, James' uncle, had already untied the box off the back of the carriage and two younger Ward cousins helped to carefully unpack the box.

As everyone watched, the box was opened, and they gently raised a beautiful clear etched glass window from the box. Everyone was oohing and aahing at the glass.

James was most impressed as well. He stepped over to the window as the cousins held it before him. He couldn't resist touching it. His hands slowly touched the shape of the etched glass. "It's beautiful."

"Well, let's get it into that hole in the wall!" Brice shouted.

James stood watching as the men moved to the window at the outside and slid the framed glass into the gaping hole. In a few moments, the window was seated into the frame of the house and safely secured. It would be sealed from the weather later.

Everyone stood back to admire the new window. Anna Wallace stood beside her husband. "What do you think of it?"

James paused to take a breath. "I think it must be as fine as anything in the cathedrals of Europe. But why is it laying down horizontal?"

Anna Wallace laughed and said, "Come with me," and they walked into the main room of their new farmhouse.

Once there, she turned James to face the window, looking out. "It's called a picture window. It looks like a picture of our landscape." She smiled up at James.

It made perfect sense now that he was inside. "Our landscape. I like the sound of that. Our picture is nearly perfect." He hugged her.

Everyone cheered from the outside and they began to celebrate the christening of the new Ward family farm.

After a while, the other families began to return home. The dark of an early December evening was fast approaching.

A fire had been started in the fireplace and it was warm in the house as Anna Wallace gave him a walking tour of their modest little home.

James noticed the ladies had put in curtains, some furniture had been put into place, and the home was decorated with pine boughs, holly branches, and some colorful ribbons. Even the fireplace mantle had two cotton stockings hanging from the wood mantle.

The kitchen area had a wooden framed stand for pots and pans. Another stand with a stone slab across it for cutting and preparing food was close by.

The stove was much older and smaller one than Miz Lizzie's current kitchen. "Mister Brice gave the stove for us from the family storage. He said they used that one a long time ago when there were only two children. He said they grew out of that one pretty fast."

She identified the areas where Brice Ward had suggested, "they could expand the house as their family grew." James smiled at that.

Anna Wallace had saved the bedroom for last. It was modest. Perhaps twelve feet by twelve feet in size.

The homemade bed was barely big enough for two and had a large headboard with some soft design chiseled in it. There was a dresser with multiple drawers to one side. "Your father made that dresser," she proudly said.

The other side of the room held a large cloak closet for hanging clothes like dresses and suits. "Your Uncle Joshua made the cedar chest for hanging our fine things. He says the bugs and rodents can't stand the cedar."

A small table stood in the corner, and it held a large bowl and water pitcher for washing up in the mornings. A galvanized bucket was just behind the table, out of sight, for bringing in fresh water each day. "Joshua did that table and the one beside the bed for us."

"Your Uncle Issac's family gave us the washing bowl and pitcher. He also had the boys dig that well by the back door."

"Uncle Nehemiah gave us the outhouse in the back. It's two-holer he says!" Anna Wallace was appropriately proud of being fully accepted into the Ward family.

Anna Wallace continued as they walked back to the main room, "Your mother has been with me the last week or two getting everything ready while you have been working with your father."

James was nearly overwhelmed as he entered the room to find Brice and Miz Lizzie standing by the fireplace. "Momma, Father, I can't thank you enough for all of this. I don't believe I could have done it by myself without a lot of time."

Brice responded first, "Family has got to take care of family. For us, that means all your family. We had the land, the lumber, and almost everything else. Just needed the hardware, nails, and windows, to make it a home. I guess the twenty dollars in gold made the difference."

Miz Lizzie laughed, "Besides, we had to get the two of you out of the house. You two make way too much noise at night! Even the girls get nervous swearing you must be killing poor Anna Wallace."

They all laughed, and Brice finally spoke more somberly, "Son, we all need you to come back. Do what you got to do and come back alive; hurt or not. But come back alive."

Brice and Miz Lizzie left them to their new home just as dusk was setting.

Their first night in their new home was most enjoyable. To them, the morning seemed to come too soon.

As James moved into the kitchen area by the stove, a pot of coffee was already brewing. Anna Wallace was washing up and getting fully dressed for the day.

James grabbed the tin cup sitting beside the stove and poured a cup of coffee. He walked toward the main room and looked at the etched glass picture window.

The Sun was just over the horizon and the rays streamed through the glass. Multiple prisms of light shown through the window and throughout the room. He stood amazed at the beauty of it.

He thought he must be rich; he had a picture window.

For some reason, he suddenly recalled the night on Malvern Hill back in July. He remembered the red-hot bullets flying in the air just above his head.

The very thought caused him to shiver in the cold December morning air.

Two weeks later, they celebrated a Sunday service on the Brice Ward farm with the entire Ward families invited. Instead of the usual service, they decided to celebrate an early Christmas for James. The early Christmas was with the promise that James would carry Stephen's Christmas presents to him upon his return to camp.

It was a joyous and yet somber Christmas. Everyone seemed afraid to say much to James, other than Merry Christmas.

Since their move to the new house, James and Anna Wallace had remained at home. James providing some improvements to the property by building fencing around the barn area, a new chicken coop, and two storage sheds. He also dug a root cellar for food storage.

While there, he hunted several times and was successful in getting five very nice deer and five turkeys. Each one was killed, dressed, smoked, and given as gifts to each Ward family, as well as Anna Wallace's family.

* * * * *

December 10, 1862

To Private Stephen Ward, Company E, 26th Regiment of North Carolina Troops near Kinston, North Carolina

Dear Stephen,

I am writing to ask you to inform Captain Brewer that I am nearly fit and intend to report to camp by December 22. I will be arriving by wagon with my Father.

The family had an early Christmas, and I will bring your gifts with me. I was told that if you had gifts to return, to give them to my Father, and he will distribute them accordingly upon his return.

Everyone reports they are fine and miss you on the farm. They wish you well and they included a new pair of boots for you. Although I told them you will probably not wear them anymore than the ones you already have.

I have much to tell you about our new home. All the families did a wonderful job of building the farm for me and Anna Wallace. I was told that I could repay them by hunting a lot more.

I must say that seeing the 26th Regiment names on the Courthouse Wall was a little unsettling for me. I was just glad not to see your name or anyone from Company E. Looking at the death roster made chills move down my spine.

I am most respectfully and sincerely,
Your Cousin, Private James Ward

CHAPTER 9

"TAKE IT TO 'EM BOYS!" MAY 1863

James and Brice Ward began the trip to Eastern North Carolina and the most recent camp for General Pettigrew's Brigade and specifically, the 26th Regiment. The three-day trip was fairly uneventful other than the many words of wisdom imparted by Brice to his eldest son.

Occasionally, James would remind his father that he was Thirty Years old at this point in his life. He knew his father meant well and the advice of his father was most appreciated when it came to the farm.

However, this Civil War was somewhat different than the War of 1812, when his father had soldiered.

It was not lost on James that they were using the very wagon that led him to Captain Webster and his enlistment at Cartersville in 1861, when he picked up the wagon as an errand for his father.

Each time that Brice Ward alluded to the enlistment, he damned the occasion. However, James always reminded him that it was because his father sent him for the wagon that caused him to even know about the twenty dollars in gold enlistment bonus.

The large wagon was used for this trip because it carried some extra Christmas presents for Stephen and James.

A more significant cargo was the beef, pork, and venison meat that Brice Ward had pulled from the smokehouse and intended for Captain

Brewer and his Company E. The smoked meat would last longer and stay safer to eat having been preserved in salt, pepper, and other spices in the smokehouse.

As they arrived on the afternoon of December 21, Captain Brewer was well pleased with the fine gift from the Ward family farms. "Sir, I cannot thank you enough on behalf of the men of Company E for your most generous offering. With your permission, I will acknowledge you and your family for its many sacrifices to this day."

"No need for accolades Captain. I was a soldier many decades ago and I know the plight of men such as your Company. Not particularly fond of this war we are in, but I am proud of you and your Command. It is an honor to help you in the fight." Brice stood back as men began unloading the wagon.

"James was telling me you served in both the Washington area and Louisiana during the second war with the British?" Captain Brewer offered in idle conversation.

"That one seemed the right war for me to help. Some bloody business, especially down near New Orleans. Survived though." Brice lowered his head and shuffled his feet in the loamy soil.

They completed unloading the wagon and the Captain offered Brice a tent for the night to rest before his return trip. Brice reluctantly accepted and secured his team.

James fed the horses and watered them for the night.

Captain Brewer invited him to eat with the officers for dinner. Brice was unusually quiet during the meal. Brewer looked to the elder Ward patriarch and asked, "Mister Ward, is there anything wrong or that I can do for you?"

Brice looked across the field table, at Captain Brewer, where they sat and said, "Captain, I need my boy back home. I would appreciate you taking special care of me in that regard. That is all I can ask as a father. Can you promise me you can do that?"

"Sir, you are not the first to ask me that question and give me that task. I will do everything in my power and the good Lord's grace to have both James and Stephen back home before this is over."

The Captain reached across the table and shook the father's hand, "You have my word on that."

"I want you to know that we don't have any slaves on our farms. We don't believe that is what the good Lord intended. There are many around us who are not so inclined. I did everything I could to prevent them boys from joining but given the circumstances, it was inevitable they would be forced into this war." Brice paused.

"Do your best Captain, that's all we asked. The rest is in the hands of the Lord, as you say." Brice turned back to listen to the music being played that night by the 26th Regimental Band.

They ate a good meal from one of the beef quarters and the soldiers all gave Brice and James a big huzzah for the meal. It was an early Christmas feast, and it was remembered with kind affection by all of Company E.

Brice got up, wished the Captain and his junior officers a good night, and walked back to his designated tent.

Next morning, Brice rose early, hitched the horses, and began final preparations for his return home.

Captain Brewer came over to say good-bye. "Sir, I see you're nearly ready to leave. It's probably a good thing. The quartermaster is starting to look at your wagon and team of horses with great avarice in his eyes." He chuckled.

Brice slipped a LeMat pistol from beneath his overcoat and showed it to Captain Brewer. "Tell him it would be the worst mistake he could make." He chuckled as well.

"Would you like to see James and Stephen before you leave?"

Brice barely paused, "No Sir. I'm afraid that would only make it more difficult to leave. No, I best get on home and let them boys do their duty. I do appreciate the hospitality, though. Besides, I'm afraid you might try to enlist me."

Brewer laughed a little louder at the father's jest. "Sir, I'm hoping we don't have to go that far. I'm very sure you would be an outstanding officer, Sir. And you never can tell if it might get that serious. But have a safe trip home Sir."

Brice climbed to the high wagon seat, placed the pistol in a boot beside the seat, and grabbed the reins. He pulled the brake, gave the reins a quick slap on the horses' rumps, and started moving away.

Captain Brewer watched for a few moments as Brice disappeared down the road. James walked up behind him just as he lost sight of his father. "That's a hell of a father you got there James."

"Always thought so Sir."

Brewer continued watching down the road, "You want to catch him and say good-bye."

"No Sir, I been watching him since he got up this morning. Didn't want to stop him from getting away." James half-turned away from the Captain to return to camp.

"You mean you didn't even want to say good-bye?"

"No Sir, we're not much for the sentimental show. Ward men are brought up to recognize, bad things happen in this world. You gotta prepare for that, and deal with it. Say your good-byes and mean it. May never be another chance. We already said our good-byes on the trip here. We're in your hands Captain, along with Colonel Burgwyn's, probably General Pettigrew's, and most likely, God's hands now and amen to it."

James finished his turn before Captain Brewer could respond and went back to the company area for breakfast.

While at breakfast, none other than Colonel Burgwyn walked over to where James had found an unoccupied tree stump to sit down and eat his ample breakfast of grits, three eggs, a couple of strips of pork fatback, some chopped chunks of fried potatoes, probably cooked in the same fat of the pork strips, and butter slathered over a one-inch slice of bread.

Seeing the Colonel approaching, James set the tin plate of food to the side and quickly stood to attention. As the Regimental Commander arrived, James posted a proper salute, "Good morning, Sir."

"Good morning to you Private Ward. I'm glad to see you back and apparently well enough for service." Burgwyn returned the salute and pointed to the breakfast plate.

"Why don't you return to your meal while we discuss a task for you?" The Commander reached over and grabbed an empty wooden box located near the fire and returned to sit by James.

"Hardly seems appropriate Sir for me to sit and eat breakfast in your presence Sir. Is it right to offer you a slice of my fatback Sir?" James extended the plate toward Burgwyn.

Colonel Burgwyn smiled and extended his hand, motioning for James to sit. "Thank you, Private Ward but Commanders have a bad habit of finding the most inappropriate times to interfere with the proper feeding and care of their troops. You eat and I'll talk." Burgwyn sat down onto the wooden box.

"James, I saw what you did with your rifled musket at Malvern Hill. I am thinking of taking a small group of men from each company and training them as sharpshooters, while we have the opportunity. I'm hoping they would be almost as good as you are to support each of their companies like you do for Company E. Captain Brewer insists, you are most valuable to him but is willing to let you take time to train other men. Will you consider doing it?" The Commander leaned back on the box and folded his arms across his chest.

"Sir, there are a lot of men in the 26th Regiment that could probably do that task better than me. I'm just a poor farm boy from Southeast North Carolina that knows how to hunt and shoot. Never tried to teach anyone how to do it. Excepting maybe a couple of the nephews growing up."

Burgwyn smiled again while nodding his head, "Well, we all know that is not completely true. Your timely and very accurate shots have saved many lives in this Regiment. I can't imagine anyone any more qualified to pass along the proper instructions for firing those type weapons than you. Please consider those soldiers as your nephews."

"Think about it and let me know by tomorrow's breakfast. If you agree to take on the task, I think you have about a week to get those men selected and trained." The young Commander, barely twenty-one years of age, stood from his box seat.

"I have secured one other Leonard Target Rifle like you have now from our captured weapons from Malvern Hill. I have also secured about two dozen British Whitworth Rifles from some friends down near Wilmington. They were kind enough to think of the 26th Regiment when they discovered they had them in a shipment from England." Colonel Burgwyn had that small boy devilish grin on his face.

He continued, "They thought those rifles would be beneficial to our men, not knowing the kind of rifles they had in their possession."

Burgwyn added, "I believe they may have been in charge of securing some contraband that was confiscated from some smugglers. Seems they got them from a blockade runner shipment coming from England."

"Sounds like you got some special friends there, Colonel." James stood up with the Regimental Commander as he was preparing to leave. He saluted again, "Sir, I'll take on that task for you. Can't guarantee any success, but I'll do my best."

Colonel Burgwyn returned the salute, "James, I'll have no doubt of your success in their training. My only doubt is the enemy to our North and front. They will have more of those weapons and men with the skill than we do. We'll get you the ammunition you need to get started."

Henry King Burgwyn Jr. turned and walked away with his shoulders a little more stooped over than a young man his age should be.

He had advanced only a couple of steps before he turned to face James again, "Oh, one other thing I almost forgot. I want to thank you and your father for the most generous and kind gifts of food and blankets. We also found several personal items of very nice gifts as well. It was a most gracious Christmas surprise. Thank you, again."

James watched as 'King' returned to his walk. From his position, returning to his unfinished breakfast, he saw Colonel Burgwyn stop near a tent where Captain Brewer and a recently promoted captain to Lieutenant Colonel named John Lane, had been watching the two men talk at James' breakfast. Lieutenant Colonel Lane was Burgwyn's Assistant Commander of the Regiment.

As he approached the two men by the tent, Burgwyn shook Brewer's hand and the Company E Commander saluted as the boy Colonel, nodded and they discussed something beyond James' earshot.

Their brief conversation ended with a returned salute from the Commander. Burgwyn and Lane continued the quiet conversation as they walked toward the headquarters located a couple of hundred yards away. They continued preparing for the many major tasks facing the Regiment, in anticipation of imminent battle.

January and February of 1863 saw the 26th Regiment tested on several occasions by incursions into the interior of North Carolina by the Federal Troops located on the Outer Banks and within the Pamlico Sound.

The 26th Regiment seemed to be everywhere at one time. They were either supporting or leading in nearly every offensive or defensive action during the late Winter and early Spring of 1863 covering the entire East Coast of North Carolina and Southeastern portions of Virginia.

The Regiment's reputation for successfully defending the homeland of North Carolina was continually growing in stature.

It was simple for the men of the Regiment, this was home. They truly believed that no one should successfully penetrate the homeland of North Carolina while the 26th Regiment was on guard.

It was personal. Politics be damned was the prevailing attitude of the men, protect the home or die trying. Nothing else was acceptable.

Their close order drill, durability, and ability to deploy, march great distances, and readiness to effectively fight the enemy on any ground made them very viable targets. Federal commanders even expressed an expectation that if they could get past the 26th Regiment, they could march all the way to Raleigh.

In between relatively minor skirmishes, James was able to train the twenty-five men requested. Many others had volunteered but per Colonel Burgwyn's insistence, he did not want too many sharpshooters and not enough troops for the attack or defense.

The newly minted sharpshooters were put to the test in late March of 1863 near New Bern, Little Washington, and Greenville, North Carolina.

General D. H. Hill's attempts to retake New Bern were repulsed, even though the 26th Regiment had successfully secured its supporting position, North of New Bern, while awaiting the main attack from General Hill's forces. General Hill's main attack failed, placing the 26th Regiment in jeopardy.

General Pettigrew and Colonel Burgwyn realized the brigade was in danger of being flanked by the retreating forces and the enemy.

Pettigrew's brigade successfully met the enemy and engaged them in force. As General Hill's forces retreated, Pettigrew instructed Colonel

Burgwyn to hold the lines until the balance of the division and the brigade could be redeployed to their next battle positions to the rear and West.

On this occasion, Henry looked over to James and said, "You ever wonder if them fools at command got any sense at all? How many times they gonna make us try to take New Bern?"

James looked to the left, over the barrel of his Leonard Rifle scope, directly at Henry. "Yeah, right pretty little town they got there, as best I recall. Not sure it's worth the amount of trouble we seem to be putting into it though."

He looked to the front, "I think I'd rather be defending the Green Swamp than this ground."

From the slightly higher ground that he and Henry occupied, James could see the array of 26th Regiment Troops deployed into hasty defensive positions along and to either side of the road below.

The Regiment was deployed with two companies on either side of the road and slightly behind those four companies, were two more companies that straddled the road. Colonel Burgwyn and his command staff were located directly behind those two companies.

Behind the headquarters, were the rest of the Regiment, in reserve, ready to deploy and reinforce the companies in front, if necessary.

James directed his personal attention to the sharpshooters tactically located throughout the Regiment's battle front. From their position, Henry and James could see nearly every one of the sharpshooters assigned to the companies deployed below.

He was glad to see that most had acquired firing positions on top of high ground like he and Henry had. Some had climbed into tall trees. A few found positions close to the hasty trenches dug by the soldiers.

While it might be necessary, James did not like the idea of getting too close to a firing position that drew attention to private houses or businesses. The thought of losing one's home or business was to be avoided as best as each sharpshooter could best determine to accomplish his task.

James reminded each of the sharpshooters to remember the same thing could happen at their home. Most of the other sharpshooters shared the same feelings on the matter.

Sharpshooters usually worked in pairs. The standing order was to find officers or senior non-commissioned officers and engage at the maximum distance, well before the enemy approached the Regiment's defensive line or less than two hundred yards.

Once the enemy had gotten to within two hundred yards of the Regiment's defensive line, they were to disengage and move back to their next defensive battle position to support any potential withdrawal or retreat.

Most of Pettigrew's brigade had cleared the lines and were moving with haste to their next battle positions in their withdrawal.

Everyone in the 26th Regiment had already performed one such move in this withdrawal and anticipated the initial artillery fire. They watched and crouched in the trenches, trees, and behind redoubts of piled dirt and logs. Ammunition was carefully laid out for ease of reloading.

James looked over at Henry, once again, and chuckled as the man was chewing on a tough slice of fatback between two halves of hard tack biscuit. "Is it dinner already Henry?"

Henry didn't even look at James while he chewed, "Well, you know, you just don't know when the next meal is gonna happen."

At that moment, the bombardment began with earnest, and the limited artillery rounds fell to the ground either well short of their position or to the flanks on the left and right. Union troops came into view, moving quickly in battle formations.

James estimated and said aloud, "I'm guessing about one thousand yards or so. What do you think?"

"I think you're the smartest man with that rifle in your hands and don't miss often. That's what I think." Henry lifted the Whitworth Rifle to his shoulder to get a proper feel for the weapon. The targets were still out of his range.

The Leonard Rifle also came up to James' shoulder. He began to scan the front looking for the right target.

He saw a particularly tall man standing at attention with his back to James, as he directed the troops in blue. James eased his right eye to the long scope on top of the rifle and found the officer.

James had already guessed the man was an officer and most likely a company commander like his own Captain Brewer.

James hesitated a moment as he thought of Brewer. He whispered softly to himself, "I hope Captain Brewer has his head down."

The Union troops were neatly organized, and the front units began to advance. All the forward 26th Regiment skirmishers from the Regiment had returned to the defensive lines. James had decided to give them another hundred yards of advance before deciding to engage the targets.

At the designated point, between eight hundred and nine hundred yards distance, James eased the Leonard Rifle up, found the tall officer to the front of his company, now facing the 26th Regiment's positions, leading his men into battle.

The scope captured the officer's torso in James' eye, the soft breath, the slow release, hammer cocked, finger gently caressing the trigger, another soft breath to hold, and the hammer dropped creating the explosion that dropped the man to the ground. James prayed softly, "Dear Lord forgive me."

As if on his command, each of the Regimental sharpshooters had similarly found their targets and began an aggressive and continuous assault on the officers and non-commissioned officers of the Union forces.

No less than eight officers and cadre had fallen in the first exchange. James estimated the sharpshooters would take at least one more shot and if not discovered by the Union troops, probably more targets would be engaged.

While successful, the hundreds of Union Troops just continued to replace the fallen soldiers and move forward toward the 26th Regiment's main defensive position.

Given his position, James could see several of the sharpshooters were already redeploying to the main force. With the effective weapon he held in his hands, James continued to find and engage the preferred targets.

The men in blue continued to reinforce their attack and were about to engage the main defensive lines of the 26th regiment. He heard Captain Brewer's command to prepare to fire. Every man rose from his position, prepared their weapons to fire, and on command, fired in mass to their front.

At that moment, the two enemy forces were less than two hundred yards apart. The effect was immediate. The defensive positions could fire, reload, and fire again in less than a minute. Given the range of the first volley, many Union troops fell to the ground, dead or wounded.

The six companies in line at their battle positions were very effective. All men rose as one and continued their fire with great impact. All the sharpshooters were back in their units and joined the fight with different muskets at hand. Other sharpshooters continued to the next position as ordered.

More Union artillery was redirected at the center of the 26th Regiment's line and while distracting, it was too few and too poorly aimed to deter the North Carolina troops from providing continuous deadly fire.

The Union commanders were beginning to deploy their reserves in support and Colonel Burgwyn verified that General Hill's Division had completed their retreat to the next positions and were ready for Pettigrew's Brigade to move into their positions as well.

James looked to his left and saw Burgwyn standing in the center with his field glasses to his eyes. The Commander turned quickly to Lieutenant Colonel Lane and gave him instructions. Lane then went to the company runners located just behind the Commander.

Two runners from other companies ran to the rear. James saw that Stephen was still standing in position, ready to relay messages to Captain Brewer, if needed. James also looked to see if he had his brogans on his feet.

"Damn, the boy's got his boots on!" James just smiled at the infrequent occasion.

Suddenly, hearing the steady thumping sound of troops at the double-quick step, James looked to his rear and saw two more companies coming forward and moving into the center of the Regiment's defensive positions.

The new insertion of the troops and continuous firing stopped the Union advance in place. The forward companies began to withdraw. The fresh companies held the center of the line and then began to fall back in the direction whence they came.

More runners returned soon afterwards with confirmation the withdrawing units had reached the next positions. The information was immediately relayed to the reinforcing companies by Lane, and the 26th Regiment began its final withdrawal from the battlefield.

26th Regiment casualties were light with forty men missing or with the Regimental Surgeon during the next day's roll call. The list of dead was even lighter at eight recorded in the unit's daily report. The Regiment had earned another battle streamer for its guidon.

Movement back to the Camp Magnolia area had been slow and methodical. The enemy had also withdrawn and with significant enough casualties for the need to protect their own rear. They returned to their camps around New Bern, Little Washington, and Greenville.

The battle status quo had remained essentially during the Christmas and early months of the New Year. North Carolina remained nearly as it was in the Fall of 1862. The State remained occupied on the coast, but no major incursions were successful by Federal troops.

Many new North Carolina Troops were deployed to the East of the State and had gotten a proper introduction into bloody conflict. They had also garnered the experience of supporting major battle in Virginia at Malvern Hill, during the Peninsula Campaigns, including Suffolk, Richmond, and Petersburg.

General Robert E. Lee, newly appointed by President Jefferson Davis, had successfully defeated a major attack by General Albert Burnside over the Rappahannock River and in Fredericksburg, Virginia in December 1862.

Lee's smaller forces successfully punished Burnside; so much so that President Lincoln chose to replace Burnside for his failure.

The result of the Winter season was many changed strategies for both sides. Both Union and Confederate Presidents recognized the need to force the issue before the upcoming elections in the North for different reasons.

For Lincoln it was to be re-elected to maintain the Union. For Davis, it was to get Lincoln un-elected President and finally break the will of the Union supporting a more protracted war.

Lincoln wanted Richmond and President Davis captured. President Davis wanted the war pushed into the North and pressure on President Lincoln. Both Presidents saw opportunities to break the status quo in April 1863.

* * * * *

January 23, 1863

To Private James Ward, Company E, 26th Regiment of North Carolina Troops, Pettigrew's Brigade, Heth's Division, near Richmond, Virginia

My Dearest Husband,

I write to you with a shaking hand as my nerves seem to desert me at this most wonderful moment. I am with a child!

It was not my intent to burden you with this knowledge before you left at Christmas since I was not fully aware of my circumstances. If I had known, perhaps it might have made you do something foolish such as deserting the army. Having you shot for desertion is no way to start our family! Your family was of a similar mind.

To say the entire Ward family and my family are happy is to greatly understate their true and obvious feelings about the impending birth. Miz Lizzie and I made a trip to see the Doctor and he seemed pleased and unsurprised at the news. He also made us aware of the local midwife for future references.

Given the size of both our families, I don't think we need a reference for a midwife. I am sure we will use the Widow Thompson as so many have in our families on similar occasions.

Your father seemed very proud that we were adding to our family. He even went to the general store to secure ten special cigars from Cuba to give to the other Ward Brothers upon the event of the special occasion.

Mr. Brice has already marked two of his prime milk cows for our baby's use. Some of the cousins have already started a small paddock for the cows to settle in close to our new barn. I know the boys will not do as good a job as you, but their hearts are really into helping any way they can.

Miz Lizzie has gone into a serious sewing fever making children's clothes. She also has suggested the need to gather the stored baby clothing from the other families.

Of course, we don't know whether it's a boy or girl, and I don't much care. However, I know you will want a boy to continue the Ward name. I will do my best to accommodate.

I would suppose that if we are not successful with having a boy, we can try again. Knowing you, I am thinking that will not be so bad as well. Curled in your arms is the safest place I think I would ever want to be.

Spring fields and planting will start soon, and the men have been busy with finding the best seeds, turning the fields with plows, and mapping out the fields for certain crops. Cow manure, soil, and old fish remains have been collected and prepared for fertilizer.

I have started a smaller garden beside our new house down by the Green Swamp. It will be more than enough for the three of us and with a little extra for our tithes to the church.

Please give my best to Stephen and I am so glad to see he is still well. I have enclosed two pairs of socks for him. I know he won't wear them unless he has to, but I thought I would make them while I was working in the sewing circle with the other Ward ladies.

Know that I love you and can't wait to see your smiling face once again. More important, I want you to see the face of your new child.

I'll let you know when it is due, probably in a future letter.

I am your most loving and expecting wife,

Mrs. Anna Wallace Ward

CHAPTER 10

"THEY'RE FOOLS!" MAY 1863

The movement North was inevitable. There were no doubts by General Pettigrew and Colonel Burgwyn that Pettigrew's Brigade, composed of the Eleventh, Twenty-sixth, Forty-fourth, Forty-seventh, and Fifty-second North Carolina Regiments were going to an area of intense battle.

Henry 'King' Burgwyn, Jr. had mixed feelings on the imminent move. He felt compelled to perform his duties as the Commander, but more than once, he had expressed his concerns about the cause for which they fought. Business was business, but this just didn't feel right.

He recalled one such occasion on the family's North Carolina plantation when his father, considering slavery so abhorrent and wrong, attempted to eliminate slavery on the family plantation by using Irish immigrants to replace the slaves. The experiment failed miserably through no fault of the slaves.

Duty was duty and young Colonel Burgwyn was determined to make his family proud, even unto death, if necessary.

After Malvern Hill, many in the 26th Regiment were not so keen on being North of the North Carolina and Virginia state lines. Of the nearly one thousand men of the 26th Regiment that boarded the train going

North on May 1, 1863, less than the number of fingers on two hands had slaves back home.

Most of these men were farmers growing crops, raising cattle, producing hogs, hunting, fishing, running small stores, and working the forges for the blacksmiths.

Like Brice Ward, most were land rich or business rich and cash poor. They worked with their hands and their wits to make a living for their families.

Buying another man to do their work was the last thing on their minds.

No, the soldiers of the 26th Regiment were more concerned about what they had seen in Virginia. An invasion from the North had occurred, and people's lives had been turned upside down through no fault of their own.

The capitol of Virginia was the grand prize sought by the Union army, and Pettigrew's Brigade was being pushed into the war to prevent them from achieving that goal.

There was no defending the homeland of North Carolina anymore. This was now a war of survival for the men of the Regiment.

On a recent trip into town, Brice Ward heard the news of the 26th Regiment performing well near New Bern. He read the newspaper articles tacked to the wall of the courthouse.

Several other people were reading the article out loud, and the crowd was continually responding to both the good and bad news with even greater emotion. Brice was not happy with the outpouring.

He turned away and before he got two steps, a gentleman reading aloud asked, "Mister Ward, don't you want to hear about your Son's Regiment? They did right proud for us."

Brice turned back to look at the man before speaking, "No. I am not interested in the report. I am only interested in hearing when my family will be returning to the farm at their earliest convenience."

"But Sir, by all accounts, your boy did well. He's a hero!"

Brice hesitated for a moment. "No Sir. James would never claim to be a hero. He would tell you he just did what he was supposed to do to protect his family."

"Well, the good news is they are going to Virginia to put an end to this war, and he'll come back home a true war hero."

This time, Brice hung his head down, took a deep breath. He slowly raised his head and looked around at the quiet crowd listening to their conversation.

Then he angrily shouted, "They're fools! Their generals are fools! Jefferson Davis is a fool! They will only find grief and savage war in the North. They will die in the hundreds, and for what?"

He gathered himself up, looked around at the shocked faces. He tipped his old beaver pelt hat on his head, "Ladies, I apologize for my blunt remarks. I meant no offense. Our boys will acquit themselves with honor and bravery. Of that, I have no doubt."

Brice, again, tipped the hat to the man reading the articles, "Sir, my apologies to you for my remarks as well. I will leave you to your oratory of the latest news." He turned with no hesitation and began his return to the farm.

While the 26th Regimental Band played, the men were busy loading equipment, supplies, cannons, horses, fodder, and tack for the animals. Officers were about, giving orders, ensuring everything was secured, and the men prepared for the final roll call before boarding the train.

It was joyous and very encouraging music with a slightly cultured sound to it. It rallied the men, even as they wondered about their fates in the North. Everyone seemed to move with a purpose by following the pulsing and deep sounds of the brass instruments and the rolling thrum of the drums.

James had gathered the well-trained and proficient regimental sharpshooters close by and were carefully instructing them on hand carrying their special weapons. He appointed men to set atop the train to offer quick response in the event of ambushes along the way.

Like James, most of the sharpshooters were carrying two weapons with them, their standard muskets for battle formations and their Whitworth Rifles for sharpshooter duties.

The other men of the Regiment's companies sympathized with these special men and their additional burdens. Someone was always offering to help the sharpshooters with their additional equipment and impedimenta. Men of the 26th Regiment knew the importance of those men to their own safety and lives.

If a soldier could be pampered, the sharpshooters were offered that opportunity. Too often, the sharpshooters kindly refused the offer of assistance with sincere thanks. To most of them, they were not burdened by their load, they were honored to carry it.

The sharpshooter was different. Unlike the soldiers in the ranks, firing in mass and not knowing whether their bullet had hit an enemy soldier or not, they knew every time they fired their special weapon, who they hit and how many souls they sent to their respective hell or heaven.

This was the true burden carried by each of the sharpshooters. They knew, there was no doubt, what they had done.

There were some that reveled in the task. There were others that struggled with the burden. Recurring nightmares were not uncommon among some of the sharpshooters.

James was neither of these. He took no great pleasure in a well-placed shot to an enemy officer. He did what he was trained and ordered to do.

He also did not worry about the consequences for the man he killed; that was between the man killed and his creator.

No, James worried more about his own soul and where it was destined to be. Being a devout Christian, he believed Jesus Christ had already fulfilled his promise.

Now it was up to James to live up to his promise to God. It was why, before each shot, he whispered the prayer of confession and request for mercy, "God, please forgive me."

James saw Stephen running down the track beside each rail car searching for someone or something. He yelled down from his position on top of his railcar, "Private Ward, where are you running to boy?"

Stephen looked up and saw James smiling down on him. "Captain Brewer wanted me to run down the cars and make sure everyone was on board. Don't want no stragglers, you know, Private Ward."

The two cousins laughed at each other, and James replied, "You need a place to ride? Got some room up here if you're interested in a view. Might get hot in the Sun, though."

"Don't mind the Sun, so much. Might like the breeze though." Stephen started climbing up to the top of the car and then settled in beside James.

"How's things happening back at the company headquarters?" James leaned back against his gear and laid his face away from the Sun.

Stephen had closed his eyes and faced toward the Sun soaking in the warmth of the morning light. "Pretty much the same. Another move to the North. Supposed to have a stop or two between here and Richmond."

James nodded his understanding, "Yeah, but what's waiting for us in Richmond?"

"Well, word is that General Lee is doing pretty good against the Yankees up around Fredericksburg again. Some guy named Hooker is on the other side of the river." Stephen paused for a moment in thought, wondering how much he should tell.

"They want us to go up and reinforce against General Hooker. Not quite sure where and what they want from General Pettigrew and this here brigade." The cousin thought that should be sufficient without getting himself in trouble for starting rumors.

"Sounds like something big, again. Heard this story before. Probably be up there a few months and go home again." James said it, but he didn't believe it, not this time.

Stephen mulled over his cousin's remark and said, "I'm not so sure this time. Think I'll catch a nap, though." He promptly rolled over and fell asleep on the moving train.

James worried about him rolling off the train. He laid his gear bag on one side of the younger Ward cousin and then propped his leg on the opposite side of Private Stephen Ward.

He then laid his head back and fell asleep as well.

The trip by rail was supposed to take about three leisurely days' time. However, circumstances in Northern Virginia had taken a dramatic turn.

General Hooker had made the decision, and at the urging of President Lincoln, to apply significant pressure on General Lee's forces at Fredericksburg. Lee's Confederate forces had won a significant victory at the same location back in December of 1862 with the Union taking severe losses.

Hooker had made the decision to not give Lee the same advantage and sought to engage him at Fredericksburg while moving North and West around the Rappahannock River and attacking Lee from the rear.

The battle began in earnest on April 30, 1863, the day before the 26th Regiment started its train ride to the North. At each stop, the train was ordered to move with even greater haste. What was supposed to be three days, took a little over two days.

They arrived at Hanover Junction on May third, and immediately prepared for battle. A temporary camp was established and then quickly dismantled as they moved toward Richmond.

By May 6, at the little farming community of Chancellorsville, the battle was over. Lee had used General Thomas Jackson's Corps to attack General Hooker's forces from the flank and push them back across the river with more heavy losses.

News of the battle and its results were humming across telegraph wires along the entire Eastern seaboard. This was bad news for the North and gave significant encouragement to the Confederacy.

Lee was sitting with the largest army the Confederacy had at any point in the war at his disposal.

With the large infusion of troops from North Carolina and other states, President Davis urged Lee to attack to the North and "punish those people like they had punished Virginia."

Davis really didn't care where but anywhere North of Washington or Baltimore would be just fine to force the war into the North's backyard for a change.

While reluctant at first, Lee saw the advantage after the results at Chancellorsville and was pleased to make use of that advantage.

The grand invasion by the Confederacy of the North was put into place.

In June 1863, Pettigrew's Brigade, including the 26th Regiment, was placed under the Division Command of Major General Henry Heth, whose division was located just outside of Fredericksburg. Heth's Division was assigned to Lieutenant General A.P. Hill's Third Corps.

The division was composed of General Archer's Tennessee Brigade, General Davis's Mississippi Brigade, General Brockenborough's Virginia Brigade, and General Pettigrew's North Carolina Brigade.

Heth was a Virginian. A man with a great deal of military experience including the War with Mexico and the Army's Indian plains wars. His promotion to Division Commander was a result of his heroic actions at the most recent battle of Chancellorsville.

General Pettigrew and Colonel Burgwyn were most impressed with their Division Commander and the feeling was mutual. Heth would look to Pettigrew's Brigade and more specifically the 26th Regiment as the center point for any future actions for his division.

From their camp, West of Fredericksburg, and even further past Chancellorsville, the 26th Regiment was getting very comfortable with their new division.

The Regiment was seen on the parade field nearly everyday drilling and preparing for battles to come. Other units and their officers would come to watch this Brigade and Regiment working hard on their skills under the hot Sun of June 1863.

What impressed them even more was the 26th Regimental Band led by Chief Musician S. L. Mickey. The nineteen musicians served up a wide variety of music while the unit practiced their drills.

Some of the music was martial in nature and others included sweet ballads providing a reminder of why they fought. Occasional Christian music would rally the troops as well.

What was certain, even the Confederate Army Commander, General Lee was impressed enough to frequently request the 26th Regimental Band play for the officers at his headquarters for dinner. Each request was most happily accepted by Mister Mickey.

Mister Mickey was proud of his band. They were all accomplished musicians, and most were from a group of Moravians found in the Forsyth County area of North Carolina.

Their repertoire included martial, classical, religious, and popular tunes of the day. If there was a tune in which they were unfamiliar, Mister

Mickey would respond, "If you can hum it, we can play it." And they did it quite often.

What was not lost on many others was the use of the band during battle. Drummers would be employed throughout the Regiment to mark time during drills, marches, and parades. Trumpeters provided bugle calls.

However, for the men of the 26th Regiment, their confidence in the band members to act as litter bearers for the wounded and dead of the battlefield was far more important.

Nearly every man took the time to visit the field hospital, share stories of back home, and slip a piece of paper with special requests if they should be mortally wounded or found dead to share with family or friend.

Mister Mickey was more than a musician, he was also a complement to the Regimental Chaplain Styring Scarboro Moore, recently appointed to that role in the early Fall of 1862.

Both men were instrumental to the mental and spiritual well-being of the men of the 26th Regiment and the Regimental Chief Surgeon at the time, Lewellyn P. Warren, who previously served as a First Lieutenant for the 52nd Regiment.

Chief Surgeon Warren had a single Assistant Surgeon to support him by the name of William Wiley Gaither and a single Hospital Steward by the name of Benjamin Hinds.

This gathering of men of the Regimental Band provided for the medical, spiritual, and entertainment for the soldiers of the 26th Regiment.

To many of the Regimental Troops, they were the conscience of the Regiment. They were the people that would take care of them in their personal moments of greatest need.

Colonel Burgwyn was of very like mind. His approach to each soldier said to them, "I will do everything in my power to see you safely back home." And they knew it to be so.

The Regimental Commander had properly conveyed that same commitment to his staff at the headquarters level. From Lieutenant Colonel Lane, the staff majors, the Adjutant First Lieutenant James Bell Jordan, the Surgeons, Assistant Surgeons, the Chaplain, Sergeant Major Montford Stokes McRae, Assistant Quartermaster Joseph Young, and the Assistant Commissary 2nd Lieutenant Phineas Horton.

Every man had his duty to perform, and every other man was assigned the responsibility to help them not fail in those duties. Each man felt it was the least they could honorably do.

Back at Malvern Hill, Burgwyn had seen the looks on the men as they faced a terrible late evening and all-night barrage of death and destruction from the hilltop filled with Union troops and cannon. The men never flinched in fear. Only patience and perseverance saw them through the night, and they survived.

Until this time, Malvern Hill was the measuring stick for intense battle. Pettigrew and Burgwyn both knew what was to come would try them even more.

Colonel Burgwyn was buoyed by the successes at Fredericksburg and Chancellorsville, and he hoped the 26th Regiment would meet muster for General Lee's newly reinforced army.

However, he worried about his promise to his men. He knew he had little power to make them safe. But he also knew they would not fail of their own accord.

The Commander of the 26th Regiment had a fitful night of sleep on June 14th, 1863.

* * * * *

June 30, 1863

To Mrs. Anna Wallace Ward, General Delivery, Whiteville, North Carolina

My Dearest and Most Beautiful Wife,
     I am in receipt of your most recent letter and happy to hear that you and the family are well. That certainly is extended to our soon-to-be-born child.
     It is good to hear of your efforts with the farm and I know it is more difficult with so many men gone from home to war.
     Our trip North has been very quiet for us, so far. I must think it is because our Corps, Division, and Brigade have been placed at the end of a huge column stretching for miles. We are nearly a hundred miles apart from front to back.
     With that in mind, maybe the battles will be fought and finished by the time we get there.
     The problem is by the time we get to our next camp each day, the pickings for the Quartermaster and Commissary are pretty well gone.
     Potato or corn soup is getting a little old. Orders have been pretty strict about not punishing the local farms but it's hard to ignore the plentiful farms and crops we see as we march through the Shenandoah Valley and into Pennsylvania.
     It is my sincere hope this trip to the North will pay us a great reward for our efforts and perhaps the Union folk will decide the war is really unnecessary.
     I pray and I hope, but I have little faith in the sanity of our two governments. It is just so hard to understand why this can't be resolved without the bloodshed we have seen already.
     I am most sorry. I did not mean to become maudlin with you. Please know that Colonel Burgwyn is doing very well, and we are most ready to do our duty. Perhaps our presence in the North will give the folks up here pause to consider the wisdom of their endeavors.

Stephen just ran by with another message for Captain Brewer and the boy never seems to stop. I'm not sure but I think he likes the army. Lord, please help the army if that is true.

Please tell Momma I love her and to pray for me and Stephen. A piece of her fried chicken, with fresh butter beans, over mashed potatoes, smothered in gravy, would be good about now. A slice of her Pecan Pie would be really good too.

We're going where we've never been before and it's a little unsettling. We are in Pennsylvania having recently crossing over from Maryland. Each small town or crossroads seems to carry different people. Some even speak different languages.

Most of the time, they just try to ignore us. They keep working in the fields, moving about the towns, as if we were not really here.

About the most frequent remarks for the 26th Regiment is people like our new uniforms we got before we left Richmond. Hope we get some boots soon. Mine are about worn out.

Tell Father, I love him as well. Mention to him that both Captain Brewer and Colonel Burgwyn frequently ask about him and his health. He seemed to make quite the impression when he brought me back to camp in December.

Well, I must be off. I have picket duty in a couple of hours and need to get some rest.

I am your most loving husband,

Private James Ward, Company E, 26th Regiment, Pettigrew's Brigade, Heth's Division, Hill's Corps, Army of the Confederacy

CHAPTER 11

"SHOES FOR MY FEET" JUNE 30, 1863

As always, Stephen was running without his boots on his feet but they were dangling around his neck. James smiled at his younger cousin. "What's the hurry cousin?"

Stephen caught his breath as he pulled up in front of James, "General Heth's about to send a brigade into that town up to the right and General Pettigrew has the honor. Also, heard some words about a shoe factory there. Might be able to outfit some of the boys with new boots."

"You got a minute?" James offered a place against the fallen log.

"Sure, what you got?"

"Just finished this here letter for Anna Wallace and thought you might be able to pass it along to get home." James extended the sealed letter, enclosed with the last few Confederate dollars he received for pay.

Stephen accepted the letter, "I'll get this back to the rear before we break for the march. Get your butt ready, we'll be pushing out just after Noon time."

Not long after Stephen had left with his letter, Lieutenant Emerson reappeared trotting down the dirt road. He pulled up in front of James again, "Private Ward, inform the men that we'll be conducting a reconnaissance mission into the local town to the North and East. Be prepared to march in column of fours at Noon sharp on this road. We'll follow company order, so we'll be near the center. Rumor has it there are shoes to be had there. Might have to lug some back. We'll be bringing two wagons in case we find some."

James had already gotten up and saluted smartly to the officer, "Yes Sir, I'll start rounding the boys up soon as you leave Sir. Are we expecting any trouble?"

The Lieutenant leaned over the saddle, "Not really sure, but we got to expect we'll eventually run into the damn Yankee Army sometime. Let's be ready if we do."

"Yes Sir!" James saluted once again as Lieutenant Emerson departed back in the direction of the Company E headquarters.

James spent the next thirty minutes moving around the company informing the cadre and troops to be prepared to march by Noon. They had about an hour and a half to prepare.

The troops knew the drill well. They would leave their personal gear in a company pile ready for pick up, if necessary. Each soldier would carry enough ammunition, personal weapons, their haversacks, a canteen filled with water, and a short bedroll if they were required to stay overnight. All other equipment and personal baggage were left behind for their return by nightfall.

"James, does Captain Brewer have any expectations for us sharpshooters on this here mission?" Henry anxiously awaited his fellow sharpshooter's answer.

"No Henry, Lieutenant Emerson didn't mention anything of the kind. We'll see once we are in formation." James finished pulling the ties on the leather wrap around his two sharpshooter rifles and he intended to march in the company formation as usual.

As expected, Captain Brewer was on his horse and watched over his troops as Company E formed in the road. The other companies of the 26th Regiment were busy similarly forming in place.

Seeing James, he pushed his horse in James' direction, "James, don't think we're going to need you boys with the long rifles today, but just keep them close, if we need you."

James responded, "Henry and me will be ready if you need us Sir." He saluted as the Company Commander returned to the front of Company E.

To James' right, Henry offered, "Well, I guess that answers that. Kinda like being in a crowd like this with the company. Nobody on the other side knows what you're carrying in that leather wrap and how dangerous you are with it. If they did, whole damned Yankee Army would be trying to kill us."

James just gave a slight smile but was thinking the very same thing. Nobody on the other side liked the sharpshooters either.

The march was about four miles to the road that led from Cashtown, Pennsylvania towards the town of Gettysburg and about three and half miles to the small town proper.

It was a moderate day, with some overhead clouds to help keep the temperatures down. There had been light rain and mist the previous night that made for some muddy spots along the road, but the road was passable.

Once on the road, Pettigrew's Brigade moved in quick time at a steady pace. General Heth was on the side of the road, observing the movement forward. Along the route, General Pettigrew's Brigade ran into a force of pickets that belonged to a Virginia Regiment.

Pettigrew, being cautious, inquired of the Division Commander to determine what was forward and in the town. The Commander was of little assistance or with information of note.

The brigade continued forward and eventually ran into a gentleman, on the side of the road, which turned out to be a local doctor performing house calls for sick patients. His demeanor and the Doctor's bag confirmed his credentials and the reason for being about the area.

However, General Pettigrew required the Doctor to remain with him as they continued toward Gettysburg to ensure he was not a Union spy. His concern was especially based upon the Doctor's speculation there were no Federal troops in Gettysburg.

Soon after, while continuing toward Gettysburg, pickets returned with information that troops on horseback were seen on some high ground West of the town.

What was unsure was whether they were local militia or regular army troops. What was for sure, was the troops they had observed, were engaged, and exchanged fire with the brigade's forward skirmishers.

The Doctor seemed as genuinely surprised as anyone by the report, although Pettigrew had his doubts about his sincerity.

Pettigrew, accompanied by his staff and Regimental Commanders moved to a better position to see the opposing forces at hand. There was no doubt in the minds of the Confederate officers, this was Union regular army cavalry.

The brigade was withdrawn to a safe place and back from any observation by the Union forces on the hill. The 26th Regiment was placed on the picket line for the night.

James found himself settling in for the night. He contemplated the incidents of the day. He was troubled. He recognized that tomorrow would be July 1, 1863. It would be one year to the day of the battle at Malvern Hill.

Until this moment, Malvern Hill was the measure of comparison for every battle by the men of the 26th Regiment. That was a bloody and terrible affair. One that would last in the memory of every man that was there and still alive.

James began to pray but stopped short of his supplications. He recalled the sermon by the Chaplain just two days ago. It was focused on the message of Jerimiah 8:20-22, "The harvest is past, the summer is ended, and we are not saved. For the hurt of my poor people I am hurt, I mourn, and dismay has taken hold for me. Is there no balm in Gilead? Why then has the health of my poor people not been restored?"

If the message could be any clearer, James could not imagine it. They had witnessed the vast fields of Maryland and Pennsylvania, filled with harvested crops and abundant wealth of food and livestock. Back home, they struggled to plow sufficient fields that could do no more than feed themselves, much less an army situated in the North.

Finally, the resounding message was even more clear to James. Everyone of God's soldiers needed to be prepared to meet the sweet Lord Jesus Christ on the other side of the veil that separates life and death.

He returned to his prayers and the time to cleanse his soul of any burden was rendered unto God and the universe. His list for prayer was long and extended to all back home and at the camp where they laid for the night.

Not lost on James was the impending birth of his unborn child and his wife. He prayed to God for their good health and thanked God for his blessings on them.

He ended the prayer with his confession and affirmation of faith as he whispered, "I believe in God the Father Almighty, maker of heaven and earth, and in Jesus Christ, his only Son, our Lord, who was conceived from the Holy Spirit and born of the Virgin Mary, who suffered under Pontius Pilate, was crucified, died, and was buried, He descended into hell, rose again from the dead on the third day, ascended into heaven and is seated at the right hand of God the Father Almighty. I believe in the Holy Spirit, the holy Catholic Church, the communion of saints, the forgiveness of sins, the resurrection of the body, and the life everlasting. Amen."

His final prayer was, "Lord, you know what this is about. You know what the right is and wrong. I leave this in your hands to divine your intent for us. Lord, I seek no justice for I am sure I am wrong way too often. What I seek is mercy, as you have promised. For mercy is truly all that will save me in your Kingdom. Amen."

With tears in his eyes, James covered himself, and set his equipment to the side, and went to sleep before his turn on the picket lines.

His dream that night was of him working in the corn fields by the Green Swamp portion of his new home. He saw his wife bringing him a pitcher of cool water and a tin cup from which to drink it. At her side was a small creature he did not recognize. It was a small boy with bright red hair.

James woke up in a misty haze. He seemed to be in a cloud that was heavy with moisture.

A hand reached out and was shaking him, "James, your turn on the picket." Stephen stepped away from James' side and pulled his blanket up close to his throat. "See you in the morning."

James cleared his head, pulled his uniform jacket a little tighter, and buttoned it to the neck. He stood up, reached for his musket and haversack, then gathered the leather wrapped weapons that went everywhere with him.

He wandered to the Commissary area and grabbed a biscuit with a small slice of fatback meat inside. He put an apple in his pocket and went to report for duty to the Sergeant Major.

"Morning James. Been kind of quiet tonight. Everybody a little jumpy, though. I think one of the boys actually shot at a rabbit. Said he was trying to get us some meat for dinner, but I think the rabbit just scared him half to death." Sergeant Major Montford Stokes McRae chuckled in the small light provided by the lantern close by the headquarters tent.

James smiled at the story as well. He knew that night picket was always difficult. Critters were always moving around at night and as the story goes, hard to tell friend from foe, two-or four-legged kind.

The Sergeant Major continued, "The Corporal will walk you down to the picket line and your position. Since it will be dawn when you finish duty, the Colonel suggested a position where you might be able to see what is out there a little better with that scope of yours. I think you're going to like that tree we picked out for you. Got some lower limbs to make it easier for you to get up near the top. Since you're eating a cold breakfast, I'll make sure you got something warm waiting when you come off the line."

"Thanks Sergeant Major. I do appreciate that. And yes, I did bring my other gear as well. I'll pass along anything that looks important to you and the Colonel. By the yonder, how is the Colonel feeling about this coming day?" James awaited the Corporal to lead him away.

McRae hesitated a moment. Thought about what he was going to say. He stood up from the campfire stool he sat on and moved closer to James. "To be honest James, I'm not sure. The Colonel will do his duty as best as any man in this army. Don't think I've seen him this quiet since I been in the Regiment. He went to bed earlier than usual. Usually, almost the last man down each night. You know how he is. Always worrying about the men."

"Yeah, I know what you mean. He will make a cat worry." James offered.

"He's studied those maps for days now. I'm afraid he's gonna lose his eyesight. He understands the plan and situation as good as anyone. I'm not worried about his plan, its them boys on the other side I'm worried about."

The Sergeant Major motioned for the Corporal to lead James to his new position in a tall tree in a nearly empty field.

As predicted by the Sergeant Major, the rest of the brief night passed by without any action on either side. The dawn came and went, and James was replaced on the picket line.

The Sergeant Major was also true to his word and had a nice breakfast waiting for James when he made his report. Two runny eggs were seeping out of two thick slices of bread, with a good slather of butter, and meat inside. It tasted a little gamey, but it did go down well with some apple cider.

"Thanks Sergeant Major, what was that meat inside the bread?"

"Oh, turns out there was a rabbit out there last night. One of the boys brought it in from his picket. Thought of you right away. Had the cook clean it and fire it for you. A little too fresh for me but the rest of that rabbit is making a mighty fine stew." Sergeant Major McRae laughed and walked away.

James returned to his position with Company E and found the camp nearly ready to move out. He found Stephen putting his personal gear away into a wagon. "What's happening?"

Stephen gave him a look of recognition and concern, "Best I can tell you all hell is about to break loose. We're moving East pretty quick, and you need to get ready. You got about thirty minutes. I got to get back to Captain Brewer at headquarters. Keep your head down cousin!"

James got into his gear and pulled a couple of additional items out of his baggage. He jammed those items into his haversack and threw his bed roll over his shoulder.

Private James Ward was at peace with his God and his Regiment. He was ready to do his duty.

* * * * *

June 23, 1863

To Private James Ward, Company E, 26th Regiment, Pettigrew's Brigade, Heth's Division, and Hill's Corps

My dearest love,

We continue to pray for you and Stephen and the rest of your Regiment. No prayers at each meal, bedtime, or church service goes by without a request to God for your wellbeing.

We had a good planting season, although it is much smaller than usual. Mister Brice is a little concerned that we may not have enough to pay some of the bills without something to bargain with. We just don't have enough people to plant and harvest the crops. We lost too much last season and ended rotting on the ground.

Unfortunately, two more of the cousins have been drafted into the army and are at training as we speak. The boys have asked to be transferred to the 26th Regiment because that is where you and Stephen are. We're not sure whether that request will be granted. Don't be surprised if you see them in the future arriving at your camp though.

We are getting by. Please don't worry about us. We have had a little concern with the local home guard though. They come by about once a month to claim that we owe taxes, and they were there to take it out of the livestock.

Fortunately, your father was able to convince them they would need a warrant from the courthouse before they took anything from our farms. Of course, he had his favorite rabbit eared double barrel shotgun in his hand and a LeMat pistol in his belt when they were here.

The rest of the Ward families are now on the watch for them and are reacting quickly to get to any of our farms they are threatening. I'm afraid it may only get worse.

They keep insisting they are responsible for getting deserters and returning them to their proper units for punishment. They say that some of our children are possible deserters.

For some good news I hope our child is well on its way. The Doctor is telling us that it should be here by mid-July.

I love you always and pray for your safe return.

I am your affectionate and loving wife,

Mrs. Anna Wallace Ward

CHAPTER 12

"STEADY BOYS, STEADY" JULY 1, 1863

James and the rest of Company E stood in formation early that morning. Tensions were high with expectations as the Sun slowly rose into the Eastern sky.

The battle began that misty morning with Heth's Division organized to move to the East toward Gettysburg. Two brigades forward, Archer's brigade on the right of the Chambersburg Pike, while to the left of the pike, Davis's Brigade was similarly positioned to move through General Pettigrew's Brigade that had secured the picket line the night before.

Heth's strategy was to move forward to find the enemy presence and then attack with heavy fire to clear them away as quickly as practical. He thought two heavy infantry brigades was about right for the task. Once through the Pettigrew pickets, Pettigrew's and Brockenborough's Brigades would center just behind those two brigades in reserve.

It did not take long for the forward brigades to make initial contact. What they found was a heavy Union cavalry Brigade with fast loading carbine rifles, capable of placing quick and massive fire on the Confederate troops as they moved in mass to the front and up the hill.

After clearing the initial hurdles of getting closer to the Union force located on the high ground to their front, Archer and Davis deployed their units from columns to ranks of infantrymen firing in rapid fashion. This required pulling down fences and pushing over low rock walls in the field. All this occurs while receiving continuous and effective fire from the high ground.

Colonel Henry King Burgwyn Jr. and the 26th Regiment were positioned in the reserve as commanded, but the Regimental Commander moved forward with his binoculars to see the battle to the front. His assistant, Lieutenant Colonel John Lane was by his side.

Burgwyn saw what was happening and anticipated what was needed. "Colonel Lane, I need for you to go back and tell the Company Commanders that we are going to be pushing forward on the right flank. We're going to have to take that ridge line just on the other side of that creek down in the bottom. I'm sure there will be a lot of Union troops in those woods waiting for us."

Lane reacted as directed. As he approached the center of the Regiment. He noted nearly the entire Regiment was laying prone on the open ground awaiting instructions to reinforce and attack to the front.

He noted the cannon fire had caused some minor casualties, but the 26th Regiment was ready to rise and move forward on command.

The Company Commanders all ran to Lane's position to receive their orders. "Gentlemen, all hell is breaking loose up there. The Colonel believes we are soon to be pushed forward along the right flank. Companies A, B, C, D, and E, you will move online, in rank order, four ranks deep. The remainder of the companies will be similarly positioned right behind the forward companies by about a hundred yards back. Forward companies, if you see an opportunity to breach the enemy positions in mass, call for the reserve companies behind you. They will follow immediately. Watch for my signal. Are there any questions?"

Captain Brewer spoke, "Sir, do we know what's in those trees on the other side of the creek?"

"Stephen, I don't think we know for sure, but there is movement in there. Can't tell if it is part of the cavalry brigade to our front or infantry supporting the cavalry. Either way, it's going to be hard getting through there in formation. With our glasses, we can tell its thick woods and brush."

Lane offered a final comment, "Gentlemen, do your duty and inform your troops. God be with you all." Lane quickly mounted his horse and moved forward to find the 26th Regiment Commander.

Casualties for the forward brigades were beginning to grow to an unfavorable level. Most of the officers of Archer's Brigade had already been shot and wounded or dead. Davis's Brigade was nearly gone. Heth had to make a fateful decision. And he did.

Everyone in the 26th Regiment knew what was happening to the front. They had seen messengers running back and forth with the latest reports of the battle.

James laid prone on the ground watching everything happening around him as if it were moving, as his Momma would say, "Like pouring molasses on a cold Winter's day." Everything moved so slowly, he felt he could anticipate all its meaning.

Even General Lee found himself near the front with General Heth and General Hill in heated discussions. The Commanding General of the Army looked perturbed but never raised his voice for James to hear.

General Hill looked unconvinced, there was even a problem. He seemed sure the enemy could be wiped from the field ahead by the wave of his hand.

Heth looked apologetic and miserable. However, he offered General Lee to push onto Gettysburg with a push of both hands.

It was obvious to most of the soldiers, this day would be much different than most. The battle had been raging for hours and even the rain of last night and the boiling July Sun would not stop what was about to happen.

Lane raised his hand in the air and waved for the troops to move quickly forward. Both Burgwyn and Lane mounted and moved to the center to better lead the Regiment.

Colonel Burgwyn, still mounted, moved across the line of men as they rose to stand in the required formations as previously directed by Colonel Lane.

The Regimental Commander pulled his saber from the scabbard and reached for the Sun with it. "Steady boys, steady." He then dismounted from his horse and gave the reins to one of his aides.

"Color Guard, bring forward the Colors." Burgwyn commanded. The Color Guard Sergeant, Jefferson B. Mansfield, brought the regimental colors forward with the flag guidon flowing with the breeze.

He then turned to the Regiment, "Follow me to the enemy. Follow these colors. Do not let these colors fall and we will win this day!"

The 26th Regiment shouted out in unison, "King, King, King!!" A tear formed in the "Boy Colonel's" eye.

Most of these men were the same men that he first met in the training camp near Raleigh, North Carolina in late May 1861. Some of them even had suggested he should not be the Commander of this very Regiment.

But now, they would do exactly as he commanded, or die trying. That was how much they trusted him and even loved him for it, to the man.

Lieutenant Emerson found James in the second rank, "James, Captain Brewer wants you and Henry to move to the end of the rank. Soon as you can, he wants you to find a place to put that damned rifle to work."

"Yes Sir." James quickly grabbed Henry by his jacket, and they moved to the right end of the rank.

"Henry, Captain Brewer wants us to find a good place where we can get a closer look at the creek. Seems to think we can do more good as sharpshooters as we can with the muskets." Henry nodded and started pulling his rifle out and slinging the musket onto his back.

James recognized the place they had slept the previous night. They had been moved to the rear and he was beginning to recognize places where he might be able to best position himself forward.

He saw the place where the pickets had been set. He saw the small grove of trees just off the Chambersburg Pike. He thought that might be as good a place for Henry as any and he nodded over to his fellow sharpshooter. "How about there?"

"Yep, that'll do." Henry immediately left the rank and ran to the trees and started climbing the very tree they had discussed the day before.

Some of the men of Company E saw James and Henry moving to the right. Several cheered at the two sharpshooter's running to their respective positions. One yelled, "Kill 'em all James!!" Others cheered them onward.

James let his attention wander to the countryside on the right side of the formation. Company E was on the far-right flank, and he was looking for a similar position, as Henry was now occupying.

He noticed a little high ground with a single tree with a nice fork in the center. A short climb up some low limbs would be easy to put him into action.

His only concern was the foliage and whether it would interfere with his ability to sight the weapon onto targets. The 26th Regiment's best sharpshooter would worry about that when he got there.

Union pickets were suddenly encountered almost immediately as they approached in front of the depression leading to the creek below. After firing an initial volley, the pickets were quickly moving into the depression and trying to cross the creek below.

While looking through the scope, James saw the distinctive tall black hats on the heads of the Union troop pickets and thought, what unusual headgear.

By then, Company E had stopped, and the first rank of soldiers prepared to fire at the retreating soldiers. The blast of noise and white smoke cleared and several of the pickets had been hit by the mass of fire. The next ranks moved forward on Captain Brewer's command and returned to a quick step march.

At that very moment, the Color Sergeant had fallen from a wound. Another soldier ran forward and gathered the colors in his hands to prevent it from falling to the ground.

Suddenly there was a massive fire from the woods just past the creek bed. The white smoke rolled out of the woods and another color bearer fell dead, the staff for the colors still in his hand.

The color guard was replaced by another soldier of the Regiment and Colonel Burgwyn kept leaning forward with the colors nearly beside him. He continued to march the Regiment right up to the depression in front of the creek. There he stood resolutely and ordered the entire front line of five companies to fire in mass.

The companies did as they were ordered, and they fired a massive volley into the wood line. Several of the black-hatted soldiers fell into view. Seeing the results and the subsequent revealing of the enemy positions, Colonel Burgwyn ordered another volley into the wood line.

The results were similar and more of the black hats fell. Burgwyn also saw the 26th Regiment being peppered with great affect by other black hats.

By this time, there had been no less than ten color guard bearers to have been wounded or shot dead. Yet, Colonel Burgwyn had not sought shelter from the fire.

Every man who saw him that day was overwhelmed with pride. They were already in hell, so he didn't need to order them to go anywhere. They just kept moving forward following their 'King.'

Burgwyn had the next rank move forward and fire another volley. Once that rank fired, he moved the next rank forward and gave the command to charge the woods.

By this time, the Regiment had moved a nearly one thousand yards from their initial position early that morning. Burgwyn knew the enemy had to be cleared of those woods across the stream. His order to charge was met by another massive round of fire from the woods.

With the command to charge, it was every man for himself. The men knew the drill: move forward, find the enemy, and kill him. Reload, find the enemy, and kill him. Don't let anything stop you.

With the command to charge, James began to search for a good location to put his rifle into action. There was a tree to his right, a large rock was beneath it, probably put there by a farmer that needed it removed from his field so he could plant his crops on this very ground.

He jumped behind the rock at first to start spotting enemy fire. His position gave him the ability to fire over his own fellow soldiers without fear of hitting them by accident.

As the 26th Regiment troops started to surge forward into the depression leading to the creek, James was provided with a number of targets. He just needed to take his time and not give his position away to an enemy sharpshooter like himself.

He began the process of selecting the most dangerous or commanding targets and put the rifle to work. Black hats were dropping at regular intervals for several minutes. As best he could tell, he had prevented several of the Company E troops from being killed during the charge.

By then, the charge had turned into a melee. It truly was every man for himself. Each man just kept moving forward. In some instances, they did not have time to reload but just attacked the enemy swinging the butt of their musket.

The group surrounding Colonel Burgwyn had thinned out considerably. The threat of being killed if they grabbed the colors was not lost on anyone that reached for those colors.

None other than Sergeant Major Montford McRae found himself reaching for the colors as another color bearer had fallen. He was mortally wounded and would soon die from the wounds.

James, seeing Montford McRae fall, knew what was about to happen and screamed as loud as he could, "Noooooo!"

The entire Regiment seemed to gather unbound strength and courage through nothing more than anger, resentment, and revenge for the loss of Montford McRae from North Carolina.

Many thought they would push those dreaded black hats to hell if necessary. They were that mad.

James continued for a few more moments at this current location but he saw the problem the boys from Company E were having just getting down to the creek, crossing it, and then getting up the bank of the creek to the woods above the creek.

The terrain was miserable. The thicket leading down the bank to the creek was covered with blackberry bushes. The thorns were so thick, they created a natural fence.

The soldiers were literally tearing their uniforms apart to get through the thicket. All this occurring while still fighting the black hats on the other side.

Worse than the briar thicket was the absolute horrendous fire being placed on the Regiment from near point-blank range. Even while in the creek or climbing the steep banks, the men of the 26th Regiment kept firing in volleys back at the enemy.

Men on both sides were falling faster than men could move forward to replace them in the line. Somehow Burgwyn kept pulling the men forward.

The Commander was everywhere, keeping order in the chaos of war. Keeping the men online. Always moving forward, even if at a greatly reduced speed.

From a distance, James could see an officer from Pettigrew's staff charging to the front lines. It was obvious that he was trying to get to Colonel Burgwyn with a message.

Not long after, the rider's horse was shot out from under him, and he was seen asking for assistance. He then moved through the creek, up the side of the thicket of briars and hand-clawed his way up the steep embankment.

At this point, James was about to have a problem with firing at the enemy without possibly firing into his own troops. He knew it was time to move to another location.

James worked his way to his right and found some higher ground that eventually let him move around to the right where the briars were not as prevalent.

He succeeded in getting to the other side with minimal damage to his uniform and equipment, but blood did flow from his hands and fingers.

The most recent color bearer for the 26th Regiment was none other than Captain Westwood McCreery of General Pettigrew's staff. The Captain had been sent by Pettigrew to give 'King' the message, "your regiment has covered itself in glory this day."

The colors had been momentarily lying on the ground having just then being lost by the latest color bearer, Lieutenant George Wilcox of Company H. Wilcox had only gone forward two steps when hit.

Lieutenant Colonel Lane, coming from the far-right flank of the Regiment informed the Commander that the Regiment was online and ready to push forward with the colors.

Private Franklin Honeycutt of Company B had been most recently assigned the deadly task of carrying the regimental colors. He too, barely made two steps when a massive volley of fire came from the woods along McPherson's Ridge.

Colonel Burgwyn quickly shared the message from General Pettigrew to Colonel Lane. Colonel Henry King Burgwyn, Jr. then retrieved the fallen colors and stood with the surviving half of the flag guidon in his hand, "Dress on the colors!! Follow me!!"

The "Boy Colonel" of the South fell to his mortal wound with the regimental colors still in his hand.

From his position on the right flank, James saw it unfolding. He was helpless. There was nothing he could do to stop it. He had failed his Commander. The Commander, ten years his junior, would never see his family again.

James immediately searched the woods to see where the bullet was fired. He saw the sharpshooter in the woods near a forked tree hidden from view when coming up the hill as the Company E had traveled. He raised the Leonard Rifle up ready to fire.

The Union sharpshooter saw James as well and was trying to quickly reload so that he might get James as a bonus for killing the Commanding Officer of the 26th Regiment.

James was as calm as he had ever been when preparing for a shot. The man on the other side of the creek knew he had a short time to reload and was hurrying the process along.

Private James Ward, sharpshooter, for the 26th Regiment, lowered his eye to the rifle scope. He firmly pulled the stock onto his shoulder. He estimated the range at about six hundred yards. He brought the hammer back and locked it into place. He caressed the trigger without pulling it too far, and he waited.

The Union sharpshooter was nearly finished loading and was about to raise the weapon when he realized he was too late. He looked directly at

James, merely extended his arms out from his body like a cross, and he closed his eyes.

James accommodated the man by placing the rifle ball right into his heart. He then whispered, "Lord, please forgive me." And then he spit on the ground.

In retrospect, James was not so sure he meant it for the first time in his life.

At that moment, it seemed the shout on the entire battlefield was, "King is dead! King is dead! King is dead!"

Lieutenant Colonel Lane was now the Commander, and he too took the colors in hand and charged up the hill to within thirty-five yards of the retreating enemy. It was at this point that Colonel Lane took a shot to the neck, through his jaw, tongue, and front teeth.

He was the last to hold the colors that day in battle as the enemy was in full retreat at McPherson's Ridge, just outside of the small town of Gettysburg, Pennsylvania.

Though terribly depleted with more than half of the Regiment dead or wounded, the 26th Regiment continued to move forward driven by Colonel Burgwyn's last command and his memory, "…your regiment has covered itself with glory today."

What was left of the Regiment moved forward with revenge and murderous intent.

The black hats and their supporting units died in the creek, the briar thickets, the woods, or disappeared into the ether. Either way, the 26th Regiment was past Willoughby Creek, through those damned woods, and well headed to the top of McPherson's Ridge.

James had finally worked himself back toward the center of the advancing 26th Regiment and found a good spot to watch the Union troops continue their retreat.

With the straggling members of the 26ᵗʰ still spilling through the woods and trying to reorganize what was left of their force, James decided he was not going to engage with the enemy unless the right target presented himself, especially with no support for himself.

As best he could recollect, he was not far from the tree where he had shot the Union sharpshooter. He thought about looking for the man but thought it unwise to make himself seen.

Instead, the spot where he chose gave him a pretty good view of the cleared area atop McPherson's Ridge. He had been there for several minutes looking for enemy targets.

He looked back and saw the devastated scene where the Regiment had charged into the woods. His heart skipped a beat.

His canteen was nearly empty, and he thought of returning to the creek to refill it. But he thought better of it and remained in the same concealed position in the trees.

Only moments later a group of officers and staff arrived within three hundred yards of James' position. They were busy reading maps, pointing in different directions, and plotting strategies.

James eased his rifle up to his chest. The foliage of the tree did a good job of concealing his position, but he did not want any sudden movements that might draw attention.

As he drew the scoped rifle to his shoulder and eye, he could see stars on the officer's collar. That would be a target he most assuredly would be willing to endanger himself to engage.

With nearly no hesitation, he eased the hammer back, pulled the stock into the shoulder again, took an easy breath, eased the finger gently to the trigger, took another breath, held it, and fired.

The officer's horse reared up and threw the man down. James did not move with the hope that his rifle smoke would be seen as only part of the drifting smoke throughout the battlefield.

Officers and soldiers all quickly checked for a pulse and found none. Others were searching the wood line for the assassin of Major General John Reynolds, Commander of the Union Army's First, Third, and Eleventh Corps.

Once past McPherson's Ridge, only Seminary Ridge stood between the 26th Regiment and the town of Gettysburg. It was there that Confederate Third Corps Commander General A.P. Hill would move more divisions forward to enter the town.

What was left of the Regiment returned to the other side of Willoughby Run. There, they would assess their losses and recover from the bloodiest day yet. Malvern Hill was not even an afterthought any longer.

Two Privates of the 26th Regiment of North Carolina troops held a blanket as a litter and carried the still living body of their Commander. Another soldier offered his help as well on the trip back toward Herr's Ridge.

In the process, another man helped, but no one recognized the man from the 26th Regiment. Burgwyn was able to ask for assistance and asked for his wound to be cleansed with water from a canteen.

The four men did so and removed the Colonel's jacket. They were washing the wound when the stranger reached for Burgwyn's prized watch strung from his neck by a ribbon. The man took it and started walking away.

One of the men from the 26th Regiment raised his musket and ordered the man to return the watch, or he would kill him on the spot. The man reluctantly returned the watch and the others demanded he leave.

Captain Louis Young, a very dear friend of Burgwyn and Captain Brewer arrived where they had stopped to address the wound.

Young was able to share several moments of joy and sadness with the young commander. No one, including Colonel Burgwyn, thought he was going to survive his wounds.

In the waning moments of his life, Henry King Burgwyn Jr. only thought of his men. He insisted that General Pettigrew be informed in his report, "Tell the General my men never failed me at a single point."

A flask of brandy was pulled from Colonel Burgwyn's jacket, and they shared a brief communion. His final words were whispered, "The Lord's will be done."

For the rest of the day, the battle and war were somewhere else other than on top of Herr's Ridge.

For those men of the 26th Regiment that survived the day, medical details were immediately deployed to retrieve the many men that were wounded, the still bodies of the dead were gathered for accountability, and finally the instruments of war that were scattered over the battlefield were salvaged to be used again.

Over eight hundred men were available for duty on the start of the day. When the battle ended for the 26th Regiment on that same day, only two hundred and twelve men were not wounded or dead. The records would show the next day that over five hundred and eighty-eight men were dead or wounded.

James Ward's Company E had only nine men, Including James and Henry left unwounded. The next day's roll call was a dismal sight with mere small sections or squads that stood in their regimental positions. Privates were now Acting Sergeants or even Lieutenants. Lieutenants were now Acting Captains. A Major was now Acting Colonel of the Regiment.

After roll call, the remaining officers and men began the task of their first official act, burying the dead in supposedly temporary, and unmarked graves. It would be a long day. Only three of nine available company commanders were left unwounded or dead. Fourteen junior officers were wounded or killed.

As bad as it was for the 26th Regiment, the very same Union black hat regiments of the Iron Brigade were even worse. The 24th Michigan had over eighty percent killed or wounded. The 19th Indiana suffered a seventy-three percent casualty rate. Nearly all those dead and wounded were directly engaged where the 26th Regiment hit them at McPherson's Ridge.

James sat by a tree on Herr's Ridge. He was mentally lost. His physical being only seemed to operate because that was what the body was supposed to do.

His thirst and hunger just did not seem to matter to him. The tragedy seemed to corrupt everything. He just could not move.

Henry leaned against a similar tree about ten feet away from James. "James, we got to get something to eat."

He pulled himself up from the tree and moved over to James. "James, please get up. You can't just stop. You're going to rot inside if you don't get up."

James looked up at Henry kneeling beside him, with his hand held out for James to take it. "I'm not sure Henry. Help me understand why I should keep going. We're all going to die on this battlefield. How do we answer God when He asked, "Why did you do it?""

"I don't know James, but I do know that I am not going to just die because someone else tries to kill me. Not sure God's going to be happy with me just letting someone end a life He has given to us." Henry paused.

He continued, "Do it for your family. Do it for your wife. Do it for that child she is about to give you. Do it for that farm you dream about all the time. Those people over there are trying to tell you how to raise your family and your farm. What are you going to do about that?"

James let his head hang down. He was trying hard to make sense of it all. He was failing miserably.

"Please James, get up and let's go eat. We haven't had anything for nearly twenty-four hours. You need rest so you can think straight." Henry stood in front of James waiting for an answer.

"I'll go. Not sure how much I can eat. But I'll go." James crawled on all his hands and knees, from the tree trunk, and stood up. He followed Henry to the cook kettle to see what was ready.

There was no 26th Regimental Band playing that night. Chief Musician S. L. Mickey and his band were too busy assisting the Regimental Surgeon and his staff with the wounded.

Malvern Hill was no longer the benchmark for the 26th Regiment. The date July 1, 1863, just moved the bar higher than ever before.

* * * * *

July 3, 1863

To Private James Ward, Company E, 26th Regiment, Pettigrew's Brigade, Heth's Division, Hill's Corps, Army of the Confederacy

Dear Son,

I wish to tell you that we are praying for you and Stephen as you receive this Letter. I am sure this grand movement into the North is significant, but we want you home as soon as possible.

Your father is beside himself with worry about you both, but he holds it inside. He is quick to temper and the children and grandchildren fear being around him.

Anna Wallace is still progressing well with the child and the Doctor is most happy with her preparations for the joyful day. He thinks it might be mid-July. Perhaps you will be back from the North by then.

I know Anna Wallace has been frequently writing letters to you, but I wanted to just share the news that recent reports from the North have been posted in the newspaper and on the courthouse wall. Your father tries to avoid it as best he can.

For the limited fields we have worked this season, it has been a good year. However, we are being levied frequently by the State government and the Confederate government for our crops, livestock, and taxes. I am not sure of how we can pay all of it and survive ourselves.

The Home Guard continues to be a nuisance here and about. The Governor says he is taking care of the troublemakers but we're not seeing much of that happening here.

Well, know that we love you and pray often. Come home safe and sound as you can. But knowing that we want you home anyway we can get you here.

With love and devotion, I am your mother,

Mrs. Louise Martin Ward

CHAPTER 13

DAY OF REST, JULY 2, 1863

The chaos for the 26th Regiment on the previous day made sleeping that night more difficult. Exhaustion had overcome those that survived, and for the rest of the Regiment, there was pain, suffering, and death continuing to fall throughout the camp on Herr's Ridge.

James struggled to get to sleep and when he did, there would be the occasional soldier calling someone's name out as they were searching for him in the dark to awaken him for picket duty.

Henry had finally gotten James to eat something and had been to the creek multiple times to fill James' canteen with fresh water. James was suffering from dehydration and had difficulty even pissing.

When James finally slept, he dreamed. The dreams were more like nightmares of the previous day. Henry woke beside him each time James stirred from a dream. Once, James even screamed.

Captain Brewer had found both Henry and James and hugged them where they sat by the fire. "Men, I can't begin to tell you how much you meant to the Regiment today. You saved lives that didn't even know it."

James seemed distant but he did respond to the Captain, "Sir, not enough. I didn't see the man soon enough. King is dead because I didn't see the bastard in that damned tree."

"No James that was not your fault. Even the Colonel was proud of you boys yesterday. If King were here right now, he would say the same thing he said to us when he died in Captain Young's arms, 'The Lord's will be done.' His death was out of your hands. God knows that."

James was not necessarily in agreement with the Captain, but he said nothing else. He rolled back into the bed roll and tried to sleep again.

As it always does, the Sun rose for another July day in Pennsylvania. Most men were like James, trying hard to overcome the grief of loss of others and suffering the guilt of still being alive.

His first thought that morning was to thank God for one more day. He was not sure God was listening, but it seemed to be the right thing to do.

Henry was sitting by the fire after throwing another small piece of wood into the small blaze. James saw him sitting there, eating a piece of hardtack in one hand and an apple in the other.

James couldn't tell any difference in Henry's demeanor that morning than from any other day the two had marched together.

His regimental friend glanced over to where James crawled out of his bed roll. "Glad to see you awake James. You had a fitful night for sure. Thought I might let you sleep in for a spell."

"Yeah, not much rest to be had last night. Too many dreams. Any food back by the Commissary?" James finished getting up and walked to the edge of the fire and extended his hands for warmth in the misty early morning.

He thought about his actions and considered the notion that he felt cold even though the temperature was already in the eighties.

"Yep, pretty good spread over there. The Sergeant got plenty, he says. Not as many to feed today, I guess." Henry realized what he said and was afraid that it would upset James even worse.

James looked at him and he too realized that hundreds of the men of the 26th Regiment would take the bread of communion in a better place this day. "Yeah, I guess he would know. I'm going to wander over and see if I can find something to settle my stomach."

"James, stay away from the Surgeon's area. They don't need any help and you're not going to find many of the boys from Company E. They already being taken care of if you know what I mean." Henry lowered his head and began eating his apple.

"Yeah, I'm thinking the same." James was beginning to realize the tragedy of yesterday and the resulting consequences were going to be felt for some time. Time may heal the wounds, but the memories of others would linger for as long as one lives. James was sure of it.

"You see Stephen this morning?"

Henry didn't even turn to look back at James, "Yeah, he was by here a couple of times last night and early this morning checking on you. Said something about we're getting time to reorganize and prepare for battle tomorrow maybe. Promised he'd be back later this morning." Henry leaned back and looked at James.

"They say Colonel Lane may not make it. Might die before the day is over." He turned back toward the fire.

"Who's in charge of the Regiment?" James asked.

"Stephen told me Major Johnnie Jones was commanding but others think it might be temporary. The boy is only a little older than King was. Sure, General Pettigrew will have something to say about that. Oh, by the yonder, Pettigrew's taken over for General Heth. Seems the General got hurt as well. Most think Heth will survive though.

James was already at the cook station and getting some eggs, a slice of fatback, a hardtack biscuit, put some butter and grape jam on the bread, and grabbed a couple of apples.

Instead of going back to his gear, James found a stump nearby and settled in to eat breakfast. He looked across the camp and could see Lieutenant Emerson heading his way.

As the Lieutenant approached, James noticed a bandage wrapped tightly around his left arm, just below the elbow. "Good morning, Lieutenant, I hope you don't mind if I don't get up and salute. Not sure I got the strength to do it. No disrespect intended, of course." James was barely able to give a slight smile.

"Private Ward that will not be necessary. Civility takes a poor place beside survival. And saluting around here just might get a sharpshooter's attention, way too easy. I'd appreciate it if you just kept eating." The twenty-four-year-old Lieutenant kneeled on one knee in front of James.

"Captain Brewer was worried about you James. Said he wanted us cadre to visit you anytime we could work it out." He paused.

"The Captain said you did some unbelievable things yesterday with that rifle. Kept talking about how many of our boys were about to be shot by the Yankees and you got a shot in to stop it. Even said he was close for done when a bullet whizzed right by his head and killed a Union soldier getting ready to bayonet him. The old man says he owes you, his life."

James just kept eating his meal. "I don't really recall the shot. Took so many yesterday. They gave me lots of targets. Sometimes I got confused on trying to select the best targets. Near the end, just kept shooting."

After putting his empty tin plate on the ground, he looked down at the Lieutenant still kneeling on the ground. "John, the only two shots that I can really remember is the sharpshooter that shot the Colonel. The other one was the shot I made on him."

"Several of the boys said something about that one. Private Setzer said the Yankee just stood there with his arms spread. Why would he do that?" Lieutenant Emerson inquired with a quizzical look on his face.

James only paused for a moment and then began, "Sharpshooters know what's on the other side. Someone with a weapon like mine can kill them if they make a mistake. He knew he made a mistake and knew he could never reload fast enough after that last shot. He gave me the one shot he wanted me to make. Wide open to the heart."

He paused again, "I obliged him. I'm assuming he was ready to meet his maker. I could see his eyes closed and him praying. I hope he got where he needed to go."

"Where do you think that was James?"

"Don't know. I'll let God sort it out. He was doing his job and I was doing mine. Pretty sure the good Lord will judge me about the same, either way." James stood up and started to take his tin plate to the Mess Sergeant.

"Captain Brewer would like to have you stop by the company headquarters tent when you're able but before Noon time."

Lieutenant Emerson looked at his pocket watch. "You got a couple of hours. Stephen will come by to find you."

Stephen showed up just before Noon and he found James cleaning his weapon after getting resupplied with the valuable ammunition.

Once again, the supply trains had an abundance of ammunition for him. James immediately thought, "Not that many left to be resupplied with ammunition either."

"Caught your breath yet cousin?" Stephen had that silly grin on his face, again.

James had to chuckle at the boy's face. "Yeah, I think I'm all right. What you and the Captain got on my mind?"

"I'm just here to request your presence at the company tent by Noon. Seems there's a big push going to happen today. Looks like on both flanks. Lots of people talking like this is going to be the big one to win it."

Stephen reached down and grabbed James' other apple and began to eat it.

"Well, Private Ward, go get your own damn breakfast, if you, so please. And I'll be ready to head to the headquarters in about five minutes. Just got to wrap everything up. Do I need to bring anything in particular?" James continued wiping down the Leonard Rifle and scope.

Stephen responded, "Well, Private Ward, I suggest you bring what the good Captain Brewer usually wants you to bring. That fancy rifle would be on that list, I believe."

Stephen put the apple core down on the stump and took off at a run back toward the company headquarters area.

James grabbed the apple core and threw it at Stephen, hitting him in the back of the head before he could go ten feet.

Later, Captain Brewer began speaking after surveying the health of both men, "James, Henry, the 26th Regiment is out of this foray today. We're trying to figure out how to consolidate troops and officers and maintain the unit. We lost a lot to both wounded and dead as you well know."

Captain Brewer paused, "Before I go on, how are the two of you right now? Your heads in a good place?"

Henry was quick to nod in the affirmative, James was a little slower in his response. He wanted to find out what this meeting was about before declaring his worth for battle.

"Good to hear. You men know how much we think of you and what you do. Here's what I know and what I can tell you. I will say, General Pettigrew has already been asked and agreed to this request, unless either of you say no." Brewer paused for their reaction.

Hearing no response from either man, Captain Brewer continued. "Very good. There is to be two large attacks. Both are to occur on the flanks of the army. Ewell's Corps is attacking to the East around the area of Culps Hill, here on the map."

After pointing to the map, he continued, "The other attack is a big push by General Longstreet's Corps over here in the East and trying to roll their flank from the East to the West. Kind of like they did at Chancellorsville."

Brewer continued, "I think the move on the West side is more to hold the Federal forces in place and the more important attack is for Longstreet's Corps."

"Sir, what's that got to do with me and Henry?" James asked.

"Good question, James. Right now, they think the sharpshooters can do a lot of harm to the limited forces near the big hill tops over here. Thought is controlling that high ground and you can lay artillery on the Yankees all the way to Washington."

Captain Brewer pointed to the map again and added, "With the open peach orchard here, the wheat fields here, and the rocky high ground here, they seem to think you can get some good long-range shots in support for their push."

As if sensing an issue, Brewer quickly added, "There is no expectation that the two of you will engage with the attacking units. You are to find targets and engage where practical. Once they finish the attack, you return to us."

Both Henry and James looked at each other. Probably to confirm that neither had an issue with the orders, so far.

"Tell us who to report to Sir, and we'll get our stuff together. Looks like a pretty good hike to get to General Longstreet's area if they're going to attack today." James continued to study the map.

"I believe that Major General John B. Hood is the man to report to. He and General McLaws are the two principal divisions in the attack." The Captain paused.

"I'll do you one better. I've got two horses for you to take to their location. Keep them and bring them back, please!" Captain Brewer had a slight smile on his face.

James and Henry immediately came to attention and saluted Captain Brewer proper, "Yes Sir!"

They turned and left to retrieve their other gear. After retrieving the remaining gear, they returned to the headquarters tent once again. Two horses were tied in front of the tent.

Captain Brewer came out of the tent and handed James an envelope. "James, these are your orders. If anyone asked you to join their lines, you must refuse them and show them these orders. I have this straight from General Pettigrew."

James took the envelope and briefly read the orders. "Yes Sir, we'll do you and the General proud Sir."

Brewer also offered, "General Pettigrew is doing this as a courtesy to General Hood. They are acquaintances and Pettigrew bragged about you men. General Hood is a little concerned about today's attack and he seemed to think your prowess with the rifle might be handy. Henry, I know the two of you work well together so I took the liberty of sending you both."

Henry responded with a sense of pride, "Like James said Sir, we'll do you proud."

It was a long ride to get to the rear of General Longstreet's Corps. They were stopped numerous times by pickets and James was required to show the orders. However, no one questioned their authenticity.

It was close to one thirty when they finally found General Lee, General Longstreet, and General Hood in conversation beneath some trees looking toward the Northeast.

James figured it was not the right time to introduce themselves to General Hood and they agreed to wait until the generals were finished with their conversation.

The conversation was quite animated, and James was sure General Lee was not particularly happy. The general finally pulled himself onto the big dapple-gray horse they called Traveler and spurred him away.

That conversation was followed by another more tense conversation between Hood and Longstreet. James and Henry waited on horseback until Hood mounted and started away.

James spurred his horse to catch up with General Hood and did so after a hundred yards. The general's staff looked perplexed by the two riders following them and pulled up forcing James and Henry to come to a stop.

"Who the hell are you boys?" a Captain asked.

James saluted from the saddle, "Sir, Private Ward and Private Rogers reporting to General Hood as ordered by General Pettigrew, Sir. Here are our orders Sir." James pulled the envelope from his jacket and passed it to the Captain.

General John Bell Hood sauntered back to the staff to inquire of the reason for the delay. The Captain passed the orders to the General. "Sir, looks like someone offered you some sharpshooters, Sir."

"Hell yes! J.J. Pettigrew's been bragging about you boys! Come on men, we'll get you situated. We got a hell of problem, and you might just be handy in this mess." General Hood passed the orders back to James and spurred his horse.

"Better ride fast, the General doesn't usually wait for anybody." The Captain and staff all spurred their horses to a full canter.

James and Henry did as well.

After the relatively short ride toward the North, General Hood dropped from the saddle with a pair of binoculars in hand. He eased up to a small stand of hardwood trees and pointed to the West.

"That there is the Emmitsburg Road. You see them two big hills up to the East?" The General waited for an answer.

James spoke for both men, "Yes Sir."

Hood then pointed slightly to the Northeast, "See that orchard over there? I think it might be a peach orchard but can't really tell from here." The General continued to look toward the spot he indicated as he handed the glasses to James.

James looked into the glasses, "Yes Sir. That's a peach orchard for sure. Looks like there might be a wheatfield just behind it, Sir?"

"You're right son. There is a wheatfield behind it and we're going to try to move through that as quick as practical with our main force. But we're also going to drive up to the right of that big bunch of rocks to get to that big hill on the right." Hood put the binoculars into their leather holster.

He turned to both James and Henry, "Boys, I'm concerned about two things, those damned big rocks up there are going to be an issue. Troops won't be able to maneuver through them in formation. We lose strength that way. I'm guessing a few Union sharpshooters, like yourselves, might be up there, as well."

Hood continued, "My boys are telling me there is a lot of activity in those rocks. They also tell me there is not any troops on that big hill up there. Hard to believe but they swore on their mother's heart there wasn't any troops up there to give us trouble."

"Sir, if you could let me see that map of yours, that might help." James responded.

The Captain quickly pulled out a map and laid it on the ground. The officers all went to a knee with James and Henry as they looked at the map.

James looked from the map and to the two locations that General Hood had provided as his greatest concerns, "Henry, you think you might be able to deal with those rocks with your rifle. I'm thinking somewhere between that fork in that creek right there." He pointed to the water symbol on the map for Plum Run.

Henry was quick to answer, "Yep, that's about right for my range James. I'm guessing I'll have to wade through those trees first."

"I'm thinking you let the first wave get into the woods and clear out any pickets. Then find yourself the best place to cover those big rocks." James added and Henry nodded.

"Sir, with your permission, I'm thinking I can move to the right and through the woods to that big hill. If it is really empty, I can make my way over toward the slightly smaller hill. From what I see from here, I should be able to get some shots off to the North onto the units around those rocks and maybe the orchard or wheat fields." James looked at the General for confirmation.

"Private, that would be a hell of a long shot. You really think you can pull that off?" Hood was not completely convinced.

Henry spoke for James, "Sir if James can see it, he can shoot it. That leather wrap he has on the horse there is the righteous hand of God on this green earth."

James slightly lowered his head in embarrassment, "Sir, I can hit most targets that present themselves to me. I'm afraid, you'll have to trust me on that."

Hood did not hesitate, "If J. J. Pettigrew says you're as good as he said, I believe you son. Do the best you can. When you're finished with us, you return back to your unit. I promised General Pettigrew I would not try to keep you."

"Yes Sir. We'll do you proud as well." James said as he and Henry smartly saluted, and the General responded with a smile.

General Hood and his staff immediately got onto their horses and rode off to address other and more pressing concerns for the Division Commander.

"I'm thinking these boys got a little while before they jump off. Let's grab a bite to eat and fill our canteens. May be a long day." James pointed to a shaded area under the trees.

"Well, we can't ride these horses up the hill and through the woods. You think we can leave them here and they'll be here when we get back?" Henry offered.

James concurred with Henry's concern whether the horses would be here when they finished their tasks. "Let's go in a little deeper where there are no troops. We'll just have to take the chance they'll still be here when we get back."

The two sharpshooters went into the woods and found a very small little clearing just large enough for the horses. Some of the limbs created a nice little corral. With a couple of yards of leather from James' Leonard Rifle wrap, they created a small corral door. They tied the horse reins to the trees.

They sat outside of the temporary corral and could see just enough of the Emmitsburg Road to know when the units would depart. However, they knew the artillery was the real start of the battle, as always.

It was a short meal of hardtack biscuits and an apple. They checked their weapons and ammunition. They then took a short rest against the trees.

At about three thirty in the afternoon, hell and chaos broke loose in the area, as artillery began its barrage onto the rocks, the orchard, and the two hills to the East.

James and Henry eased out toward the road to get a sense of where the main enemy positions were located by the direction of fire. By four o'clock the Confederate troops moved in mass toward the Peach Orchard just as General Hood had described it.

Good progress was being made toward the orchard and wheat field except there was more enemy there than Hood had estimated.

Where those troops came from nobody on the Confederate side knew, but they were having a dreadful effect on the advance.

Henry had made his way, as planned, and he soon found himself being decisively engaged. As suspected, there were Union sharpshooters located within the big rocks. He could see Confederate enlisted and officers already being targeted and taken down.

James had made his way to the right as planned and with no Union troops to be seen, he was able to get to the far right of Hood's attacking force. While getting up the big hill was strenuous, it was not much more than a long walk in the woods back home.

As he got near the crest of the big hill, the action to the North was becoming vicious. Each side was attacking and counterattacking, time after time. Reinforcements were being pushed into the line by both sides.

Henry did finally find a place where he could get some shots off. He focused his attention on the group of rocks. The closer he got, the more difficult for his ability to engage the enemy. He found himself looking at a maze of rocks. Every turn was a killing field, as small as the field was.

Henry had already dispatched four Union soldiers, but it was the two Union sharpshooters that were his most difficult targets. They hid themselves well and obviously were not firing at random targets. They were after Hood's officers and cadre.

It took some time, but Henry continued to work closer to get the shots he needed to take out the sharpshooters he could reach. After that, he continued to search for more targets and was successfully hitting most of his shots.

Henry saw a Union officer stand up on the top of one of the large rocks, a rock the size of a small house back in North Carolina. The officer held his pistol out ready to fire. He carefully raised his Whitworth Rifle and was about to pull the trigger when the man pitched forward and fell out of sight from his position on the rock. Henry immediately recognized the man had been shot from behind.

James had finally made it up the hill but to very little advantage. Seeing the tremendous forest of trees, he knew he had to move to another location. His first reaction was to move toward the smaller hill to the North.

There he saw pickets positioned close to the swell that sloped toward the smaller hill. With a single rifle, he was no match to take on a section of Union infantry by himself. He thought it strange to see no troops to the South of their position.

James whispered to himself, "could we be on the far-right flank of the entire Union Army?"

He continued to work his way toward the rocky area that General Hood found so concerning. When he finally got closer, he was able to pick out limited targets between trees.

From this position, he began to see Confederate troops moving up the hill and toward the smaller hill. He waved to them to get their attention. He pointed in the direction of the small section of Union infantry he had discovered.

The unit commander waved back and pointed his sword in that direction. The unit charged up the hill in mass, not knowing what was exactly there but he did seem to trust James knowing it was the enemy.

The new position actually provided James with two views. First, he could see the exchange with the Union force on the smaller hill. Second, he was able to see the rocky place and the targets of Hood's concern.

He watched as the Confederate units made attempt after attempt to take the little hill. James thought as he watched between shots of his own on the rocky place, the Confederate troops were very close to taking the hill.

Two of the last charges had resulted in hand-to-hand fighting between the foes. James was sure they only needed one more massive push to take the hill. He wanted to yell encouragement but knew that would only get himself killed.

As best he could recall, he had already hit six targets. He would have hit more but the trees were too thick for him to use the Leonard Rifle. He then thought, he wished he had brought his Whitworth Rifle with him.

By late afternoon, James realized the Union had held the small hill and he could do little else to help General Hood. He began to work his way back down the big hillside and hoped to work his way close to Henry's position down by the rocks.

As he got closer to where he had left Henry earlier that afternoon, he realized getting to Henry's original position would be dangerous. He made it across the Emmitsburg Road and worked his way toward the place where they left the horses.

"Wondering how long you were going to stay up there on that big hill." Henry pronounced as James came into view.

"Yeah, not able to do a lot up there. No real long shots like we thought. I tried to work my way over to you to help but looked like the Yankees were holding onto those rocks pretty good." James eased himself close to the ground.

Henry inquired, "What time you reckon it is?"

James pulled his watch from inside his jacket. "Looks like past five thirty."

"You think we should wait for General Hood? Or should we go on back to the Regiment?" Henry kept leaning on the tree.

"Looks like a lot of our boys are coming back across that road. I'm thinking the General's not going to be very happy if they didn't take those hills up there. Let's wait about another hour and if we don't see him, we'll head back. Besides, I'm tired of climbing up and down that hill." James fell to the ground and tucked his haversack under his head.

It was several minutes later that Henry gave James a nudge with his boot. "James, look at this."

James and Henry worked their way closer to the road. There, they saw some of General Hood's staff carrying him on a blanket and moving toward the rear.

"I'm guessing it's time for us to go home." Henry said as he turned and walked to the makeshift corral.

It only took five minutes to get everything packed up. From their position, they had to pass through nearly the entirety of General Longstreet Corps. It was a bloody mess.

James and Henry walked the horses slow. There was no hurry to work through the throng of wounded and dying. Both were reminded of just twenty-four hours ago and McPherson's Ridge. They mounted and spurred the horses into a trot to quickly leave the area.

They got about half-way back to the 26th Regiment's previous location when James saw a rider coming hard down the trail. He recognized Stephen in the saddle. The Ward cousin pulled the horse up quickly to a stop.

"Hey boys, Captain Brewer was concerned you boys might try to desert us! Said I was to bring you back double quick." Stephen had that grin on his face.

"Good to see you, Stephen. We were on our way back. Might want to be a little quieter. These boys been in a sausage grinder, kind of like we were yesterday." James whispered.

Stephen looked about and saw the troops helping others back to the rear. No one was taking the time to pay any attention to the three riders on the trail. "Sorry, didn't realize what was going on. They do look a bit shot up, though."

"Yeah, let's get on back to the Regiment. Seen enough of General Longstreet's Corps." James spurred the horse again and they continued to trot down the trail, trying hard not to notice what was happening around them.

* * * * *

July 8, 1863

To Private James Ward, Company E, 26th Regiment, Pettigrew's Brigade, Heth's Division, Hill's Corps, Army of the Confederacy

My Dearest Husband,

We hear and read so much about the Northern Campaign and its importance to the Confederacy's cause. I fear for your safety and the safety of our family.

My latest visit here at the farm by the Doctor was most pleasant in that I was informed the baby would probably be born very soon. Perhaps within the week. He had high praise for the position of the child and said it should be a smooth delivery. Given it is our first born, I am glad to hear those words.

Many in the family are speculating about it being a boy or girl. I, of course, want a boy for you. We can have girls for me later. We should make sure we have someone to carry on the family name, although, given the size of the entire Ward family I can't imagine how the Ward name could not be perpetuated.

Miz Lizzie has forbade me from doing any farm work and to travel no further than the bedroom, kitchen, and the privy for any reason. I must admit, it is very nice to be relieved of other duties. I feel as if I am a princess from a foreign land with servants to meet my every need. That will change with the baby's birth and your return. I have no doubt. We have a farm and family to build.

As for the farm, Mister Brice has actually sold a few acres of land to cover some of our expenses. I know that is something you don't want to hear.

However, with the reduction in crops to plant, harvest, and sell, he had to do it. You certainly know your father; he will incur no debt if at all practical.

We are comfortable. New cloth and materials to make clothes is very expensive. Everyone is doing their best to save but we're just running out of ways to make ends meet.

Well, enough about our small problems. You have enough to worry about for the whole world. I sincerely regret your having to listen to my whining and complaining. I sincerely promise not to ever do it again.

Know that I love you and cherish you. Please come home soon to our new child.

I am your most devoted and loving wife,
Anna Wallace Ward

Postscript: I have added an additional five pages of writing paper for your next letter.

CHAPTER 14

A LOUD SERENADE! JULY 3, 1863

Nighttime was coming fast as Stephen led the two sharpshooters to Herr's Ridge where the 26th Regiment was still trying to identify how badly they had suffered on the first day of battle. As they entered the camp, campfires were beginning to sprout in the darkness.

Even in July, the fires were invaluable. They were gathering places where lonely men, frightened men, even men that had thought they had seen the worst of humanity already, could sit and be warmed by the fire.

It was not the warmth of the fire they sought. It was the fear of the cold-hearted death about them that caused them to gather. They needed light from the darkness. For in the darkness, each man had to deal with his fear and perhaps, his shame.

No, it was not the warmth of the fire. It was the light they truly sought. They gathered because they needed each other. Men who shared the same real nightmares of war.

James and Henry quickly moved to their personal gear and gathered their things. Henry asked the Quartermaster, "Where's Company E situated tonight? I need something to eat and some sleep. I'm plumb tired."

The Quartermaster looked at him with a strange look on his face. "Son, I'm sorry to say there ain't much left of Company E. If'n you go about a hundred yards that way, I think you'll run into Captain Brewer. Not sure he's got much more than ten or so soldiers in the company."

James and Henry looked at each other in shock. When they had left that morning, to assist General Hood, they knew the killed and wounded total for their company was bad enough; but they struggled to believe the entire company was nearly gone.

They headed in the general direction the Quartermaster had pointed. Neither man wanted to ask the question, "Who is left?"

James saw Captain Brewer sitting on a stump close to another campfire. The company headquarters tent was all that reflected a company designation. The company flag was limp in the gentle breeze of the night.

James nudged Henry and headed in that direction.

Stephen Brewer had a coffee cup in his hands, and he nursed the cup like it was a prayer. He saw James and Henry coming in his direction and stood, "Don't even try to salute. Just damn glad to see you boys back." He sat back down, cup in hand.

"There's some fresh coffee in the pot there. Mess Sergeant got us a nice little stew going on the fire. Bread in that box over there." Brewer looked like a broken man to James.

Henry responded first, "Thank you Sir. Surely that's for the officer's and not for us."

The Captain gave a half smile, "I wish that were true Henry, but I'm down nearly every officer. Lieutenant Emerson is still alive. Did get a slight wound on his left foot though. Orren Hanner is still with us. Bill Lambert as well. Other than that, we're down to about twenty boys able to lift a musket. Picked up a few more from the Doctor today. No, you go ahead and eat Henry. We got plenty right now."

James was getting really agitated with that sentiment, "we got plenty because they're not that many to partake anymore." To him, it seemed to demean or belittle the men that were not there.

"Is it that bad all over the Regiment Sir?" James said as he laid his gear down.

"Pretty much. No doubt the companies to the center took the worst of it. Major Jones is telling us that we're being consolidated with some other regiments as well." Brewer kept nursing his tin cup of coffee.

"Does that mean we're not the 26th anymore?" James started to ladle some of the stew into a tin plate.

"Nope. Good news is the 26th Regiment is still functional. Some others in Heth's Division took some heavy losses and they're going to be moved into some of our units. They'll be part of the 26th Regiment. You know that Regiment 'that was covered in glory this day.'"

Brewer's comment regarding General Pettigrew's message to Colonel Burgwyn, just before he was shot, had both anger and pride in it. If anything, Brewer was unsure whether he should be proud or sad. The glory was just not very evident at that moment.

Captain Brewer seemed to recognize his own demeaner and suddenly sat up straight, "So, how was your work with General Hood today?"

James offered his report between each spoonful of stew. "Sir, the General put us where he thought we could do the most good. Really didn't have a lot to offer him for advice but his thoughts were pretty plain." He paused for another bite.

"Henry did a good job working in that part around them big rocks. General Hood said it was called the Devil's Den. Seeing how many men died there today, from both sides, I can see why they call it that." James grabbed a piece of bread and started sopping the juice from the stew.

"I worked my way around that big hill near the top. Got off a few shots but the terrain and those thick trees didn't give me a lot to work with. Nearly run into a bunch of Union boys about halfway down the little ravine between the hills." He paused again.

"You know Sir, I might be wrong, but I believe there wasn't another Yankee on the other side of that hill." James stopped and looked at his Captain.

Brewer stood up, "You mean to say you were on the absolute flank of the Union army? Why did General Hood not move around them?"

James looked down, "Can't really speak for the General Sir, but he was not particularly excited about how General Lee and General Longstreet wanted him to attack that high ground."

"What was Hood's reaction when he found that out?" Captain Brewer sat back down.

"Sir, General Hood was shot up pretty bad when we saw him last. By then, the attack was pretty much over. That's when me and Henry headed back here." James sat his plate down by the edge of the fire.

Brewer continued in a monotone voice, "Yeah, I heard that both flanks remained in Union hands at the end of the day. Well, you boys eat all you want. There are a couple of tents over by the trees. Use 'em and we'll see what happens in the morning."

Henry grabbed another plate of stew and James grabbed another piece of bread. He saw cheese near the fire and smeared some of it on his bread.

They wandered over to the tents and laid their gear inside one of them shaped like a shelter. Both men were tired and decided to split a shift of guard duty nearby. James took the first shift and was in bed by ten o'clock that night.

He was in a deep sleep for the first time in days. He dreamed this night, for the first time in weeks. This dream was not a nightmare of Gettysburg. It was a dream of home. He was able to recall a November day in 1862 while he was on furlough recovering from camp-inflicted dysentery. Anna Wallace and James were walking around their new home.

James remembered the etched glass that had arrived. He remembered it was placed into the front windowpane. He also remembered the Sun rising and coming into the house through the glass. It was breath-taking.

He remembered propping his head against his hand while looking at his sleeping wife. He caressed her body until she was aroused and awakened to find her husband smiling at her. They satisfied each other several times that morning.

His dream carried him out of the house and walking down by the stream near the Green Swamp. He remembered the air was slightly chilled and Anna Wallace had a shawl around her shoulders. He couldn't tell what, but he was sure she was different. He was about to ask her what was wrong.

A little after midnight, Henry entered the makeshift shelter and shook James by the shoulder. "James, get up. Gather your gear, we're moving out shortly."

James' hated Henry at that moment. His dream was cut off and he could not hear Anna Wallace's answer.

After shaking his head, he realized the noise going around the tents. It was the obvious sounds of Company E getting ready to move.

"What's going on? Where are we going?" James pondered the questions and shook his head to clear the grogginess from his brain.

Henry responded as he continued to gather a couple more pieces of equipment and placed them over his shoulder, "Can't give the particulars right now. Captain just said to rouse the men up and get ready to move out. Said something about going over to that big ridge over to the East. I think he said it was Seminary Ridge."

James moved quickly and gathered his own gear. He rolled his bed roll and tied off the leather binding straps. He crawled out of the shelter and grabbed the ropes holding it between the two trees.

Once the shelter was gathered and rolled, he placed it into his larger bag. He gathered the haversack and canteen around his neck and off of his right shoulder.

With everything on his shoulders, in his hands, and off his back, James stood straight up to balance the load. He looked around and the few people that were left of Company E seemed as unsure about what was happening as he felt.

What was more concerning was the number of people from Company E that were missing at yesterday's roll call that had suddenly reappeared. Many of those faces he recognized right away.

It was obvious that Captain Brewer had been tasked to gather everyone from the field hospital that would walk, carry a musket, and able to fire the weapon. Nearly everyone from the original Company E, retrieved from the Surgeon's care, was present that night with at least one bandage clearly marking a wound. Several had more than one wound, some of those still bleeding.

James was also surprised to see several men that were unrecognizable, getting into the Company E ranks and preparing for the march.

First Sergeant James Brooks was moving about the area organizing the troops and preparing for the march.

"First Sergeant, any idea where we are heading and what we need to prepare for?" James stood in front of the senior sergeant for Company E.

"Wish I could tell you James, but the Captain just said to get you boys up and ready. Said he would be back shortly with more instructions." He paused for a moment.

"James, could you help me get these new boys in the ranks. Try to calm them down a little. They ain't seen anything quite like this before tonight."

"I surely will First Sergeant. Can you tell me where they are from?" James was looking over to the new faces that shown in the night campfire light.

Sergeant Brooks replied, "Mostly boys from North Carolina. Not from our Regiment though. Others are from a Virginia bunch left over from yesterday's fight."

Sergeant Brooks stood up and surveyed the company for a final look, "Someone got the notion we could just jam these new boys into the middle of the ranks, and they would know what to do."

James nodded in the weak light, "I guess they're going to get a lesson real quick."

Suddenly, out of the darkness, James saw Stephen Ward walking toward First Sergeant Brooks. Both turned to face Stephen.

"Morning James, First Sergeant!" He had that silly grin on his face again.

Pulling his pocket watch from his coat, James checked the time. It was just past one o'clock in the morning. "Well, at least you got the time right." James said.

Stephen smiled slightly again and then turned to the First Sergeant, "Captain Brewer wants you to have Lieutenant Emerson form the company into four ranks and march them directly behind Company D to your front. We'll move in regimental formation until you get to the new location."

The Company E messenger watched First Sergeant Brooks to ensure he understood the instructions to that point, "Once we get to the ridgeline, I'll lead the company to its new location."

Stephen paused again, "Final orders will be given later this morning after you arrive. Do you have any questions?"

"I surely do Private Ward, but I'm sure the good Captain will explain everything when we get there. Do we know what we're going to be doing once we get there? Are we attacking or defending?" Sergeant Brooks looked concerned for the answer.

"Can't answer that for sure. I guess it will depend on what General Lee says this morning. If I had to guess, I'm hoping we're defending." As Captain Brewer's messenger, he knew he was not to expand on any message that might confuse his orders.

He looked at James, "But I am most afraid we're going to be attacking again." Stephen held his breath for just a moment, then turned on his heels, and he was running down the trail, back into the darkness.

As ordered the newly reorganized 26th Regiment and more specifically, Company E, marched that early morning for about two hours.

Pettigrew's Division, formerly Heth's Division had moved from Herr's Ridge, then turning South while crossing Willoughby Run.

McPherson's Ridge and the woods where the Regiment suffered such terrible loses on July first, were passed by in the darkness. Survivors of the first day of battle knew just how close they were to that deadly spot. They were in quiet fear as they passed.

The early morning march continued past the Hagerstown Road and turned on a Southeasterly direction. They stopped just West of Seminary Ridge and found temporary rest behind a wooded area just Southwest of the town of Gettysburg.

It was just after three o'clock in the morning. Morning nautical twilight was close at hand. Light would begin to slowly peel away the darkness very soon.

General Pettigrew had ordered his Regimental Commanders to position their units in preparation for an imminent attack by Union forces. However, the units were also told not to waste time on major defensive fortifications. More details were promised.

The Regiments and their men, prepared very hasty positions, set out pickets, and collapsed to catch some sleep in the early hours.

To the Northeast of Pettigrew's and the 26th Regiment's position were Generals Rodes' and Pender's Divisions. To the right of Pettigrew was the Virginia Division of General George Pickett. All of Pickett's brigades and regiments were new to the Gettysburg battlefield, having just arrived the night before.

The men of the 26th Regiment numbered less than two hundred and fifty men. That included the newly inserted troops from the night before. This number was being asked to perform the same heroic feat of July 1, on McPherson's Ridge when the Regiment was attacking with almost nine hundred able-bodied and trained men.

The early morning light made most men nervous that morning. Were they to defend or attack? Either way, it would be bloody. If it was a defense, the Union would have the advantage of moving downhill all the way to the woods of Seminary Ridge. If an attack, the Confederate forces would be attacking uphill all the way to top of Cemetery Ridge at a great disadvantage.

Captain Stephen Brewer found James Ward curled up beside a tree trying to sleep while he could. When he saw James, he almost turned away to leave him alone to sleep.

But he knew he could not do it. He had a job to do. He also knew that Henry Rogers could not be far away either.

Brewer placed his hand on James' shoulder and gave him a slight shake.

James immediately reacted by swinging his arms forward to cover his body and face. He saw his Company Commander. "Sorry Sir, didn't mean to hit at you." He tried to get up from the ground.

"Rest easy James. Besides, I should have known better than approach a man like that. Not safe at all." Captain Brewer stepped back to give James room to stand.

"Still sorry Sir. Shouldn't be hitting your Company Commander though." James slapped the dirt and debris from his pants and jacket.

"Why don't you grab a bite to eat and meet me up by that big Oak Tree over there in about a half hour." He pointed to a particular tree that was on the edge of the open field in front of Seminary Ridge.

"Yes Sir, I can do that. You want me to bring anything special with me?" James glanced down at his Leonard Rifle still covered in its leather wrap.

Captain Brewer smiled to acknowledge the purpose of the task at hand. "Yeah, bring that, your field glasses, and wake Henry up over there. We might want his opinion on this matter as well."

"Yes Sir, we'll be up there in thirty minutes." James was about to salute the Company Commander, but Brewer put his hand out to stop the Private.

"Not necessary here James. Some Yankee is up there on that hill just waiting to find me right now." Brewer walked away.

"Henry, get your butt up. I think the Captain's got some work for us." James started gathering his gear.

"Yeah, I heard the man. Damn, I just got off the picket less than an hour ago. What's a man got to do to get some sleep in this here army?" Henry threw the bed roll blanket away from him and crawled out of his makeshift bed.

"What ya think the Captain needs us for?" Henry moved to grab his haversack where he pulled out a hardtack biscuit and a chunk of cheese.

James did the same and quickly cut an apple in half and tossed one piece to his fellow sharpshooter. "I'm guessing he's gonna ask us to personally kill General Grant, if'n he's here, from that big Oak Tree over there."

Henry chuckled, acknowledging the joke, and knowing full well that Grant was nowhere to be seen on this battlefield.

Fact was, both men had no idea General George Meade was the new Commander of the Union forces to their front. Not that it would make any difference to the two of them.

At the given time, James and Henry made their way to the designated Oak Tree where Captain Brewer was already looking across the open area with a set of field glasses.

James spoke first, "Sir, we're here as ordered Sir."

Brewer lowered the field glasses and turned to the two men. "Gentlemen, do me the favor of taking a look at the field to our front. Look toward that high ground running along that ridge line. Tell me what you see."

After a couple of minutes for each man to use the field glasses, James responded. "Sir, if you think we can hit those boys up on the top there from here, I'm gonna say, not much we can do. That's definitely beyond my range with the scope. Pretty sure that Henry's not going to be able to use that Whitworth at all and expect to hit anything other than the few pickets they got out."

"James' is right, Sir. I'm afraid the shot would fall way short of even their pickets right now." Henry nodded in agreement as he brought the glasses down.

"Henry, what if I could get you about a half a mile closer? Could you hit those boys then?" The Captain had a slight smile on his face.

"Well. Yes Sir, I think we could but how you going to get out into that field and not get yourself killed?" Henry started to hand the glasses back to the Captain.

Captain Brewer pushed his hand out for Henry to keep the glasses. "What if I could get you to the big barn over on the left? Think you could make a difference from there?"

James looked at the big whitewash painted barn and the adjoining building where Captain Brewer was pointing. He estimated that it was over halfway up the sloping hill. Yes, he thought that would make a difference.

Henry put the glasses back to his eyes and looked at the terrain they would have to traverse to get to the barn in question. "I'm pretty sure that James would make a big difference. My Whitworth might be tested a bit." He paused.

"I can't see anybody over there. Who we got near that barn?" Henry turned to James, who promptly took the glasses.

"Pender and Rodes has their people over there in force. They're just below the place. Might be able to work our way forward and have your backs covered by them." Captain Brewer was postulating a scenario that would require some coordination. He was not sure they had the time.

What Captain Brewer did know was the regiment would be attacking up that hill today. What he did not know was when and exactly where the 26th Regiment would be in the attack?

"Tell you what, I'm going back to see Major Jones and get his permission to try to get you in position. If he approves, be ready to move out along our left line. I will coordinate with Anderson and Pender and get you safe conduct. Until I get back, get some rest." Brewer left the two men with the field glasses.

James studied the entire field. Given the general direction of Pettigrew's Division and more specifically the 26th Regiment.

The Regiment had to move nearly a mile to reach the high ground where the Union troops seemed to be in a constant state of movement through the field glasses.

He chuckled to himself for thinking about the beehives back home. It was a source for sweetness and adding flavor to cured meat, especially hams. His mouth watered with the thought. His stomach only growled at him for the mere thought. James couldn't think of why he thought of the bees back home.

Henry offered some insights on the terrain as well. "You notice those artillery pieces up on the left? See 'em, there near the end of the stone wall? Might be some good targets to hit there. I'm guessing three hundred maybe four hundred yards."

"Yep, I see 'em. They got a bunch of guns along that stone wall all the way to that bunch of trees to the center. Those cannons gonna tear us up." James added.

James paused and lowered the glasses. "You notice anything in particular about the ground going up?"

After a pause to look at the lay of the land, Henry responded. "James, it almost looks like waves on the ocean. Goes up, then down, back up again. Gets a little steep the further up you go."

"I'm thinking those little swells might be a good place to make sure we're in good order. Tighten the ranks and lines, maybe fire from those locations. Makes it a little harder for them boys up there to get a clean shot at us." James suggested.

"Yeah, I see what you're saying. Might want to mention that to Captain Brewer when he gets back." Henry paused again, "James, you notice those fences up there near the top?"

They exchanged the glasses again and James took the time to follow the fence line from the entire left to right view. "Damn! You see how many rails they got and how high?"

Henry thought for another second, "I'm guessing you got to either tear 'em down or climb over them. Only other thing is to start firing from those fences, not sure you're close enough though and those split rails ain't gonna stop those cannons right in behind them."

The more the two men looked through the glasses, the more concerned they got. Privates didn't get this kind of information before the battles. They were told to follow the colors, just keep moving forward, and kill whatever was in front of you.

For privates, it was war in its simplest form. But here, the two men could see the future and it was bleak, at best.

Within a half hour, Captain Brewer was back with permission from Major Jones, Acting Commander of the 26th Regiment, to put the sharpshooters to work. Additionally, they were provided with instructions to hurry.

Time was getting short. It was just past ten o'clock on July 3, 1863.

Captain Brewer coordinated with General Davis's Brigade to the immediate left of the 26th Regiment. A small force of eight men volunteered to move forward and provide any covering fire for the sharpshooters.

James was not particularly pleased with the offer, given the attention the small group of troops moving forward would create for them.

However, the group had performed some scouting forward and offered advice for the sharpshooters to use the depressions of the ground to stay out of sight from most of the Union troops on the ridge.

Within another half hour James and Henry were in the barn. They first moved throughout the barn to ensure no one was there. Even the stalls and paddock were empty.

"James, you think you can get the best shots from that top floor of the barn. I can handle the targets closer to us from the shed door. We'll let those boys down there in the lower ground take care of our backs." Henry waited for James' answer.

James had already started walking to the ladder that would take him to the large barn door on the second level. "Yeah, I'm thinking that's best for me. "You get in trouble, you let me know soonest. Let's not get caught back here by ourselves. I'm thinking the whole Union army is in front of us."

Both men immediately moved to their chosen locations and began to assess the targets available for their different weapons. Henry had offered to let James start firing before he would shoot. This would give James the advantage of hitting targets much further away and without drawing direct attention to the barn.

James climbed the ladder, found a couple of old hay bales, and positioned them just inside of the opened barn door on the higher level. He was in the shadows. Anyone that looked to the barn would see the same thing, a white barn, a door open, old hay bales, and nothing else.

As they agreed, James needed to find a way to minimize the artillery where he could. Henry would focus on the pickets, officers, and cadre nearest the stone wall that were within his range.

They went to work. James had hit two gunnery sergeants and one officer near the two artillery batteries closet to the angle in the stone wall. At one point, he noticed an open ammunition caisson just to the rear of the battery. In the caisson were the powder bags loosely attached to the rounds to be fired. He could see enough of the powder bags with his scope to get off a decent shot.

His shot was dead on, the powder was hit, the explosion was massive, and the caisson flew high into the air. By the time it landed on the ground, it was splinters and burning. Several of the gun crews were similarly hit by the flying debris from both shot and shell.

Henry's position was just inside of a small shed attached to the barn. The shed door had previously had a glass window, but it had been broken out for some time. He was able to fire from the broken window without being readily seen from a distance of several hundred yards.

He too, had success by hitting four different pickets, an artillery sergeant, and he thought he had hit a lieutenant as well, but the man continued to stand at his post, holding onto his arm as he provided orders to the gun crews of his battery.

They were starting to be noticed by the Union forces to their right front. Fire was being placed on to the barn by musket fire and most of it was poorly placed and certainly not very accurate.

James was the first to notice the field piece being repositioned to fire in their direction. "Henry, I think it's time for us to leave. Meet me at the back of the barn, quick!"

Henry couldn't see the artillery piece, but he knew something bad was happening for James to urge him to the back of the barn.

Just as James and Henry met inside of the barn, the cannon was fired, and the artillery round landed. It hit the ground in front of the barn and exploded but did not hurt the two men. At that moment, one of the men that had led them to the barn came running into the back barn door.

"We got to get outta here! Yankees are coming up fast from the West." He turned on his heels and ran out of the door.

James and Henry quickly followed only to be fired upon by a bunch of soldiers in blue. They were still some distance away and their fire was not very accurate.

"You boys go ahead and clear the way for us. We'll be right behind you shortly." James lifted the Leonard Rifle to his shoulder and picked out an officer with a sword in hand.

The Confederate soldiers saw what James was doing and immediately fell in line with James and prepared to fire their own weapons.

Henry had also brought his Whitworth Rifle up and selected his target as well. James fired first, Henry was a very close second, and the rest of the men fired as one volley.

An officer fell to the ground. A sergeant also fell. One other man fell as well. The Union troops seemed to falter for a moment and someone else yelled for a charge.

All of the Confederate soldiers made a hasty run for the sheltered ground and continued to move with haste to the woods on Seminary Ridge.

As James and Henry returned to the 26th Regiment's location, they were met by Captain Brewer and just behind their Company Commander was Major Jones, the Acting 26th Regimental commander.

Captain Brewer spoke first. "Well done boys. We could see with the glasses you were doing some good."

Major Jones stepped forward, "Can you boys give us some advice on what is up there?"

James looked to Henry and shook his head in the affirmative. "Yes Sir, I believe we can. But you're not going to like what you hear."

Both Brewer and Jones had grim faces with tight lips pursed together.

James and Henry got some water, took several deep drinks, and splashed some more on their faces.

For the next several minutes, both James and Henry explained the ground in front of them and what obstacles they were going to face going up that hill. By the time they had finished answering the Commanders' questions, five other company commanders of the 26th Regiment were listening as well.

Major Jones began to formulate some thoughts on the order of battle. No one could really argue with his thoughts. No matter what was offered as suggestions, they were quickly dismissed as not being practical or no less dangerous.

Jones said he would pass this information to General Pettigrew and perhaps they would have definitive orders by the time he returned.

Everyone went their separate ways.

The battle of the cannons continued off and on for two hours. Damage was done on both sides, but nothing changed the consequences.

Both armies were determined that this was the time and place for deciding the outcome of this war. The serenading cannonade had begun in earnest by midday.

However, in between the cannonade and destruction, a Chaplain's service had begun. Prayers were spoken. Redemption was offered and received. Hymns began to drift through the woods of Seminary Ridge.

Across the breeze of the hot July day, the 26th Regimental Band began playing the song "The Sweet By and By."

In the anticipation of what was surely to come, men began writing or finishing letters home.

* * * * *

July 3, 1863

To Mrs. Anna Wallace Ward, General Delivery, Whiteville, North Carolina

My Dearest wife and future mother of our child,

This is a significant day. I know not what the Lord intends but I can say with little hesitation that what occurs on this day shall be memorable for years to come.

We are about to enter into a battle that most assuredly will make the previous days of battle insignificant in comparison. I fear for my soul and my family.

For my family, I bequeath any and all properties held in my name to my loving and devoted wife. May she use and dispose of it as she deems appropriate. I give these things to her out of great love and concern for her well-being.

To my Father, I have left a locked box in the barn where several items of mine are left for him to use as he deems most appropriate.

For my Mother, I ask her to love, nourish, and care for my wife and newborn child as one of your own. If he is a boy, teach him the proper way to treat a woman. If she is a girl, teach her to be just as loving as you are as a mother, and as beautiful as her mother.

I sincerely hope that his letter serves as proper notice that if I die, these are my last wishes. If I do survive this battle and war, may the God, Lord Almighty, and Jesus Christ, His Son, have mercy on my soul. I seek no justice, for there is none, but I ask for mercy and forgiveness for all my sins.

I am most respectfully and sincerely,

Private James Ward,

Company E, 26ᵗʰ Regiment, Marshall's Brigade, Pettigrew's Division, Hill's Corps, Army of the Confederacy

CHAPTER 15

"LORD, HELP US!" JULY 1863

The competing cannonades were nearly over. Confederate artillery batteries were nearly down to nothing in reserve. Resupplies would take too long. They could barely support the impending attack up the hillside.

Cemetery Ridge was a name that was both ironic and symbolic of the consequences of such an attack. However, before the cemetery could claim its prize, there must be a battle for the hearts, minds, and souls of a nation.

Once all of the strategizing and planning were discussed and finally agreed upon, there was nothing else but to execute the plan. However, these plans were made by men and as men, these plans were flawed.

The distance up the hill to the crest of the ridge was just a little short of a mile at its closest point. It was as much as a mile and a quarter at the farthest point. No matter the distance, it was over open ground. Only folds in the earth seemed to change the view.

Fields lay open before both sides that many a farmer could conceive of working back home, in the North or South. All they could see was a wheat field, an orchard, stubble coming out of the ground where the first crops of corn had matured and had been harvested.

They saw pastureland where cattle, sheep, and horses had grazed, empty now, each animal taken by the owners or the men from either side for use by their respective armies.

The mid-afternoon Sun was hot, and men sweated profusely beneath its unrelenting rays. Somewhere, around that sweat, a tear or two was falling, reflecting the nervous anticipation of the order to move forward or prepare to defend.

Either way, no man with any common sense, on either side, would believe this battle would be survivable.

In the last seventy-two hours, General George Meade's Union forces had accumulated nearly fifty thousand men. Even with the casualties of the last forty-eight hours, his effective forces on July 3, included nearly thirty thousand troops along and behind their lines.

The Union forces were tucked neatly in an integrated crescent of death and destruction waiting to be let loose. Union commanders could move troops in mass within minutes to any part of the battlefield.

At the bottom of Cemetery Ridge lay the crest of Seminary Ridge and over fourteen thousand Confederate troops to be committed to the attack. Their battle lines ran concurrent with Seminary Ridge and their only protection was the wood line on the smaller ridge where they prepared for the attack.

Federal artillery lay heavy fire on the woods as the Confederate soldiers waited for the order to move into position and begin the long and dangerous trip up the hill.

Nearly every regiment on the line of attack were seasoned veterans of this war. Only General Pickett's Division had not previously been engaged in the last two days of conflict.

Those units used on July 1 and July 2, were greatly depleted to both wounds and death. They had been quickly reorganized overnight by combining units that had been used over the previous two days. What was unknown to most was there were nearly 13,000 Confederate soldiers that were fresh and available to General Lee to reinforce the attack or defend their ground.

When the order came down the line along the wooded Seminary Ridge, division, brigade, and regimental commanders began to form the troops into the prescribed battle formations.

The main attack was simple, two divisions would move straight up the hill, converging on a clump of trees that stood at the center of the battlefield. One division would be General Pickett's Virginia Division focused on the trees. The second division would be Pettigrew's Division focused on the left side of the angle in the stone wall.

James could hear and see Captain Brewer relaying the commands to the front of the company. "Fix bayonets!"

With some difficulty, James' hands shook as he pulled the bayonet from his scabbard, inserted the bayonet socket onto the barrel, and gave it a quick twist to lock it into place.

He smiled to himself as he recalled the last time, he had used the bayonet to move the fallen tree by the road just a few short days ago.

Henry was to James' immediate right side. Both men had reluctantly left their preferred sharpshooter rifles back at the rear. Today, they were foot soldiers and would perform as they had been trained by Colonel Burgwyn for over two years. James flinched at the thought of going up the hill without Colonel Burgwyn leading the charge.

"Don't seem right. It just ain't right!" Henry harshly whispered.

James gave his friend a quick look. "What are you talking about?"

"Well, it's bad enough they wouldn't let us bring our rifles, but then they make us carry these muskets, loaded, and we're told not to fire until we are given the command. What the hell?" Henry Rogers was incensed by the order.

"Well, it won't make much difference if we only get one shot anyway. We'll be dead by the time we get the shot off." James was almost laughing, perhaps from nervousness.

The order to form was made by the commanders at all levels. Captain Brewer walked along the line, talking to the men. "Steady boys, you know your duty. Do yourself proud today. If a man goes down to your front, man in the next rank move forward. Man goes down to your right or left and no body fills the line, tighten up to the man closest to your left or right."

Everyone knew what to do. Even the people newly inserted into the 26th Regiment knew the drills. Henry Burgwyn would have been proud if he were alive this day.

James was near the left side of the rank in his place within the company formation. From his position, he could look far to the right and see on the horizon, rank after rank, line after line as far as he could see.

Flag guidons with unit colors waved in the breeze. James remembered the parade ground, where they departed, outside Fredericksburg, just a few weeks ago. The pass and review in front of General Lee and his staff that day was a day to remember. It was glorious! That day was a grand affair. James whispered to himself, "This is not going to be a parade."

To the left, he could see the other regiments of Marshall's Brigade. The entire brigade was properly aligned and ready to move forward.

For a moment, James was confident the sheer size and organization alone would carry the day. However, the brief moment of confidence melted away when he turned his eyes toward Cemetery Ridge.

From the barn, he had seen the problems they would face as they moved forward. The moment of thought was punctuated by an artillery burst which fell just behind them.

Both Henry and James had pushed hard for the commanders to plan and prepare for how to deal with each of those obstacles at the summit. Those fences were starting to make him very nervous.

Finally, the order was given, and the grand parade began. Every unit stepped out smartly. The formations were held in line by the company sergeants with sabers in hand and directly behind the troops to keep up their pace.

The Company Commanders were usually positioned to the left of the ranks and the First Lieutenants would be positioned on the opposite side of the ranks. James immediately noticed most Company Commanders were directly in front of their respective companies.

That was where James saw Captain Brewer and he could not have been prouder of his Commander. He also noticed that about two steps to the left and two steps to the rear of the Captain was none other than Private Stephen Ward. He also noted Stephen had his boots on.

At the quick step march command, they were making satisfactory progress up the hill. Muskets at the ready with bayonets shining brightly and pointed toward the afternoon sky. They moved with precision but not rushing. The troops were instructed not to fire but to save their ammunition for the attack into the Union lines.

The 26th Regiment came to one of the folds in the ground that took away the pressure from the Union guns. About that time, The Brigade Commander, Colonel Marshall, fell from his horse shot by Union fire.

As planned before the battle started, Major Jones, Commander of the 26th Regiment was moved into command of the brigade. That was when James realized that none other than Captain Stephen Brewer was running with Stephen right behind him to the front and assumed the command of the 26th Regiment.

There were many great and heroic men of the 26th Regiment but for Company E, there could be none better than Stephen Brewer. If there was such a thing, he was a natural born leader of men in combat.

James fought the urge to run forward to be beside the new Regimental Commander. He felt obligated to protect him. He pushed the urge down and then only focused on Stephen to his front. His thought was, "What in God's name is that boy doing up there?"

James looked around himself and noticed men had fallen around him and others had moved forward to fill the gaps in the line. He smiled for a moment and thought "just like 'King' taught us". Daniel Carter went down to his right front, wounded in the chest. Randal Cheek went down to his right; shot in the knee. Johnny Dowd went down with a right arm wound.

David Foster fell from the rank directly in front of James with a wound to the upper chest. James politely stepped over the body trying not to look down at the fallen soldier.

Willis Jones was not too far away when he fell out of the formation. Jeff Mansfield was shot in the foot and couldn't walk. Sergeant Bill Merritt was near the company guidon when he fell with a wound.

John Mobley took a shot to the head almost directly behind James. James almost tripped when John's body recoiled and caught him on the back of his left leg. After getting up, he looked at John and saw the look of peace on the man's face.

The brigade had taken a quick stop at the last fold in the ground before the assault on the fence line. He grabbed his canteen and continued to look at John Mobley. Henry poked him on the shoulder, "He's dead James. Nothing you can do for him. Look over there."

James did as Henry pointed to the white barn where they had used their long-range weapons to good purpose. The barn was now in flames and a smoldering ruin. The shed door, covered in black soot, was where

Henry had been located. It was obvious an artillery shell had landed and tore the shed door into splinters. "Guess, I'm lucky not to be still in there. Don't you think?"

James Tally was just finishing his drink of water from his canteen when the bullet struck him clean in the stomach.

Bill Welch went down shortly after reforming the company lines and ranks. Bill had remembered being wounded on July 1, 1862, at Malvern Hill. He had said last night, by the fire, he had a bad feeling about this battle.

The ranks were thinning out and they still had not made it to the high split rail fences on both sides of the Emmitsburg Road.

To the right, only about two hundred yards away, George Pickett's Division was receiving rapid gunfire and poisonous lead. They were also dealing with the fences, and they had no better solution than James did.

As the 26th Regiment advanced on the first fence, their efforts to pull down the fence proved even more difficult than they imagined, given the number of men trying to pull it down. Finally, the first rank of the 26th Regiment moved forward, took aim at the Union forces only two hundred yards away and fired a massive volley.

The Union troops recoiled from the fire. There were many gaps in their defensive line and the men of the 26th Regiment continued to pull down the fence as another rank of the unit came forward to fire another volley into the enemy lines.

Both sides, simultaneously, fired, and the men fell in mass on both sides. As usual, the color guards had suffered badly in the exchanges. Sergeant McRae had already fallen, wounded in the arm, and could not continue to carry the colors forward. First Lieutenant John Emerson was down, Second Lieutenant Orren Hanner wounded, and Major John Jones, the previous acting 26th Commander, wounded on July 1st, was wounded again by an artillery blast.

James looked to his immediate right, where Henry Rogers was still moving forward. He smiled for a moment, the fences were finally down, and the Regiment surged across the road.

Everything seemed to slow down for James. He saw things happening that he had no ability to influence. Henry fell backwards. Captain Brewer had reached for the colors. Stephen Ward was right beside him holding the brave and wounded Captain upright.

Brewer turned his head and yelled at the men to charge the lines. James looked only fifty yards beyond the officer and saw the Union artillery sergeant reaching for the lanyards on two cannons.

Stephen saw the sergeant as well; he looked back at James and only smiled.

The cannons, with double canister shells, exploded and the smoke was so massive as it rolled into the charging Confederate troops, hiding everything that was alive for several moments.

The battle at the angle of the stone wall was turning badly for General Pickett. What was left of the division was surrendering, being shot, bayonetted, or for a very few, retreating back down the hill.

James' eyes were burning from the smoke, and he could not see anything. For a moment, he thought he must be in heaven. Everything was white. It was after the smoke from the guns engulfed him, and left him chocking, that he realized it was not heaven but an earthly form of hell.

He heard the muskets firing in rapid succession. Lying there, James was tempted to reach up and catch the rounds before they hit someone. For some reason, he again thought of the honeybees back home. He also recalled the cold night on Malvern Hill where he thought about reaching up and catching the hot rounds.

James heard a slight groan to his right. He turned in that direction and saw Henry just a couple of feet away. "James, I'm pretty sure I'm killed. I'd appreciate a taste of water if you please."

Staying low, James reached over to Henry and gave him his canteen. He saw the blood covering the upper chest, it was quickly spreading just to the right of the heart. A little spital, mixed with blood, eased down the corner of Henry's mouth.

Seeing James' reaction, Henry responded to his friend and fellow soldier, "Don't you worry about me my friend. I'll find you on the other side."

Henry was still smiling as he closed his eyes. He never opened them again on this side of heaven.

James rolled onto his stomach and felt the pain as he did so. He was afraid to look and see how bad it was. He propped his head up to see toward the front of the stone wall.

To his surprise, he saw Captain Brewer moving in the grass just past the road and the last fence line. Stephen, always there for him, was helping the Captain up, once again.

Beyond where he could see the most recent Acting 26th Regimental Commander and Stephen heading back down the ridge, James saw two tattered and weary bodies making their way forward, with their heads down as if leaning against a hurricane on the East Coast of North Carolina. Without seeing where they were headed, they moved steadily toward the stone wall with the 26th Regimental colors in hand. Neither soldier had a weapon on them.

First sergeant James Brooks of Company E, 26th Regiment of North Carolina Troops and another man from Company E, that James didn't immediately recognize, but he did see neither one of them realized how close they were to the stone wall until they almost ran into it. Both had closed their eyes in that final moment anticipating the shots that would kill them.

Instead, they were greeted by the battery sergeant that had fired the fateful rounds into the solid mass of the remaining 26th Regiment's troops while watching the regiment's charge disappear from this earth.

The sergeant stepped one leg over the stone wall and said to the two men from North Carolina, each still holding onto the colors flag staff, "Come over men, come over to the right side of God."

The sergeant moved the two filthy men back a few yards and told them to sit down and be still. He told them he would come back for them. As he turned back to the carnage that laid before him, the artillery sergeant whispered, "My God, their all gone!"

What had been a solid mass of nearly two hundred men, spread across over thirty yards in that last charge, and led by Company E troops, had truly disappeared.

From his position, some thirty to forty yards away from the wall, James saw that Brooks and the other man, though wounded, were alive. Captain Brewer and Stephen were no longer to be seen.

James fell back for a moment to catch his breath, as it was becoming more difficult to breathe. He could see the swath of death the cannons had made of the 26th Regiment. As best he could tell, the death and destruction of the men caused the bodies to be piled against each other.

All around James, most of them dead, he saw the few faces from the old Regiment and the many new faces of the latest members of the Regiment lying in rest or nearly to death.

Noise was continuing all around, but it seemed so trivial, at the moment. Who won or lost was the least of James' concerns at the moment.

He gathered his thoughts, took a drink from the still open canteen, and rolled onto his back. He looked high into the blue Pennsylvania sky.

James closed his eyes and thought about Anna Wallace and the rest of his family. He recalled the recent dream of Anna Wallace introducing him to a two-year-old red-headed boy. He just couldn't remember which family member the boy belonged.

He took another deep breath and exhaled, as he started to dream of Anna Wallace once more. This time, he recalled the morning they woke up for the first time in their new home near the Green Swamp.

James also remembered the beautifully etched glass in the window bought using that twenty dollars in gold bonus he received for enlisting in the army. He recalled it looked like angels coming through the clouds and sunlight etched on the window.

He smiled that sly smile he always gave to Anna Wallace when he requested her gracious favors as his wife. She smiled back at him and told him, "James, it's time to see the light."

Private James Ward opened his eyes and looked into the Sun. He saw the soft wings of the angels in the glass again. His last thought was of Anna Wallace and a small red-haired boy.

* * * * *

July 7, 1863

To Mrs. Anna Wallace Ward, General Delivery, Whiteville, North Carolina

Dear Mrs. Ward,

I am in the deepest of regrets to inform you of the untimely death of your late husband, Private James Ward of Company E, 26th Regiment of North Carolina Troops, of Marshall's Brigade, Pettigrew's Division, A.P. Hill's Corps, of the Army of Northern Virginia, in service to the Confederate States of America.

Private Ward was wounded and died of those wounds on a battlefield near the town of Gettysburg, Pennsylvania on July 3, 1863.

James was a devoted soldier, loved by his fellow soldiers of Company E throughout his service, and a true patriot. I cannot name another that gave so much and asked for so little of others.

I was witness to his heroic charge and his leadership at critical moments of the battle in question. He fought to the very end and died close by his dear friend, Private Henry Rogers.

On a personal note, there are few men in this army, including a great many generals, that I would trust with my life more than James. On many occasions, he saved this officer's life, and several other senior officers owe their lives to his skills with a rifle.

My sincerest condolences to you and James' family as well. James' father, Mister Brice Ward, was kind to the company and the entire regiment. We are greatly indebted to your entire family.

Unfortunately, the battle conditions did not allow us to take possession of his body for a return to his home.

In that I am currently captured, at a Union hospital near Gettysburg, I am making official requests to the Union commanders for access to the location of his and other regimental soldiers remains, for both official record and for your consideration regarding the return of his remains.

James, on the previous night before his demise, provided a brief message addressed to you, with a lock of his hair, and a silver cross. I have enclosed those items herewith. You were always in his thoughts.

The men and officers of the 26th Regiment offer our sincere prayers and thoughts for you at this most troublesome time.

I am your most obedient servant,

Captain Stephen Brewer, former Acting Commander, 26th Regiment of North Carolina Troops

Union Hospital, Gettysburg, Pennsylvania

CHAPTER 16

"HOW LONG DO WE RUN?" JULY 1863

By sundown of July 3, it was obvious that both sides had suffered horrendous casualties. While some on either side suggested that immediate counterattacks were in order to destroy the other side, perhaps cooler heads prevailed. Neither army made advances up or down that open field by Emmitsburg Road.

Private Stephen Ward, wounded in the hip, somehow, pulled Captain Stephen Brewer back from the killing field directly in front of the stone wall. An occasional musket round would hit near them, but they were soon out of range from the Union troops along the wall.

Brewer, now the Acting Commander of the entire Regiment, kept trying to give orders. Stephen Ward just acknowledged the order and focused on getting the Captain back down the hill. "Sir, the troops are reforming back at the ridge. We need to get you there, so you can organize the Regiment."

As Stephen half carried and half pulled the Commander down the hill, he clearly saw there were no troops to reorganize, prepare for a defense, or make another attack. He muttered to himself, "Damn, there all gone!"

Captain Brewer was barely conscious and only mumbled more incoherent orders. Stephen ignored those too. Halfway down the hill,

Brewer suddenly became lucid and alert, "Dress on the colors! Dress on the colors!!"

Stephen Ward looked back up the hill to where he had last seen the colors, directly in front of the stone wall. He couldn't see the colors lying on the ground on the other side of the stone wall.

He returned his attention and a firm grip on his Commander, "We got 'em Sir. They're waiting for us down on the ridge." He said it as if the Captain was nothing more than a picnic basket, he was carrying to Sunday homecoming at church.

Members of the 26th Regimental Band had come onto the field and helped get Captain Brewer back to the rear of Seminary Ridge.

Brewer's condition was determined, by the Surgeon, to be severe enough, that movement from the area would be difficult and dangerous.

In two days, Captain Brewer was left behind with many other Confederate soldiers in similar conditions. They were at the mercy of the Union army.

Most of those captured wounded soldiers were treated and later moved to Federal prisons at various locations in the North. This included Lieutenant Hanner, First Sergeant Brooks, Bill Caviness, Middleton Cheek, Jim Dorsett, Issac Edwards, Lab Ellis, Manly Forrester, Nat Foster, Joe Hackney, Jim McDaniel, Marty Nall, John Powers, Dan Thomas, Bob Welch, and Issac Wilkie.

Many would die within days including Dan Carter, Randal Cheek, Bill Ellington, Everett Page, Wiley Smith, Jim Tally, and many others from the 26th Regiment.

A few would make it through all three days at Gettysburg without a single wound. But they were too few and far between.

On the morning of July 1, 1863, the 26th Regiment had eight hundred and forty-three men ready for battle, including the band and support staff.

By the end of the day on July 4, 1863, only sixty-seven men and three officers were able to retreat from the ridges around Gettysburg.

July 4, 1863, saw the two sides watch each other and try to anticipate what was coming next. Union generals knew that Lee had many more troops available to attack them again. If anything, they were convinced that Lee's next attack could be the Union forces' undoing.

For whatever strategic or tactical reason, Lee did not do it. Perhaps his generals finally convinced him that Gettysburg was not the best place to push the Union army. Regardless, he recognized the vulnerability of his entire army.

Perhaps the only saving grace for either side on July 4th was the torrential downpour of rain for nearly the entire day. No one could see what the other was doing.

What Lee was doing was getting his wounded and supply trains out of harm's way. The process was painful for the wounded. Those not able to march rode in wagons over very rough terrain.

By the evening of July 4th, the Army of Northern Virginia was effectively and efficiently withdrawing to the safety of the Potomac River. If the soldiers could not walk and fight, they were left behind, to be captured by the Union forces.

It took two days for General Meade to realize the Confederate troops were not going to attack. His staff proposed probing attacks on the flanks to keep track of the enemy.

It did not take long for Union cavalry to discover Lee's forces were in general retreat. Token forces were being employed to keep the Federal troops at bay, while the Confederate army crossed the Potomac River and back into Virginia.

The remains of the 26th Regiment continued under the command of General Pettigrew's Division. Their primary mission was to offer covering forces against the enemy until the army was safely across the river. They suddenly found themselves as one of the buffers against the Union Cavalry.

The trek across the Pennsylvania and Maryland countryside, included over twenty thousand Confederate men and being covered by a small force when the heavy Union forces made contact at the Potomac.

The Union cavalry had found and caught the train of wagons filled with wounded soldiers by July 5th. They harassed and captured some lingering wagons over the following two days.

Most engagements were not major battles, but the smaller Confederate covering force quickly massed to repulse each attack. The engagements were short, violent, but usually inconclusive.

Major General Heth had mostly recovered from his head wound of July 1, and he resumed command of his division from General Pettigrew. The North Carolinian resumed command of his own brigade, including the 26th Regiment. Major Jones had likewise resumed command of the 26th Regiment from Captain Brewer, deemed too injured to move from Gettysburg.

Finally, by July 12th, the army was nearly across the river in mass. Pettigrew's Brigade had set up the defensive wall against potential danger and harm during the actual crossing.

Pettigrew's scouts indicated that an attack was almost imminent during the day. While still harassing, the Union forces still did not make a major attack.

That all changed on July 14th when a small force of Yankee Cavalry appeared and attacked the much larger force of the infantry brigade. The results of the five or ten minutes of chaos included twenty-nine Union cavalrymen killed, wounded, or captured.

Unfortunately, tragedy struck again for the Confederate troops from North Carolina. General Pettigrew suffered from two major wounds. The first wound was to his right arm from the battle of Seven Pines. His second wound, and probably most significant, was his smashed left hand that was bound to his shoulder from the attack in Gettysburg, on July 3rd.

A Union cavalryman decisively charged and engaged with Pettigrew. The two adversaries fired at close range at nearly the same time. Pettigrew wounded the man, but the general would die for his efforts. The Union cavalryman tried to run away but he was brought down by Private Nevel Staten of the 26th Regiment.

Nev Staten looked to General Pettigrew's condition and saw his Brigade Commander in great pain. He was incensed beyond control, "Damn you Yankee!!"

He picked up a large stone near the garden where Pettigrew had positioned himself in the battle. He threw the stone onto the chest of the enemy cavalryman and killed him by crushing his chest.

Pettigrew was still alive and refused to leave the field of battle. Four men quickly took responsibility for their general using a blanket as a litter and moved him around the field until they could safely withdraw.

As Pettigrew's Brigade and the 26th Regiment made quick progress back to the river, they stopped, formed ranks, and fired a massive volley that stopped the advancing Federal cavalry.

The 26th Regiment had once again done its job well. They were the last unit to cross the river. General Pettigrew was with them.

A wounded but able to walk Private Stephen Ward was holding a corner of the blanket carrying the general. "Sir, if you don't mind me asking, how long do we have to run?"

Through the pain, General Pettigrew said, with a slight smile, "Son, I am of the opinion that Hell itself isn't far enough."

The General survived until the early morning of July 17th. He awoke that morning as the Surgeon stepped over to his cot. The general said, "It is time to be going." General James Johnston Pettigrew also saw the angels coming.

The Regiment, Brigade, and the Division cried nearly the whole day. For days, his name was whispered in prayers. By July 24th, Major General Pettigrew's body laid in state in the North Carolina Capitol of Raleigh.

The mere mention of Pettigrew's name in Major General Henry Heth's presence, in his own words, always brought a clinching feeling in his chest, a chocking sound from his mouth, and tears that slipped from his eyes.

The 26th Regiment moved with Heth's Division to the Culpepper area of Virginia and began to rebuild once again. Once on the South and Western side of the Rappahannock River, Lee's Army felt safer.

The wounded from the Northern campaign had the opportunity to recover. They would also be the core of the companies and regiments that would continue the fight for nearly two more years.

Even after watching humankind try to kill itself, these men knew what it took to perform their duty, as God gave them the ability to see their duty.

* * * * *

July 24, 1863

To Mrs. Anna Wallace Ward, General Delivery, Whiteville, North Carolina

Dear Anna Wallace,

I am not sure whether you have received the news regarding the battle in Pennsylvania. It was most terrible.

I regret to inform you that James was killed by Union forces at that battle. I was able to see him, for only a brief moment, yet, I knew he has gone to see the Lord. He looked to be in peace.

We lost Colonel Burgwyn, Lieutenant Colonel Lane, and General Pettigrew. We may have lost Captain Brewer as well. We had to leave him and a bunch more in Gettysburg because of their wounds.

I just don't see how we can win this war when you lose good men like that. We have taken a lot of casualties and it is hard to see how we can win this war. The damn Yankees just seem to keep coming. They got more men, more guns, more artillery, more food, more of everything. I just don't see how this is going to go well.

Please let my family know that I have received a couple of wounds. The one at Gettysburg was the worst but I was able to get out of the fight before dying.

The new Regimental Commander, Colonel Martin has said we'll all have to recover with the unit. I will not be able to come home on furlough like James did.

I would dearly love to see North Carolina one more time.

Regardless, I made a promise to James, that if he did not make it home, that I would take care of you. As God as my witness, I will make good on that promise.

I'll try to write more on the next post. Please send writing paper, like you used to send to James.

I am your devoted cousin,

Private Stephen Ward, Company E, 26th Regiment, Martin's Brigade, Heth's Division, A.P. Hill Corps, somewhere in Virginia

CHAPTER 17

"PAPA LET'S GO HOME!"
JULY 9, 1863

The news was coming fast but in too many pieces. Newspaper accounts of a big battle in Pennsylvania was coming with both cheers and sudden fears.

Large crowds formed around the outside near the courthouse wall every day, waiting for the latest information. Not least of importance was the actual death rosters and rosters of wounded or unaccounted troops.

The wall had become so busy because two major fronts to the war were taking a lot of space on the wall. Major battles in Vicksburg, Mississippi to the West and Gettysburg, Pennsylvania to the North were almost too much to ponder.

Farm reports, births, and local news were being covered over, by battle reports on the wall. It was July 7, 1863. The battle on July 1 had people nervous. The 26th Regiment, the same Regiment that included large numbers of families from this community, was heavily engaged.

Not least of concern was the loss of both Colonel Burgwyn and Lieutenant Colonel Lane, both beloved men of North Carolina. There was even an article about General Pettigrew recently being promoted to Commander of the Division in Heth's absence.

On this day, the crowd was especially large because of the posting of results of the battles near Pennsylvania. This subject garnered most attention and space on the wall.

A large contingent of the entire Ward brothers' families had come to town. Brice had determined that with some of the local hostilities by the home guard becoming more prevalent in the community, it was best to travel with a large armed group.

They had five wagons with them carrying most of the youngsters, with the purpose of getting supplies. The Ward brothers and a couple of the older boys had pistols in their belts or carried hunting rifles and shotguns across their arm.

Brice Ward had both a pistol and shotgun at the ready as he rode his horse ahead of the wagons. The horse moved at a slow but purposeful pace, Brice looking only straight ahead while noticing any unusual movement from either side.

Miz Lizzie, Anna Wallace, and most of the Ward ladies were riding on the front wagon and were dressed in their better go-to-town clothes.

They smiled and waved at the folks passing by and the shop owners that sought their business. Even at ten o'clock in the morning, it was sunny and very warm.

The Ward caravan looked as if it was a grand parade.

They were near the center of the town when Brice brought up his hand in a motion to stop and pulled to the side of the street.

He turned in the saddle, "Jer, why don't you and a couple of the boys go down to the blacksmith shop and get those plow blades we need. Might want to get a few shoes for the horses and mules. When the farrier comes this Fall, I don't want him charging us some outrageous price for his shoes, like he did last time."

He continued, "Lizzie, you and Anna Wallace go see the Doctor. I know both of you are concerned about the baby. If you're able after that visit, you and the ladies can go over to the general store and get those things on your list you wanted. I'm sure we'll find you down by the mercantile store before we're finished."

Brice looked back at the third wagon where his brother Josh had the reins in hand. "Josh, I have an order at the feed store. You and that boy of yours get that loaded up. Should take all of your wagon to carry it."

"Issac, you go and help. They'll need some of your wagon space for the rest of it."

Finally, he turned to his brother Nehemiah, sitting on the fifth wagon. "Nem, how about you go with me to the hardware store. I'm thinking we need some more seeds for the corn and wheat. Gonna have to plant at least one more crop if we want to make it through the Winter." Nem nodded his head, popped the reins on the two mules, and headed for the hardware store.

Brice pulled his pocket watch from his vest and looked at the time. He then gave his final orders to everyone. "All right, it's now ten after ten. I want everyone to meet back at the farmers market down near the end of town by one o'clock. I'm sure they'll be something to eat down there for us. We'll have our afternoon meal and then head home."

Everyone acknowledged the Ward family patriarch's directions and moved in their respective directions.

This event took place every first or second week of each month. Brice collected the family funds, to pay for the family needs. He negotiated the deals for everyone. By buying as a group, they got a better bargain than buying separately.

Things like plow bits, blades, horseshoes, and farm equipment, were equally shared by the each of the farms. Just like the family laborers helped each other's farm and just like their own farm received help in kind.

The Ward farm was known for its collective farming method. When things did not go right for one, it had an impact on the others. Each family had a special talent or skill and they shared it religiously with each other.

Brice would always say, "If you can't trust your own family, who can you trust, other than God almighty?"

The monthly trip to town was progressing well. By one o'clock the entire Ward family had circled their wagons at the end of town. In the center of the circle was a fire pit. Over the already well-burned embers of the fire, was a spit with half a cured hog over the fire.

The heated fat dripping from the spit sizzled as it hit the fire. One of Josh Ward's sons was gently turning the spit. It allowed the meat to evenly cook.

A smaller fire contained a black cauldron half filled with water. Chunked potatoes, cobs of fresh corn, sliced onions, carrots, and cut pieces of green bell peppers were dropped into the pot. Slices of fatback pork were dropped in the cauldron as well.

Most ingredients were coming from the stalls of farmers gathered to sell the results of their own farming efforts.

Miz Lizzie had procured most of the food while Issac and his family had built the temporary fire pit and got a good fire going. The half hog came from the Ward farm.

The aroma of the farmer's stew was overwhelming. The family was partaking of the great feast, and as usual, friends, neighbors, and other farmers would wander by and were soon offered a farmer's meal of stew, slices of pork right off the spit, and fresh bread with butter and honey.

While not expected, the other farmers would offer to pay for their meal. Miz Lizzie was adamant about not taking their money. In her presence, Brice always said no as well. But everyone knew there was a little tin box, sitting just behind where Brice leaned against his wagon.

Everyone knew Brice Ward didn't take charity. They also knew Brice would always turn his head as the few coins fell into the box.

There wasn't much in the tin box because everyone there was in the same financial strain from the war as the Ward family.

As proud people tend to do, they always found a way to pay for their own contribution. In this case, it was the other farmers that offered ingredients for the meal.

It was nearly three o'clock when Brice saw the temporary fire pit cleaned up and the ground covered. Everyone was ready to head home. The ride with all their family and supplies would take about two hours.

They moved steadily back through town and saw the crowd at the side of the courthouse had grown even more.

The alleyway between the buildings could not take anymore. People were backing up and into the street.

As the Ward family wagons approached, people recognized Brice Ward at the front and center of the family return trip home.

They became quiet as the family got closer. By the time Brice had stopped, the crowd was absolutely breathless.

Brice had frequently expressed his opinion of people that read the reports and the emotional responses to the bad news by many. He almost had a sneer on his face as he looked toward the crowd.

Unbeknownst to Brice, Anna Wallace had found a way to crawl down from the wagon seat beside Miz Lizzie and was walking toward the alley way. She walked slowly and tried to smile to the few people she recognized.

As the crowd parted for Anna Wallace, Brice could see from his horse that several people were crying at the wall of paper. Seeing Anna Wallace, he called out, "Anna Wallace, come back and get in the wagon."

Anna Wallace ignored Brice's call and continued toward the wall. Once again, Anna Wallace recognized families that had members of the

26th Regiment standing in front of the wall. Some were crying openly, and others contained their emotions to mere tears down the cheek.

Finally, having reached the wall, Anna Wallace held the shoulders of a woman of similar age. She too, had a husband and soldier in the 26th Regiment. His name was Henry Rogers.

The young woman looked at the hands on her shoulders and turned to face Anna Wallace. The crying woman said nothing. She hugged Anna Wallace without hesitation.

She stepped back and wiped her face with a handkerchief. She then stepped aside and gave Anna Wallace room to walk to the wall.

Anna Wallace turned and stepped to the wall. She stood perfectly straight, especially for a woman soon to have a child. She stared straight ahead. She gave no visible reaction to what she read.

The crowd continued to remain absolutely still. Even the wind and the birds made no sound.

By this time, Brice had become irritated and seeing no reaction from Anna Wallace, he stepped out of the saddle and to the ground. He walked with quick strides to Anna Wallace.

The crowd found even more room to step aside for Brice Ward to get to his daughter-in-law. Everyone took at least one step backwards to give him more room than necessary.

Without looking at the courthouse wall, Brice placed his hands on Anna Wallace Ward's shoulders with a soft hand. "Anna, please come back to the wagon. I want to go home." There was a small tremor in his voice.

Anna Wallace stood for a moment. She then turned to Brice Ward and softly whispered, "Pappa, I love you!"

She stepped away from Brice and started walking toward the wagons, everyone in the Ward families, watched with great concern, as she turned. They saw nothing from her but small tears running down her face.

Brice Ward watched her gracefully leave. He saw people watching her and then at him. He faced the courthouse wall once again. This time, he could not miss the obvious.

As if the print for James' name was enlarged by ten times, Brice could not have missed seeing the death roster showing **Private James Ward-Dead.**

No mule could have kicked him in the chest any harder. No shock could have been worse. No result could be more meaningful.

Brice Ward threw his hands onto the wall, pulling at the paper as if he could change what it said. He screamed a deathly sound from hell itself. "My God, they've killed my son!!" He fell to his knees and cried in sobs that would restrict any man's ability to breathe.

Seeing Brice on the ground, Anna Wallace returned to Brice's side. She kneeled in front of the man, took his hands in hers, and said, "Pappa, we need to go home."

She stood and pulled at Brice's arms. He rose still crying. She kissed him on the forehead, took his hand, and led him to the wagon.

They both made their way to the wagon seat, and she allowed Brice to sit by Miz Lizzie on the return trip home.

Anna Wallace went to Brice's brother Josh and asked him to take Brice's horse home. Josh's son took the reins to his family wagon while Brice's younger brother prepared to lead the patriarch's wagon home.

She crawled into the back of the wagon, with some help from a younger nephew, who placed a straw bale on the ground to help her onto the wagon.

As they started to move again, she heard someone from the crowd say aloud, "Well, Mister Brice Ward ain't so proud now, is he?"

Anna Wallace Ward showed her disdain for the man by offering a brief hand gesture. Her immediate thought was, "Not very lady-like but most appropriate."

* * * * *

The state of affairs in the North Carolina Capitol was chaotic. Governor Vance, former Commander of the now renowned 26th Regiment was not happy with President Jefferson Davis.

Relations between the two leaders was starting to fray to the point of conflict. Davis was requiring more troops from North Carolina to reinforce the recent losses in the North. And he wanted them in Virginia very soon.

Vance argued that over twenty-five percent of the troops at Gettysburg were from North Carolina. Of those killed and wounded Confederate soldiers in the battle, one in three were from the Old North State.

The Governor vehemently pushed back and suggested that North Carolina was not going to send her sons to fight in a war for Virginia. He also expressed exacerbation at North Carolina being the central logistics depot for Lee's army.

"We're being constantly levied for men, uniforms, weapons, food, and supplies. Our railroads seemed to move filled to the North and empty when they return. At the very least, you could bring back our wounded to recover." Vance offered.

He continued, "You expect us to hold off the Union army and navy off our coast and protect those rail lines. If you continue to take our people, we'll lose the few ports we have now, and the blockade runners around Wilmington are going to be destroyed. Mister President, the State of North Carolina cannot supply the entire South!"

Davis replied with another unveiled threat regarding "the neighbors" surrounding Vance's state."

To the clear threat, Vance responded with a typical curt remark, "Sir, to hell with our neighbors! If we must fight, we'll fight for our State, not for you and this Confederacy."

Vance added, "Given you have lost a major battle in Gettysburg and a similar and perhaps worse defeat in Vicksburg, I'm not sure how many neighbors we have left!"

* * * * *

Cooler heads prevailed between the two men and their respective cabinets. North Carolina continued to reluctantly levy for new troops.

Many of them would join the 26th Regiment and other North Carolina regiments in and around Richmond and Petersburg, Virginia.

The railways would remain active for the next two years. Disenchanted North Carolina deserters would begin to find safe havens in the caves and woods in the mountains of North Carolina.

Locally, the levy offices throughout the state were met with loud and increasingly violent receptions. The levy for young boys soon replaced a levy for men. It was clear, a levy for older men would probably be next.

Families, especially those that had already lost a loved one in the war, found ways to lie about birth dates and hiding the young men in secret cellars or places on their farms.

To enforce the levies, the Home Guard roved throughout the state. They received a mission to enforce law and order. They went far beyond that mandate.

While some of the Home Guard actually did reluctantly enforce the law and protect the people of the area. Too many of the Home Guard found their newfound authority too tempting to pass for the exploitation of the local community.

Too many were nothing but marauders, stealing livestock, crops, and the minimal personal accumulated wealth of the farmers and shop owners.

When the marauder's demands were not met, they effectively demonstrated their abilities at burning farms, beatings, hanging, rape, and murder.

The infamous woman recruit, of the 26th Regiment, Private "Sam" Malinda Blalock, would run a group of marauders in the western area of the State. She would share that infamous behavior with her husband Kess Blalock. There was apparently no crime they were not willing to commit to enrich their own lives, even after the war.

* * * * *

The success of the Union army at both Gettysburg and Vicksburg gave real hope, although not spoken in public, to the slaves of the South. Even in North Carolina, uprisings were occurring more often.

What was little known by many was the famous "underground railroad" ran through North Carolina. The area along the East Coast became a holding area for runaway slaves moving from the South to the potential safe havens in the North.

From the beginning, the battles around New Bern, North Carolina were significant in that those safe havens were bordered to the East by the Atlantic Ocean and controlled by the Union navy. The Federal army facing to the West of the ports on the coast, toward the center and defending against the State of North Carolina.

By preventing the recapture of the ports of New Bern, Bogue Sound, Greenville, and Little Washington, little control was left for the State other than the North and South roads and railroads.

These became the lifeline to Virginia. Those were being hard-pressed by those same Federal troops occupying the coastal area.

After the Union victories at Gettysburg and Vicksburg, rumors of the terrible swath being cut across the South by General William Tecumseh Sherman were in the papers nearly every day.

The news was not good.

Governor Vance did not like what he saw. Utter destruction inflicted in Tennessee, Alabama, Georgia, and South Carolina meant North Carolina was not far behind.

A military genesis wasn't required for anyone to understand that North Carolina was being squeezed from the North, soon the South, and the State was under constant pressure from the coast.

The unwanted war in North Carolina was fast approaching from many directions.

* * * * *

On the Ward farms, everything was moving much slower. Suddenly farm chores and life lost its urgency.

The livestock had been greatly reduced to pay both taxes and meet levies for supplies for the army. By the Fall of 1863, The Ward family brothers decided to reduce the cost of feeding the animals and use the rest for the levies to offset their taxes.

Fields and crops were not being plowed or planted other than enough for the Ward family farms to subsist for their personal needs. Small portions were being sold to other farms in need of food for the community.

To pay taxes, they were forced to reduce their land by nearly a hundred acres. They were paid in Confederate currency, paper money that was essentially worthless.

The good news at the Brice Ward farm was the birth of a new baby boy in mid-July. He was beautiful to look upon by nearly all that stood over him.

He had soft blue eyes and a shock of red hair. A neighbor, without thinking, said upon seeing him at his baptism, "My Lord, he looks just like James."

Brice Ward nearly ran from the church. He often visited the child, while the baby slept in his crib. He would stand watching for minutes without saying a word.

When Miz Lizzie caught him in such a visit, she asked, "Brice, what are you thinking?"

He said without hesitation, "Why do we bring them into this world only to be slaughtered like hogs? Why would God do this to them?"

Miz Lizzie hung her head, "I can't speak for the Lord Brice. But He has always been kind to us by giving us good children." She paused.

"James was with us for thirty years. He was everything you would want in a son. He revered you for your service and he felt like this was a war he had to fight too." She waited for her husband's response.

After a moment of silence, he said, "I didn't want him to go to this war. It wasn't right and I told him so. He didn't listen to me. He did it for twenty dollars in gold, for God's sake! I would have given him the money!"

Lizzie gently embraced his arm, "Brice, the boy did what he thought was right for him and Anna Wallace. He didn't think he would ever leave the State. You know that he would have been levied into service either way."

Brice pulled his arm from his wife and left the child's room in their house. Lizzie followed him to the kitchen area, "Lizzie, I'm lost. I don't know what to do." He whispered.

"You need to pray on it with the Lord Brice." Miz Lizzie offered.

"I'm too mad at God to pray to him right now!" He quickly left the house before she could respond.

Anna Wallace Ward was a new mother with no husband to help her. She had a farm but no one to help her run that farm.

Miz Lizzie insisted she bring her small family of two and live with them at the Ward farmhouse where she already had a room waiting. Lizzie was most persuasive, and Anna Wallace just had no idea what to do by herself.

By mid-August, a small sea trunk was delivered to the farm by two soldiers of the 26th Regiment. "Sir, I'm Private Nathan Brewer of Company E, 26th Regiment. This here is Private John Brooks. We were instructed by Colonel Martin, the Regimental Commander to deliver this here box of personal possessions of your son, Private James Ward."

The soldiers were greeted with great fanfare by the family. It was obvious that both men were still recovering from their own wounds. Neither of the very young men made any pretense of their conditions.

Brice encouraged them to stay overnight given the lateness of the day. They kindly accepted the invitation. What appeared as a great feast was placed before the men, and they were surrounded by the entire Ward extended family.

He asked them, "Gentlemen, may I ask how old you are?"

Nathan responded first, "I'm nineteen Sir, I join in March of 1862."

John Brooks responded as well, "Sir, I'm not too far past twenty Sir. I joined at Cartersville at the same time James was enlisted."

Both men explained why they had been assigned this duty of delivering personal possessions to families while recovering from their wounds.

While a little younger, Nathan seemed to be the one in charge. John Brooks was the quieter one.

Both of the boys had been shot on July 1, at McPherson's Ridge. Their wounds were bad enough to be in the hospital and not in the battle on July 3. They were bunked close by each other along Herr's Ridge until July 4th when they were placed into wagons and retreated with the army toward Virginia.

Brice asked if they would recount what happened on July 1st. "Can you tell us anything about what James was doing?"

Nathan hesitated to start the conversation. This was not the first time he had been asked the question and he knew how it would probably end, only in more sorrow for the family.

"Sir, what I know is that James and Henry Rogers were hell with them special rifles they used. Captain Brewer used 'em all the time in the best places. He was good at it, Sir. Not sure I can say a whole lot more." Nathan took another drink of the previously offered good and sweet apple cider.

John Brooks almost whispered, "He hated the shot he didn't get off before 'King' was killed. It weighed heavy on him for sure. Felt like he failed not protecting the Colonel. Wasn't nothing he could do, though. God just decided it was King's time to go. He did right by killing the man that shot the Colonel though."

The rest of the evening took a somber tone. It went just as Nathan Brewer knew it would. It always did.

Sometimes, war stories don't need to be told.

Someone mentioned Stephen Ward and the mood changed dramatically for both young men. They started telling all the great stories about Stephen never wearing boots, being the best messenger Company E ever had. How he saved Captain Brewer from certain death on July 3rd.

Both men were exhausted by the end of the evening from eating, drinking, and telling stories. The extended Ward family started drifting away towards their own homes.

When sleeping arrangements were offered by Miz Lizzie, the men suggested they could stay in the barn for the night. Brice pushed back on the suggestion and said the family would find other arrangements more appropriate for their distinguished guests.

Anna Wallace suggested, "Pappa, let me take these young men to our cabin. We have two rooms where they can sleep on a comfortable bed. Why let it go to waste?"

She continued, "I will lead them to the house, and they can secure their wagon in our barn for the night. I will return before it is too dark."

Brice drew up from the suggestion, but Miz Lizzie gave him a look and said, "Be quiet Old Man!"

The Ward Patriarch took her advice but did add, "I'll take care of the wagon here Anna Wallace, you take Jer's hitched wagon out by the barn to get them situated. I'm sure Jer can take it from there to home." He nodded at his brother.

Anna Wallace did as he suggested. She went inside her home for the first time in weeks. There was a little dust, but the two young soldiers remarked it was a fine home.

Anna Wallace blushed at the comment. She sat down for a moment in the living area to ask a question. "Kind Sirs, I want to thank you for bringing my husband's possessions. It is a true kindness, and I would ask that you express my great thanks to the Colonel. Before I leave you to your rest, may I ask you a simple question?"

Nathan spoke, "Yes Ma'am. If I can answer it, I will."

Anna Wallace pressed her dress forward with her hands and took a deep breath. "Was my husband a good soldier?"

Before Nathan could respond, the quiet voice of John Brooks spoke with tears falling from his cheeks, "Ma'am, he was the bravest, most selfless, and most God-fearing man I have ever witnessed. He is a better man than me and he deserves to be where he is today, on the right hand of God Almighty."

Nathan Brewer lowered his head, "Yes Ma'am. You just heard it." He raised his head and he too had tears in his eyes.

Anna Wallace stood up, walked to each man, and whispered in their ear, "Thank you. God bless you." She kissed each on the forehead and walked out the front door.

* * * * *

Brice extended an invitation to stay a couple of days, but the young soldiers refused saying they had other similar deliveries to make before their return to camp in Virginia.

Brice Ward saw both men and their wagon on their way the next day after a large breakfast and a basket with more food for the road.

After they left, Brice went to the barn where James' chest was initially stored. Beside the chest were a couple of other items that he recognized without knowing what was in the wraps.

When he opened the chest, it contained many packets of letters from the family James had received throughout his service. They were bundled and tied with ribbon, tobacco twine, or any string that could bind them together at the time.

There were more than a hundred letters. They were labeled by address, "From Anna Wallace," "From Momma," "From Family," and others. James' canteen with his initials carved on it was there beside a butcher knife in a scabbard he had made from leather pieces. The LeMat pistol that Brice had given to James was still in the leather holster and the cartridge box looked as if it had never been used.

James' pocket watch was inside his haversack. Several wooden pencils were inside along with blank writing paper. The canvas bag included his writing notebook. A journal, covered in soft leather, was also there with many pages left to be completed. Its last entry was dated the morning of July 3rd, 1863.

When Brice looked deeper into the chest, he saw at least eight additional journals. He was afraid to even open the books to start reading. He put them back in to the chest and the haversack laid to rest on top of the other journals.

He closed the chest and walked over to the other two wrapped packages. He opened the first wrapped leather bag and found the rifled musket that James had carried with him to his new unit.

It had been cleaned with immaculate care. The polished wood shined in the sunlight. The gun mettle was a deep blue like a midnight sky in a Carolina Summer. The oil wiped across it had protected it from rust and corrosion for the entire war.

Last of particular note was a small tin type photograph obviously taken after recently arriving in Virginia in 1863. He was in his new 26th Regiment uniform that followed the unit in April 1863 and then issued to the Regiment.

His pose, while sitting, he held in his right hand the standing Leonard Rifle. On his knee was not a kepi hat or any other formal head gear that many units wore of the day. The knee held the same floppy felt field hat he wore when he left home.

He found the other leather wrapping and carefully untied the leather straps and opened the waterproofed leather. He reluctantly slid the rifle out of the cover.

Brice Ward nearly fell to his knees and braced himself against the chest. He sat down on the ground and draped the rifle across his lap. He silently cried for several minutes, eyes closed, and whispered, "James, why didn't you stay home?"

* * * * *

As Brice Ward stood in the shadows of the large Oak Tree, there was a gentle breeze to soften the late Summer heat of the day. He sat down to rest.

He surveyed the property from an old slat chair that always seemed to be there when he needed it. Brice held an old pipe filled with tobacco and contemplated striking the match to light the cured leaf.

What he saw before him was a sprawling farm that expanded to as far as his old eyes could see. Brice wondered how the farm would survive if the war continued to bleed the South.

The union of the Ward brothers was under some pressure. Between the government taxes, marauders, and broken families from the war, a couple of the brothers were considering selling their property and going West.

Brice knew that running from the war here and taking on the troubles of the West would not make their lives any better. Trying to convince his brothers it was a mistake would serve no great purpose. They would decide what was best for their family and not necessarily for the extended family.

No final decisions were made. However, Brice saw, when the families gathered, where the discussions were leaning each Sunday afternoon. The youngest of the Ward brothers, Issac, and Nem, were pretty confident in their minds.

The older Ward brothers, Brice, Josh, and Jer were too set in their ways to contemplate restarting their lives. They would stay for as long as they could keep their dwindling farms.

Brice could only imagine what he would have bestowed on James, if he were still alive. He had closed James' chest and put a lock on it. He stored it inside the attic of the family farmhouse.

He gave the tin type photograph to Anna Wallace, and she was most unnerved by the photograph. Brice was unsure whether it was seeing her husband in a photograph or was it him in a uniform with the weapons of his trade?

Either way, she gave the photograph back to Brice to keep it to remember his son.

The very thought of James always caused anger to grow inside his chest. For a man that held his emotions in check so well, he found tears falling down his cheeks too often these days.

* * * * *

May 18, 1864

To Mrs. Anna Wallace Ward, General Delivery, Whiteville, North Carolina
In Reference To: Collection of Remains

Dear Mrs. Ward,

I am in reference to your recent letters regarding the location of the remains of your late husband, Private James Ward, of the Army of Northern Virginia and his demise during the Battle at Gettysburg, Pennsylvania.

We offer our Christ-felt condolences on his passing and with the understanding of your desire to return his remains for burial in your family cemetery located in North Carolina.

For your consideration, Private Ward's remains were carefully wrapped and placed into a temporary grave near the Gettysburg Cemetery. His remains were clearly identified by Captain Stephen Brewer, who we understand was his company commander, and was in a Union hospital during that period. Captain Brewer has since recovered from his wounds and is now held as a prisoner of war in Ohio.

Upon notice of your expected arrival, Private Ward's remains will be removed from its temporary grave and prepared for their return to your home.

Please carry this letter with you for safe passage on your journey. We offer our best courtesy and consideration as you truly deserve for such a solemn occasion.

With your permission, a small service will be prepared for Private Ward's transfer to your custody. I await your instructions and notice of your expected arrival date.

I am most sincerely and in the Lord's name we pray,

Pastor David Jones, Superintendent of the Gettysburg Cemetery

CHAPTER 18

LONG JOURNEY HOME, JUNE 24, 1864

The arrival of the letter from Pastor and Superintendent Jones had been hoped for but was still a surprise after so much time passing since the July 1863 battle.

It was sealed and was read with great care. Each sentence was parsed to interpret its proper meaning. The Pastor seemed to make it clear that James' body was found and could be conveyed from Gettysburg back to North Carolina.

The real question was, how would they cross the States of North Carolina, Virginia, Maryland, and Pennsylvania and past two great armies engaged in open battle.

A quick telegraph message to Raleigh resulted in a slightly longer telegraph message from Governor Vance asking for courtesy and consideration for the passing of the family through their many obstacles on their journey.

On a separate message, Vance offered doubts about his message having any weight in passing into the Union forces. However, he wished the Ward's well and advised them to post a white flag on their conveyance.

There were many discussions regarding transportation. It was suggested that taking the train would be the fastest method, but the trains from North Carolina would only run to Richmond. Catching a train North would be impossible since Richmond was now under siege.

A single wagon on the road would be harassed by both armies and with a very small group, they would be easy prey for Home Guards on either side. With a steady pace, it was estimated it would take about two or three weeks to get to Gettysburg. This assumed no extended delays for weather or the armies.

Then there was the question regarding who should go. This was a much greater debate for the entire Ward family.

Brice was of the opinion that he and one of the other Ward brothers would go to retrieve the body. He was quickly stopped in his thoughts.

Miz Lizzie was the first to put up her hand, "No, I will get my son's body out of the ground if I have to dig it up myself and no army on either side is going to stop me!"

Anna Wallace made it very clear that she was going as well. Brice pushed back on that remark and offered, "Who will take care of the child while we are gone?"

She was just as quick with a response for her ten-month-old child, "He is going to find his father too!"

No matter how hard Brice pushed, neither of the Ward women were relenting. War or no war, they were going to get the body of their beloved son and husband.

It was finally decided that there would be six members of the family traveling to Gettysburg. Brice would lead the family in one wagon that included Miz Lizzie, Anna Wallace, and the baby.

The second wagon would include brothers Josh and Jerimiah Ward. Their wagon would contain food, water, and supplies along with tentage for the group to cover themselves at night or storm.

Brice also wanted both of the older brothers so if either army considered pulling them into the war, they would be considered too old.

Both of the brothers were in their mid-sixties. While there were men in the sixties in the war, they were fewer and far between.

What made all three of the Ward brothers the better choice for the trip was their proficiency with their weapons. They could be handy in an armed conflict.

After all arguments and plans were made, the journey began with a large gathering at the Ward farmhouse. Prayers were offered, instructions provided for all emergencies while the group was gone, and finally hugs were shared by brothers, sisters, cousins, nephews, and nieces.

They left the Ward Farm on May 23, 1864. They had previously sent, by letter to the superintendent, their intention to arrive at the cemetery by the 24th of June but no later than June 30th.

Getting through the Confederate lines had been relatively easy. Most senior officers read the letters of safe passage with understanding and sought to accommodate the family as best they could.

By six o'clock each evening, they had set up their small camp, prepared light meals from their supplies and the food that both Miz Lizzie and Anna Wallace had prepared in advance.

Their supplies included fresh corn, tomatoes, potatoes, onions, and flour in abundance. Cured meat was carefully covered in cheesecloth wrapping and portions were cut off each day to place into the small black cauldron that hung on a spit over the open fire.

It was Brice's intent to purchase vegetables and fruit along the way but even during this period of early harvesting, the pickings were thin.

When horse apples were found in the wild, they took advantage and pulled as many as they could. Some were still too green but could be boiled for some small hand pies for the next day.

Within the first two weeks, they were out of eggs and the flour was getting low. By this time, they were well into Virginia. Confederate pickets were frequently encountered, and their letters were presented, as required. They were just past Richmond when they met a picket that provided valuable information for the rest of the trip.

One of the pickets informed them the Union army was all around the area after a big battle to the West in the woods earlier in May. They called it the Battle in the Wilderness.

"We lost a bunch a boys when all the cannons set the woods on fire. Bad enough to have to fight the damned Yankees but too hard to fight them and the fire too. Just burned 'em to a crisp." The picket offered.

"Most of our boys are over by Spotsylvania right now. Seems General Grant's taking it personal to run right through us. I'm sure General Lee will have something to say about that." He paused for a moment.

"Folks, I'm sorry for your loss and I wish you well on your journey. I'm sure your son would be most happy to see you. By and by, you might keep your eyes open for some of the Home Guard. They're a mean bunch and the fools try to steal everything." To Brice Ward, the man on picket duty looked to be in his mid-twenties.

He was in rags for a uniform. The hat had at least two bullet holes through it. His toes showed through on one boot. He was filthy with dirt and grime.

He saluted Brice before they departed. Brice instead reached out his hand to the soldier. "Thank you, young man. Keep your head down and stay alive. Someone has the tell this story."

They moved toward Fredericksburg and were soon met by the Home Guard as warned.

Home Guards back in North Carolina were not well thought of and Brice had no reason to believe they were any better in Virginia.

Brice, Josh, and Jer eased their hands under the wagon seat to ensure their weapons were close and ready to fire, if needed. Jer had a musket and a LeMat pistol that Brice had given him before they departed on the journey. He had the pistol cocked and ready to fire.

"Halt and be recognized!" Shouted the apparent leader.

While reluctant to do so, Brice pulled the reins in and stopped the horses. "We're the Ward family on our way to Gettysburg to retrieve the body of my son and this woman's husband. Let us be on our way."

The man laughed and looked at the five other men on horseback. "Well, Mister Ward, how do we know you're not some Yankee spy caring valuable information to that butcher General Grant?"

"Sir, as you should easily be able to identify by my accent, I'm from North Carolina and I'm sure General Grant would have no more place at my dinner table than you would." Brice eased the reins to Miz Lizzie.

She took the reins and said with a sly smile, "Now Brice, don't be rude to the nice gentlemen."

"Yeah Brice, be nice to me. What proof do you have of your journey?" The leader moved closer to the wagon and looked in the back.

"Well, what we got here?" He said with a sneer on his face.

Brice said, "She's my son's wife. She is holding his baby boy. Like I said, we're going to get his remains and take him home." Anna Wallace was laying back against the opposite wall of the wagon with the baby between her legs.

The leader nodded to one of his men to move toward the other wagon. Josh held the reins in one hand. Jer was sitting there smiling and nodded in greeting to the rider. The wagon break was on, and Josh wrapped the reins around it.

"I have documents to attest to the purpose of our journey. We even have a message from the Governor of North Carolina." Brice slowly reached for the envelopes just inside his coat pocket.

The leader edged the horse up closer to Brice's wagon, "I don't give a damn about the Governor of North Carolina, and I'm only interested in what you got in these wagons."

Instead of the envelopes promised, Brice pulled the LeMat pistol and pointed right at the leader. "Let me be clear, Sir. I don't give a damn about your interests in the least. What I have in this wagon is your imminent death. Ride off and leave us alone."

The leader eased his horse a bit away from the wagon, "Well now Old Man, ain't you the brave one? I'll bet that old piece don't even work anymore. What do you think Horace?"

The man named Horace responded, "Well Boss, he's pointing it at you and that makes me feel better. Besides there's six of us and three old men. I don't think he can take us all."

One of the other men had slipped to the side of the wagon and near to the back of the seat where Brice sat with his pistol.

Brice fired directly at the leader and dropped him from the horse. His next shot was at the man they call Horace. With two shots, Horace dropped from his saddle to the hard road.

The man by Jer's wagon came face to face with the other LeMat pistol and the man fell where he stood with a surprised look on his face.

The man on standing on the ground directly behind Brice's wagon seat reached for his gun. Suddenly a shotgun fired into his chest from the back of the wagon. His last look was of the young woman with a baby between her legs and the shotgun smoking from the barrel with her shawl draping over the weapon, less than three feet away.

A horse for one of the men reared up and the man was thrown to the ground. His neck was broken with the fall.

The last man sitting on his horse had seen enough. He spurred his horse and disappeared down the road toward Richmond.

Brice was already on the ground standing over the leader. The leader was still breathing but his wound was mortal. "Boy, what did I tell you? You should have just let us go. But no. You had to try and take advantage of old and helpless people."

The leader had a wry smile on his face. "Not so old and helpless after all." He closed his eyes and died.

"Josh, strip these boys down of weapons and ammunition. If they got any valuables grab it and we'll use it for trade. If you can catch any of those horses, put the gear in the wagon and we'll use that for trade too. Tie the horses to the back of my wagon." Brice was already getting the earthly remains of the leader and dragging his body off the road.

In a few moments, Josh and Jer had already caught two of the horses. As directed, they had stripped the horses tack and put the saddles and bags into his wagon. "Brice, these boys must have been some poor thieves to just walk up like that. The saddles and bags are in pretty poor shape, and I only found about eleven dollars between those two back there."

Brice had been a bit more fortunate. The leader had fifty-eight dollars in gold, thirty-six silver dollars, and another hundred and fifty-two dollars in Confederate currency. His saddle and bags were of a slightly higher quality and contained some small jewelry such as rings, necklaces, and brooches. He found three gold watches, two with gold chains attached.

He smiled back at Jer, "Yeah, I'm glad we spent a little time working on such occasions as this before leaving. We just got to be watchful and beat them to the trigger."

The baby was crying from all of the noise and Anna Wallace had already reloaded the shotgun and was soothing the baby. "Anna Wallace, you, and the baby all right?"

"Yes Pappa. We're fine. Just a little too much excitement." She eased her little finger onto the baby's lips, and it began to suckle it.

Miz Lizzie had helped with capturing the Home Guard's weapons and personal possessions. All such items were being placed into a box directly behind the seat of the wagon.

"Brice, we gonna give these boys a proper burial?"

"No, we'll let someone else or mother nature deal with them now. God will take care of the rest." Brice climbed back up into the seat.

"I thought you and God weren't talking anymore." She said with small grin.

"Well, we're at least talking again. Can't say much more than that right now." He slapped the reins on the horses' rumps, and the wagons leaped forward.

Several hours later, as they approach Fredericksburg, they ran into Union cavalry moving toward them. Once again, the Ward family warily watched the horses arrive and discreetly prepared to defend themselves, if necessary.

The Captain of the cavalry troop of about thirty men pulled up, blocked the road, and troopers moved their horses around the two wagons. "Halt and identify yourselves!"

Brice's first reaction was, here we go again. He recalled the exact command of the Home Guard leader that tried to rob them.

He did, as ordered, and stopped the wagon. Brice pushed the brake on the wagon and tied the reins around the brake handle. He placed both hands on his knees.

"Captain, we're the Ward family and we're about the business of going to Gettysburg to retrieve the remains of our son and this woman's husband. We would respectfully ask you to let us pass and be on our way. I believe we still have a ways to go." Brice spoke clearly and without disdain in his voice.

"I am Captain Joseph Stahl of the Army of the Potomac Sir. Do you have papers to support your claim?"

Brice answered, "Sir, I have letters in my vest pocket. They include a letter from the Governor of North Carolina requesting safe passage. If I might be allowed to withdraw it Sir?"

Captain Stahl squinted his eyes just a bit but responded, "Mister Ward, you may ease those documents out, but Sir, make sure they are documents and not a weapon or you and your family will be placed in serious danger. Do you understand?"

"I do understand Captain Stahl." As directed, Brice eased the envelopes from his vest pocket. He promptly passed them to a young cavalry soldier that stood on the ground near the seat of the wagon.

At that particular moment, Brice suddenly remembered the drills they had practiced back home. He had no doubt that Anna Wallace had the shotgun eased into position between her legs, and ready to fire. He could only hope she remembered the part about not firing until threatened.

Anna Wallace and the shotgun were silent.

The young cavalry trooper handed the envelopes to his Captain.

Captain Stahl read each letter at least twice. He placed the letters back into the envelopes and got off his horse. He walked casually over to the wagon and handed the documents back to Brice.

"Mister Ward, my condolences on your family's loss. Lord knows we've all seen enough of that already. At Gettysburg, you say?"

"Yes Sir. It was at Gettysburg that he was killed. He was with the 26th Regiment of North Carolina Troops. Colonel Burgwyn's Regiment. General Pettigrew's Brigade." Brice took the envelopes and returned them to the vest pocket.

The Captain bowed his head at hearing the unit that James was associated. "I lost my Corps Commander, General Reynolds to the 26th Regiment on the first day. Also had the misfortune of running into General Pettigrew on July 12th at the river. I'm guessing we both lost a lot that month."

Brice could tell the man was sincere with his expressed emotions as he could be regarding both his son and the men the Captain had lost on the Union side.

"It was a damned fools war to begin with Captain and hopefully we'll learn to do better once it's over. My condolences to you, your men, and your families as well."

Captain Stahl reached his hand up to Brice to shake. Brice responded with equal strength. The Captain returned to his horse and stood in the stirrups. One of the troopers ran up, leaning into the Captain's horse. They shared a brief conversation in whispers.

"Mister Ward, we've had a rash of ambushes by some men that claim to be the Home Guard. They're really just a bunch of thieves though. I would suggest you be alert at all times for such men, until you get well past Fredericksburg."

The Captain guided his horse a few paces behind Brice's wagon and eyed the two horses tied to the rear. "I see you have extra horses with you?"

Brice was more than a little uneasy by the question. "Yes Sir. Brought them as extras if we had one of our other horses go down. Sounds like good advice you've given to me, Sir. We'll be sure and be ready for them if the need arises."

The Captain returned to the side of the wagon and sat even with Brice, both men looking forward and down the road. He slowly turned to look Brice Ward straight in the eyes, "Mister Ward, you wouldn't have seen any of those type men on your recent journey, would you?"

Brice never hesitated or blinked. He looked the Captain in the eyes. "No, Sir! But if we do, we'll be ready!"

Captain Stahl smiled, "Of that I have no doubt. Whatever fate those men might have with such an event, they will probably deserve the result. Don't you think?"

"Of that, I am very sure and have no doubt Sir." Brice almost whispered to the Captain.

"Mount up men, we need to move up the road toward Stafford before we can rest." He tipped his hat, "Have a safe journey Mister Ward."

Brice and the family relaxed after the Union cavalry moved up the road. He turned to Jer and asked, "What was that all about?"

Jer shrugged his shoulders, "That Union boy wiped some blood off one of those extra horses you got tied up on the back of your wagon. He also got a little pale when he saw that brand on the rump of one of them."

The Ward family patriarch took his handkerchief out and wiped his sweating brow. Miz Lizzie asked, "What's wrong Brice, they left us to our journey?"

"Yeah, they left. The Captain knew what we had done, and he didn't care. We just eliminated one more of his problems." He wiped again, took the reins, and gave the horses another smack on the rump.

For two more days of similar encounters with Union forces, they pushed forward into Maryland. What Brice noticed was the further North they moved, the less problems they encountered when providing their documents.

By late June, the early crops of corn, wheat, and vegetables were well in store. Unlike so much of the South, here food was aplenty.

There also seemed to be an abundance of respectful people that understood the shock of war and what the Ward family was trying to accomplish. Even when offering to pay or barter for supplies, the family was being well provisioned. No one tried to take advantage of the family. On more than one occasion, they were invited to attend church with their new benefactors.

Brice accepted one such invitation to a church but would not attend another one after that. His response to Miz Lizzie's question why he wouldn't attend was, "Me and the Lord aren't there yet."

They had finally made it just South of Emmitsburg, Maryland on June 21, 1864. The trip had gone fairly well after skirting to the West of Washington and Baltimore. They stayed away from the Shenandoah and the mountains to the South and West to avoid any major conflicts in Virginia.

Brice knew they had a few days to spare before they got the Gettysburg and decided that a day or two of rest was better for the tired Ward family. He also knew they were going to need to resupply themselves for the long trip back home.

They found a farm nearby and asked permission to set up camp for a couple of days by a small lake just South of Tom's Creek. The owner, Mister Issac Hager, was suspicious at first, but once he read the letters, he quickly offered his farm and home to the Wards.

Brice thanked Mister Hager for his family's hospitality and offered to pay or work the farm while he was there. The man kindly refused his help.

They set up camp near a small lake not too far from the main farmhouse. Brice was looking at the list the family had put together over dinner the previous night, assessing their situation physically, emotionally, and financially for the return trip home.

Josh had been busy taking care of the wagons and horses. Some traces and halters needed to be repaired and at least two of the wagon wheels needed to be repaired and tightened.

Jer had been fishing, with permission, at the lake and caught some nice Bream and Bass. He was busy, at the side of the camp, cleaning the fish for supper tonight.

Miz Lizzie had offered to make some of her family's favorite dish of chicken and dumplings for the farm owner and his family of five. She suggested tomorrow's evening meal as her way of saying thank you in return for their kind hospitality. All that was requested was some flour, four chickens, and a little lard.

The farmer and his family were descendants of Quakers from Europe and the offered meal was somewhat unfamiliar to them. They happily accepted the invitation and provided Miz Lizzie with her requested items.

Anna Wallace had also offered to milk the twelve cows in the milking barn for a single pale of milk. The milk would be primarily for the baby.

The children of the farmer were very excited to accept the offer of Anna Wallace taking on their chores with glee.

The two teenage boys and one older teenage girl offered to help Anna Wallace with the milking. She accepted their advice and help, knowing full well, she was very familiar with this work back home.

Each of the children brought stools, milking pails, and large milk cans for the milk. Throughout the milking session, the three children cascaded Anna Wallace Ward about everything Southern, North Carolina, being married, and having children.

Their questions were not difficult subjects for Anna Wallace to answer.

"Do you own slaves?" Thomas, age sixteen, asked.

"No. We farm like you do. With our family." Anna Wallace replied.

"Why did you leave the Union?" David, age fourteen, asked.

"We didn't leave the Union. We didn't vote that way. We were made to leave the Union by politicians." She firmly answered.

"Are you a Southern Belle? You and your baby are so beautiful!" asked Louise, age eighteen.

Anna Wallace had to laugh at that one. She looked down on her clothes. They were thread-bare in places, a couple of tears near the hem, her shoes were scuffed without color, and her hair hung long and low on her head, snarled and tangled in places.

She had just had the first bath in nearly two weeks just last night. Beautiful was not the word she would use to describe her appearance.

"I am a married woman of the South. I am not a Southern Belle of the gentry. I am a common farm girl, just like you. But you are more beautiful than I can ever hope to be."

Louise nearly fainted from the compliment. She swooned in delight and ran over to hug Anna Wallace. She nearly knocked over the milk pail.

They were in the barn for nearly two hours. Anna Wallace spent most of the time answering questions as fast as she could, while milking cows the whole time.

Once she completed the task, the boys took care of the extra milk and they rushed to the house, milking chores completed.

Louise took Anna Wallace to the cold cellar where she pulled out four one-pound cakes of butter. "Here Miss Anna Wallace, put these somewhere in your stores to keep it from melting. I would suggest some wet cheesecloth wrapped around each pound. Wet them down each day and they should last you quite a ways home."

Anna Wallace thanked her and started out the cellar door when Louise asked her, "Miss Anna Wallace, may I ask you a delicate question?"

The tone of the question concerned Anna Wallace a little, but responded, "I'm sure I will try my best to answer your question Louise, but I make no promises."

She almost knew the question before Louise asked it. "What's it like to lay with a man?"

The young girl was eighteen years old and obviously had never had that discussion with her mother. Then Anna Wallace recalled, Louise was of Quaker upbringing. It would be a hard discussion to have.

Anna Wallace smiled at Louise. "Don't you think that is a question best answered by your mother?"

"I have asked her on several occasions, and she seems too embarrassed to tell me the answer." The young woman seemed perplexed by her dilemma.

Anna Wallace softly smiled and took Louise's hand in her own. "Trust me, when I say, I understand your situation and more so, the need for answers to your question."

"The answer is very important to know before you do anything foolish with a man you are not married to." Anna Wallace pressed and smoothed her dress with her hands as she always did when nervous.

Anna Wallace continued, "If I tell you these things, will you promise not to mention it to your family what I have told you? Do you understand that you must not do these things until you are properly married?"

"Yes, I will tell no one. I promise that I won't do these things until I am married to my husband, as you were." Louise grinned from ear to ear.

Anna Wallace knew it was a bold-faced lie. Afterall, what woman would turn down the attentions of a young man in love? However, she also knew every young girl needed to know the truth of a woman's virtue without the interference of an ill-fated affair with a man.

They remained in the cold cellar for over an hour. Both women later walked hand-in-hand to the farmhouse with soft smiles on their faces.

Anna Wallace returned to their camp to see if she could assist with the supper of fish, cut potatoes and onions, and fresh bread.

Brice sat on a wood box, under a big Oak Tree, catching the late afternoon breeze on the late June Summer day. The tentage they had set up was just behind him anchored and supported by the tree and its heavy limbs.

"Josh let's keep at least two of the best horses we got and see if we can trade up for a couple more. If we have to, we'll sell the worse two and use the money to buy one if we need it going home. Get rid of that one horse with the brand on it. We don't need that following us around." Brice continued checking down his list.

He saw Anna Wallace returning down the farmhouse road with a pail of milk. He smiled as he looked at the young woman and the mother of his grandchild. For the first time, in quite a while, he saw her smiling.

The cooking fire and spit were already at work and Miz Lizzie was nearly finished as the Sun got low on the horizon.

Jer was ladling the fried fish and potatoes from the cooking oil of the large spider skillet. The fish were coated in a corn bread mix of ground yellow corn meal, salt, and pepper. They were using the last of their ground corn meal to make corn bread.

Some Summer squash and fried green tomatoes were thrown in as well. Early apples and fresh peaches were cut up into slices for dessert.

Anna Wallace had washed, dried, and laid out the tin dishes, cups, and flatware of their meager feast. For the second night in a row. They had their fill and got comfortable by the fire as it cooled down to small embers.

The conversation was light and recounted the brief adventures they had on the Hager farm that day. Not much was said regarding the purpose of their journey.

Everyone slept well that night.

It was June 22nd, and each member of the group had their task to accomplish for the day.

Josh went about bargaining for some fresh horses at a farm nearby and as referred by Mister Hager himself.

Miz Lizzie began her initial preparations for the supper meal this very night at the Hager home. She would get all the preparations done at camp and then borrow the Hager kitchen for the cooking.

Anna Wallace would take care of the baby for most of the day, but she had acquired the young Louise Hager to assist her with tending to the Ward baby. The two women continued their risqué conversation in the privacy of the camp near the lake.

Louise kept giggling with each part of their conversation. Anna Wallace couldn't help laughing at her. "What is so funny Louise?"

"Anna Wallace you must be playing a funny trick on me. I can't believe you would let a man do that to you! I would be so afraid!" She put her hands to her blushing face.

Anna Wallace only smiled, "Louise, when you truly love someone, like I loved James, it will seem so natural, you won't even think about it. And, if he truly loves you, and you love him, you'll never want to be apart again."

The giggle went away from Louise's mouth, and she whispered, "I want that, Anna Wallace. I want someone like your James. That would go to war for me."

Anna Wallace reached out and slapped the girl with her open hand, "Don't ever say that again. Don't ever wish that for your family. I've lost my husband. My son has lost his father. I'm on a journey to retrieve his remains. I don't even get him whole to take back. Is that what you really want?"

"I'm sorry. I'm sorry Anna Wallace. I didn't mean to say it like that. I just meant I want the kind of love you had with James. I'm so sorry." The girl hung her flushed face down into her hands as she cried.

Anna Wallace immediately regretted her outburst. "No, I'm sorry Louise. I was wrong to hit you. You are very right to want a love like we had together. We never imagined anything could break us apart. This is what happens when you love so much. It hurts. And you deserve the right to love someone the same way."

She paused. "I'm sorry."

She hung her head this time, "Just don't let the lust for love become greater than the love being offered to you. Love them as your very best and trusting friend, someone that would never willingly hurt you. So, then love them as one, as we discussed, because you share a common love for each other and not the love of lust."

Louise got up from the ground beneath the tree, walked over and sat down beside Anna Wallace. She leaned into the older woman, laid her head in Anna Wallace's lap, and said, "Anna Wallace, I'm sorry if I hurt you. I love you." Tears were sweeping down her face.

Anna Wallace hugged her close, kissed her on the forehead, and stroked the farm girl's soft brown hair. The young girl fell asleep.

The evening meal was wonderful and appraised by all as a feast worthy for the angels. It ended with some minor wishes for a safe journey and an exchange of postal addresses for future correspondence. Hugs and well wishes ended the night with an exchange of small gifts.

Miz Lizzie offered Mrs. Hager her prized recipe for her North Carolina Chicken and Dumplings. Jer offered a string of nice Bass caught from the lake, cleaned, and wrapped in cheesecloth by Josh.

Anna Wallace offered a blank leather covered journal that she had recovered from James' chest. "Louise, I wish to offer this journal for you to write your thoughts down each night. The next day, I want you to read what you have written and think about what you wrote. Ask yourself, did I write my real feelings down or just for what I wanted at the moment?" She gave Louise a wink and smile.

Brice was the last to offer gifts. "Mister Hager, Mrs. Hager, I cannot thank you enough for your hospitality and help. We were near the end of our rope with not much to offer. You took us in as if we were a special part of your family." Brice paused.

He pulled two gold pocket watches from his vest. They were both used but in good working order.

Brice handed one of the watches to each of the Hager boys. "No man should walk around without a proper watch to tell time. A good man must know the proper time to ensure he meets his obligations. I offer these watches to you young Hager men as a token of my appreciation for your good Christian help to me and my family in need. Thank you." Each boy beamed with excitement as they opened the watches to see the face of the timepiece.

He continued, "Mister Hager, I don't need to give you a watch to remind you of your obligations. You have shown that courtesy to my family already many times over. I know you said you would take no money from us in our time of need, but my son joined this damned war for twenty dollars in gold to buy glass windowpanes for his new bride. I'm offering you twenty dollars in gold to you, Sir and sincerely hope you put it to good use."

The Hager patriarch stepped over to Brice Ward, extended his hand and said, "Mister Ward, I accept your kind offer in the spirit in which it is intended, a love offering. May you and your family go in peace. You've seen more than enough of this war."

The evening ended with hugs, promises to stay in touch, and prayers for a safe journey.

As the Ward family made its way back to their camp, Miz Lizzie, with her arm tucked into Brice's arm said, "Didn't I recognize those two gold watches from those thieving men we killed on the road?"

Brice didn't miss a step or acknowledge the intent of the question, "Yes Ma'am. You did recognize those watches. Seemed like a good way to get rid of ill-gotten gains by putting it to a good purpose. Don't you think?"

"Well Brice T. Ward, you crafty dog, and with such eloquent words!" She laughed as they kept walking.

On June 23, 1864, the Ward family got up bright and early. Everything was packed and loaded onto the wagons. Only one extra horse remained attached to the wagon, and it was one of Brice Ward's original horses. The other four horses were fresh from Josh's visit to the local horse farmer.

They continued through Emmitsburg proper and found the bustling streets and prosperous business a bit disquieting. Nothing like this was to be found in their hometown. The war obviously meant something totally different here.

It took most of the day to get to the South side of Gettysburg, and they went straight to the cemetery as required by the letter from the superintendent.

They arrived after four o'clock in the afternoon and found the superintendent's office. "Ah, Mister Ward, we are glad to see you under these most trying circumstances. Based on your correspondence, we were expecting to see you closer to the 30th."

Brice offered, "Yes, Sir. We got an early start not knowing the problems we might run into. Also, we made good time with both weather and avoiding any conflicts along the way. Do we need to raise the body of my son?"

"Oh, no Sir. We'll take care of that. In fact, with your permission, we would like to offer you a brief service and prayers before you leave. If that is permissible to you and the family." The superintendent offered.

Miz Lizzie spoke before Brice could respond, "Sir, we would be honored to have a service with prayers. We're Methodist if you can accommodate us."

He quickly responded, "Oh, Yes Ma'am, we have an excellent Methodist minister as part of our staff. If you will allow us, we'll raise the body tonight. It will be prepared in proper linen and placed into a coffin for travel. We'll have a short service at that time. The body will also be prepared for travel. However, there will come a time when the smell may get a little rank."

Anna Wallace almost retched at that moment and quickly ran from the office.

"I'm so sorry, I did not mean to offend the young lady." The superintendent profusely apologized to the family.

The Ward family left the cemetery and found the local inn the superintendent offered as a place to stay for the night. Brice, Jer, and Josh stayed in one room and Miz Lizzie, Anna Wallace, and the baby stayed in the other room.

Brice still had a few gold and silver coins and some US currency as well. He didn't intend to use any of the nearly worthless Confederate currency until they reached Richmond or beyond.

They ate together in the little boarding house near the cemetery side of Gettysburg, and it was a good meal of roast beef, potatoes, fresh carrots, and green beans. Miz Lizzie commented on the flavorful beans with a little salted pork in the bowl. "Just like back home, I couldn't have done better." She said.

It was a fitful night of sleep for nearly everyone. Between Brice and Jer competing for snoring rights and the baby being a bit agitated and restless, they made it through the night with some sleep.

After breakfast they packed their possessions into the wagons and headed for the cemetery. Very little conversation was passed between the family.

On June 24th, 1864, the Ward family met the superintendent and several men of color standing by the fenced entrance to the temporary graveyard.

Several of the graves were open and Brice could not help but notice how shallow they were. The shallow graves facilitated the process of removing the bodies to more permanent graves or the return of the remains for families like the Wards. It did not take long to dig the bodies up, when required.

"Ah, Mister Ward. It is good to see you on this morning. I had the diggers recover your son's body from its temporary grave." He offered a warm smile.

"Thank you, Sir. We appreciate your consideration. May we see the body?" Brice requested.

The superintendent offered a frown at the question. "Mister Ward you may certainly view the body, but I must remind you, it has been nearly a year since he was laid to rest. I'm afraid the body is not what you would readily recognize as your son."

Anna Wallace offered another insight, "I must know that it is my husband wrapped in the shroud." She chocked the words out with tears rolling down her cheeks.

The superintendent knew such a request had occurred on similar occasions. "Yes Ma'am. I do understand. If I may offer, here is a small bag of items that were recovered from the body. They stayed with him until he was placed into that grave. As you can see, we have marked the tag on the bag with his grave number and name." He offered the bag to Anna Wallace.

She pulled the string at the top of the bag and opened it. Anna Wallace carefully poured the items into her hand.

A white silk handkerchief with some dirt and smudges on it was the first item. In the corner were the initials AWW sewn in by her own hand. Her gift to him when he left home the last time.

Folded inside the handkerchief was a wedding band that she had given James on their wedding day. It was the second item she recognized. On the inside of the band were the initials JW.

Lastly, she unfolded a cloth with a tin type photograph of James sitting with his rifle at his side. Brice recognized the photograph as the same as the one he had found in the chest they received last year. She didn't need to see anything else and there was very little left to see.

Anna Wallace held the bag with the items in her hands as she knelt by the wooden coffin where the newly wrapped body was waiting. She held the tears as best she could. "Oh, James, when will I see you again?" She promptly fainted to the ground.

After recovering from Anna Wallace's faint, the family stood together by the wooden coffin and listened to the Methodist minister renew a heart-felt eulogy. Prayers were offered all around and blessings bestowed.

The minister offered this message, "Dearly beloved, it is most proper, at this time, that we gather unto one another to grieve for the loss of this man, Private James Ward, of North Carolina. To all here, I truly mourn your loss. We stand here surrounded by the Summer Sun, a warm breeze upon our faces, and we are surrounded by fields freshly made for the harvest. No matter the time of the year, nothing is more certain than life comes to an end. God and nature reclaim its own. We must accept this fact of life, there is death on this earthly home." He paused.

"Yet, it seems to hurt more when it comes too early in a life, as it has for James. We feel cheated by fate, we rage at its unfairness, and perhaps we even blame God for our loss. Even in the bright Summer of light, we feel the darkness within ourselves, and we feel alone. We think of all our memories and those we shall never share with James. We dwell on our loss and not the wonderful times we shared with him, and he offered to each of you." He continued.

"There are many ways to lose a loved one, and this is the way we lost James. It is unfortunate that his life has been cut short and he leaves a family to grieve for him. However, we know this to be true, God loves his children and knows when they need to come home. Love our God for knowing when James was ready to face his Lord of all. Amen."

Two of the grave diggers came over and closed the coffin, nailed it tightly shut, and placed candle wax around the wooden box edges to seal it for the long journey home.

Brice inspected the effort and then Josh supervised the coffin's placement into the back of his wagon with Jer's help. Brice walked over to the six men in the grave diggers detail and handed each man a silver dollar. "It's not much, men but we appreciate what you have done here for our family. God bless you all."

The Ward family moved toward the wagons after offering thanks and goodbyes to the superintendent, the minister, and his workers. Brice offered two gold coins to both men, but they kindly refused the offer.

As they approached the wagons, Brice noticed a flag staff with a white cloth pennant mounted to the back portion of his wagon seat. "What's this?"

"Ah, Mister Ward. We would offer this as a way to make your trip less complicated on the way back. We have found that a flag of truce helps in the cause and helps others to see that you are not part of any army." The superintendent smiled once again.

Remembering the message from Governor Vance, Brice responded, "I see what you mean. That might help us for sure." Brice climbed onto the wagon seat besides Miz Lizzie.

The superintendent stood below the seat and passed another envelope for Brice to carry. "Sir, I believe this letter from me should also assist your journey. It clearly states you are returning your son to his home for proper burial. We hope you arrive with God's love and speed."

Brice took the letter and slipped it into his vest pocket along with the others he had brought on the journey. He gave a nod to the superintendent and "Thank you again. May God bless you and yours."

The Ward family headed South. As they left the town of Gettysburg, they could still see remnants of the battle from nearly a year ago.

From the temporary grave site, the superintendent offered the general location where James' body was found after the battle.

When walking to the place indicated, Brice, Jer, and Josh looked across the field toward Seminary Ridge to the South and West. Brice staggered on his feet as they looked at the field that was crossed by James and the 26th Regiment nearly a year before.

"Brice, I never went to war like you. How could a man come up that hill and survive" Jer found a seat on the stone wall before he fell.

"Jer, if what we've been told is even half right, there is no way. And given what we've just received from the cemetery, I believe that answers your question." Brice settled down beside him and they both cried. Josh stood near the wagons with Miz Lizzie and Anna Wallace.

Brice had worked out a plan to shorten the trip home. First, they would make their way South to Richmond. There, they would sell the wagons and extra gear for the cost of a railway ticket to North Carolina.

From Richmond, they would get a ride on the frequent railroad trips by the Confederacy to North Carolina. They would ride in the empty railcars along with wounded, and other soldiers.

Before leaving Richmond, Brice was able to send a telegraph message to town to have the other brothers bring wagons to meet them at the station in Kinston.

After arriving in the Kinston area, they were able to purchase two very poor excuses for wagons and a single mule for each wagon. They loaded remaining supplies, baggage, and the coffin of Private James Ward for the much shorter trip home.

They met Issac and Nem Ward when they were halfway home.

EPILOGUE

The war turned ugly on every front for the Confederacy. Any attempts to regain the momentum after Chancellorsville was lost in the North. Between Vicksburg and Gettysburg, The armies of the Confederacy didn't have the men, supplies, equipment, weapons, and even a government worthy of the title.

* * * * *

Robert E. Lee and his many generals found ways to keep the Union armies at bay, but they could not stop them. General Meade and the newly appointed Commander of the Union Army, Ulysses S. Grant, were pushing the Army of Northern Virginia right into the front door of President Davis's office in Richmond.

Grant knew he couldn't take it without great loss, but he knew he could break it over time. Grant was committed to being relentless in his pursuit of Lee before he could reconstitute his army.

By early 1864, Grant was successfully doing just that but at the terrible costs he feared.

* * * * *

The 26th Regiment was caught in the middle of the push. They were bounding from one battlefield to the next, trying to keep Grant from flanking Lee's army. To do so would cut off all help from North Carolina and the rest of the South.

The Regiment found itself being used to march almost continuously from the Battle of the Wilderness from May 5-7, then to Spotsylvania Courthouse, May 8-21, and then Cold Harbor from May 31 through June 12.

The early months of 1864 were bloody affairs for both sides.

Eventually, they were pushed into the siege positions for nine months around Richmond and Petersburg from June 9, 1864, until March 25, 1865.

* * * * *

When General Grant began his Spring offensive in May 1864, he had nearly one hundred and sixty-three thousand men at his disposal. After the blood bath at the Battle of Cold Harbor, in mid-June, he had lost forty-eight thousand killed, wounded, or captured. It represented nearly a third of his Army of the Potomac.

General Lee's numbers were over fifteen thousand men less than General Grant's casualties. However, he could not afford to lose over thirty thousand men dead, wounded, or captured. He only started that Spring with sixty-one thousand men. He had lost nearly half of his Army of Northern Virginia by the end of June 1864.

* * * * *

Grant's strategy called for his other main force under the command of General William T. Sherman to march from a successful campaign to take Vicksburg and move across the South.

The march across the South would be performed in leaps from Chattanooga, to Atlanta, and then a bloody and as harsh run across the State of Georgia to the Atlantic Ocean to Savannah.

The scorched earth policy of destroying everything in the path of the Federal army would be to capture, burn, destroy, or make unusable anything that prevented Southern production of any resources to support the Confederacy.

Freed slaves became members of his army, only because Sherman didn't know what to do with them. By Christmas of 1864, he was in Savannah, Georgia with an army of former slaves almost as large as his military force.

* * * * *

This foretelling of what was happening across the South was seen by the North Carolina State Government with great concern that created fear throughout the State. If they were divided about entering the war, the debate was how to prepare for a potential similar fate of the State as was inflicted on Atlanta, Savannah, Columbia, and Charleston with nearly utter destruction.

The populace was in uprising. The Home Guard was even more brutal and lawless. They hung or shot anyone they deem deserters, including old men and women.

Pleas were being sent to the Governor in mass batches calling for assistance and an absolute unwillingness to continue to actively assist in the war.

* * * * *

None other than the President of the United States, Abraham Lincoln, sent notice to General Grant of the situation in North Carolina and suggested that the scorched earth approach should stop at the North Carolina border. Lincoln reminded Grant that North Carolina never wanted to leave the Union but was forced into it by Jefferson Davis.

He also suggested, however, that if the North Carolina resistance was too strong, they should be dealt with accordingly.

General Grant sent a message to that affect to General Sherman.

* * * * *

Lincoln had been reelected president. Richmond was nearly in ruins by March of 1865, and General Lee had nothing to fight for in the Capitol of Richmond.

President Jefferson Davis and most of his cabinet had already vacated the city and heading for North Carolina. Some, in Raleigh, suggested Davis and his cabinets' stay should be short-lived. Feelings regarding the Confederacy were not that welcoming.

* * * * *

Lee hoped to move away quietly before Grant knew he was gone. His plan was to go to North Carolina and meet with his old friend General Joseph Johnston, who currently had over twenty-five thousand men, many with no training and so young, that they may not be able to properly hold the musket.

However, for Lee, it was an army worth consolidating with his dwindling forces in Virginia.

* * * * *

General Sherman was well on his way to North Carolina. His primary goal was to get to North Carolina before Lee arrived to consolidate his forces with Johnston.

He anticipated a relatively quiet welcome to the State. He was only partially correct.

The last major bastion between ultimate access to the State and victory was the port of Wilmington. The river and the railroads that ran from the port were lifelines for the Confederate Army.

The blockade runners were notoriously brave and successful for years. The Union Navy had simply chosen to avoid the port until the right forces could meet and take Fort Fisher and Fort Anderson, which guarded the port and city of Wilmington.

The engagement would be the largest combined Federal Army, Navy, and Marine battle of the war. Nearly sixty ships would support the attack with naval artillery, and Union Soldiers to take the once undefeated forts.

The three-day battle was decisive and with the land forces moving onto the fort, the Confederate force was defeated. But not without a fight. Five hundred and eighty-eight Confederate soldiers were killed in the land invasion.

However, of the just over nineteen hundred men inside of Fort Fisher, nearly all nineteen hundred were captured and made prisoners of war with little resistance.

They were almost immediately turned into labor for the reconstruction of the fort and other facilities.

Fort Fisher became a port of entry for the Union forces that began an active campaign up the Cape Fear River to take Raleigh.

* * * * *

Lee's last gasp effort to get to North Carolina would end at the small community of Appomattox Courthouse, Virginia on April 9, 1865, where General Lee met General Grant for the terms of surrender.

The 26th Regiment of North Carolina Troops would be the last unit to lay down its weapons, given it was the designated honor guard until the end. Each man was required to sign his pledge to no longer take up arms against the Union and receive his parole.

Thus, began the long journey home to North Carolina for so many.

* * * * *

Meanwhile, in North Carolina, with some smaller battles at hand, General Sherman offered the same general terms of surrender to his old friend General Joseph Johnston on April 17, 1865, at Bentonville, North Carolina and just outside of Raleigh.

Sherman was somewhat concerned about the impact the assassination of President Lincoln would have on the whole affair. The two spoke about the subject as Sherman shared the news, he had only received the night before.

Johnston shared Sherman's concerns but also shared with Sherman that President Davis had left with most of his cabinet for Charlotte on the previous day. They agreed that would be good news for both sides.

For all intents and purposes, the American Civil War was over. However, the policy of reconstruction was still to come.

* * * * *

Private James Ward was finally laid to rest in the Ward Family cemetery in July of 1864, just over a year after he was killed. The entire extended Ward family would be there and hundreds of others from the local community attended what was supposed to be a small family gathering.

* * * * *

Brice and Louise Ward would find farm life almost too difficult to bear without their son, James. With Reconstruction, the farm would continue to decrease in size and production. What had been over a thousand acres of Ward family farms dwindled down to one hundred and fifty-six acres near the Green Swamp. Within a single generation, they would be down to a single farm, no longer "land rich and cash poor." They were now, just poor dirt farmers.

* * * * *

Cousin Stephen Ward would survive his wounds at Gettysburg. He would reluctantly leave his Company Commander, Captain Brewer in Gettysburg to be captured by Union troops as a result of the seriousness of his wounds on the final attack of July 3. Stephen would ride in one of the medical wagons back to Virginia where he would recover and eventually be in the ranks until he was captured at Hanover Junction, Virginia May 24th, 1864.

It was recorded in a letter that he was captured because he had stopped to pull off his boots. He was imprisoned at Point Lookout, Maryland and transferred to Elmira, New York, where he was later paroled and exchanged for Union prisoners on February 20, 1865, near Norfolk. As promised, he would remain near Anna Wallace Ward and help her with her small farm until she remarried several years later.

* * * * *

Captain Stephen Brewer, Commander for Company E, temporarily Acting Commander of the 26th Regiment during the final attack on July 3, was left near Seminary Ridge on July 5 after the last Confederate force had vacated the battlefield. He, along with thousands of wounded men, would be left for the hoped-for care and comfort and the good graces of the people of Gettysburg and General George Meade's army. Those were offered to Brewer and others with little animosity.

Brewer was one of the most well-regarded officers of the 26th Regiment and nearly any mention of the heroes of the 26th Regiment always included hushed tones when Brewer's name arose in the conversation.

His wounds were sufficient for him to remain unmoved from Gettysburg for some time. He was moved from Gettysburg for additional hospitalization in Baltimore, Maryland and by September 1863, he was transferred to a Union prison camp located at Johnson's Island, Ohio. He was finally paroled at the camp and then transferred to City Point, Virginia for prisoner exchange on February 24, 1865.

Brewer was with Colonel Henry King Burgwyn, Jr. when he was shot and removed from the battlefield. He led the final attack onto high ground at McPherson's Ridge on July 1, where he saw Lieutenant Colonel Lane shot in the neck, and was the last man to pick up the regimental colors from the fallen Colonel Lane.

His last act for the Regiment occurred on July 3, when he retrieved the colors and attempted to reach the stone wall, directly in front of the remains of the Regiment. He often remarked, "I don't know why I was not killed."

Once returned to home after the war, he became a beloved sheriff for Chatham County.

* * * * *

First Sergeant James Brooks was one of the two men that was offered the hand of the Union Artillery Sergeant at the Stone Wall on July 3. Brooks was imprisoned and was part of a prisoner exchange in March 1864. By early 1865, he was with the 26th Regiment again, where he was wounded and captured once again. He was finally paroled in June 1865.

* * * * *

Colonel John Randolph Lane was a true North Carolinian. Simply, that means he is dedicated to his State, its people, and telling a proper story of the officers and men of the 26th Regiment.

After being shot through the neck, mouth, losing part of his tongue and the bullet shattering his teeth, he recovered from his nearly mortal wound. From that moment, he was unable to speak clearly and with some effort and practice, became an articulate gentleman orator of the South.

He recovered from his wounds of July 1, 1863, at Gettysburg and returned to duty with the 26th Regiment, as its official commander. He would remain with the Regiment and be wounded several times before the end of the war. In March 1865, he would be wounded again and not be present for the surrender at Appomattox.

Upon return to civilian life, he was industrious, prosperous, and very successful in his community in Chatham County.

As a former commander and well-versed in the history of the 26th Regiment, he was asked to speak at various functions, including major anniversaries of the Battle of Gettysburg. On certain occasions, he would actually wear his old regimental uniform, still containing both worn holes and blood from previous wounds.

He was regaled as a man of conciliation. One who gallantly fought a war he was uncertain about. However, he fought with the full commitment and valor once involved.

On July 3, 1903, John R. Lane was a keynote speaker at the fortieth anniversary of the famous battle, in the town Gettysburg. Two great moments occurred on the day as Lane gave his speech and shook hands, across the stone wall on Cemetery Ridge, with the very man that had shot him on July 1, 1863, at the top of McPherson's Ridge.

In typical fashion, Lane began his speech with some light comments.

"I want to thank you for this organization and for what you are doing. But I must warn you that you must not expect a highly wrought oration from me. I was once a solder, never a speaker. Besides, our good friends, the enemy took good care of this field of Gettysburg that I should never become an orator, for a Yankee bullet ruined my throat and took away a part of my tongue and deprived me of my teeth. Yet with your kind forbearance, I will do my best to tell you something of the personnel, spirit and conduct of the 26th Regiment, in whose honor I am pleased to think you have invited me to be with you."

Lane would continue his oratory by describing the men that were in the 26th Regiment and the State they represented in the conflict.

"Pardon my pride, I do not ask you to pardon my loving remembrance of them, and the tears that gather in my heart, and rise to my eyes, but pardon my pride, when I say a finer body of men never gathered for battle. May I mention some of the things that went to make them good soldiers? In the first place, the soldiers came of good blood. I do not mean that their parents were aristocratic, far from it; many of them never owned a slave. They were the great middle class that owned small farms in central and western North Carolina; who earned their living with honest sweat and owed not any man. They were good honest American stock, their blood untainted with crime, their eyes not dimmed by vice. The boys had grown up on the farm and were of magnificent physique. Their life between the plow handles and wielding the axe had made them strong. They had chased the fox and the deer over hill and valley and had gained great power of endurance that scorned Winter's cold, or the parching heat of a July sun. Again, these men, many of them without much schooling, were intelligent, and their life on the farm, and in the woods had taught them to be observant and self-reliant. They were quick to see, quick to understand, quick to act.... Finally, these men had native courage, not the loud-mouthed courage of the braggart, but the quiet, unfaltering courage that cause them to advance in the face of a murderous fire.... The men of this regiment would never endure an officer who cowered in battle. They

demanded in the officer the same courage they manifested themselves. At this time, the men had come to understand and to trust the officers, the officers the men, and like a mighty well-arranged military engine, it was ready, with one spirit to move forward. The noble band of men, God bless them! God bless them!"

On this occasion, John R. Lane would meet the man that shot him in the neck on McPherson's Ridge. It was a former Sergeant Charles H. McConnell. On the day of the fortieth anniversary, Union Sergeant McConnell was a successful pharmaceutical executive. After some fanfare, the two men met at the stone wall, exchanged handshakes and warm embraces, and the solemn and tearful statement by Sergeant McConnell, "I thank God, I did not kill you."

For the short time left for both men to be alive, they became and remained good friends.

Typical of Lane and his devotion to his men, he always gave this reminder; *"Your valor is coming to be regarded as the common heritage of the American Nation. It no longer belongs to your State alone; it no longer belongs to the South; it is the high-water mark of what Americans have done and can do."*

On that day, and every day that he was asked to speak, Lane wept for the memory of the men of the 26th Regiment of North Carolina Troops.

AUTHOR'S FINAL THOUGHTS

How do you know where you're going if you don't know where you've been? Whether Native Americans (to use that title) or immigrants (as nearly everyone in this country are a descendent), we owe our personal history to those that preceded each generation.

We may all have some smart and successful people as ancestors. However, I'm willing to bet there is at least one branch or character in each of our family trees that was a little notorious and the family chooses to ignore them.

Sometimes, those bad tree limbs fall away or are long forgotten. Perhaps their actions were so horrible or successful they could not be ignored. Either way, reality tells us the family tree has some interesting branches stretching over time.

The American Civil War was such a blemish on our American heritage tree. It's the "infamous" relative we sometimes don't want to claim. It's the branch we wish had never grown. History says you can't forget them but must learn from them. Ignoring them will not work.

However, as Jesus of Nazareth proclaimed, "... *Let him without sin cast the first stone...*"

What happened over one hundred and fifty years ago was a terrible event in America's history. Unfortunately, it was an event that had to happen to change or eliminate the "sins" of our national past.

Paraphrasing Jesus again, the nation had to learn to *"...go and sin no more."*

My story began in the Summer between my twelfth and thirteenth birthday on the Summer of 1961. As usual for me, the weekend following the end of every school year meant traveling to Southeastern North Carolina to the Ward (Dad's side of the family) and Thompson (Mom's side of the family) farms.

It was on such a Summer, that I discovered a "secret" staircase behind a closet door. On a Sunday afternoon, with nearly everyone catching an afternoon nap after church and a big farm lunch, I climbed the staircase to another door. Behind that second door, I found an attic, not unlike lots of attics. I saw old furniture, wooden boxes, several hanging framed portraits, and clothes hanging on makeshift lines.

My attention was quickly caught by a medium sized sea chest. It was made of wood slats bound by metal strips. It had a large metal lock on the front side. Being curious, I eased the metal lock open and lifted the top of the chest.

It is dusty in the attic of most farmhouses. As I lifted the chest lid, dust swirled in the air, and some got into my eyes. With a little effort, lots of blinking, and wiping the tears away, I was able to see the contents in the chest.

A tray covered the top inside of the chest. I could see lots of letters and other documents bundled into small packages bound with colored ribbons, tobacco twine, and thick strings. What got my real attention was a large bayonet and some military decorations.

As I lifted the tray of bound letters, I found other military equipment, most of it much older than that of contemporary military wear. Even I, at that young age, recognized it was from a different era.

I returned to examine the top tray and looked at some of the letters at the top of the bundles. I saw 1861 and later dates. I pulled the ribbon off of one bundle and read one of the letters from a Private James Ward, of Company E, 26th Regiment of North Carolina Troops.

Most of that afternoon, while most of my extended family was napping, I discovered that I had history in my hands. Not history from a textbook, but actual history from someone that had been there.

I spent that afternoon and many more visits before I mentioned anything to my Grandmother Gertrude Ward.

"Grandma, I found a chest in the attic with letters and things. Where did it come from?" I asked.

She looked at me with a wrinkled brow, "Where have you been boy?"

I explained finding the secret closet door, to the hidden staircase, to the attic upstairs. She listened intently and finally remarked, "Son, I had completely forgotten about that old chest. The family has had that for so many years, I've lost track of the last time I saw it."

She went on to further explain that the family all knew about James Ward and his exploits in the "War between the States," as she referred to it.

Grandma Gertrude also offered that my grandfather Brice Ward (her husband and the name I used for one of my characters) had gone to war in Europe in 1917. She lowered her voice and said, "He wasn't the same man I sent to that place when he got back. He changed a lot."

In today's vernacular, my Grandfather had PTSD from the trenches of Europe. I asked her if I could continue reading the letters and she said, "Yes, but don't mention it to anyone else and do it after all of your chores are done each day."

It was a promise I was most happy to agree to keep. For the next several years, I found time to read each and every letter. Some were a little more virtuous than others and some were a little more salacious between a man and his wife. But it was emotionally moving to read of the accounts of his life and her life on the farm.

This adventure in history fueled an even greater curiosity for history, US History in particular. For the next sixty years of my life, I spent more time on battlefields, museums, libraries, and purchased nearly everything I could find about the period leading up to, through and after the US Civil War. However, I do not consider myself an expert.

I was already in the Army when I received a call from my mother, and she informed me that the Ward Family farmhouse had gone up in flames on a cold winter's night. The entire house had burned to the ground. Nothing other than the family had survived the fire.

My treasure trove in the attic was gone, but the letters I read and the messages they conveyed were not lost. My personal notes and better than average memory captured most of the abbreviated letters used in this novel. I only slightly modified some of the content without the horrors that were described and the more tender moments of my descendants' thoughts.

While in the Army, I was sent to the Combat Studies Institute at Fort Leavenworth, Kansas where I was trained and certified to be an Assistant Professor of Military Science, so that I could instruct and train others in the US Army's Reserve Officers Training Corps at Appalachian State University, in Boone, North Carolina.

This course taught me to use the Battlefield Staff Ride as an excellent technique to put the contemporary soldier into another time and place, using the nine principles of war we teach in our military doctrine even today.

I have conducted battlefield staff rides in Guam, South Korea, Bastogne Belgium, Fulda Gap in Germany, Gettysburg (seven times), The Little Blue River, Nashville, Shiloh, Antietam, Manassas, Vicksburg, Guilford Courthouse, New Bern, Fort Fisher, and Bentonville.

Finally, after numerous visits to the North Carolina Museum of History, I had captured nearly every major record of the 26th Regiment of

North Carolina Troops. I have poured through and noted thousands of citations, attended lectures by renowned authors and historians such as Shelby Foote, Bruce Canton, and Stephen Ambrose.

I had extended conversations with Ken Burns, Executive Producer of the ultimate video presentation of the Civil War at the Casemate Museum while stationed at Fort Monroe, Virginia. I have read no less than thirty-nine books and personal diaries, of those who lived to tell the tales, and I was able to piece this story together.

Why this story? What makes it any different than any other story of the Civil War or any other war for that matter.

My answer is simple. This is my story. The results of all of the people, events, timelines, and decisions came to the very incarnation of my existence, my birth.

If James Ward had not gotten dysentery in camp in the early Fall of 1862, He would not have been at home on furlough. If he had not been on furlough and recovering from his illness, they would not have made love on those fateful nights in November and December 1862.

If not for those fateful nights, my direct ancestor would not have been born. My Great Grandfather and his Grandfather Ward would not have had my father Howard Carl Ward. And finally, I would not have been born for the opportunity to share my family's story with you.

Let it be known, the Ward family has almost always been the direct descendants of poor dirt farmers. The land was all that we really had other than our family.

I entered the Army as a Private during the Vietnam War era and for thirty years, I made a career as an officer out of a sense of duty for my country, as was expected by our family traditions.

Why would my family today hinge on such a coincidental moment like the impregnation of a very young bride in North Carolina in the Winter of 1862?

I really don't believe in coincidences. I believe in God. I believe God never makes us do anything. I believe He gave us free will and as such, we create our own hells and heavens.

Hell can be on a battlefield. Heaven can be in the arms of the one you love. We only get those moments when we see them in front of us. We can't plan them, shape them, or delay them. We can only enjoy the moment when they present themselves to us.

When my father was lying on his death bed, while trying to recover from a stroke, he was unconscious for several hours and for the last six hours of his life, I was holding the only hand he had with any feeling.

He opened his eyes and looked at me. Gently, tears ran down from his eyes, he could not speak clearly, and yet, I knew exactly what he was thinking and trying to say at that very moment.

"I tried to make you the best man you could be. I'm sorry if I ever hurt you. Please take care of your Mother and the girls. I love you and I'll see you on the other side."

I knew this to be his intent at that moment because we had both said them when I was thirty-eight years old. We had finally reconciled our grievances with each other after nearly twenty-five years of hurtful words on both sides of the argument.

The Civil War was necessary. Our Nation was at a critical moment in time, just like my father and me. As a nation, our temporary compromises were just that, temporary.

It would take a schism like the Civil War and the following period of reconstruction to remedy the wrongs of the past. The Civil War and the following period of Reconstruction were not particularly great successes either.

For me, that schism meant being a member of a community that wanted no part of the Civil War and yet, when put to the task, we did our duty as others dictated to us.

The title of the novel is simple. James Ward did his duty for nothing more than twenty dollars in gold for windowpanes and his love for his new wife. Following the thoughts of the vast majority of the State, at that time, he expected to serve his duty in North Carolina and then return home after a year of duty.

He thought he was protecting her, his extended family's life, and the land they worked so hard to make successful, "land rich and cash poor." They did this with not a slave to be found.

They were self-educated by using a family Bible as their teaching aide. They believed in God, Jesus Christ, and the Holy Spirit, and the grace and providence provided to all.

In author Richard Paul Evans' book, '**The Locket**', his protagonist recalls his views on how we gain from our life's lessons, *"Through the course of my life I have come to believe that life is not lived chronologically, by the sweep of a clock's hand or the sway of its pendulum, but rather, experientially, as a ladder or stair, each experience stacked upon the previous, delivering us to loftier planes. Perhaps this best describes my concept of God-the-architect of that divine ascent, the hidden arm that slashes our swath through the overgrown flora of destiny, best revealed in the evidence of our lives."*

So, we are here, not by coincidence but by the grace of God, still trying to learn our lessons with one experience "stacked upon the previous lesson."

We cannot hide from our history; we must remember its joys and its horrors by embracing one and repulsing the other. As author Joseph Campbell describes it, we're merely on the "Heroes' Journey" of life.

When will we ever really learn?

ABOUT THE AUTHOR

A. C. "Carl" Ward lives at the beaches of Southeastern NC with his wife, Jolene and the family cat, Heidi. Carl retired from the Army after 30 years of military service and continued providing consulting services for Government and Commercial enterprises regarding Defense and Homeland Security. Over the last 20 plus years, he continues to write and tell stories that convey messages of importance to him: family, courage, integrity, and faith. Their Children Brian and Adrienne, have their own families and successful business relationships in Los Angeles, CA and Naples, FL areas.

This story is based on a true story. After over a century and a half, the story has changed with time, just like our contemporary times have changed in the United States. While many may choose to ignore or forget history, I believe it is imperative that we study and understand what drove some men to fight in a civil war for what some call "the heart and soul of our nation" really means. As historians, we are taught as Sir Winston Churchill paraphrased George Santayana's famous quote,"… those who fail to learn from history are condemned to repeat it." How can we understand others if we don't understand ourselves? Instead of ignoring our history, or worse yet, obliterating our history, why not recall that we all have our own story to tell. This account is personal because it acknowledges what my historic family has gone through over time and the impact it has made on me as a direct descendant of one of the many who fought in the hot Sun of July 1863 in a little community known as Gettysburg.

My goal is not to justify or explain what leads men, and even women, to make the decisions they made regarding the war. For me, sometimes, it can be for nothing more than "$20 in gold" to purchase window glass and hinges for a partially built cabin for a soldier's new wife on a simple farm in rural North Carolina. Many have suggested that North Carolina has a unique history as it relates to the Civil War. My role in the novel is not to justify that decision either. I just want to tell a hidden story lost in the facts of history. I will let the gentle reader decide if those decisions were right or wrong.

Printed in the USA
CPSIA information can be obtained
at www.ICGtesting.com
LVHW020824310823
756530LV00035B/237/J